ALSO BY JADE BEER

The Almost Wife

JADE BEER

What I Didn't Say

bookouture

Published by Bookouture in 2018

An imprint of StoryFire Ltd.

Carmelite House
50 Victoria Embankment
London EC4Y 0DZ

www.bookouture.com

Epigraph by Burchill, Julie. From "Music to the ears."
The Guardian, 10 May 2003.

ISBN: 978-1-78681-937-6
eBook ISBN: 978-1-78681-745-7

Previously published as *Promise Me*

To Stephen,

For keeping all your promises, I love you

X

'My favourite spectator sport is watching people, who should know better, searching for something (and often claiming to find it) where it never could be.'

Julie Burchill, writing for The Guardian

Chapter One

Jenny Archer

If only, just for once, my shift had finished on time. I wouldn't have been swallowed up in the throng of early-evening commuters en route to Paddington tube station, pushed the longer way back towards Marble Arch. And she wouldn't have seen me.

By the time I round the corner onto Connaught Street, past a vet's with its window filled with colourful doggie outfits and a café serving flavoured macchiatos, the chill October air is already biting at my face. I realise my gloves are still sitting in the staffroom next to the family-sized tin of Christmas-is-coming Quality Street chocolates. There is a moment where I consider going back for them but the crowd marching forth behind me, their heads bowed penguin-like to the wind, is more of a barrier than I can be bothered to deal with.

I try really hard not to notice at first. I even cross to the other side of the street because I can see what's coming. But the boutique's floor-to-ceiling glass windows wrap around the corner it sits on, making it impossible to miss. The walls inside have been painted a dark grey and the bright light is bouncing off every one of those white dresses, illuminating the entire shop like some giant searchlight calling me home. It's all so pristine and orderly, the exact opposite of the frantic mess I've just left behind.

As she steps out from the fitting room, I can't help it, I cross back over the road, not even bothering to look for oncoming traffic, and as I get closer, I can hear the warm laughter and giddy squeals enveloping her. *Who are they*, I wonder? It looks like her grandmother, a sister perhaps and a bridesmaid or two. Then I see what must surely be her mum. They share the same pretty almond eyes and confident smile. She's seated in a deep blush-pink chair and as her daughter steps forward she starts to rise, her hands moving slowly up to her heart.

Oh my goodness, that dress! Clearly, I don't know one end of a wedding gown from the other, but this one looks *regal*. There's so much of it for a start and the closer I look, the more I see: tiny glass beads that catch the light, sequins that seem to shower down the skirt like precious raindrops. Whoever made this knew what they were doing. She looks like she's been stitched into it; it fits her so perfectly.

I step closer to the window now, place the tips of my fingers onto the pane of glass and watch, completely absorbed, as her mum gathers her beautiful daughter up in her arms. *The love*. I can feel it through two inches of toughened glass and I realise I'm holding my breath. As my fingers creep higher up the window and my nose gently touches it, I see how everyone is so lost in the moment. There could be a riot going off on the streets out here and none of them would notice. My thoughts flick to my own mother and her last letter, 'When You're Missing Me' written on the envelope in unusually untidy handwriting – perhaps the pain or medication was starting to overwhelm her by then.

There's something about this time of year, when the weather turns and the first signs of Christmas start to magically appear overnight in all the shops on Oxford Street when no one's looking. After dark, the windows of Selfridges fill with an explosion of designer colour, an exciting surprise for all the commuters passing on the bus the next morning. For me it just means I'm coming to the end of another year without her and I can feel my spirits physically sag inside me at the thought of it. Twelve years now and I still miss her desperately and the way she used to dismiss every problem with a cheery 'Everything will be alright in the end. And if it's not alright, it's not the end.' Well, not always, Mum.

Oh, the bride is twirling now, sending a whoosh of air up under that skirt, and I have to use my freezing fingers to wipe my frosted breath from the window pane to get a better look. Her mum is crying. No big heaving sobs, just a few delicate little tears picking their way down her perfectly made-up face. Then she's pulling out an embroidered hanky and dabbing at the corners of her eyes. I bet this family are going to have the most magical Christmas together. I'll be working.

It was last Thursday when someone decided we needed to sort out all the Christmas rotas at work – those with husbands and young children bagging all the best days off, those without (me) getting lumbered with everything else. I went straight home, untied the little bundle of notes Mum left for me and gently teased the *missing me* one open through sad little sobs. I've read so many of them since Mum lost her battle with breast cancer when I was just sixteen. Dad read them to me at first. We used to sit on my bed, under the star-scattered canopy and a string of fairy lights that Mum had spent one afternoon putting up and I could never bring myself to take down, and off he'd go. Letter in one hand, my tense little fingers squeezed in the other, forcing himself not to cry because that's not what she wanted. First Boyfriend, First Broken Heart, Graduation Day. How she had the strength to write those letters, I'll never know, and as a vulnerable teenager sometimes I couldn't bear to listen to them. Now, I tackle them myself.

Come on, Jenny, you're made of tougher stuff than you know. Remember, you are me and I am you. Promise me you won't let anything ruin the big, beautiful life you are yet to live – not even if you must do it without your mum. What is it we used to say? Pull on your big-girl pants and get on with it! That always made us giggle, didn't it? It makes me smile now as I'm writing the words again. You can do it, I know you can. Try your very, very best. Think of the fun times we shared, then go and find your own fun, because there is plenty out there waiting for you. Don't waste your tears on me, darling, they won't bring me back. I haven't gone, I'm watching you every day…

I'm not sure if it's the cold or the memory of her, but I'm starting to shake a little. I need to go. Just as I make that decision, the door to the boutique flies open and the friendly smile of an older woman holds me there. Her face is so inviting and kind. She looks like the sort of woman who floats elegantly through life, one who would never get her hair wet at the swimming pool. I try to make my escape, muttering a quick apology, stepping back guiltily from the window, but she's pulling me in.

'Are you wanting to make an appointment? I won't have you standing out there in the cold until we've finished. Come on, I can book you in quickly.' She's fiddling around by the till now, pulling out a huge concertina file. 'What's your name?'

'It's Jenny, but I er…' The bride-to-be's family have noticed me now and I'm feeling a bit ashamed of the bobbling Topshop duffle coat I thought I'd try to get one more winter out of. I see my reflection from the other side of those huge glass windows. Urgh! Major hair fail. Attacked by the cold evening air, it has erupted into a giant lollipop of frizz. My cheeks are unflatteringly flushed and, now that I'm in the warm, I can feel my nose start to run and I'm wondering if I can get away with a quick wipe on my sleeve. I am so far from the vision of styled perfection in front of me.

Naturally, everyone else is a bit dressed up for the occasion. This is special, right? The mum's in a pastel tweed skirt and jacket while the girls are all cream cashmere, chic cropped trousers skimming above pretty embellished flats – the sort that always seem to make my ankles look thick – or floaty floral dresses belted at the waist to show off their neat figures. Even Granny looks all elegant in a midnight blue dress that flares at the sleeves, a ring of tiny pearls at both wrists.

'OK, you are in luck, Jenny, because I have a cancellation tomorrow at 6 p.m., otherwise you're looking at a six-week wait, I'm afraid. And I'm so sorry, I haven't even bothered to introduce myself. I'm Helen, I own The White Gallery.'

'I'd take it if I were you.' The bride, who's got to be a good three years younger than my twenty-eight, is turning her full attention to me now. 'I've been to just about every wedding boutique in London and Helen knew immediately that this dress was the one for me, long before I did. She's the best there is.'

'It's from the Elie Saab Fall 2018 collection,' smiles Helen, looking all proud of herself. And rightly so, she's nailed it. 'A dress that has about 230 hours of handwork in it. See the way all the detail cascades down over the tulle? Only the very finest embellisher could create something so beautiful, so faultless.'

'OK, tomorrow it is!' Then – crazy woman alert – I actually start to do a quick bit of mental arithmetic to see if I'll have enough time to leg it back here when my shift ends tomorrow. No! I need to get out of here before I start inviting them all to my big day. I can always call and cancel it later and no one will be any the wiser. Anything is better than admitting I just got busted having a right good nose at total strangers enjoying such a private moment.

'Perfect! I'll see you then.' Helen squeezes the file shut, sending a waft of warm air up into her immaculately blow-dried hair.

Then I'm back out into the flow of determined commuters, hurrying against each other, fighting to make the lights, fighting to dive into the last seat on the tube, then fighting to be the first out the sliding doors when it finally flies into their station. The whole thing is exhausting. As I sit, counting down the ten stops to East Putney, I can still smell the day on me. I wonder if the man sitting next to me, legs splayed open so he's helping himself to more than his fair share of my seat, can smell it too. My thoughts drift back to Mrs Rodgers, and how she struggled to get her newborn to latch on – the reason I was so late finishing today. That and two births, one very stroppy matron and a delivery ward full of dads-to-be convinced '*we're* contracting'.

Sweat, tears, blood, vomit, urine… I've had it all on me today. From the second my shift started at St Mary's, it was brutally busy. I got Mrs Johnson, a first-timer who'd done her homework and produced a birth plan three sheets long. As she handed it over, she looked at me and asked the same question most of them do: 'Are you a mum?' Then I watched as the confidence drained from her face when the answer was no. It's not a medical thing, I'm sure she knows I can do my job. But just then, right at the beginning when she's scared of everything that's about to happen to her, she needs to know *I know* how terrified she is and that I came out the other side and everything was OK. I can't offer her that, but I feel her worry. It's hard for me too. Every time I ease a new life into this world, I wonder if I will ever be on the receiving end of that most precious gift. Will my hands, the very first to touch every newborn I deliver, ever cradle my own? Will I ever open the letter marked 'You're a Mum!'? And now I think about it, why was she so sure I would be? I suppose it's not quite the same, writing 'Now that you've been barren for fifteen years', is it? Mum's letters didn't come with instructions, I guess she only wanted me to open them when they're relevant. But she must have known I'll eventually open them all regardless, just to hear her voice dance around my head again.

By the time I force my key into the lock of my basement flat and step over the mountain of unpaired shoes that Marianne, my frequently absent and chaotic flatmate, has dumped there, I'm struggling to feel my fingers. I should have gone back for the gloves. That lovely bride might have been out of her dress by then and on her own way home too.

But I can't get her out of my head. I'm thinking about that dress as I'm stabbing the fork through the film of a microwaveable meatballs and rice; her mum's face as I'm picking up Marianne's trail of clothes that are running from her room down the dark, narrow corridor to our shared bathroom – always falling short of the laundry bin; and as I draw the curtains across the metal security bars that criss-cross the window and sit on my bed to eat dinner, I'm thinking about what feels like the next letter Mum intended me to read. The one that says 'You're Engaged!' on the front. I can tell from the exaggerated exclamation mark how excited she was trying to feel when she wrote it.

I don't know why I decide to read it tonight. I'm about as far away from an engagement as Marianne is from owning a pair of rubber gloves. But I do. Maybe I just want to feel close to Mum again. To hear the sound of her voice surround me. To pretend for a moment that I am fulfilling all the hopes and wishes she had for me.

How old are you, I wonder, poppet? I was twenty-seven when your father proposed and that felt just about the perfect age to me. And now, here you are! On the tip of something so magical, I barely know how to describe it to you. The thought that you have found someone you love so much that you want to spend the rest of your life with them is all the comfort I need today. The knowledge that someone else out there loves and adores you is no surprise at all.

The truth is, if I was there, I'd be a mess. The thought of letting you go to build a life that might include me a little less used to keep me awake at night, even when you were just a little girl. It would stir up so much sorrow and excitement in me, leaving me staring at the ceiling for hours. I used to drive Dad nuts, worrying about things he said didn't need worrying about.

I've thought a lot about what advice I should give you at this point in your life and actually, it's far simpler than you think: just love each other. Sounds obvious, doesn't it? But when life gets in the way, don't let him be the thing you push to the bottom of your list. Cherish him and be sure he does the same for you. Be kind to each other. Let him be the one person who never finds fault in you. Let you be the one person he can talk to about anything – everything. Build a little wall around you both so no one can ever hurt you.

And your wedding day! I've written another letter for you to open that morning, Jenny, but since you'll be planning it now, this is what I say. Go Big! Go white! Go over the top! Don't shy away from what should be a huge, joyous celebration. Buy the enormous dress, order too many flowers, drink too much champagne, overspend (a little!) on the honeymoon. Don't ever look back and wish you'd gone for the six-tier cake. Have it! You deserve it, my darling. We've made sure the money is there for you, so now is not the time to be sensible!

I'm so sorry I'm not there to help you with all the wonderful planning – we would have had so much fun together – but perhaps I will guide you in some way neither of us expected. Think of me when you're smelling those roses, or choosing the scent you'll wear on your wedding morning. I'll be there in every twinkle of the cut-glass crystal during your toast, I'll be the sound of laughter travelling across your reception after the speeches. Don't cry any tears for me on your wedding day, Jenny, it would break my heart to think of that. Instead, place a beautiful bouquet of flowers where I might have sat.

And know that I will love you forever, even longer if I can. I won't waste my words being sad about what might have been, just like you mustn't waste your time being sad for what you'll miss. The fact you have opened this letter at all is all the peace I need. You've found him. You'll be happy and I can rest now. Congratulations! I honestly feel like I might explode with pride. Love Mum x

That's when I dig out Mum's engagement ring from my bedside drawer. Dad gave it to me the day before he proposed to Sylvie, sixty-four days after we buried Mum and another twenty-eight before my heartbroken older sister Lulu packed up her own life and took the marketing job up North. It's an Art Deco emerald-cut aquamarine, encircled with a halo of diamonds. She never took it off, until Dad had to. She loved it. And so do I, because it carries all the promise of a life so much more glamorous than my own. Perhaps that's why I decide to keep it on now.

I slip it on to the third finger of my left hand, like I have many times before. But I leave it there this time and huff back into the kitchen to dump my half-eaten excuse for dinner into the bin. If they're going to advertise this as 'Meatballs & Rice', they might have the decency to put a meatball in it. I open the fridge to retrieve the Curly Wurly I've hidden at the back behind the out-of-date Greek yoghurt and some cheese that's really starting to whiff. I've Post-it-noted my name all over the chocolate but, no surprise at all, Marianne has beaten me to it and helped herself. Still, nice of her to leave the empty wrapper in there for me to bin.

Perhaps I shouldn't entirely blame my thieving flatmate for putting me in this devil-may-care mood, but I decide there and then not to cancel Helen tomorrow. For once, I'm going to be the silly one and do something spectacularly stupid.

Chapter Two

Natalie Butler

Whoever is banging that hammer against the inside of Nat's head really needs to sod off. The hangover! It's tearing through her, waves of nausea swaying up over her, setting her stomach to sea as it twists and churns under – oh hell – last night's dress. It's still glued to her and rather sadly, stinking a bit, smattered in what she hopes is buttercream but could just as easily be toothpaste – a starting gun for the first unwelcome flashback from yesterday. That mortifying dance the bride made her do up the aisle to Taylor Swift's 'Shake It Off' – damn YouTube and its never-ending gallery of inspirational 'Our Wedding!' films. It's not the first time Nat's had to publicly humiliate herself in the name of being a bride-slave and sure as hell won't be the last. But she can see it all now: the two girls sat three rows from the front, clearly having a damn good bitch about her as she fixed a determined grin to her face, threw her hips from side to side, pumped her head back and forth and ploughed on towards the celebrant as quickly as the lilac spray-on satin sheath would allow; the bewildered faces of everyone over the age of twelve who just didn't understand what the frig was going on. Still, that's what the bride wanted and so that's what she got. One of the most toe-curling starts to a marriage ceremony Nat has ever been part of. And considering this is her fifteenth time up the aisle this year, that's no small brag.

Urgh! Why does she do this to herself? *Why would anyone do it to themselves*, she wonders again, as the last bit of moisture evaporates from the back of her throat and she starts to contemplate the Herculean task of getting out of bed. Not just the expense and the big show-off but why marry at all? Aside from the important stuff she is yet to work out the answers to – like, is there any such thing as true love? Could she ever conform to someone else's timeline of the perfect life or happily cast aside all those feminist objections about one man giving her away to another? Aside from all that, there is the *seriously* big stuff: someone else insisting she picks her knickers up off the floor; sharing her bed every night with someone who might do something as grotesquely anatomical as break wind. How would she stop herself getting bored with him quicker than most people migrate from Pret's double-berry muffin to the white chocolate and cranberry? Plus, she likes her name and wants to keep it, and could she ever, with any sense of dignity, pull on a white dress when she's bonked as many best men as she has? Nat makes a feeble attempt to raise the duvet from her sticky, sweaty body then drops it swiftly as the stale smell of last night's booze and fake tan hits her nostrils. Rank!

No, there is a good reason why she once got savaged by a bride for physically punching away the bouquet toss and why, yes, she can handle being an enduring disappointment to most people for not *even* being engaged. Because the idea of her own wedding, even a low-key one in a registry office where the previous customer might have been doing something as devastatingly romantic as renewing their driver's licence is just not that appealing. There will be no Godly union for this girl because she is yet to convince herself that even the most thrilling moment – tearing the wrapping off the new pepper grinder from the gift list – is going to enhance her life in any way.

Oh, for a Nurofen within arm's reach right now! She stretches for her mobile instead to check the time: eleven o'clock. Not bad. As a rule, she doesn't get hammered at weddings. Tipsy, yes, for sure. But yesterday was different. Apart from the aisle dance there was also the dedication she was forced to sing in front of the entire three-hundred strong reception, the words to which charted the passionate love affair between bride and groom. All to the tune of 'Oh Happy Day'. Every word that screeched out of her made her skin flush a deeper shade of fearsome red. No one could get through that without booze. So, in between endless reassurances to the bride that she looked more ravishing than the groom's ex, who, unfortunately, he'd invited, Nat was knocking back the gin miniatures from the hotel minibar. And when they were done, it was out with the half-bottle of prosecco that she always carries with her for such emergency situations – resulting in the sort of messy post-wedding situation that she is glad only she has to witness. How wonderful to be single. Earning her own money, and blasting it just as quickly in Space NK. Dating is easy, thanks to the captive audience of up-for-it single men hanging off her at the weddings she's constantly attending and, well, she prefers her own company most of the time.

She's still festering in bed, three floors up in the new-build block of flats where she can hear every toilet flush and the wake-up alarm of the couple living next door to her, which is not ideal when they get up as conventionally early as they do. She has to match their TV viewing or be forced to listen as their soundtrack competes with the noise of her own widescreen. Feeling the migraine swell within her, she looks down at the pastel-coloured spots stuck to her cleavage. Once moist confetti, it's now crusted hard there. She can hear the buses passing on the main road outside, rattling the window frames as they make their way into Wimbledon town centre. It's Monday morning. Maybe it's a good thing she hasn't got a proper job. One that might require her to be at a desk by now. Although, she can't carry on like this forever either. But for now, her day is going to consist of a half-head of highlights – her brassy yellow locks begging for the familiar fingers of Charles Worthington. Then, major perk of the job, dress shopping.

OK, she's not going to feel bad about yesterday's performance. At least she's being honest with herself, not something she can say for every woman she follows up the aisle, including Miranda Forbes – now Mrs Christopher Barings – the New York investment manager who prioritises personal wealth over private friendships and whose train Nat was fluffing less than twenty-four hours ago. Miranda flew in to London on business two years ago and Nat was her relocation manager at the estate agency, sourcing the Mayfair apartment she needed for three months while Miranda stopped a very wealthy client taking his family's business to a rival bank. As Nat went above and beyond the call of duty, accompanying Miranda to theatre productions, spending weekends exploring the capital's visiting exhibitions and helping her hammer the plastic in Selfridges' personal shopping department, the two became close. Inseparable, even. There was no one else Miranda wanted to spend four hours trawling the beauty hall in Harvey Nichols on her behalf, hunting down the best waterproof mascara. It had to be Nat. Her best friend in the world – despite living on opposite sides of the Atlantic. That was their story and they were sticking to it. Everyone swallowed it. Even Christopher. No reason not to.

*

Nat finally wrestles herself free of the duvet, drags herself through into the kitchen and drinks enough water to fill a goldfish bowl, noticing in the window that her skin has all the telltale signs of yesterday's abuse. It's blotchy, make-up smeared, tired and grey. No high-street face mask is going to sort this out. She needs something weapons-grade; an overdose of vitamin C-rich serum and a level of hyaluronic acid that could double as bathroom cleaner.

She moves into the lounge and scans the mantelpiece above her faux-coal fire. Lined up in date order are invitations to the eight other weddings she will attend this year, the first indication of the kind of day each will be. The pristine white, bevelled card from Smythson, embossed with smart bronze lettering that sits perfectly within its tissue-lined pale blue envelope. The bespoke cartoon of a couple bungee jumping together. The pop-up 3D country house that's the couple's venue. Far right is the invitation to the last one of the year, on Christmas Eve. OK, a bit of a pain in the arse to be needed aisle-side that day, but what the hell? It's an illustration of a girl with a mop of blonde curls leaning over a man at a typewriter above the words 'Our Love Story'. This bride has been amazingly low-maintenance so far, leaving it entirely to Nat to find the designer and order the invitations. Nat's loved her over-to-you approach from the start. This one will be a doddle.

*

One restorative bacon double cheeseburger and two hundred quid's worth of caramel highlights later and Nat is breezing into The White Gallery on Connaught Street, feeling jubilantly near-human again.

'Helen, how are you?' She's perfectly on schedule by the looks of it. The boutique's owner already has a fresh brew waiting for Nat, requisite bone china teapot positioned on a rose-gold, glass-topped table, together with a gilt-edged plate of pale pink macaroons. It's like Helen knows Nat's sugar slump is about to hit.

'I'm wonderful, Natalie, my dear. And I am so happy to see you again. Come on, tell me how yesterday's wedding went?' She has both arms around Nat's shoulders and is guiding her into the boutique. 'I honestly don't know another woman alive who gets invited to as many as you do.'

'Ha! Just perfect, thank you, Helen. And I loved the dress so much, I woke up in it this morning!' As usual, she'll spare Helen the more unsavoury details of what she really looked and smelt like in that dress when the hangover forced her awake.

'Thrilled to hear it! Now, everything is ready for you, exactly as discussed. You're choosing the dress you'll wear to Alice's wedding today, I believe? Make yourself at home and I will bring your rail through to the fitting room.' Helen is everything that Nat is not. Together, ordered, sensible and very clean-looking. While Helen busies herself with the rail, Nat shoves a macaroon into her mouth whole, with the intention of seeing another off before Helen returns.

Despite her own lack of bridal aspirations, Nat has to admit this place is pretty awesome. She's been here so many times and loves how entering Helen's world seems to bathe her in a gloss of refined elegance that is not naturally hers. Now that she is through the huge black lacquered door onto the polished parquet floor, she is once again distracted by the two rails of bridal gowns that run either side of the boutique towards the back of the shop. The ultimate dressing-up fantasy, Nat has often thought about buying one, so she can howl at everyone's reaction when she wears it to the pub. Each rail is straining under the weight of full-length white gowns of every conceivable fabric and shape. Tulle and chiffon sweep over heavier organza, onto gowns of satin and silk. Then come the heavily embellished dresses with all their showy sparkle before the modern crepes and the expensive regal laces. Nat has lost herself so many times in those gowns, when she should have been in the changing room helping another weepy bride make a decision. She always appreciates the works of art, despite never having the inclination to fulfil their purpose herself.

There is a gold lattice frame leaning against one of the walls, onto which Helen has hung a selection of delicately embroidered shrugs and bridal cover-ups, and a glass cabinet filled with some of the most beautiful accessories Nat has ever seen. Strings of vintage pearls, glass beaded belts, soft faux-floral headpieces, Swarovski hair clips and bell jars that are filled with exquisite cream chiffon corsages. As she steps forward for a closer look, Nat can see Helen has updated her inspiration mood board too since her last visit. She's added some new fabric samples, a truly stunning piece of gold embroidery, some loose appliqué pink flowers, netting studded with gypsophila, images from some of her designers' latest shoots and a photograph of a shoe with intricate mother-of-pearl inlays worked around the heel. The boutique also smells divine, thanks to the vast number of café au lait dahlias, potent, pale yellow freesias and clouds of soft white hydrangeas filling various urns around the room.

'OK, Natalie, shall we?' Helen has returned and is ready for business, small white notebook tucked under one arm and her usual brown leather bag of pins and clips in the other. 'So, you said Alice is having a full white wedding and the bridesmaids need to be wearing white too, is that right?'

'Correct, Helen. But I'm the only maid so we don't need to co-ordinate with anyone else. The wedding's not until next year, I'm just getting ahead of myself and this will be the bride's fourth attempt at choosing the right husband so she's very happy to leave the dress choice to me. Come to think of it, this might be the closest I ever come to the real thing myself, so let's make it a good one, shall we?'

'Absolutely! Is the bride going to be joining us today, or has she specified whether you need to be long or short?'

'Nah, she's happy for me to decide so I say short, then I can get the legs right out.' Nat is stripping off her jeans and sweatshirt now while reaching for her third macaroon.

'OK, let's say goodbye to the multi-way wrap dress then and the off-the-shoulder bohemian number. I think what we need is a bit of *this*.' Helen is lifting a dress aloft, looking delighted with her early choice. 'The ballet-inspired midi dress has tiny silver cut beads on the bodice and a pretty ruffled trim that edges the neckline. You'll have your legs and arms exposed, but the grosgrain ribbon at the waist and the soft tulle skirt still keeps it feminine. What do you think?'

Just as Nat opens her mouth to say she loves it, Helen's mobile springs into action and she hastily tries to reject the call.

'I'm so sorry, Natalie, I never normally have that switched on during an appointment. I must have forgotten to flick it to silent at lunchtime. Let me just do that now. I can see it's my daughter. She's getting married. On Christmas Eve, can you believe? The invitations have just gone out. A really sweet illustration of her and her fiancé, Jacob. He's a novelist. Well, trying to be.'

'Ahh, lovely!' ventures Nat, immediately suspicious that all is not entirely well here. 'What did you say your daughter's name is, Helen?'

'Oh, I didn't actually, but it's Betsy. It's possible you may have seen her in here on one of your visits, she has brilliant corkscrew curls. Well, when she's not flattening them with those straightening irons of hers.' Helen is all smiles, the super-proud future mother-of-the-bride.

But those names are horribly familiar to Nat. 'And he's a writer, is he?'

'He's working on his first novel as we speak. That's why they chose to have a typewriter on the invites. A little random if you ask me, but there you go.' Helen dismisses the mild criticism with a fleeting wave of her hand.

That sounds remarkably like the invitation that's sitting on Nat's own mantelpiece at home. The one she chose and had printed because the bride was showing no interest whatsoever in doing it herself. *Now is probably not the time to share that piece of information*, thinks Nat. Women hire a professional bridesmaid for many reasons: they want high-level organisational skills without the need to reciprocate all the good deeds; they take a look at their own friends and realise no one's up to the job or they have torn loyalties and elect to appoint a stranger rather than offend a sister or an old school chum. But all of them, without question, want and need one simple thing: her total discretion. Nat's become a victim of her own success. What started as a bit of low-level hen do planning has spiralled now so hiring her often negates the need for a separate wedding planner. In truth, she prefers it that way. It's easier to conceal and invent when you have eyes over every part of the deception. And it pays well – maybe *too* well. It was never Nat's intention to build a career from this, but the large and regular payments hitting her account are making her reluctant to break free and get a proper job – one that doesn't involve lying for a living.

And that's exactly why Nat shoves another macaroon into her mouth before she can say anything that might expose lovely Betsy or force Helen to question the real motivation behind her daughter's big day.

Chapter Three

Betsy Whittaker

The 6.50 a.m. from Birmingham New Street to Euston is not a lot of fun. Not when Betsy has to fold herself in half to accommodate her own body, a backpack, her sloshing-everywhere morning coffee and a laptop twice the size of the wobbly fold-down tray harbouring the remains of an earlier commuter's breakfast. Still, she's on the train, she has a seat and, as yet, no one with any severe personal hygiene issues has chosen to sit next to her. There is also the prospect of another inspiring day in the London office awaiting her. Which is surprising.

When her boss at the recruitment agency promoted her to account director earlier this year it came with the initially horrifying downside of at least twice-weekly trips to the capital. But that negativity quickly evaporated when Betsy arrived on day one and was assigned a young, super-keen team to manage and told she would be reporting directly to Dylan, the agency's managing director.

Dylan: the man who has helped her nearly double her monthly earnings with his bold approach to candidate and client management and a level of charisma that seems to floor everyone in his path, male and female. The *confidence* of the man. Completely comfortable hearing his clever views project across the office, never for a second stilted or awkward with the new girl, he has welcomed Betsy in and promptly set about fast-tracking her up the league table of company high performers. How can she not be impressed? And want to impress him. Her already sky-high levels of organisation are being ratcheted up. First in, last out every day, never missing a beat. Jumping on any new business leads with the ferocity of a hungry wolf, leading meetings like her life depends on it. Motivating her team to work harder and smarter.

Gone are her trademark blonde corkscrew curls, replaced by a sharp, edgier bob that's more rampant bed-hair than wash-and-go. The unstylish work wardrobe has been upgraded with hip-skimming pencil skirts, one with a zip that runs tantalisingly from the waistband down between her legs to the hem. Shirts are diaphanous, revealing a hint of well-chosen lingerie, and the heels have climbed higher and higher. She's upped her game, no denying it. This job, and excelling at it, is everything now. Wedding planning? Well, on the back-burner. Just like her fiancé's plans to publish his first novel.

It's more than a year since Jacob proposed and the two of them excitedly started Googling wedding venues. But then his long-awaited and prematurely celebrated book deal fell through – a new sales director at the publishing house just couldn't be convinced of the selling power of his sci-fi trilogy. Overnight he's retreated to the dumping ground that is their second bedroom, carved out some desk space in amongst the broken clothes horse and his neglected dumbbells, where he well and truly wallows in it. Taking the promotion and alleviating their money worries seems like the naturally supportive thing to do. Betsy can hardly be blamed if it switches her ambition into overdrive, can she? Anyway, the space that her trips to London affords them is a good thing, giving Jacob ten hours of uninterrupted peace and quiet as he starts on draft four of the so far failed manuscript.

The only person to beat her in this morning is Dylan. She can see him in his glass office, scanning the business pages online with one hand, mobile in the other, already making things happen. He isn't expecting anyone in for another half an hour so his crisp pale blue shirt is still slightly unbuttoned with the sleeves rolled back to the elbows, revealing lightly tanned arms and the sort of watch that hints at the number of deals he's already closed this year. His chocolate brown hair is peppered with a hint of mature grey, casually un-styled and pushed back off a face that is slightly weathered and rugged from being all outdoorsy when he's not in the office. She tries not to think of him bare-chested and pulling himself up the side of a mountain with just his hands.

She's also momentarily reminded of what Jacob looked like this morning when she left, shuffling around their house in an unflattering dressing gown, moaning because there was nothing for breakfast and he had six hours of writing ahead of him. She has every sympathy for him, knowing he has to motivate himself with absolutely no promise of a pay day at the end of it all, and she wishes she'd been more supportive – but there was a train to catch.

Dylan ends his call and turns to see Betsy has arrived. She watches the smile break over his face before he shouts, 'Morning, trouble! Get in here.'

'Morning, boss. Who was that? The London Stock Exchange wanting your permission to open the markets?' From that first morning a few months ago, Betsy felt comfortable enough in Dylan's company to slip into an easy, early-morning banter.

'Yep, I've told them to hang on, my chief advisor isn't in the building yet. But now that you are, talk to me about what our year-end is looking like. I need revenue forecasts, a view on where our contractor numbers are, the realistic prospects of any new business leads, any new pitches for preferred supplier lists and the number of new roles coming on. But before all that, go and put those incredible red velvet heels of yours on. I can't focus properly until you do.'

Betsy pauses for a moment, not entirely sure of the correct response here. She takes half a step back, feeling her cheeks start to warm to the colour of those shoes, as Dylan erupts into hysterics.

'Bee, I'm bloody joking! What d'you take me for? I know I'm a product of the seventies, but credit me with a little more sensitivity, will you?' He's holding his sides, looking like he is thoroughly enjoying having the upper hand, and, if she's not mistaken, rather pleased he can make her blush so easily.

The fact he's noticed the shoes at all is interesting.

'Er… right. Well, all those reports are ready on my system so when I've finished lodging a complaint with HR about your gross sexism, I can present them to you any time you like.' She's relieved his sniggering is as convincing as her faux outrage.

'I look forward to it. Although my diary is rammed today so let's chat it through at the drinks tonight, shall we?'

It's not really a question, she knows that. No one says no to Dylan. Not because he's a bully, but no one ever wants to disappoint him. Or look ungrateful for his unlimited generosity. Tonight, he'll be putting his gold card behind the bar at Dirty Martini's like he does every last Friday of the month and there it will stay until the final member of the team leaves. That cannot be Betsy. She has to make the 9.20 p.m. from Euston or Jacob will already be in bed and grumpy as hell with her tomorrow morning. And she's promised to read the three new chapters he's intending to write today.

'Yep, I'll be there. And I'll fill you in on the meeting I had with that MD of the new digital marketing business I was telling you about. He's got the investment in place now and I've almost persuaded him to partner with us, bringing the first five senior execs in. It's a whole new sector for us so could have great growth potential.'

'Does anyone ever say no to you, Bee?' Dylan is giving her the look now, the one she has seen him use countless times to defrost uptight, *you-can't-flirt-with-me* female clients. Full eye contact, the slightest smirk on his lips, one that suggests he's thinking about something very different to work. She always marvels at how quickly women unravel in his presence. Except she can feel herself doing it too now and is keen to escape before he notices.

'Ha, no one with any sound business sense, obviously!' She's turning to leave but just catches Dylan say, slightly under his breath, 'I have to admit, they are bloody great shoes, though.'

And so starts a day of relentless phone bashing, only disconnecting from her headset to glug back the three litres of water needed to keep selling for nine hours or to troubleshoot ideas with her team. She loves the three of them: Lauren, fresh out of Bristol University with an inexperienced but razor-sharp strategic mind, who is yet to work out how powerful her natural beauty is going to be; Anton, who joined from a rival agency last year with obvious ambitions to be the next Dylan but also a host of bad business habits that Betsy is having to unravel. Then there's Kirsty, the only one with a young child so consequently the one who makes the best use of her time before she flies out the door on the nursery run.

By six o'clock Betsy can practically taste the first chilled glass of Sauvignon Blanc in the back of her throat. As she gathers the team together an email arrives from Dylan explaining he'll meet them there, as he's having a quick drink with a client the other side of town. She can't deny she's a little disappointed. The evening won't really get going until he arrives and she's keen to show off the progress she's made with the new digital client. If she can pull this off, it will mean a whole new revenue stream for the agency and the warm glow of Dylan's approval, perhaps even the prospect of another promotion in the new year. She throws her phone, purse and a bunch of reports that she needs to read overnight into her bag before pausing for a moment. Then she kicks off the black ankle boots she's had on all day and replaces them with the much-higher red velvet heels.

Dirty Martini's is heaving but they've reserved their usual table in the corner and everyone starts to drop bags, unpeel coats and sink onto the low gold leather seats and footstools. Betsy tries her best to reserve the seat next to her for Dylan but Anton plonks himself down and immediately starts a verbal assassination of a client who got the better of him today. A waitress in a microscopic black skirt and vest, and with the sort of legs Betsy thought only existed in the movies, appears with cocktail menus and a couple of bottles of prosecco. 'They're from Dylan,' she explains. 'Until he gets here.' Betsy is first in. If she has to have this conversation *again* with Anton, then a little light lubrication won't go amiss.

'No client can expect us to spot absolutely bloody everything on every single CV we see, for crying out loud!' Anton's had all day to get over this but it's like he's saved up all his annoyance to dump on Betsy now.

'Well, as I've already said, Anton, it was a pretty big oversight. Not spotting a three-month break in someone's employment history, and then leaving it to the client to discover those three months were actually spent at Her Majesty's leisure for GBH at a football match is really not ideal, is it?' So far, Betsy has protected Anton by not sharing the details of this balls-up with Dylan, but Anton's inability to just accept he's wrong and apologise unreservedly to the client is really starting to rankle with her.

'But he should have told me about it when we first spoke, how am I supposed to—'

'Unless you drill down on this level of detail, you leave yourself, and this agency, wide open to these kinds of mistakes, you know that.' She needs to shut Anton up before Dylan arrives, or he'll want a full account of it all. And the last thing she wants is for it to reflect badly on her. Betsy's eyes are at the door again but there's still no sign of him.

'The client was expecting this guy to start the role, they had rejected all the other candidates, which now means they are right back to square one with the recruitment process. And we've suffered reputational damage. You have to be more thorough.'

Betsy's relieved it's so dimly lit in here, helping to disguise her increasing lack of interest in Anton. He can wait until next week; she's had enough work chat for one day and is happy to be distracted by what's going on around her.

The place is packed with girls in their twenties who have clearly spent a good half an hour in the office loos with the bronzer and dry shampoo, now throwing back the Peach Bellinis and Negronis. Thirty-four's not exactly old, but it suddenly feels like it, although she's grateful to be out of this dating warzone. While Anton continues to blather on uninvited, she notices a girl in an emerald green mini dress being near-pinned to a wall by a man who's finding himself more amusing than she is. On the other side of the bar another girl with a high glossy ponytail, wearing a black silk jumpsuit, is doing a valiant job of looking interested in a guy who's just bought her a glass of wine. As he's speaking conspiratorially into her right ear, he's pushing his groin backwards and forwards in time to the resident DJ, perhaps giving her a little taster of what delights might await her if only she would agree to go home with him tonight. It's all so… unsophisticated.

Eight o'clock and still no Dylan. Betsy's thoughts flick back to Jacob, and whether he hit his three-chapter target today. Well, whatever he's managed, she'll be reading it tonight and loving it. He badly needs the confidence boost or the entire weekend will be lost to another one of his epic moods. The thought forces another glass of prosecco down her throat.

As the last of the heady fizz disperses around her mouth, her mobile vibrates in her lap. She looks down to see a text that reminds her of the wedding date that is looming roughly ten weeks from now. The dress that is yet to be chosen. The menu that remains undecided. The flowers she hasn't given a second thought to.

Hi Betsy, remember I'm looking at bridesmaids' dresses soon, so if you could come back to me on the shortlist of options I sent you, that would be amazing!

As she finishes reading, Betsy hears a cheer and glances up to see that Dylan has finally arrived at 8.45 p.m., just as another text pings through.

Timing is tight. Need to decide at the first fitting so do let me know, love Nat

Despite feeling an immediate connection with Nat, like she could trust her with anything, Betsy still feels uncomfortable about her decision to hire a professional bridesmaid. It's not exactly the sort of thing women do every day of the week, is it? And she does have plenty of genuine friends to choose from. The ad popped up on her Facebook feed as she was leaving her mum's place after a weekend of concerned remarks about the lack of progress on the wedding front. And her mum, Helen, should know. Owning and running two successful bridal boutiques, she couldn't *not* be aware of how horribly behind her daughter is. Betsy is trying to make eye contact with Dylan, but all she can see is the look of sheer joy on her mum's face the day she announced her engagement. Joy that is so needed in their family right now. In the days that followed, her mum's excitement was palpable in every gushy text she sent and the daily calls they shared. After helping with so many other big days, finally, she was going to do it for her own daughter and she was raring to go. It's just that Betsy's not: she's pulling back, not charging forwards, and hating herself for the stain of disappointment she's casting over her mum's eager anticipation. She wishes she could say she is merely protecting her already-busy mum from the burden of the extra workload, but there's more to it than that.

Hiring Nat seemed like a convenient way to keep the ball rolling, just to get something ticked off the list, buy her some time and satisfy some of the questions she doesn't have time to consider. From the first moment they met in a discreet Italian coffee shop behind the tube station, Betsy knew in another life they might be firm friends. Nat strode in, pulled her into a hug without waiting to see if it might be appreciated, then announced, 'Your stress is now my stress,' and Betsy was sold – on the woman and everything she could do for her.

And, to be brutally honest, having Nat has helped avoid forcing conversations with Jacob he never seems to want to have because he's editing, rewriting or talking game plans with his beleaguered literary agent. Now, as the weeks have rolled on and she's pushed more and more tasks Nat's way, effectively promoting her from bridesmaid to full wedding planner, she feels completely disconnected from the whole process. Jacob hasn't even bothered to ask who this bridesmaid is, but Nat is amazing. Not cheap, but taking a ruthlessly professional approach to it all, which is what Betsy loves – and needs – right now. She fires a quick text back:

Whatever you think is best. I know you won't get it wrong.

Dylan is waving at her from the bar, one hand tilting towards his mouth, the universal shorthand for 'what d'you want to drink?' as she works her way through the throng. He has already attracted the attention of the ponytailed beauty, who sidesteps her gyrating companion to get closer to him. There are another five or six colleagues swarming him too, keen to hear how the meeting went. It's nearly nine o'clock, twenty minutes until her train leaves Euston. The only way she'll make it is to go right now, grab a black cab and beg the driver to floor it down Great Portland Street. She gives up on Dylan, darts back to the table, grabs her bag and coat and is out the door, straight into an idle taxi. Then the driver is on and off the accelerator, speeding around corners and braking late at lights until she is feeling every bubble of the four glasses of prosecco start to climb back up her throat.

Six minutes to spare. She throws a tenner at the driver and sprints across the concourse at Euston, now seriously regretting the pointless shoe switch, to her usual platform three. No time for the loo, she's going to have to use the vile facilities on board. No train! She belts back to the concourse, towards the information boards, until she is close enough for the letters and numbers to shift into focus. The 9.20 p.m. to Birmingham New Street, platform twelve. Shite! – it's always platform three! She knows she'll never make it but runs anyway, praying for once it might just be delayed – an extra two minutes is all she needs. As she rounds the corner to platform twelve, there it is, crawling away from her. All she can do is watch as it gathers speed.

Her phone is jumping to life again and this time it's a text from Dylan:

Wow, that hurt. Running out on me like that. You're a proper heartbreaker, Bee.

She slumps down onto the cold metal station seating, knowing she has forty minutes to kill before the next train and that dinner will now be whatever dregs are left in the Starbucks' chill cabinet.

When she finally tiptoes through the front door of their house at 11.30 p.m. the place is in total darkness and Jacob is nowhere to be seen. He did at least leave her a note before he went to bed. It's on the work surface, next to the kettle and a plate of stone-cold chicken stir-fry:

After being such a grump this morning, I thought I'd make you dinner, but it looks like you've had a better offer. Don't wake me up when you come in. Two of the three chapters still need writing so I'll be up early. That's my weekend sorted, I suppose. And we were meant to have a Skype call with a caterer tonight. Did you forget about that too? Everything was way too expensive, in case you're interested.

Sometimes she feels there is nothing she can do to make Jacob happy. Only getting this book published is going to achieve that. She re-reads Dylan's text six more times before finally switching her phone off and climbing into bed. She can think of many things she'd like to text back, but decides against all of them.

Chapter Four

Helen Whittaker

Lunch at Scott's is going to be *fabulous*. And Helen has dressed for the occasion today in her favourite rosehip silk dress, cuffed at the sleeves, with a high V-neck and diamond seams that allow it to flare out playfully around her knees. She's meeting Nick there at 1 p.m., leaving just enough time to confirm the full day of appointments she has booked in tomorrow – and to chase her daughter, Betsy, about her wedding dress, *again*.

It's just ten weeks now until Betsy will marry her fiancé, Jacob, in the beautiful nineteenth-century church that sits opposite Helen's other boutique in the village of Little Bloombury in the Cotswolds. But progress on the wedding planning front has been painfully slow. Helen is keen not to harass her daughter about the now urgent decision-making she needs to tackle, but she's struggling to understand her reluctance.

When Betsy arrived at her cottage to break the engagement news more than a year ago, she couldn't have been happier. It was all hugs, happy tears and dress predictions before they belted downstairs to Helen's boutique below the apartment and started loading Betsy up in veils and tiaras. Now, rather tired of waiting for any sort of update since then or even a steer on the colour palette for Betsy's big day, Helen has ploughed on, buying her own outfit weeks ago. It's a carefully chosen, works-with-anything pale blue and silver jacquard dress by Bruce Oldfield. The pretty floral print, fitted bodice with its fuller skirt and distinctive sailor collar, looks just grand enough. As she stepped out of the fitting room in Peter Jones on Sloane Square that day, she thought she saw a flicker of pride in Nick's eyes as he said it suited her perfectly.

He's been the most wonderful friend to Helen over the months it has taken to get her new London bridal boutique open for business. His firm of architects pitched for the job of transforming the site into the elegant space it is today and under Helen's confident direction, he's been a much-needed sounding board ever since. It was Nick's suggestion to push the ceiling a little higher, reducing Helen's storage space upstairs but giving a wonderfully airy ambience to the boutique, where it really matters. When the builder told Helen she couldn't hope to save the original parquet flooring, Nick armed her with the facts to make sure she could. And after the neighbouring Italian coffee shop complained that all the building works were adversely affecting their passing trade, he personally negotiated new working hours for the builders that meant no white vans taking up all the parking spaces at peak times.

But the real glory belongs to Helen. Her first boutique opening in the Cotswolds, when life felt so fragile, was done tentatively, with little confidence but plenty of passion. This time it's different. Spurred on by the growing demand for her expertise, endless calls from London brides who want to see her, but don't have time to travel into the countryside, Helen took the leap to the capital. And she did so with all the ambition and drive needed to guarantee success. The financial risk means little, such is her soaring self-assurance now. Safeguarding her professional reputation is everything and on that point, she surely cannot fail.

Helen was the one who suggested lunch today as a thank you for all Nick's help. Then, before she had a chance to book anything, Nick left a message on the boutique voicemail with the restaurant name and the time of their reservation. Just one more thing he's prevented her from worrying about.

As she's sending the final email to confirm the last of tomorrow's brides, Helen is thinking back to the first time she and Nick met; how he came alone when he could so easily have sent someone more junior, as most of the other firms did. How, when he walked into the hotel lobby where they had arranged to meet, she was momentarily intimidated by him; his six-foot frame, the shock of well-styled, glossy grey hair, the perfect teeth. But within two minutes of him sitting opposite her and extending a warm hand to shake, his gentlemanly good manners put her entirely at ease. They've spoken almost every working day since then.

Helen tries one more time to connect with Betsy's mobile, but as it clicks to voicemail for the fifth time this week, she gives up. Is her daughter deliberately avoiding her? Surely not. No time to worry about it now, she doesn't want to be late for Nick. It's a cold but bright day and Helen is going to walk towards Oxford Street and into Mayfair to Scott's restaurant. But as she steps out of the boutique and turns to lock the door, something roots her to the spot, halting her own breath inside of her. A man in smart chinos and a winter trench, clearly in a hurry, swerves around her and as their bodies briefly brush together, she's unable to move for a moment because there it is. *That smell.* One she hasn't enjoyed on a man for nearly five years. Her accidental assailant is mumbling an apology and checking Helen is OK, but her mind is somewhere else entirely.

It's the middle of summer and she and Phillip are lying down, feeling the fresh, green grass prickle the backs of their knees as they squint up into the sun, its intense heat stinging their cheeks. His arm is draped across the front of her softened belly and he's whispering how she has made him the happiest man alive, while a gurgling baby Betsy lies between them. The smell of him, that unmistakable soft woody musk that she loved, mingles with the comforting freshness of his own skin. She remembers it on Betsy's hair that day too, after he'd picked her up and cuddled her. It's the smell that started every day they shared together, and told her he was home from work. Its deep blue glass bottle was the last thing she always bought to finish off his Christmas stocking.

As the tears are streaming down Helen's face through short, sharp breaths, she is struggling to force the key back into the lock of The White Gallery entrance. Once inside, she drops her bag to the floor and collapses onto one of the blush-pink chairs. She pulls out her phone and with unsteady fingers, sends the briefest text to Nick, warning him she'll be a little late. Then she's digging through her bag for the wet wipes, still shocked by the force of what just happened, feeling the adrenaline start to slowly ease back, no longer feeding her panic. Helen stands in front of the boutique mirror, ready to reapply her make-up, and she sees before her the strained, suddenly unsure face of a woman she thought she'd said goodbye to months ago.

*

The smart box hedging that fronts the windows of Scott's is perfectly neat. Just like the doorman who pulls the heavy glass door open for her and the sharply pressed host who takes her coat and bag into the cloakroom before leading her through to their table. Nick is waiting for her and stands as he sees her approaching. *Gosh, he's impossible not to notice,* thinks Helen, not for the first time. There's no denying he's in incredible shape for a man in his early sixties. His skin is more radiant than most of the stressed-out twenty-somethings she spends her days advising and there is not the faintest hint of a paunch under the black cashmere sweater he's wearing today.

'Wow, what are we celebrating?' Helen notices the two glasses of chilled champagne already on the table, as she reaches up to place the briefest kiss either side of his face.

'Oh, I'm sure we'll think of something.' He's smiling through the words as he helps Helen into one of the green leather dining chairs. 'And if nothing else, then let's at least drink to the past six months, the opening of your second White Gallery and to what I'm sure is going to be the most successful year ahead for you, Helen.'

'Cheers to that! And to you, Nick, for all your wonderful support. I really couldn't have done it without you. Honestly, you've been incredible.'

They clink glasses, Nick letting his eyes linger on Helen's in a way that makes her gulp back a little more fizz than she intended. The little alcohol spike is needed. Her emotions are back under control but the incident at the boutique has unnerved her. She would hate to unravel like that again in front of Nick. And somewhere as refined as Scott's.

Just being in here feels exciting. There isn't a spare seat at the marble-topped seafood bar in the centre of the restaurant, where a circle of well-heeled men and women are working their way through a mountain of iced oysters. Everywhere Helen looks, people are having a tremendous time: corporate colleagues, tucking into the lobster thermidor and not caring how much it costs; older ladies, with perfectly set hair and overly rouged lips, slowly nibbling on the beluga, more interested in the gossip than the food. And diners like herself and Nick, rewarding themselves, celebrating something special.

'I'm so pleased you could join me today, Helen. You deserve a treat after all the hard work.' Nick's hand rests briefly on top of Helen's and, surprisingly, she is in no hurry to wriggle it free.

'It was supposed to be my treat, Nick.' The last thing she wants is for him to think she has conveniently forgotten her promise to buy him lunch.

'I know, I know, and please forgive me but you *are* the client and I like to consider myself extremely lucky to be at your disposal, so there we are. I hope you can live with that? Now, please tell me about Betsy, have you managed to persuade her into action with the wedding plans?'

Plate after plate of langoustine, simple smoked salmon with muslin-wrapped lemons and potted shrimps come and go, as Helen fills Nick in on the increasingly distracted Betsy. He listens intently, never attempting to change the subject, just letting her get it all off her chest while he keeps the champagne coming. Then a beautiful crystal highball glass of sloe gin jelly, that Helen doesn't remember ordering, is placed in front of her. She's lost all sense of time, failing to notice that most of the other diners, well-oiled from the mix of fine wine and caviar, have retreated to the other delights of Mayfair – or returned to their offices, clients happily sloshed and with their lunch deals all tied up.

She is aware that Nick is silently smiling at her.

'What? What have I said that is amusing you so much, Nick?' She's giggling but also vaguely aware that the fizz has loosened her so much she may not be making as much sense as she thinks.

'You're just so wonderful, I love spending time with you. My greatest worry, Helen, is that now the boutique is up and running, you may not need me any more.' His mood has shifted to being more earnest, not that Helen has noticed.

'Oh, don't you worry! Give it another month and you will be well and truly sick of my calls about cracking plasterwork and whether I should extend the boutique to give me another fitting room.' She's spooning the last of the jelly into her mouth and chuckling at her own imagined neediness.

'No, I won't. I won't ever get bored of hearing from you. I can't imagine anything worse than *not* hearing from you.' His eyes are on her, waiting for Helen to read the change in his tone. Gone is the light-hearted charm. He takes a huge intake of breath and waits, willing her to understand the point he's making.

'Oh. Well, er, that's very kind of you.' She's fiddling with the napkin in her lap, not at all sure how to handle such a direct compliment.

'I'm not trying to be kind, Helen. I'm trying to tell you that I don't want to be apart from you.' He's so intense, not in the slightest bit embarrassed about sharing his feelings so honestly, so openly.

Helen looks at him, sees all over his face how much thought he has given to this. How he might have imagined this conversation, planned it, even.

'I want to see you every day, not just be someone you call when you need a recommendation for a good plumber. I love you, Helen, I have done for months. And I don't want to hide it any more. You're everything to me.'

All she can think is, *how has this happened? How could I possibly not have seen this coming? I was just being me and now…*

'I… I… thought we were just friends, I had no idea you felt this way.' Her mind is racing back over all their calls, all the time they've spent together and how much of it was strictly necessary. How much did he instigate? How much did she suggest? There have been moments of real tenderness between them – a slightly lingering kiss on the cheek at the end of one lunch, a brief touching of hands as he steered her across a busy road and one surprisingly frank dinner where he confided that his biggest regret in life was never marrying – but nothing in Helen's mind that strayed beyond good friends who care for each other.

And then the words she thought she would never hear again fall out of Nick's mouth.

'Marry me, Helen. I love you.'

She recognises the little red box immediately. Cartier. It sits on the white tablecloth between them, like a panic button no one wants to touch, having left Nick's fingers but not yet been embraced by hers. It's impossible to ignore.

'Open it, please.' It's the first time she's seen Nick anything close to nervous. His breath has deepened and he looks slightly pained, like it's dawning on him far too late that this might not go the way he intended it to. It's making Helen panic, knowing she won't be able to spare him the embarrassment and awkwardness that's coming. Not because she doesn't hugely respect the man sat in front of her, a man who makes her feel special every single time she's in his company, someone she looks forward to seeing more than just about anyone else she knows. She should be elated, she knows that, but… a marriage proposal?

'Oh, Nick. I wasn't expecting this at all, I'm not sure I can…' Unlike Nick, who seems oblivious to anyone else in the room, Helen sees they are starting to attract the attention of one or two waiters who are hovering nearby, no doubt waiting for the instruction to unleash more champagne.

But he *can* see she has no intention of taking the luxe little box, so he reaches forward and opens it for her, revealing the most beautiful diamond ring Helen has ever seen. A central pear-shaped diamond, surrounded by a spray of smaller ones. It's large, quite breathtakingly so, and enough to force Helen to her feet.

'Helen, *please.*' Nick's standing too now, searching for a hand that doesn't want to be found. 'I know this is a surprise and I hope I haven't upset you. I want nothing more than to wrap my arms around you now, to kiss you. Please, will you at least give my question some thought?'

Helen can feel the tears choking up through her and has no choice but to mutter a rushed *I'm sorry*, before she is skitting back across the dining room towards the cloakroom.

A quick glance over her shoulder tells her Nick is going to let her go. She sees him close the lid of the ring box and place it back in his inside jacket pocket before she is out onto Mount Street, into the first black cab she sees, and disappearing away from him.

Chapter Five

Jenny

Ten minutes until my shift starts and the staffroom is its usual chaotic mess. The central coffee table is strewn with all the hallmarks of an intensely busy nightshift. Half-eaten sandwiches – some with only a single bite mark out of them – have been left to get limp and warm next to a tower of Diet Coke cans and Tupperware boxes of homemade leftovers that were started but never finished. It's the biscuits and sweets that have been demolished, the things you can grab on the run when the chance of an actual break in your twelve-hour shift is pure fantasy.

No one looks up as I enter the room, already too caught up in the rushed chat before the shift starts. It might only be 7.15 a.m., when the rest of the population is just starting to stir in their beds, but here the banter is already raucous, unedited and consuming. People often seem to think there is something saintly about being a midwife. They'd change their minds soon enough if they spent ten minutes in here. Maybe pulling on the burgundy coloured scrubs makes you a little anonymous to the nine other women sharing your shift and therefore free to say what you wouldn't otherwise? Perhaps it's just pure release from the stress of what we're all about to go through together. Surely you can only rummage around between the legs of total strangers so many times before your ability to judge what's appropriate and what's not becomes clouded and irrelevant forever. Whatever it is, the air is already blue with talk of anal bleaching, married sex – or lack of it – and the fullness of bush we should all be aiming for.

'I prefer the full winter coat, myself, thick and fierce when it's that cold outside. Not a pair of knickers on earth that could hope to contain it, and my Keith is quite happy with that, thank you very much!' Lucy is one of the most experienced midwives in the unit, with seven years' service at Queen Mary's, three of her own grown-up children and an ineffectual husband who unwittingly provides most of the entertainment in this staffroom. But right now, he's getting a brief reprieve.

'Really? A full thigh invasion?' Jean is our head of midwifery. An ordinarily quite refined woman in her early fifties, something of the librarian about her, she's generally unshockable, unless we're talking about pubic hair. She has a limitless supply of gumption and experience, a proper roll-up-your-sleeves type. I've seen her get results from the most tired women, who truly believed they couldn't go on; motivate useless fathers-to-be with her 'no spectators in here!' approach to childbirth and keep a room free from panic when everything and everyone else around her was starting to unravel. She garners huge respect from the medical team here – and from me. I've always admired her, although I'm not sure she notices me much.

The next ten minutes, between last hurried bites of buttered toast and gulps of too-hot tea, is devoted to a frank discussion about what a woman's approach to personal grooming says about her – one chat I'm happy not to be asked for my input on. Full pelt? You're strong, womanly and capable, apparently. Landing strip? Too controlling. Mannequin bald? Angry with the world. Shaped or coloured—

'Now, *that* I just don't understand.' Lucy is pulling her wiry dark hair back into a loose knot, removing her impractical hoop earrings and sunglasses – that always seem to perch on top of her head, regardless of the weather – all while simultaneously pushing her feet into the ugly black work shoes we all tolerate. 'All that self-love and adulation. Really, who can be bothered?'

I dump my bag on the side next to a microwave that's full of soup spills, and the pile of magazines that no one will get a chance to flick through today. Then I check my phone one last time and make a mental note to call my sister, Lulu, this week. We haven't spoken properly for weeks and I could do with one of our downloads – if she can fit me in between delegating her life out to the cleaner, nutritionist, personal trainer, dog walker… I'm sure I'm missing someone.

As the team from the nightshift clocks off, with the pallid grey complexions that usually accompany brain-numbing tiredness, we all file into the central office where a giant white board charts the progress of every woman still in the department. Most of the action has happened overnight and the new mums have been moved to the postnatal ward. We've hit a lull so I'm assigned the one thing no one ever wants to do: admin. I'm refilling supplies, date-checking medications, and making sure every trolley in the place is stocked with all the swabs, delivery packs and latex gloves it needs.

It means my mind can wander to my six o'clock appointment with Helen at The White Gallery. The briefest flick onto Instagram last night turned into an indulgent two-hour marathon through lavishly laid banqueting tables, brightly coloured bouquets, huge floral arches, dessert tables covered in every conceivable cake and enough wedding dresses to fill Helen's beautiful boutique a thousand times over. I can't quite believe I'm going to keep this appointment. As I'm replenishing the supply of stitches and mesh knickers, I'm thinking I should just call her on my first break and cancel. It seemed like an amusing idea last night but now, knowing later on I'll have to stand in front of her and fabricate the vision of my perfect wedding day? It's just ridiculous. I can't waste Helen's time, she's obviously busy and, lovely as she seems, I'm sure she won't appreciate that. No, I'll call to cancel.

As I'm tormenting myself with it all, I hear the breathless, low moan of a young woman who has just arrived at the reception desk. I push the last of the protective bed sheets into their designated boxes and march back around the corner towards the sound. She's alone, bent over the counter, and weeping, clearly struggling to remain upright while she chokes out her name and contact details between contractions. My instincts take over immediately. I want to care for her, to take away the fear she is feeling. I place one arm around her shoulders, gently easing her upright, and the other loosely across her bump, feeling how taut it is.

'Oh God, help me, *please*. I can't breathe.' She can't be any older than twenty-two, twenty-three, perhaps.

'I've got you. Everything is going to be OK. Just lean on me and we'll get you straight to a room so I can examine you.' Being a midwife is like being an actress in many ways. I adapt my performance to suit the woman in front of me and what she needs. This one is scared. I can see it in her wide eyes and feel it in the unrelentingly tight grip she has on my hand.

'Room four is free, Jenny.' Our receptionist can see this woman hasn't got long to go. 'This is Sarah Richards. She's in good health, full term, first baby, no complications. Maternity notes are in her bag. Husband is on his way.'

Room four is my favourite. It's big with plenty of space for women to move into different birthing positions. It's dimly lit and has a chair that reclines so that partners can be almost horizontal if things go on through the night, as they so frequently do. I don't think Sarah will have to worry about that.

'I can't do this!' She's wailing between sobs as she lowers herself onto her elbows over the bed. 'I'm not ready, I haven't got my candles or my labour playlist. I can't do it! I can't do it! Where's Matt? You won't leave me, will you?' Despite the pain, she doesn't take her eyes off me, terrified that I might disappear into the corridor, leaving her to cope alone. I never would.

She's flailing around the room, working herself up into a panic that will help no one, least of all her unborn baby, wasting all that vital energy she's going to need. Between contractions that I time as four minutes apart, I wrestle her out of her clothes and into a green hospital gown. She screams for all she's worth for an epidural that I decide not to tell her isn't coming. It takes three of us to keep her still enough to get her onto the bed so I can examine her, and while I'm confirming she's seven centimetres dilated, Lucy is giving her a crash course in how to use the gas and air.

'Long, deep breaths, take as much in as you can. Try to control your breath, Sarah, don't rush it.' Lucy's trying her best but it's having little effect as Sarah pants rapidly into the mouthpiece, hearing none of the advice she's being given. She's flushed and sweating, so far from being in control of herself, I wonder if I will be able to get her back on track. Lucy is needed elsewhere, so it's all down to me. I know what's happening: she's caught in that sticky place between what the antenatal classes have told her to expect and trusting her own body to do what it has been designed to do – to try, despite the pain, to just go with it.

'Sarah, listen to me, you are doing brilliantly. I just want you to listen to me now, do exactly as I ask you to and very soon you are going to have a baby.'

'Not without Matt!' she's yelling at me.

I try to distract her with questions about baby names and whether or not her parents have any other grandchildren. I give her a handheld fan and offer her some iced water. Then I lower the lights a little further, get her to lean over the end of the bed while I hold a cold wet flannel to her forehead with one hand and massage the small of her back with the other. But she's fighting me all the way, too far into her own private panic room to see a way out.

Just as I reluctantly think I may need to get Jean involved, the door swings open and it's her husband, Matt. He strides across the room in two big steps, gathers her up in his arms, where she stays, completely cocooned by him.

'Please could you play this?' He's handing me a Waitrose carrier bag containing an iPod and docking station. 'Just hit play, it's all ready to go. Thank you.'

The room fills with the sound of Etta James's 'At Last' and the two of them start to sway from side to side. He's leading her in the most romantic dance I've ever seen. They're circling the room together while I take a seat in the corner, on a birthing ball. I'm not needed now, it's my chance to catch up on the paperwork as I keep an eye on them both. They continue like that for another couple of hours, her heightened breathing the only clue she's in any pain at all. She returns to lean on the bed for extra support only when the strongest contractions hit. Then, with no warning, she lowers herself into a squat using the bed frame to hold her position and calmly says, 'I need to push.'

Their baby daughter is delivered easily into my waiting hands and, as Matt kneels beside Sarah on the floor, kissing her forehead over and over again, he says, 'You're incredible, I love you, I love you. I can't believe what you just did, you truly amazing woman!'

There was a time when I briefly believed this might happen for me. Not the baby, but Sam, a visiting student doctor at St Mary's who used to hold me tight and full of urgency, letting his blond locks tangle with mine. But I mistook his cravings for love, stupidly believing he was all mine. The patronising look on his face when he, very honestly, he thought, explained I was one of many, will stay with me forever, I think.

I can feel the tears starting to run down my face. All three of us are crying now – well, four, if you count the baby. And this is why I love what I do, why I first decided to become a midwife. Being there, doing whatever I can to bring a new life into the world, holding a mirror up to the most intimate moment a couple will ever share. I want some of that hope. It's such a privilege, this job. But there is a downside: perhaps it's not fair to expect such career highs without the personal lows it forces on me too. Sharing these tender moments with a couple I barely know can only make me question my own place in the world, such as it is. Will I ever be a mum? Will I ever open *that* letter from my mother? I know she always thought I would.

I leave Sarah, Matt and their new daughter curled up together under soft candlelight – he remembered those too, bless him. They're all so content, I even manage to duck out a little earlier than I should. The night shift will be coming on soon, someone will be round with the tea and toast. I'm pleased I never got a chance to cancel Helen after all.

*

I take the ten-minute walk down Southwick Street and around Hyde Park Crescent to Connaught Street and The White Gallery. I'm relieved I spent so much time online last night. During all that social scrolling, I discovered a feed called 'All About Us', a stream of defining wedding photos from big days all over the country. My favourite was one of the more intimate ones. The couple had exclusively hired a country house in Wiltshire for the perfect low-key, home-away-from-home, house party wedding. With a church at the bottom of its garden, huge sash windows for gazing out onto manicured grounds, deep collapse-onto teal sofas, an open-all-hours cocktail bar and a ground floor designed to party in, it was the perfect choice. And it could, in theory, be *my* choice, couldn't it? I'll just borrow their wedding day if Helen asks. Talk about how they, *I*, plan to fill the drawing rooms with vases overflowing with powdery cream peonies and how I'll mark the walkways with giant white orchids. How guests will dine on English veal and Cuban rum babas. How at midnight we'll all be tucking in to Cotswold wagyu beefburgers and dancing the night away under the stars in the glasshouse. Perfect. I feel prepared. I can do this. I remember just in time to take Mum's ring out of the inside zip compartment of my handbag and slip it on.

Helen is waiting for me. Oh God, maybe I'll just come clean to her. She seems nice enough, I'm sure she'll understand. It may not even be the first time it's happened.

'Come in, Jenny! Ahhh, my final lady of the day. Now, I had a good look at you yesterday and I've selected some styles that I think will suit you perfectly. They are all on your rail, back there in the fitting room. Shall we take a look? And you can fill me in on all the details of your plans so far.' Helen is reaching for two champagne flutes from a glass side table. 'And, as you are the last appointment of the day, how about a few bubbles, too?'

'Yes, please!' After the day I've had, I'm more than willing to take up her offer of some free fizz.

'How about we start with the Hayley Paige?' Helen is handing me a flute as I'm kicking off my flats and starting to wriggle free of my jeans.

Whoa, the Hayley Paige is magnificent! Probably exactly what I would have chosen, if Helen hadn't been so spot on with her selections. OK, I'm doing this. I need to see what that dress looks like on me.

'It's Hayley's blue willow embroidered ballgown, with a tiered tulle skirt,' she's telling me as she's lifting the dress up over my hips and gently fastening it behind me. 'I just had a feeling this was going to look divine on you and I'm happy to say, I'm not wrong!'

This dress is everything and I'm wondering why any woman would ever try another after it. The delicate blue embroidery is glistening off the bodice, bringing the whole thing to life before it erupts into layers and layers of skirt. As I start to move, it's gently lifting outwards, growing in size, and I have to stop before I knock over our champagne.

'Step back into the shop for a moment, Jenny. You'll have a little more space there to really see what this dress is capable of.' Helen takes my hand and I follow her back to the giant mirror that is resting against a wall there.

'Wow!' I can't help myself, I'm spinning around, lifting the skirts with my hands and letting them drop again dramatically, imagining for a moment how they might look during my first dance. Stupid, yes, but bloody magical, too. The dress is swishing from side to side, performing its heart out for me, almost begging to be bought. And if the ring on my left hand was really meant to be there, there is no doubt in my mind that I'd be buying this dress.

'Shall I take a picture so you can show your mother, Jenny? She wouldn't want to miss this, would she?' Helen is looking around the boutique for her phone so she can snap me.

'You don't need to, actually. She's…' Even after all these years I still struggle to say the word 'dead', knowing it will cause faces to flush and eyes to drop to the floor. 'She passed away.'

'Oh, I'm so sorry to hear that.' Helen's eyes stay fixed on mine. I think she's weighing up whether I need a hug, as her mouth shifts into the warmest smile. 'Would you mind if I take a photo anyway, Jenny? You look beautiful and I feel like we should record this moment, don't you?'

'Yes, I agree!'

'I'm going to grab you a veil, wait there.'

I watch with a huge smile on my face as Helen practically skips off back into the fitting room, where she's placed a few key choices.

Then, as I turn back round to the mirror, something catches my eye in the window of the boutique. I have to squint to make it out at first, battling against the reflections from inside that are projected there. There's something about it that tells me it's not supposed to be there; that I'm not going to be pleased. Then a face becomes clear. The wiry hair, the sunglasses on the top of her head, the hoop earrings: Lucy. Her jaw has dropped open and, as I stand and stare motionless, feeling like the fraud I am in this puff of tulle, both her hands move up to cover her gaping mouth. Then, before I can react, she bursts into laughter and starts pointing at me, mouthing the words *Oh My God* through the glass.

Chapter Six

Nat

For every bride who makes Nat's job a blast, there is one like Grace, who confirms beyond doubt that weddings really do bring out the worst in humanity.

On the plus side, Nat looks incredible in the gown that Helen so expertly chose for this big day. On the downside, the very long list of demands this bride has made of Nat in the run-up to her wedding is now culminating with one request that she is really not sure she can fulfil.

'Sorry, you want me to do *what*?' They are standing outside Chelsea Town Hall. Vows have just been exchanged. The new Mrs Fletcher-Lawson is resplendent in a Vera Wang that costs more than some people earn in six months. All should be rosy, but Grace is pulling Nat to one side, making her well-wishers wait before they can deliver their congratulatory kisses.

'The second we arrive at the reception, I want you to spill something on Maria.' Grace is hissing out the words, jabbing her head backwards, in the direction of a beautiful young woman with cascading golden hair flowing all the way down the back of her white silk dress. 'Then she'll *have* to change.'

'Are you serious? You really want me to do that?' Nat can already see from the look of pure venom on her miserable face that Grace is indeed entirely serious.

'Of course I bloody do! She's wearing *white.* How dare she? We made it very clear on the invitations that the dress code was *do not disappoint.* Well, this disappoints me a great deal and I'm not tolerating it, so it's up to you to sort it. And do it properly. Red wine or coffee, something there will be no chance of rinsing off in the loos.' With that, Grace's own head of glossy locks is tossed so violently skyward that her monstrously large tiara is in danger of taking flight.

Nat should have known something like this would happen today, that this bride was never going to be happy, regardless of how the day might unfold. All the warning signs were there but Nat ignored them in favour of the large fee. For a start, she was hired not because this bride wanted to spare her friends the hassle of all those bridesmaid logistics but because Grace wanted to add to her long list of employees. She wasn't, like some lovely brides before her, looking to spare anyone's hurt feelings, nothing nearly as altruistic as that: Grace wanted to have total control over the person doing all the donkey work. The pouting perfectionist planner Bruce – who was overheard quietly seething this morning, 'I will reject any canapé that exceeds twenty-five milimetres diameter!' – could make everything look pretty, while Nat was left with all the jobs no sane person should ever say yes to. And the job description has been long and arduous.

When one of Grace's invited guests announced her own engagement and confirmed the wedding date would follow a month after the Lawsons', Grace exploded in a rage down the phone to Nat. She made it very clear it was Nat's job to call the girl in question and explain that this was Grace's *year* and only a change of her own wedding date would continue to secure her an invite to *this* one. Next, when it became obvious Grace wasn't going to hit her target weight in time, it was Nat who had to call Helen and beg her to rush through another gown. The one already on order would of course fit, Helen had made sure of that. But Grace wanted an identical gown, two sizes smaller, to be photographed on its hanger. 'It's one of the key shots!' she had moaned to Nat. 'Just bloody well make it happen, will you.' Then finally, when Grace discovered a week before the big day that twelve guests were yet to contribute to the wedding fund, it was Nat's job to call each and every one of them, reminding them of all the necessary banking details. And no, Bruce couldn't be expected to dirty his hands with this task. He would be busy blowing warm breath – Grace insisted it had to be his – onto each and every one of the peonies, making sure they eased beautifully from bud to their full blousy best in time for the wedding day.

The only thing keeping Nat in this game is the knowledge that she is charging this woman a day rate way beyond her usual sum – and my goodness, is she earning it.

The entire wedding party of eighty guests plus the groom make the short walk up the King's Road to the Bluebird restaurant for the reception. Well, all except Grace and Nat. Grace has to have a chauffeur-driven Bentley because it's a third of a mile away and *you can only expect so much from a pair of £800 Manolos*. It's also her final opportunity for a private briefing before the party begins:

'Please speak to the photographer as soon as we're there, will you. He's taking far too many pictures of all the pretty young women.' Grace is talking to Nat but not actually looking at her. She's looking seductively into a handheld mirror while she reapplies a slick of red lipstick to her plumped-up lips. 'I don't know why. None of them are making it into my photo album, so what's the point? Oh, thank goodness for delicious Bruce, he's the only one who continues to blow my mind with his creativity!'

'Yep, no problem.' Nat isn't really taking this in. She's staring out of the window at everyone enjoying an innocent and uncomplicated day of shopping, wondering how she is going to get Maria out of her white dress without having to resort to Grace's outfit-ruining plan. *Oh God.* She needs to start being a little more choosey about the clients she takes on. Is any sum of money worth what she is about to do? *Think.*

OK, the options are limited. She could front her up, tell her how much offence her outfit is causing and offer to provide something else for her to wear. They are on the King's Road, after all, so no shortage of upmarket fashion boutiques. But the woman could – and probably will – say no, and Nat doesn't really fancy haemorrhaging the cost from her own pocket anyway. Option two: is there anyone else in the bridal party who could realistically talk some sense into Grace and get her to change her mind? No, because that would involve confessing what she has demanded in the first place and, despite the craziness of the situation, Nat has a code, not to mention a contract, with Grace that she must honour. Which just leaves option three: do what she's being asked to do. It's hideous, but it's the only option or she can kiss goodbye to her fee and all the weeks of pandering to this lunatic will have been for nothing.

All the guests are gathering on the ground-floor terrace for the champagne reception so Nat starts to circle the crowd, looking for Maria. She spots her on the far side, surrounded by a group of young men, all apparently auditioning to be her date for the afternoon. As Nat approaches, she can hear the men talking about Grace.

'I can't believe he's gone through with it, to be honest. Really thought old Fletch would have seen sense and called it off long ago.'

'Come on, Piers, she can't be *that* bad.' Maria is actually going to defend Grace, it seems.

'Well, you tell me, you're her yoga teacher. Does she seem very Zen to you?'

'Maybe she's just got a bit bent out of shape in the run-up to the wedding. It happens to a lot of women, you know.'

'Oh, it goes *way* beyond that. The poor bastard! We've all tried to talk him out of it over the years. I thought pulling that stunt at their engagement party would have been the nail in her coffin, but he even forgave *that*.' The men are doing nothing to keep the volume down, obviously not worried who hears. *Perhaps everyone has the same low opinion of Grace*, thinks Nat. It wouldn't be entirely surprising.

'What stunt? What did she do that was *so* bad?' Maria's smirk says she is not expecting this to be anything more horrendous than a bit of mild intoxication. A few ungracious comments about her future mother-in-law, perhaps?

Nat slides in closer, just behind the group: she needs to hear this too.

'She chose the best-looking woman in the room, a real beauty she was – Grace had been scowling at her most of the evening, if I remember rightly. Then, she offered to pay this woman £2,000 to try it on with Fletcher, more if she succeeded. You know, to really test his resolve and to flatter her own fragile ego that he wanted Grace more than any other woman, I suppose. But it backfired royally because what darling Gracie didn't realise was that she was propositioning one of the new partners at his law firm. First thing Monday morning, Tanya called Fletcher into her big glass office and downloaded the entire sorry story to him. It still amazes me that Grace managed to bawl her way out of that one.'

There is silence for a second or two while everyone takes that little anecdote in and Nat raises her eyes to the heavens, thinking again what a bum decision it was to take this bride on. Then Maria takes a deep yogic breath, presumably letting any unkind thoughts flush out of her pure body and refuses to be drawn into the bitching.

'Come on, guys, doesn't that just show how incredibly insecure she is? Anyway, they're married now, that's bound to put an end to all that nonsense.'

Nat's here to prove how wrong Maria is.

People are starting to be called through for lunch, so Nat tags on to the group so she can see exactly where Maria gets seated. There are two long banqueting tables in the Gallery room and both are groaning under the weight of crystal candlesticks and a metre-wide arrangement of fragrant mixed white flowers running the entire length of each table. Every place setting is marked with an exquisite gold charger plate onto which have been etched the couple's initials. On top sits a glass dinner plate and a thick white linen napkin tied with a textured white ribbon, a single garden rose head placed at its centre. Tucked into each napkin is a personalised menu for each guest, walking them through the five courses they are about to have lavished on them. The heavy white tablecloth is covered in gold votives and each of the gold dining chairs has a white velvet cushion. Then, suspended above each table is a canopy of dense white wisteria, hung with tiny lanterns that are flickering like mini flash bulbs.

It is absolute perfection, thinks Nat as she enters the room. Beautiful Bruce *has* excelled himself.

Maria is seated on the table nearest the balcony, the opposite one to Grace. Nat is watching everyone milling around, finding their places. She glances around the room, keeping one eye on Maria and another searching for the bride, who enters the room on Fletcher's arm. Maybe, Nat prays, Grace has cheered up or had a few glasses of the fizzy stuff and will no longer care about what anyone else is wearing, but as a mild, unenthusiastic ripple of applause starts, she's mouthing the words *do it* across the room at Nat.

Nat feels sick as she stops a passing waiter and orders the glass of red. All this white, it's going to make such a mess. She pictures the moment when the blood-coloured liquid pours down Maria's back, causing her to screech and every pair of eyes in the place to fall accusingly on Nat. She drains the last of the fizz in her glass and hands the empty flute back to the waiter in exchange for the wine. Then she starts her journey around the table to where Maria is already seated. As she approaches, she can see Maria is taking care of all the introductions around her, making sure everyone is comfortable and chatting, that everyone's glass has something in it before she lifts her own.

Nat is behind her now and can feel her hand start to tremor as she lifts it, ready to tip the entire contents onto this lovely, unsuspecting woman – the only person she has met so far today who has had anything pleasant to say about Grace. She steals a last look at Grace who is nodding slowly, chillingly from the other side of the room. As the glass is tilting, Nat feels the tears coming and closes her eyes briefly, absolutely hating herself for what she is about to do. Just as the liquid is about to plunge over the lip of the glass, she feels a hand, tight on her other wrist and quickly rights it.

'Don't.' His voice is strong and authoritative. He's not asking, he's telling.

'Sorry?' Nat's voice wavers as she loses control of her bottom lip.

'Don't do it.' Fletcher is moving her now, out onto the balcony and out of earshot of any other guests. 'I know exactly what you were about to do.' He looks sad rather than angry and a denial from Nat right now seems a little insulting.

'Really?' She gulps in the fresh air, trying to bring her heart rate back down to something approaching normal.

'She asked you to do it, didn't she? Grace. She asked you to ruin that poor woman's dress? Come on, I've seen the way she's looked at her all day, we all have. Christ, I thought she was beyond all that! Who are you, anyway?'

'I'm Nat, the bridesmaid.' She hangs her head, wondering how on earth she's going to talk her way out of this one. He's totally onto her – and Grace.

'Nat the bridesmaid. Right. One of Grace's friends from yoga, aren't you? Tell me, how d'you like the scorpion? Or are you more of a peacock sort of girl?'

'Um, sorry, what?' Bloody hell, this is a disaster, Nat's never going to see that fee now.

'You're not Grace's friend. You don't do yoga. Is your name even Nat?'

'Yes.'

'Well, here's the deal, Nat. Whatever she's agreed to pay you for this total charade, I will cover it, on the strict understanding that you don't attempt any more stunts like the one I just prevented.'

This is a first. She's never been rumbled before. But then she's never had a bride push the boundaries of human decency quite like Grace before. Perhaps this outcome was inevitable.

'Agreed.' She's failed to meet Grace's expectations, this is the only way she's going to get paid and she knows it.

'Just get through the meal to avoid any more awkwardness, then you can go. Here's my card.' He reaches into his breast pocket and hands her his business card. 'Email me your details tomorrow and I will sort the payment. Now, let's both get back in there and pretend none of this happened. Can you manage that?'

'Yep.'

He turns to walk back into the dining room.

'Fletcher?' She catches him just before he makes it back to the glass doors. 'I'm really sorry, this whole thing just spun out of control a bit today. I really hope I haven't ruined your wedding day?'

'No,' he says, his expression sad but accepting. '*You* haven't. I think you'll find Grace is the captain of her own *Titanic*. I don't know why she does it.' His head drops, defeated and tired. 'You'll have to excuse her, Nat. She convinced herself a long time ago we would never last, that one day I'd get fed up and leave her. Even my proposal failed to quash her doubts. I just don't want to be that predictable. Deep down, she's good, I know she is. I just hope people will get to see that one day, if she ever finds it in herself to trust me properly.' Then he's gone, caught up in the backslapping and congratulations from around the table.

Nat takes her seat opposite Grace, who can see her requirements will not be met. She saw Fletcher's intervention, the two of them come back in from the balcony and, well, there's Maria still wearing white. Nat watches as Fletcher takes his seat next to his new wife, who reaches out her hand to take his, testing how hostile the waters might be. He squeezes it. 'It's our wedding day, Grace,' Nat hears him say. '*Please* try to enjoy it.'

So, the bride barely touches a mouthful of the £200-a-head meal her parents have paid for, but she does, over the course of the next three hours, polish off seven glasses of expensive French wine. Nat watches her sink each one as the mascara starts to smudge down under her lashes and her lipstick feathers out across her mouth. It's as if the window dressing is coming down and the room is finally seeing the real Grace.

Thank the Lord the speeches are planned for later, Nat couldn't bear to sit through that right now. Watching Fletcher cope is one sight she's happy to be spared. Every nice thing he planned to say about his new wife melting the crowd but not making a dent on her hardened heart. Nat hopes Grace realises what a lovely, forgiving man she's married before her fears about him leaving her become a painful reality.

At six o'clock Nat rises from the table to make her getaway. She gets as far as the cloakroom before Grace catches up with her. She's a drunken, sobbing mess and at this moment Nat feels nothing but mild loathing for her.

'Nat, wait, I need your help.' She's staggering around like some awful hen-do pretender in a big white dress.

'I'm going home, Grace. I think I've done enough.'

'It's just, I think I've made a terrible mistake. I think I'm in love with Bruce. He just *understands* me so well, totally gets me. I think he feels the same way too, don't you?'

'Your parents have paid him a lot of money to totally *understand* you, Grace. The man who really loves you, the one trying to understand the madness of you, is upstairs. And I can't help feeling you're pretty lucky to have him.'

Then she's out into the welcome fresh air, leaving Grace to cry all over someone else.

Chapter Seven

Betsy

If you ignore countless calls and texts from your mother and make no attempt to answer the gazillion wedding-related questions she's been firing at you for weeks, then you can expect to pay the price. Just like Betsy is now.

She woke at eight o'clock, after a night of imagined encounters with Dylan, none of them appropriate, to a text from her mum.

I'm in the Cotswold boutique today and there's a last-minute cancellation. You could be here in just over an hour. Come, please. There is so much to do.

She's been summoned. And as much as she's not in the mood to talk tulle, neither can she remain in denial. The wedding date is closing in on her. Plus, a day tiptoeing around their tiny two-bedroomed house, ducking the mood swings and snarky comments from Jacob is even less appealing. The thought propels her out of bed, through the shower and into the kitchen for breakfast before he has even stirred.

She's pulling together the meagre amount of wedding research she's done – some hurriedly torn pages from bridal magazines and a few designer lookbooks, all of which she only has because her mum posted them to her – when Jacob eventually mopes into the kitchen.

'Good night, was it?' He's unshaven and starting to look flabby, thinks Betsy. All those sedentary hours staring into a computer screen are catching up with him. There's definitely a bit of belly overhang at the top of those pyjamas and the corners of his eyes are crusted up with the remains of sleep. Fairy dust, her mum used to call it. But on Jacob this morning it looks, she's slightly shocked to think it, repulsive. As he brushes past her to reach for the kettle she can smell his breath too, sour and stale and the faintest tang of body odour coming from a t-shirt she knows for a fact hasn't been washed in at least a week.

'Not really, no. I'm sorry I was late, I just missed the train by a couple of minutes.'

'Yeah, I had a feeling you might. Forget it. You going out? Someone needs to go to the supermarket if you are. We're out of bin bags again.'

Betsy's eyes flick to the tower of rubbish stacked next to the overflowing kitchen bin. Endless crisp packets have been stuffed inside empty cereal boxes. There is an upturned carton of milk, its dregs already pooled into a dry white circle that will really whiff by lunchtime. It's surrounded by teabags that have been thrown but missed their target.

'I'm going to see Mum for the day. Try on some dresses, catch up with the venue while I'm there. Anything you want me to ask about?' She sounds considerably more enthusiastic than she feels. One of them has to make an effort.

'Nah, not really. I'm going back to bed.' And with that he swipes his mug of tea and retreats back to the darkened bedroom where she knows he'll stay, watching crap weekend TV, until he can procrastinate no longer.

*

As Betsy's VW Golf finally turns off the Fosse Way into Little Bloombury, she lowers the driver's window, letting the proper countryside fresh air blast away the negativity she's been holding inside her all the way here. The village looks so pretty at this time of year. The small stream that runs through it is perfectly calm, disturbed only by a couple of ducks making their way towards the old mill. The smell is one of the changing seasons, a mix of wood fires, horses and wet Barbour jackets. Willow Manor sits grandly against a cloudless blue sky, like it's presiding over the village and everyone in it, its striped lawn untouched this morning by a footprint or dog paw. It's just opposite the Manor that her mum's first bridal boutique is positioned, the one Betsy proudly remembers Helen opening after losing her husband and Betsy's father, Phillip.

The thought of him makes Betsy pause for a moment. She sits on a bench overlooking the stream, lets her head fall backwards into the bright autumn sun and thinks about the good man he was, how he looked after them all and how unimpressed he'd be with Jacob's work ethic. Now she's thinking about it, maybe her dad's absence explains at least some of her reticence about this wedding – no adored father-of-the-bride to hold her hand. It somehow seems a little hollow without him. She's reminded of how utterly broken her mother was when she lost him to lung cancer. But she had refused to stay that way, finally selling the family home in Bristol and buying the business here, where they had both shared so many happy weekends together. Before too long, it was so successful and she had built such a good reputation that the London store was planned and opened. Just at the point when most women her mother's age are calming down, clearing their diaries and making a little time for themselves, hers was firing up to London on the train, meeting architects, charming the bank manager and driving her business forward. She knew that a part of her mother, the shadow of that cautious woman she once was, would be scared, but she was doing it anyway and Betsy has such huge respect for everything she's achieved. How she has transformed herself from devoted housewife and mother to savvy, ambitious businesswoman – one who charges back and forth between London and the Cotswolds to keep both boutiques running with minimum help. But it's here, to the countryside, Betsy loves to come; where the pace slows and there's room to breathe, to think and to plan.

She knows her mother will have a client with her, so Betsy enters around the back, climbing the small uneven flight of stairs up to Helen's apartment above the boutique. She pings her mum a quick text to let her know she's arrived, then makes herself at home. As usual, the place is immaculate. The mantelpiece is lined with thank you cards from happy couples, and Betsy starts to read through a few of them. There is one from a Jessie and Adam Coleridge with a beautiful photograph clipped inside of the couple in the grounds of an impressive stately home, with what looks like both sets of parents stood behind them. All six are beaming out of the picture, probably because in Jessie's lap, bundled up so tightly so you can barely see it, is a newborn baby. They couldn't possibly look any happier.

There are also framed pictures of Betsy and her brother, Jack, all over Helen's orderly bookshelves and another gloriously happy one of Helen and Phillip on their wedding day. Betsy is about to pick it up for another closer look, but is distracted by a colossal bunch of flowers positioned on the small fold-out antique dining table. They are far too grand to be something her mum would buy for herself, and Betsy can see a card nestled in amongst the yellow rose leaves. She dips her head to smell them and pauses. Should she read it? It feels like an invasion but then her mum would have hidden the card if she didn't want anyone to see it, surely? She pushes the stalks apart so she can make out the words:

I'll wait as long as it takes for your answer, Helen. With all my love, Nick.

Who the hell is Nick? Her mum has never mentioned him before. Betsy's assuming it's a him. Maybe it's not? Women don't send each other flowers like *this* though, do they? Feeling that she probably shouldn't have read the card after all, Betsy moves back across the room to the window overlooking the grounds of the Manor and then hears her mother's footsteps approaching up the stairs.

'Betsy! You're here!' Helen bounds into the room, throwing her arms around her daughter and squeezing all the air out of her. 'I'm so glad you came. My lady is just getting dressed. Give us ten minutes, then pop down, OK?' Betsy watches her mother's eyes dart to the flowers and then back to Betsy. Helen moves forward, pretending to rearrange the stems, humming casually to herself, then she swipes the card and pushes it into the pocket of her wool trousers.

'Great! I'll be down in a bit.'

Now Betsy *knows* she shouldn't have read the card.

*

'OK, we've got an hour and a half until my next lady. Let's make some real progress, shall we, catch up on everything we're behind on?' Her mum clearly means business, Betsy can see that, but this is starting to feel a little like a job interview that you stupidly haven't bothered to prep for.

'So, thoughts on the dress… There's not enough time left to have something made bespoke, Betsy, I hope you know that? But if I call in some major favours we can still take an existing dress from a current collection and have it made to measure for you, possibly with some mild design tweaks, if you want them. What kind of gown are you imagining?'

The two women are sitting next to each other on Helen's new cream leather chaise longue, illuminated by the rails of white dresses surrounding them, as if shining a spotlight on Betsy. There is nowhere to hide. No way of avoiding the exposing line of questioning Betsy fears is coming.

'I don't know.' It's not the best start.

'Ballgown, fishtail, A-line? Were you thinking about a high neck or off-the-shoulder? Long sleeves, empire line, full-length, short? Come on, Betsy! You seemed to love the ballgowns when we first talked about your dress, all those months ago. Do you have *any* more thoughts about it now?'

'I really don't know, Mum. Er… what do you think?' This is hardly helpful. But Betsy hasn't done the sort of legwork needed to be able to answer these questions with any certainty. And, the truth is, she just can't picture herself in a wedding dress, no matter how hard she tries.

'I know exactly what I would choose for you, Betsy. It's hanging in the fitting room now. The Harmonie gown by Mira Zwillinger – an ivory silk ballgown that's scattered in roses with sleeves made entirely from the flowers' petals. They will drape and fall from your shoulders into a dramatically low back. It was made for you, Betsy, the sort of dress I always imagined you might wear on your wedding day.' She's obviously spent years thinking about this. 'But I think the point is, it needs to come from you, darling, at least some of it. How do you want to feel on the day? What kind of dress is going to capture this moment for you, one you will remember for the rest of your life?'

Blank. *How can she possibly follow that?* 'I just haven't had the time to think about it, Mum. I'm away in London more and more, there again on Tuesday… I just haven't had the thinking space.' It's lame, but it will have to do.

'OK, let's approach this a different way. Have you thought about flowers, or the way you'd like the church to look? How we might set the tables for your wedding breakfast? That can all be a useful starting point that might lead us to the dress. And you have sent the invitations out, haven't you?' Her mum's face is starting to drain of all the pleasure she was showing at Betsy's arrival and is now clouded with concern.

'Of course I have! But I haven't thought about any of the rest of it.' The last thing Betsy wants to do is start crying in front of her mum but the way her breath is starting to quiver out of her suggests it's coming.

Thankfully, Helen is reaching for some designer lookbooks and is yet to notice, because a hand on Betsy's shoulder right now is probably all it would take to set those tears free. And she can't handle the sympathy and knows she doesn't deserve it either.

'I know work is really busy for you and probably taking up all your time but who are your bridesmaids, Betsy? Can they take on some of this for you? That's kind of what they're there for. Who did you choose, Rebecca and Harriet?'

It's completely logical that her mum would assume she'd chosen her oldest school friends, the girls she shared everything with before everyone got obsessed with climbing the career ladder. But Betsy has seen so little of them both recently, another reason she has farmed the job out to a professional.

'No, actually. It's someone from work.' Why is it that lying to your mum is more difficult than lying to just about anyone else on earth? Because Helen doesn't deserve it, because she's only trying to help, but Betsy knows she'd be horrified if she knew the truth about Nat. She'd love the woman herself, Nat's business-like efficiency and the way she genuinely combines it with all the warmth and concern of a best friend. But the fact she's hired her? It would be official and final confirmation that Betsy doesn't care about this wedding nearly as much as she should.

'Does she have a name?' Her mum has swivelled around on the chaise longue so she is directly facing her now.

'Sorry?'

'Your bridesmaid. What's her name? And why don't you bring her in? I'd love to meet her, Betsy – and ideally, before the big day.'

A pause grows between the two women while Betsy seriously considers, for a split second, just blurting the truth at her mum: *I'm struggling to get excited about this wedding and to stay excited about Jacob. Oh, and my bridesmaid is a fake.* But she changes tack, switching the conversation down a very different line of enquiry.

'Mum, who's Nick?' She knows she's intruding and can't quite hold eye contact while she's asking a question she feels fairly sure her mum won't want to answer.

'Oh. Um...' Helen's cheeks are immediately colouring. 'He's a friend.'

'A friend?' The arch of Betsy's eyebrows conveys how unsatisfactory this answer is.

'A very good friend.' Helen tries again. 'He was the architect for the London shop and, well, I saw rather a lot of him while all the work was being done and we've got… close. I'm sure you'll meet him soon enough.' That's clearly her way of putting an end to this chat but Betsy wants to dig a little further.

'What did he ask you?'

'Ask me? What do you mean?'

'What is he waiting for an answer on? The card, Mum, on the flowers – I read it.' This is full-on prying now and her mother's reaction could go either way. She watches as Helen's shoulders slump and the irritation huffs out of her.

'Betsy, I'm not sure that's any of your…' Her mum is on her feet now, trying to busy herself, unnecessarily rearranging a pair of pretty lace gloves fanned out on a side table.

'Sorry. I was just interested and, well, I like the idea that you may have found someone who…' Betsy doesn't want to say 'might replace Dad', it's not what she means but she's struggling to string the words together, knowing so little about this relationship and what it might mean to her mum. Still, if Helen does have someone new in her life, that can only be a good thing. Betsy hates to think of her spending night after night alone – splitting her life between the never-ending possibilities of London and the quiet beauty of the countryside but with no one to share any of it.

'You're putting me on the spot, Betsy.' Helen has deliberately moved to the other side of the shop now, where she keeps all the pretty dress sashes. She's straightening them, allowing her to keep her back to her daughter.

'Isn't that what you're doing to me too, with all these wedding questions?'

'Oh… I thought I was helping. You're supposed to be getting married in ten weeks and we don't have a dress, shoes, lingerie, a veil.

Nothing.' Now she's no longer the subject of the conversation, Helen has spun back round to face her daughter.

'Ten weeks is plenty of time, it's months!'

'It's not, actually. I do know a thing or two about this.'

'Actually, Mum, do you mind if I grab some fresh air? I'm not feeling a hundred per cent.' This is pointless. Helen isn't going to elaborate any further about this mysterious Nick and Betsy can't give her any of the answers she wants so it's safer to switch back to avoidance tactics.

'Take all the fresh air you need, darling. Just remember, I'm your mother so I know when something is wrong. You're not fooling me.'

There's the invitation. If Betsy wants to unload what she's really thinking, now is her chance. But she can't.

She steps outside, leaving her poor mum to spend the afternoon worrying about her. She walks into the grounds of the Manor that sits directly opposite the run of pretty Cotswold cottages housing The White Gallery, then makes her way round the back, where she'll be more out of sight, and perches on one of the stone walls that separates the Manor from the church grounds. This is the church she should be marrying in, overlooking the lawn where her marquee should be pitched. Everything around her looks so idyllic, just as it should be. The gardens are wonderfully ordered and neat and there is the cheerful chorus of birdsong carrying through the air. Couples are starting to explore the gardens of the Manor, hand in hand, happily planning their futures or just enjoying the freedom of a weekend away in the country – lovely, unplanned days filled with pub lunches and long walks, making memories together.

Betsy pulls out her mobile and her mood instantly lifts as she sees she's had another text from Dylan. Weird that he should get in touch at the weekend.

Morning, Trouble! That digital client wants dinner next week. Can you do Tuesday night? It will be a late one so you'll need to stay over, expense a hotel? Let me know. Dylan. PS we need to discuss New York plans too!

She pings a quick one back.

Yes, of course, I'll book somewhere. Bee

New York. She's yet to break this bit of news to Jacob. Will he care that she is spending time away in an exciting foreign city with another man, albeit her boss? Will Jacob even register the excitement she knows she will be unable to hide when she tells him about it? Because right now, the idea of three nights in Manhattan with Dylan and all his capable, manly, go-getting lust for life is considerably more attractive than what's waiting for her at home.

As Betsy climbs back into her car she decides she's not going to head straight home, she's going to detour to Cheltenham. She saw an incredible dress in the window of Whistles last week. Heavy black satin, the sort of fabric that will slide over her curves, pulling her in and pushing her out in all the right places. It's cut low into a sweetheart neckline and with a slit that she knows will sit noticeably mid-thigh. Exactly what she has in mind for her dinner with Dylan on Tuesday. And it will look perfect with those red shoes.

Chapter Eight

Helen

Helen presses the doorbell and waits, heart banging a little inside her chest. *Is she doing the right thing?* She's not sure. Something has to be done, they can't go on as they are. She has to press it twice more, then hammer hard on the letterbox knocker before she finally sees signs of life inside. It's eleven o'clock on a Tuesday morning but you wouldn't know it from looking at Jacob when he finally edges the door open, face filled with irritation.

He's obviously not expecting her. He's not expecting anyone. He's shrouded in a ratty old dressing gown that's fraying all along the hem. Even from the doorstep Helen can see how dirty it is. He hasn't bothered to tie it properly and it's falling open at the front to reveal a t-shirt that might once have been white but is now covered in what looks like last night's dinner splatters, the sort of mess you might expect to see down the front of a three-year-old – or someone who has eaten in bed, plate balanced on a pillow.

'Oh, er… she's not here. She's at work.' Jacob is squinting into the bright morning sunlight, clearly seeing it for the first time today.

His future mother-in-law arrives unannounced on the doorstep and that's the sum total of his concern, thinks Helen, who's going to have to be a lot politer to Jacob than she wants to be.

'Good morning to you, too, Jacob. I know Betsy's not here, that's why I chose this morning to come. I wonder if you might spare me a little of your time? I think we probably need a chat.' This is already worse than Helen was expecting. The state of him. She knows her daughter well enough to be sure she would be equally unimpressed by the mess stood in front of her. And Jacob is doing nothing to hide his reluctance to let Helen in.

'Sorry, I'm working.' He's standing firm, not showing the slightest indication that the door will open wider to welcome her.

'Forgive me, Jacob, but you don't look like you're working.' She hasn't come all this way, an hour's drive from Little Bloombury, to her daughter's unremarkable two-up, two-down on the residential outskirts of Birmingham to be denied access now.

'I'm about to start.'

Wow, this takes some rudeness, thinks Helen before she has another go at getting in. 'It really won't take long.' Her voice is soft, but persistent.

'If you'd called…'

'If I'd called, you would have said you were busy, and I think we really need to talk. It's about Betsy. I need ten minutes of your time, Jacob. No more.'

The door finally edges open wide enough for Helen to step in, accompanied by the longest sigh she's ever heard, one that Jacob looks unaware he's even unleashing. The house smells, as if the windows haven't been opened for weeks. The carpet is covered in fluff, crumbs and who knows what else; no question now that Helen will keep her shoes on. She follows Jacob through to the kitchen, where all hell has broken loose.

'Er, you'll want a cup of tea, then?' Jacob is wiping a hand across his face, trying to revive himself.

'I'm not sure you have any clean cups.' Helen's eyes are all over everything. There isn't an inch of work surface that doesn't have something festering on it. Saucepans are encrusted with old food and the door of the dishwasher is hanging open like someone considered making a dent in the mess and then gave up. She can see it's over-stacked with a week's worth of dirty dishes that will take about three cycles to get somewhere near to clean again.

'Why don't you go and take a seat in the lounge and I'll wash one up? How d'you have it?' Jacob's voice is heavy with exasperation, he's hardly keen to ingratiate himself with her.

'Do you have Earl Grey, by any chance?' Helen knows Betsy drinks it.

'No.'

Perhaps he just can't be bothered to look for it. 'OK, just white with no sugar, please.' *It's sad*, thinks Helen. *This man is about to marry my daughter and we've spent so little time in each other's company that he has no clue how I take my tea.* A small thing, perhaps, but it says a lot to Helen. She walks back down the narrow corridor to the lounge, stepping over some recycling that is yet to make it out to the bin. *Is it really so hard to muster some polite enthusiasm, even if it is totally fake, for the ten minutes I'll be here?*, she wonders.

The lounge looks like it has become an extension of Jacob's office. There are papers and books and notepads strewn everywhere, in no discernible order. Not to Helen, anyway. Half-finished mugs of tea are dotted around the room and there is a plate with what looks like the remains of yesterday's toast crusts wedged in between two sofa cushions. She decides to stay standing. As she's looking around the room it occurs to Helen that there is nothing of her daughter here. No favourite books, no framed pictures of her, with or without Jacob, no Betsy touches – a scented candle, a familiar ornament, a vase of flowers, a discarded item of clothing. Nothing at all that indicates her daughter lives here. Neither is there anything of Betsy and Jacob, the couple. No joint invitations on the mantelpiece. No photographs of the two of them having fun. No keepsakes that Helen can see that talk of a history together.

There was a time, not long after they met, when Betsy and Jacob would disappear for long weekends together, squandering all their holiday allowance – when Jacob had a proper job – because they just wanted to be together, with no interruptions. Helen barely saw Betsy over those months. Salaries were blown on concert tickets, city mini-breaks, and most weekends they would spend a fortune having friends over for dinner, doing that cosy couple thing. Judging by the state of the place, that hasn't happened for some time. They chose to marry on Christmas Eve because that's the day they first met, at a friend's drinks party. That Christmas Betsy spoke of nothing but Jacob and by New Year's Eve it was obvious they were going to be together. But now?

Just as Helen starts to pick the dead leaves off a houseplant that gave up living weeks ago, Jacob calls through from the kitchen.

'Did you say you *do* take sugar?'

Perhaps it was when Jacob decided computer programming wasn't for him and novel writing was that the balance shifted between them, thinks Helen. She knows Betsy agreed to it, but it hasn't been easy, her daughter having to support them both, stretching her not-huge salary to cover everything. Helen knows because the requests for mini loans increased. Then came Betsy's promotion and things seemed to ease; at least, the handouts from Helen stopped, but when Jacob's book deal fell through, it seems to Helen their relationship followed it down the black hole. It just isn't until today, right now, standing in their home with all the trappings of their careless daily life around her, that she can see quite how far it's fallen.

'Here you go.' Jacob hands Helen a mug of grey tea.

'Thank you.' There is no chance she's going to raise it to her lips and she looks around for somewhere, anywhere, to place it. As she leans over the arm of the sofa, stretching to reach the side table, she spots something, shoved underneath on the floor there. A crate full of cards and envelopes. She dips a little lower, trying to make out the picture on the front of one of the cards. A typewriter. It's all one hundred and twenty of their wedding invitations, unwritten, unaddressed, unposted, despite Betsy's insistence otherwise. She can hear Jacob wittering behind her, but she can't pull her gaze away from the box. *My God, why would she lie?* It's not like Helen doesn't know they're behind with everything. This isn't Betsy and it's worrying, seriously worrying. Helen can feel her skin prickle from the realisation that what is unravelling here is more than just a bit of wedding planning and slack housekeeping.

Jacob cuts in.

'So, what's up? What's the problem with Betsy?' There's no concern in his voice, thinks Helen. He could be talking about the woman who lives three doors down, the one who lends them her lawnmower every summer.

'She's staying in London tonight, I gather?' Helen needs to ease into this gently. The last thing she wants is to upset Jacob and then have to explain herself to Betsy later.

'Is she?' He's shifting newspapers off the other sofa, trying to make space to sit down, not in the least bit bothered.

'Yes. Didn't you know that?' *How could he not know that?*

'She might have told me, I can't remember. Anyway, what's wrong with that?'

Helen is starting to wonder if he would actually notice if Betsy was home or not. 'Nothing, but I am getting a little concerned that the wedding planning has stalled, Jacob. Do you talk about it much? Do you need some help from me?'

'I dunno. We haven't spoken about it for ages. As you've pointed out, she's not always home. It's not really my priority right now. Listen, is this going to take long, Helen, because I could do with getting on?'

Helen can see this is pointless. 'Do you mind if I pop to the loo?' It's obvious Jacob isn't going to be any use, she may as well be on her way. A two-hour round journey completely wasted. She starts to climb the stairs to the bathroom, dreading what might be awaiting her there. As she reaches the landing, she turns and passes their bedroom. The door is open and she slows, sneaking a quick look inside. Betsy obviously packed for London in a hurry – there are clothes everywhere, thrown over the wardrobe door, piled up on a chair next to the bed and almost completely covering the ottoman that sits at the end of it. Helen can hear Jacob clattering around downstairs, so steps into the room. She's not even sure what she's looking for, but being in the house feels as though it might be like stepping inside Betsy's head. It's a confused, jumbled mess. Hard to live in, certainly impossible to be happy in, Helen suspects.

There are a few quality carrier bags on the floor next to the bed. Betsy has been shopping. None of the new buys are here so Helen can only assume they have been packed for the client trip to London. A receipt has tumbled out of one of the empty bags onto the floor and Helen bends to pick it up, pausing for a moment while she questions the ethics of what she's doing. But the receipt is in her hand now, much harder to put it back down than steal a quick look.

It's from a lingerie boutique in Cheltenham. Helen knows it because so many of her clients head there for the racier honeymoon pieces. She can see from the printout that Betsy has bought a black corset, panties and a suspender belt totalling nearly £300. Whatever this is, it's not her bridal lingerie, Helen knows that. And it seems pretty unlikely she's thinking about the honeymoon when the wedding is so disorganised. A horrible thought briefly passes through Helen's mind, one she does not want to believe her daughter is capable of. Perhaps Betsy is simply trying to reignite something that's gone out with Jacob? Although that's equally hard to believe, considering what's crashing around downstairs, wrapped up in the sort of dressing gown that most sixty-year-old women wouldn't let the milkman see them in.

She drops the receipt and heads straight to the loo, emptying her untouched tea down the sink while she's in there. And suddenly it's like she's stepped into the beauty hall of an upmarket department store. The shelves are lined with expensive cosmetics: Chanel, YSL, Givenchy, it's all here. For a girl who used to think a quick swipe of clear lipgloss and a dab of cheek colour constituted being made-up, Betsy's beauty expenditure has obviously gone through the roof. What is *very* Betsy is the way the products sit orderly on the shelves, lined up in ascending height order and grouped helpfully together – lips, eyes, cheeks, skin. It's the only part of the entire house where she can feel her daughter's calm organisation. The only part of the house that smells clean. It feels like Betsy's sanctuary, away from the mess and madness of everything else.

Helen makes her way back down to the kitchen, where she adds her mug to the mountain Jacob is shifting into the sink, making no attempt to actually wash them. She leans back against one of the kitchen units and watches him. There is a noticeboard on the wall in front of him, covered in all the paraphernalia of a life that is running away from them – unopened bills, an overdue car MOT reminder, Betsy's to-do lists with nothing crossed through. Helen takes a couple of steps forward. There is something in the middle of the board that looks faintly familiar, a business card, partially pushed under an old picture of Betsy and her friend Harriet clinking cocktail glasses on a girls' night out.

'How's the book going?' It's a blatant attempt to distract Jacob with something he might want to talk about while she gets closer to the card.

'It's getting there.' It's the most positive thing he's said since she arrived. 'Lots to write and rewrite today but there is a plan, at least. I'm going to rework one of the major characters, making him more…'

Helen isn't listening. She's leaning in, getting closer to the card. She raises a hand to push the photograph to one side, giving her clear sight of it now. 'Oh, I love this picture of Betsy,' she says, as Jacob looks to see what she's doing.

Natalie. Just one name on the card with a small illustration of a wedding cake and a mobile number that she feels sure her fingers may have tapped out before. It couldn't be *her* Nat though, could it, the girl who has been coming to The White Gallery time and time again for bridesmaid dresses? No, why would it be? When Helen mentioned Betsy's wedding to her just recently, Nat didn't say anything about knowing her daughter at the time. And yet, that mobile number does look so familiar.

Helen needs to chat all of this over with someone – someone with a clear head, some perspective and a little distance from it all. Someone she knows will care…

Helen and Nick have exchanged a few short texts since that mortifying lunch at Scott's but nothing more, just confirmation that she will think about his offer. She's been too embarrassed to talk to him properly. She misses him, though, his absence making her realise that her reaction that day was much more about her shock at his depth of feeling than any sense she doesn't want to have him in her life. And if there's going to be any future for the two of them, she needs to share every part of her life with him, however messy it might be, doesn't she? Betsy seemed so keen to find out more about him too. Perhaps it's time to acknowledge he's important enough for all of them to meet?

'Jacob, there is someone I would love you and Betsy to meet soon.' Helen takes a deep breath, knowing she is about to utter his name and make this whole Nick-and-Helen thing far more official. People will start to have an opinion about them and to ask what the future might hold for them. She'll be expected to have a view herself.

'Oh right.'

'It's a close friend of mine, Nick. I wonder whether the three of us might get together for dinner with him sometime soon. Would that be OK?'

'Probably best to check with Betsy, she's the busy one. And the last time I tried to check her diary, I couldn't get into her phone – there's a lock on it now.'

Helen knows Betsy has furnished Jacob with the details of her past life, it's Betsy's too, after all. Jacob knows about Phillip, the months and months of pain that followed his death, her retreat from life until she finally found the courage to re-emerge. So, his lack of interest, his failure to grasp the significance of what Helen is saying, is so hurtful. She doesn't want to be in Jacob's company for a second longer. She makes her excuses, sees herself to the door and leaves, feeling even more concern for Betsy than she did when she arrived.

*

Helen saves making the phone call to Nick until she is back in Little Bloombury. She needs the drive home to prepare herself for hearing his voice again and the heart-fluttering effect it might have on her. She parks the car behind the boutique then takes a walk through the village, feeling the warm glow from the Cotswold stone cheer her up. She takes a seat on one of the benches in the churchyard and searches for his number in her mobile, suddenly so nervous. What if he's annoyed it's taken her this long to call? Their lunch at Scott's was weeks ago now. Maybe he's just talked himself out of caring so much? Forced himself to mentally move on after such a public rebuttal from her? But then he did send the flowers with a note that reassured Helen at the time she wasn't forgotten. She makes the call. He's probably in a meeting anyway and she'll be able to get away with leaving a more cowardly voicemail.

He answers almost immediately.

'Helen?'

'Yes. Hello, Nick. How are you?' She can feel the nervous quiver in the back of her throat as she's saying his name and hopes he isn't hearing it.

'Absolutely delighted to hear from you. Are you OK?' *Isn't this all anyone wants*, thinks Helen, *someone to ask you if you're OK and to genuinely care that you are?*

'I'm fine, thank you. I wanted to call and say thank you for sending such beautiful flowers. It was such a wonderful surprise and, well, I'm not sure I deserve them but thank you nonetheless.'

'I miss you.'

She can feel her heart rate picking up and she wants to blurt the same words back at him but they're just not coming.

'I'd love to see you, Helen.' His voice is full of intent, he clearly doesn't want this call to be just a polite but necessary thank you for the bouquet. It's making her wish more than anything he was here with her right now, wrapping his arms around her and pulling her in to his chest. It would all be much easier if he was.

'I know you're very busy with everything but I wondered if I could introduce you to Betsy and her fiancé, Jacob? Would you have time for that?' Why is she sounding so formal? She doesn't mean to, she just can't relax enough to be normal with him.

'If you'd like me to, I'd love to. Dinner one night?'

'That would be lovely, I'll get some dates together.'

'Can I see you alone, too? I don't want to trouble you, Helen, I just want to be with you. I want to hold your hand and just be with you, alone, just for half an hour, that's all I ask.'

She wants to tell him to jump in his car and get over here now but instead she mutters a passive, 'That would be fine. I'll see you soon, then.'

Helen disconnects the call and then sits there for a few minutes, allowing herself to daydream about what life with Nick might actually be like.

Chapter Nine

Jenny

Never have I dreaded a shift more. Lucy will be working with me this morning and there will be no avoiding what I know is coming. The hundreds of questions firing my way. *Who is he? Where did you meet? When's the wedding? How did he propose?* I'm timing the walk from the tube station to the main entrance of St Mary's so that I have the least amount of time possible in the staffroom with her. I'm praying for once that the night shift has been manic, that the handover to the day shift will be swift and that there will be no time for the grilling she'll want to give me. I just need to get through this. When I get home tonight, my sister, Lulu, will be there, visiting for a few days and maybe I can share the whole sorry thing with her. In between some lovely shared stories about Mum, she'll make me see the funny side, I know she will. Mum wrote letters to Lulu too and over the years we have shared them with each other. Never the letters themselves, but the content of them. I think we both understand that her words are like a private conversation for each of us to hold close.

Right now, I need to get my story straight. I've given this serious, endless thought, since Lucy's sighting of me in the wedding dress last week. I'm gonna keep it simple: what she didn't see was my friend in the fitting room – the real bride. I was simply trying things on for *her* after she got an attack of the nerves. Urgh, it's pathetic and they probably won't believe it, but I've got to say something and that's the best I've got. Then we can all move on. Perhaps there will be some incredulous mocking behind my back at break time but I can suck that up.

Fifteen minutes until I start. I'd normally be enjoying a few last relaxed minutes with a cup of tea and *Grazia*, and instead I'm lingering in the hospital's main reception, killing time, watching visitors and patients try to navigate the warren of wards and departments that branch off confusingly from here. I need to get up to the maternity unit or I'm going to be late and I'm not sure I can handle one of Jean's disappointed frowns today.

As the lift doors open onto the second floor, I can hear the din from the staffroom. It will be rammed in there now, with everyone from the night shift trying to finish up and everyone from today's shift rushing to get ready. As I turn the corner and start my walk towards it, I can see it's even busier than usual. Odd. Some of the support staff are in there, and some of the doctors, even our two usual cleaners. What's going on? Whatever it is, it's going to give me the diversion I'm hoping for, thank goodness.

Then I see it.

There's a giant foil banner draped the length of the staffroom with the words *You're Engaged!* screaming across it. And balloons, silver and gold, with horseshoes and wedding bells printed in white across them. Someone must have hit play on the iPad because as I freeze to the spot that horribly familiar tune 'The Wedding March' – *da da da-dah, da da da-dah* – booms out at me.

'Here she is! Make way for the bride-to-be, everyone!'

I can see from the ecstatic smile on Lucy's face that she is loving being the source of this revelation. I can also feel the tears coming. I'm not going to be able to stop them, I know I'm not. And I give up trying almost immediately. I'd like to say it's a few subtle, ladylike tears that slide down my face and look endearing, but no, this big, snotty bawl jumps out of me like a builder's belch. And once it comes, there is no stopping it. Why am I crying? Because this is about as mortifying as life – *my* life – can possibly get. Because I'm touched, *really* touched, that my colleagues have gone to so much trouble. Because the picture of my mum's beautiful smiling face is suddenly filling my mind. What the hell would she make of this? It's all of it, all crashing around in my head, while I know I am going to have to say something. The crowd will go silent and I'll have to speak.

There is a moment of stunned hush while everyone registers the bawl, raised eyebrows and sideways glances, and then the arms start flying in around me.

'Give her some room, the poor thing. This is all a bit overwhelming,' bellows Lucy protectively.

She has little effect. Someone thrusts a bouquet of flowers at me and plants a big kiss on my cheek, while someone else plonks a plastic kid's tiara on my head. Bloody hell. I'm sweating under this duffle coat and my cheeks must look sunburnt from the sheer embarrassment of it all.

'Wow!' is all I can manage as I'm dragging my snotty nose along the arm of my coat again; I need to get this thing dry-cleaned. Some of the men are saying congratulations then making their excuses and leaving, sobbing, hysterical women being all a bit too much for seven o'clock in the morning, probably.

As a horseshoe of midwives forms around me, Lucy moves to the front of the crowd, keen to remind everyone, I think, that this is all her doing.

'Was that *the* dress, Jenny? Because it looked absolutely beautiful on you.'

I look at everyone's expectant faces, the ring of unbroken smiles, all directed at me, and I know what I need to do: come clean and deal with it, whatever shitty response will come my way when they all realise they've wasted their time and money.

Come on, Jenny, it's time to do the decent thing – the sane thing!

'I think so!' I'm grinning like a maniac and I can hear my own forced, hollow laugh in the back of my throat. Why isn't my mouth sticking to the plan? Too late now. This story has started and every excitable woman in this room will be with me for months until we all see how it ends.

'Come on then, who's the lucky man?' Jean is moving towards the front. She places a soft kiss on my cheek, a comforting arm around my shoulders and pulls me into her. And it feels wonderful. 'Congratulations, Jenny. It really is the most wonderful news.'

'Thank you. Um, his name's…' *Think, think, think, they need a name!* Sam? No, let's not go back there. Um… 'Will.' It's my sister's husband's name, and the first one that pops into my head. 'We met online a while ago. It's all been very quick, really.' No choice but to embrace this now, I'll just skirt over it all with as little info as possible.

'Well, we want to know all the details,' adds Lucy. 'Leave nothing out. Dates, venue, where's the hen do, are we all coming?'

Despite the enormity of the bullshit flowing out of me with surprising ease, there is something so lovely about what these women are doing for me. The planning that went into the surprise, all the phone calls needed to co-ordinate everyone, getting them all here half an hour before an already chronically early start to set it all up and the fact they all care enough to ask. We sit down on the low, blue foam chairs, minutes to spare before the madness of the day shift begins. Someone puts a cup of tea in my hand and one by one, every woman in the room appoints herself my chief wedding planner.

'The first thing you need to do is confirm a venue, then everything will flow from there.'

'Think about seasonality, it will save you a fortune on the food and flowers.'

'Whatever you do, don't buy one of those awful face veils. It looked a bit serial killer on our Sally, which I'm pretty sure was *not* the look she was going for.'

Everyone starts to share the best bits from their own wedding days; the nerves they felt walking down the aisle and the heart-soaring moment when all the scary official stuff was done and he planted the first married kiss on her lips. I don't want it to end. We're suddenly just a normal group of friends, planning someone's wedding. Jean is sitting next to me and picks up my hand, leaning in so no one else can hear her.

'You know, I never had children, and always felt such terrible sadness that I would never be planning my daughter's wedding. I would be so honoured if you would let me help? Give me any job you like, something no one else wants to do, perhaps?'

'Thank you, Jean. How are you with seating plans?' *Oh my God, what's wrong with me?* This is nuts, but I love it. And how marvellous that all it's taken is this teeny little fib to make Jean feel she can confide in me. I must make more effort. Yes! I'm going to start taking a view on all the important things in life – well, in this staffroom anyway – the peri-menopause; what to do when your pubes start going grey, or how to cope with a husband whose snoring could drive you to reach for the sharpest knife in the kitchen.

We collectively decide to start a WhatsApp group called GetJen-Married and a private Pinterest board that we can all drop pictures into. Fun! Jean uses her entire morning break to start filling it with beautiful images of guest escort cards – I particularly like one where they are attached to mini bottles of fizz for each guest – and seating plans grandly displayed on easels in thick guilt frames. Love it!

*

By the time I head home, I'm whacked. Two babies delivered today and all the excitement of my impending nuptials has taken its toll. As I exit East Putney tube and cross Upper Richmond Road, it starts to drizzle. Thankfully, I don't need to deviate into the kebab shop tonight. Lulu was letting herself in this afternoon and has promised to knock up her legendary – and my favourite – mac 'n' cheese. She'll cover it in crispy, garlicky croutons that will go soggy from the rich creamy sauce. My belly is roaring all the way up Putney Hill until I finally make it to the mansion flats on the right at the top. A much grander description than the 1920s block deserves. The estate agent might think it 'superbly proportioned' but in reality it's a breathy, uphill pain in the arse to get to, unless you want to wait for a bus full of sweary school kids. No, thanks!

Marianne's wheelie case is blocking the front door, preventing me from pushing it open, and I have to holler her name until she finally comes to move it.

'Alright, keep yer knickers on!' She's wearing so much make-up, I can only assume she's had another marathon session on one of her favourite YouTube beauty channels.

'Where are you going?' She's barely in the flat these days and seems to time her exits perfectly with when the place needs a clean or there is a big food shop to do. I'm not sure she's contributed to the grocery bill since about August last year.

'Just thought I'd bugger off and give you and Lulu some space while she's here. She can have my bed if she likes? And, well, it's a bit of a date. I'm going away with a guy I met on Tinder, who is *touch-yourself* hot!'

Christ, I'm not even going to ask! I'm more worried about the fact I'll now be stripping every item of her bed linen before I can possibly suggest Lulu sleeps in there. In the three years we have shared this place together, I haven't once seen Marianne wash her bed sheets. It only ever happens because I do it for her. Why? I suppose I just hate the thought that whatever's festering underneath her duvet might somehow make it into my room. And looking at her now, I can see that's more than possible.

'Marianne, that's my dress, isn't it?'

'Yeah, you don't mind, do you? Anything that's clean is in my case and I had nothing else to put on.'

'And how much of what's in your case belongs to me?'

'Yeah, a fair bit, to be honest.' The words cackle out of her like I imagine they might if she had just successfully shoplifted three hundred quid's worth from Topshop. 'Listen, I've got to go or I'll miss my train. Tell Lulu the cheesy pasta was pretty good, needs more pepper. I'm not sure she cooked enough for three, but I couldn't help myself!'

As Marianne totters up the steps from our basement flat to street level in the sort of platform shoes that belong on a drag queen, I see she has hitched my dress right up, pulling it out over the top of a thick black belt so it's much shorter than it was designed to be. By the time she gets to the top of the stairs I can see everything that exists between her legs – and God knows I've had enough of that for one day.

'Marianne!' She halts at the top and I can feel the giggle building in me at quite how ludicrous she looks for the tube ride to Victoria train station.

'Yes, babes?'

'Oh, don't worry, I'll see you in a few days.' *What's the point?*

As I turn back into the flat and close the front door, Lulu explodes into hysterics behind me.

'I really have no idea how on earth you ended up living with someone like that, Jenny!'

She's collapsed against the wall, tears streaming down her face.

'Let me refresh your memory, I had no choice. The lovely girl who worked at the British Library had to pull out of signing the lease at the last minute because her parents wouldn't stump up the cash. Marianne was the next person who called and I was desperate.'

'Oh, come here!' She gives me a big messy squeeze, so I'm somehow chewing on her hair and one of her earrings. We head through to the tiny kitchen and spend another ten minutes gently assassinating Marianne – the greedy cow has eaten half of what Lulu cooked – before we opt for the sofa, food on laps and a movie that neither of us is really going to watch.

'How's Dad, have you seen him?' I ask.

'Yes. Will and I went down there a few weeks ago.' By down there, she means the pretty little Cornish cottage he and Sylvie bought early this summer. Although I can't really attest to how pretty or not it is since I've yet to go.

'And? How was *she*?'

'As you'd expect. Busy stripping out every original feature in the place, giving it the sort of sanitised makeover that would make Kevin McCloud shit himself. They both asked about you a lot, though. They really want you to go and visit.'

I can tell from the unchallenging way she says this that Lulu thinks I should. It just feels so disloyal, even after all this time. I've made so little effort with Sylvie over the years, it will look completely disingenuous to rock up now, when the prospect of free summer holidays in Cornwall is suddenly a possibility. And, OK, if I'm being really honest, I don't think Mum would like Sylvie. She's cold and mechanical, the exact opposite of everything Dad loved so much about Mum. I'm happy he's happy, but I can't be bothered to force myself to like her too.

'Maybe I will.'

Lulu knows I won't, her long sigh tells me so. 'They're going away for Christmas this year, skiing.'

'Dad? Skiing? He's never shown the slightest interest in it.'

'Yeah, well, she thinks they need to stay as active as possible, so this is their new thing.' Lulu's face is clouding. Something tells me I'm not going to like what's coming next.

'And it's my turn to go to Will's parents' place this year so we'll be up north. But I'm worried about you, Jenny, what will you do?'

The prospect of sharing a crappy roast chicken – because what would be the point cooking a turkey for two? – with Marianne is too tragic to consider. And anyway, she'll be off gallivanting somewhere else in a microscopic Santa suit and no knickers, probably.

I'm not giving Lulu the quick 'don't worry about me' she was hoping for and now she really looks pained.

'I could ask Will if you can come with us? I'm sure his parents would be more than happy with that.'

I like Will a lot – he's big on fitness, owns a couple of gyms and clearly spends hours using them. He's in great shape, and I should know, I spent a not small amount of time admiring him from afar before they moved back up north from London. He's not like one of those health types who comes for dinner and then ruins the evening for you with endless talk of macrobiotic nutrients, though. He drinks, he stays up late, he makes you laugh – he just makes sure he works it all off on the treadmill the next day. But do I want to spend Christmas with him, or more to the point, his family? I barely know them.

'It's fine, Lulu, I'll work something out.' It's hard sometimes when your sister's so sorted in life. Great job in marketing, earning good money, married to a hot guy, children surely only a matter of time away. They'll be beautiful, too, their kids. The gene pool won't fail them. I'm suddenly feeling a lot like the runt of the litter here.

'Well, the offer is there. Please do say because I know it won't be a problem.' Lulu's reaching for the wine bottle to fill us both back up. 'Oh my God, the funniest thing, I almost forgot to tell you. Before you got home, the phone rang and Marianne shouted for me to get it, said she was waxing, and I didn't want to think what part of her. Anyway, the woman asked for a Jenny and then claimed to be from a bridal shop and said she needed to confirm your next fitting for the wedding dress you loved!'

'Oh, right. That *is* funny. How strange!' This is definitely the time to fill Lulu in on the madness of the past few days but I'm worried about how it will come across now: loser, lonely sister with no one to spend Christmas with, goes into bridal boutique and pretends to be engaged. *Actually* tries on dresses. Worse, chooses one. No, best to dodge this, for now at least.

'She said her name was Helen. Don't worry, I set her straight.'

Urgh! I drain my glass in three needy gulps, then reach for another swift top-up. Lulu definitely won't be helping me fill that Pinterest board tonight!

Chapter Ten

Nat

This might be the first time they're meeting, but Nat knows Susie *very* well. In the month leading up to this appointment, she's watched as Susie's brushed her teeth first thing in the morning and been frustratingly fascinated by the way she takes her make-up off last thing at night. She's hung out with her in hip cafés all over London, where she pretends to eat stacked burgers and drink cappuccinos decorated with cute chocolate hearts. Then there was that incredible skiing trip to Verbier at the beginning of November, where the diminutive beauty wore nothing but head-to-toe Dior. She did very little skiing but looked immense: mountain backdrop, immaculate full face of make-up, eyes drawn wide, and long caramel dip-dyed hair tossed back into winter sun that bounced off every one of her perfectly aligned teeth. Her bright red ski suit, the only bold stab of colour against all that flawless, untouched snow, the images all said, *too right, I'm fabulous* to her not yet cynical 573,000 followers – those who swipe up ten times a day to find out #WhatSusieSaw

Today, they've arranged to meet in London's eye-wateringly expensive Eaton Square, where, in Susie's words, *it'll be a couple of quick shots, then we can chat.* That was an hour and fifteen minutes ago and Susie's still not happy with the pics Nat is taking of her. It's the classic. Girl, with super-long legs in over-the-knee black boots, strides purposefully past black iron railings fronting a white stucco property (like she just stepped out of it on her way to lunch with equally fabulous friends). Her ridiculous handbag (the same one every high-profile blogger was sent this month) swings from her arm so casually she's almost forgotten it's there. *At least that's what she wants you to believe*, thinks Nat. The flirty floral dress is nicely lifting on the breeze so her audience will all get an envy-inducing flash of tanned, toned thigh.

It's one of those biting, but bright November mornings, set against an icy-blue sky. Nat can feel the chill freezing her insides with every breath she takes as Susie walks back and forth over the same six paving stones for the thirty-fifth time.

'You need to catch me at the precise moment my legs are at full stride, my head is back and I've started to laugh.' Susie's directions might sound straightforward but Nat is trying to balance an iPhone, the giant Starbucks she was instructed to pick up for Susie on the way here and the notebook she was hoping to use if they ever make it to the pre-arranged chat.

'OK, that's better, we're getting there. But this one has to be perfect. We're aiming for around 15,000 likes and then you can hit them up for my wedding accessories.'

'Sorry?' Nat is really not at all sure what Susie is suggesting she has to do, or to whom.

'The bag designer. They have a gorgeous range of cream leather clutch bags. I want one for the ceremony and their nude calfskin heels. I think if we can get them on side, they might also stump up for my honeymoon wardrobe, but they're a tough one to crack. They've been working with the same three influencers all year and I need to oust one of them somehow.'

Is this really what it has come to? This hardly – *surely* – does not qualify as anything like normal bridesmaid duties. Isn't this more in the realms of a celebrity agent? *Think about the day rate, Nat, think about the day rate.* She's also aware that if she does a great job for Susie, the referrals could mean *lots* more bookings.

Half a dozen more pic attempts, endless filter manipulation, some quick cropping and the image is uploaded. Finally, they can talk.

'Right, let's go back to mine and then we can go through everything I need.' Susie hails a black cab, gets Nat to snap her bending to get into it, revealing all of both thighs this time, then slings the driver a fiver, telling him that actually, they'll take the tube. On the ten-minute walk back to Sloane Square, Susie doesn't talk to Nat – she's got a global audience to update, via an Instagram Live. And nothing is too banal for discussion, as far as Nat can see. What mascara is Susie wearing? What did she feed her cat for breakfast this morning? What will she watch on YouTube tonight? Most of the comments from men are asking her out. Many of the ones from women are begging for a job working with her. Nat's trying to make her mind up about this bride-to-be and potential high-paying client. She knows, from a few hours spent trawling her social feeds and YouTube channel, that this girl means business. And she's doing very good business, by the looks of it, which is why her house is such a disappointing surprise.

It's tiny and nestled in amongst dozens of identical ones on the modern housing estate they've arrived at in Croydon. A white PVC door opens onto a tiny hallway and corridor that are covered with plasticky, pretend wooden flooring, the sort that squeaks and gives a little too much when you walk over it. It leads into a boxy IKEA kitchen, just like the one in Nat's flat. As Susie shows her around, which takes barely a few minutes, Nat recognises all the features of this mini film set. The all-white room from where Susie delivers her bedroom confessionals, one leg always curled suggestively out over the covers, forcing her audience to question just how naked she might be under there. The duvet, where the strategically placed plate of poached eggs and avocado is always sat on one of the fashiony weekend supplements. Nat sees the white ceramic kitchen sink where Susie unwraps her weekly bouquets and the sofa where she curls up with Nicki Minaj, her spiteful-looking Siamese cat. Except today, the white throw has been removed and what lies underneath is a horrible brown nan sofa that looks a little discount retail outlet, circa 2007. *Not very on brand*, thinks Nat. Susie leads her into the biggest room in the house, her office.

'You follow me, I assume, so you know how insanely busy I am,' starts Susie.

'I have looked at your feeds, yes. It all seems pretty full-on.' Nat's trying not to let any trace of judgement lace her words. Not to give away the sense of utter fakery that seems to be this girl's reason for living.

'My followers live and breathe me, so time out isn't an option.' Humility is not one of her obvious characteristics either, it seems. 'There's no digital detox coming for me at Christmas. No honeymoon that my followers won't be invited on. That's why I need you, Nat. I haven't got time to plan a wedding and I don't want to hire one of those awful planners who'll just want to trade off my connections and reach. I can't expect my management team to do it. They're too busy bringing in the book deals, presenting jobs and landing me my own line of homeware products.'

'How can you bear it? Never just being… you?' Nat has naively assumed this might be a barrier to enjoying this way of life.

'All these people follow me, commit to me, so they expect me to commit to them too. If I take a break, they'll turn on me. It's always your most loyal fans who become your trolls, every blogger knows that.' Susie is switching on the giant Apple screen, bringing up her online diary and giving Nat a frightening glimpse into how pre-planned her life is. Every day has multiple colour-coded entries that denote when she should be posting content and to what channel.

'I'm not living my life, I'm curating it. I'm art-directing every single day. Not everyone can do this. As you can see, my life doesn't dictate my posts, it's the other way around. It can be bloody exhausting, but that's what it takes to get to the top in this game. The important thing is this, Nat, I shouldn't need to spend a penny on this wedding and I need *you* to make sure that's the case. Venue, dress, flowers, booze, I want all of it – for free. Obviously. Find me sponsors.'

Wow! The hustle. *She's not even trying to hide it*, thinks Nat. Where's the charm? What happened to the prudishness we Brits were supposed to be renowned for? Aren't we all supposed to quietly go about the business of making money but never be so crass as to actually discuss it? Where's the self-deprecating good humour? There's none of it here today.

Nat changes tack. 'Tell me about your fiancé. Who are you marrying?'

'Jason Reed. Obviously, you've heard of him. He had the fastest-growing online audience of any male fashion blogger last year. Made it onto the Forbes list of Top 100 Disrupters. People are falling over themselves to offer him the honeymoon so we don't need to worry about that.'

Nat is watching as Susie pouts into the large round mirror sprouting from the top of her computer screen. *Even when she isn't on, she's never off*, thinks Nat.

'But what's he like? How did you meet?' Nat is searching for some sign that underneath all this pretence, there might be some real emotion, some depth of feeling. Anything that will make Susie seem less of a shameless blagger and more one of us, underneath that inch of foundation.

'Oh, the usual.' It's obvious that time really is money to this girl, and she clearly can't see the point of wasting it talking about something that isn't going to advance her earnings. 'Having this wedding keeps us relevant. As we get older, our followers get older and we need to keep putting content in front of them that speaks to their own life stage. The entire day will be filmed so any brands coming on board will get massive exposure. Film edits of the day and the lead up to it will be shared across all channels. It's probably going to be the easiest job you've ever been offered, Nat.'

Susie's phone goes, giving Nat the freedom to sit there for a few minutes in a room that has effectively been wallpapered with images of Susie but none, as far as she can see, of the over-achieving Jason, and think about her own love life. It's sporadic, random, there is no one special and hasn't been for a long time. But that's OK. Nat's having fun and loves that this job puts her in the path of so many interesting and diverse people, ones with lives entirely different from her own. But this? It's so utterly soulless. So transactional. What sort of children might these two inflict on the world? Nat's reminded of an interview she read recently in one of the weekend papers, some celeb agent dishing the dirt on a former child star whose earnings had far eclipsed, by the age of fifteen, anything the agent could ever achieve. It had all gone wrong, because the child's ego had raged out of control and film studios started refusing to work with them. A celebrity's mental age freezes, the agent said, at the precise point at which they achieve fame.

The point at which they stop being treated like a regular human being by everyone around them.

Perhaps that's what's happened to Susie?

Or could it be that Nat's got it all wrong? Should she be more ruthless – with men, her career, her finances? Like most things in Nat's life, this slightly barmy professional bridesmaid thing of hers was just born out of a random series of events. A friend-of-a-friend's bridesmaid let her down a week before the wedding and another mutual friend suggested Nat step in. The bride, Rebecca, needed someone to keep the other in-fighting maids in check and insisted that she would pay. Nat did such a great job that two more paid-for weddings followed. One was a colleague of Rebecca's, who needed someone to blame for all the decisions her future mother-in-law was hating. Then, a couple of months later, another bride, Joanna, who was eloping without her family's knowledge and needed someone to make all the arrangements, minus a paper trail back to her. Being an undercover pro-bridesmaid is the perfect foil. The family look at Nat and see a treasured friend, albeit one they don't remember meeting before, not the arch manipulator of plans she so often is. She's free to slip under their radar in a way a regular wedding planner, who everyone feels they can have access to, never could.

So, being uncalculating and letting life take Nat where she should go has worked so far, hasn't it? Most weddings she's masterminded have been wonderful in their own way.

When the emails started to land in Nat's inbox, she was suddenly turning down the waitressing shifts and ordering *another* bridesmaid dress, having more fun and earning a lot more money. Any advertising has been very low-level, vague posts on Facebook and some very discreetly worded business cards. Susie called after hearing Nat had renegotiated all the venue fees for one woman's big day after a major double-booking balls-up. But what Susie wants is on a whole different level, one that actually doesn't seem terribly fair to Nat. Why should Susie get everything for free when so many lovely brides have to save and pay for it themselves?

'So, I'll give you a list of the brands I want associated with this wedding and you can do the rest.' Susie has ended her call and spun around on her office chair, presumably to see Nat's ecstatic reaction at such good news. 'Whatever your usual day rate is, double it. I'm sure you'll be worth it. Then we can talk specifics. For starters, I don't want you in any of the pictures. I'll only be photographed next to people with a comparable following – and that's not you.' Nothing in Susie's emotionless face belies the sheer arrogance of her last statement and it makes Nat's response an easy one.

'Thanks, Susie, that's very kind of you. But… I'm going to pass.'

'What! You're joking, right?'

Even through all that make-up, Nat can see Susie is going very red in the face. 'I'm afraid not. I only work with clients that I feel a connection with – I'm sure given the business you're in, you can understand that.' Nat is up now and heading for the office door, knowing she needs to exit before this gets nasty.

'Everyone in this business wants to be something they're not, Nat, I'm sure you're no different. Close the door on your way out.' Susie is already gazing back into her giant mirror, arching her head back, getting ready for another post from the frontline of nothing-of-any-significance.

Nat steps out into the last rays of the day's fading sunshine and feels a surge of pride ebb through her, the sort of feeling you only get when you know you've just done precisely the right thing. But it's edged with a far less comfortable feeling of exposure. *Everyone wants to be something they're not.* Did Susie see something in Nat that she hasn't been brave enough to admit to herself yet? She glances down at her mobile phone for the first time in hours and sees she has two missed calls from Helen at The White Gallery. Just as Nat's checking the time of her calls, a text pings through from Helen that immediately makes her stomach tighten.

Can we chat please, Nat? It's about Betsy. Come and see me as soon as you can.

It's been a day of firsts. The first time Nat has ever disliked a potential client enough to turn down her business. And, dear God, let her not be right about this – the first time she has somehow blown a bride's cover before she even followed her up the aisle?

Chapter Eleven

Betsy

Betsy hasn't been able to look Dylan in the eye all day. She spent an excruciating twenty minutes in his office earlier, while the two of them tried to plan their strategy for the client dinner tonight. He was all ideas and clever thoughts, while she sat there, palms sweating, looking like she'd left her brain at home and thinking only about the contents of the overnight bag that's tucked under the desk, out of sight from colleagues. And the slightly ludicrous sum of money she's spent on what's in there.

It's amazing how you can convince yourself that these things are necessary, not extravagant, if you need to, she thinks. Just normal buys that are long overdue for a woman who does a lot of client entertaining and needs to look and feel the part. Nothing wrong with that. Except it has forced her to dip into the wedding fund and she knows she hasn't spent the best part of three hundred quid to impress the client. And if the shopping trip was so innocent, why did she feel like she had to stuff the dress and new knickers into her case before Jacob spotted them? And why has she also spent all morning worrying about the bags and receipts she forgot to dispose of before she left in a tearing hurry this morning? It's Dylan's attention she wants more than anything, she just can't entirely admit that to herself because that would make her pretty stupid, wouldn't it? Planning a wedding to her long-term love but spending every idle moment – and plenty when she should be working – imagining what it might be like to have Dylan's hands all over her.

And is she imagining it or is there a tension between her and Dylan today that hasn't been there before? A nervousness. She certainly feels on edge and he seems a little jumpier than usual too. Or is it just her? One thing's for sure, there's no work getting done today. She may as well not be here for all the use she is to anyone. Lauren's new business proposal isn't getting signed off, she can't focus enough to read Kirsty's end-of-month report and she's struggling to contain her irritation with an unnecessarily bullish Anton. Can't he just have an off day, for once? Slack off and calm down, just today? She decides to give him some competitor analysis to get stuck into, anything to stop him bugging her every five minutes. Then Betsy goes back to the wonderful daydream about what might – *could* – happen in her hotel room tonight, thoughts that are making her feel a way that's definitely not appropriate in the middle of a busy open-plan office.

Dylan recommended the hotel. It's just a few doors down from the restaurant they are dining in tonight, in a cobblestoned corner of Covent Garden. Very discreet. There's no obvious signage, just a huge black lacquered door that leads into the converted townhouse. Her room is full of special little touches: a giant pink velvet headboard, a walk-in rainwater shower big enough for two, a beautiful gold tray filled with make-your-own cocktail ingredients. Now that she's here, she decides to do just that as she's hanging up the Whistles dress and laying out her lingerie and make-up.

Betsy takes her time getting ready. After a shower, she removes every trace of hair from her legs and armpits, then covers herself in a rich layer of sweet-smelling body cream, working it all over her thighs and bum. She paints her nails a chic shade of gunmetal grey and blow-dries her hair into its usual choppy, sexy bob. She takes her delicate Chloé scent and dabs it behind her ears, and down between her boobs.

Then she sits on the edge of the bed and spends the next fifteen minutes wondering what the hell she's doing. She even brings up Nat's number on her phone, knowing she'll talk her in or out of whatever might happen tonight, then thinks better of it – she'll just be implicating someone else in the mess. She likes Nat too much to do that to her.

What does she actually want from tonight? Just some mega-strength flirting with a man she knows will have the attention of every woman in the restaurant tonight, whether he knows it or not? Or more? All the evidence would suggest more – but could she? Why is she even asking herself these questions? Yes, she's attention-starved at home. But it's more than that. She hasn't thought about Jacob in *that* way for ages. Sex has been infrequent and functional, or, worse, needy, when she felt like he wanted cheering up after a bad day at the laptop, when he was frustrated at his own lack of progress and needed something to take his mind off it for ten minutes – her body present but her mind a million miles away. Both of them know it's no good, but neither has had the guts to say anything because it's just easier to pretend it's not happening until this book deal is landed and all their problems magically disappear. It's a phase, a blip – all long-term couples have them, right? She shouldn't judge their entire relationship on how she's feeling right now. Of course there are good reasons she agreed to marry Jacob, they've just become harder to remember in amongst all the work, wedding and managing Mum stress.

She takes a large, strong gulp of the Negroni she's made and then starts to hook herself into the new corset, not easy on her own. But the effect is incredible. Her waist is suddenly tiny and it has smoothed out every lump and bump around her middle, gently pushing her chest skywards so that a touch of forbidden flesh will be visible above the neckline of her dress. The knickers sit super-low on her, just about covering what they're intended to. Like the corset, they are black, sheer, and edged with a line of expensive black ribbon that bows at the back just above a heart-shaped hole that reveals the gentle, womanly curve at the very base of her spine. Even after draining the cocktail, she can't bring herself to put on the hold ups. The slit in the dress runs too high, making the deep lace top of them just visible. It's too obvious, too much. She's going to have to go with bare legs instead but the dress is long enough, just below the knee. It still looks professional. Just.

Betsy scans back through her notes on the client, refreshing herself with the proposal put forward; the number of roles they'll recruit for, the percentage they'll charge, the size of the team they'll put on it and the deadline by which they guarantee to deliver the candidates. It's all locked in. She's baby-stepped the managing director, Mark, through this for weeks, doing all the groundwork that she hopes will now see her and Dylan land an important new account together.

Betsy is the first to arrive at the restaurant and goes straight to the table, the less self-conscious option than perching alone at the bar. Dylan has, obviously, made the perfect choice. It's all dark, woody and leathery in here, and the detailed stained-glass windows make it feel even more exclusive, no prying eyes from the street outside. There are private booths tucked away for more intimate dinners but Betsy has been seated at a table for four in the centre of the main space. An aproned waiter approaches to smooth the white tablecloth, deliver a menu, some bread and to take her drink order. She feels excited and full of anticipation now so orders a glass of champagne. Before he returns, both clients arrive at the table, thrilled to see her. Mark, the oldest and the founder of the company, bends to kiss her on both cheeks, while Jonathan, his finance director, who Betsy is meeting for the first time, settles for a firm handshake.

'I'm so pleased you could make it, Betsy. We both loved the proposal you put together and I really wanted you to meet Jonathan, too.'

There's something so comfortable about Mark, so unlike some of the smug upstarts she meets through work. He's charming and unassuming and she warmed to him the moment they first met.

'And I'm delighted to be here! It's been great getting to know your business, and I hope we're going to get to work together a lot more. Now, what can I get you both to drink?' It's such a positive start that Betsy is feeling totally on top of this, not in the slightest bit worried about a now faintly delayed Dylan.

'Looks like you've made the perfect choice, so I'll join you on the fizz,' says Mark.

'Yep, works for me.' Jonathan is definitely the better-looking of the two, younger and with bright blue eyes that are already appreciating the effort Betsy has made tonight.

There was a time she would have been intimidated in this situation but not any more. She knows her stuff and has researched their business so well there is no risk of being wrong-footed. And she feels incredible tonight, knowing that she looks just the way she planned to; sexy, capable and in control.

While they start to chat through the week they've all had, Betsy sees Dylan enter the restaurant from across the room. As the hostess is helping him out of his Burberry mac, she can see he's changed into a deep petrol-blue suit and freshly pressed white shirt with no tie. Just one look at him, and the mega-watt smile he's treating the hostess to, is sending a surge of energy right through her, totally distracting her from the chat around the table. She can hear Mark and Jonathan answering her questions, but their voices are suddenly muffled, receding into the background, unimportant now. As Dylan reaches them, he bends to greet her first, placing a kiss on the side of her cheek, one that lingers long enough for her to feel his warm breath on her skin and to smell his expensive cedarwood aftershave that she loves so much.

'Betsy, thank you for holding the fort, bloody traffic around the Strand is at a standstill, as usual! I'm so sorry to keep you all waiting.'

'Let me introduce you.' Betsy does the intros and pours Dylan a glass of fizz, while the three men immediately slide into easy chat about the nightmare that is London traffic and how they've been looking forward to eating at this place for months.

Then Jonathan turns his attention to Betsy, asking how long she's worked with Dylan and paying endless compliments about how well respected the agency is within the industry.

'I know Mark is enormously impressed with all the work you've done, which is so much more thorough than anyone else we pitched the business out to. And now that we've met, I can see you're going to be the best partner for us.'

'That's great to hear!' It sounds to Betsy like this business is all but in the bag and Dylan's end-of-month figures are going to swell pleasingly higher than expected.

'So, tell me about *you*. What do you do when you're not driving the business forward?' Jonathan has angled his chair towards her and has noticeably switched off work mode.

'Well...' *Mmmm, where's she going to start with this*? Thankfully, she's saved because Dylan, who is to her left, is reaching an arm across the table towards her and pulling her into his conversation with Mark.

'Remind me, Betsy, what was the name of that piece of business you worked on last year? Where the client took all the other suppliers off the job because you delivered what three recruitment agencies had been hired to do, in half the time?' She can see the pride in his face, and Betsy is loving that she is able to give him something to show off about to Mark and Jonathan.

'It was the online marketing start-up, I'm still advising them now actually. We have a really supportive working relationship with them.' Dylan has absentmindedly left his hand on her arm and she can feel his thumb gently caressing her skin there. Betsy watches as Jonathan's eyes fall from his glass to that exact spot on her arm. She can feel herself start to tense as his gaze is lingering, then flicking between her and Dylan, searching their faces for confirmation of what he thinks he's seen. *And where might this go if they were alone at this table tonight*, wonders Betsy.

'She's bloody amazing and I'd be lost without her.' Dylan tops up Betsy's champagne glass and breaks into a smile that she knows is intended just for her. The two of them lock eyes and for a moment there *is* no one else at the table.

'So, how long have you two been together?' Mark forces Dylan's attention back to him.

'Sorry?'

'You and Betsy, how long have you been together? Not sure I've ever worked with a couple in this business before.'

There is the briefest moment of awkward silence before Dylan regains himself with a gentle chuckle.

'My goodness, in my dreams, I'm afraid. Betsy is far out of my league, Mark. But I'm lucky to consider her my work wife, since we spend so much time together there.'

'Oh, I'm sorry, I saw the engagement ring and just assumed…'

They need to move on quickly, because Mark is starting to look like he's made some hugely embarrassing blunder.

'Yes, I'm planning a wedding for later this year, but don't think that means my eyes will be off the ball at work.' It's up to Betsy this time to fill the silence.

'You don't need to convince me, Betsy. In fact, that's why we were so keen to have you here tonight. Dylan, if you can guarantee me that it will be Betsy who heads up this account, then the business is yours. But I want her on it, that has to be the deal.'

Dylan's gaze flicks to her, quickly assessing this is OK, but surely knowing she wouldn't have it any other way. She landed this business and it should be her that runs it.

'Looks like we have ourselves a deal then!' The delight all over Dylan's face has sparked the order of another bottle of champagne.

While Mark and Jonathan talk quickly about getting contracts drawn up early next week, Dylan leans in close to Betsy so that his lips just touch her ear, his head turned towards her so no one else can hear what he's about to say. She can feel his hand on her left thigh, his fingers briefly playing where the slit of her dress stops.

'You know this is going to happen, don't you? Tonight. I'm not going to be able to help myself.' He's whispering the words, his voice uneven, a little breathless but full of intent.

It's all she can do to stay sitting upright. She allows her hand to drop beneath the table, lacing her fingers tightly between his and allowing him to push them upwards so they move briefly between her legs. Silent confirmation that she is as willing as he is.

More champagne comes and goes, courses of Peking duck and truffled chicken are followed by a velvety chocolate mousse before finally, Dylan is asking for the bill and ordering the clients a taxi. As the four of them spill out into the cold evening air, Dylan waits until Mark and Jonathan are disappearing out of sight around the corner of Henrietta Street before he takes Betsy's hand and starts to stride towards the hotel.

They don't bother with a drink in the bar, diving instead into the lift and heading straight to her room on the third floor. He doesn't say a word, just grips her hand, and Betsy is too pumped full of adrenaline, despite the five glasses of fizz, to know what to do with herself. She's leaving it to him; Dylan is deciding what happens next.

As they reach the end of the dimly lit corridor, Betsy's room is there in front of them. They pause briefly while she delves into her tiny clutch bag, trying to locate the credit card room key that is going to make this door fly open so the two of them can do what Betsy has been fantasising about for months. As her fingers grapple with the clasp on her bag, she can sense him behind her, moving in closer. Then his hands are reaching around the front of her, gripping both her thighs and pulling her dress upwards. *Where is the key?*

'Bee, have you any idea what I want to do to you right now?'

She turns to answer him and as she does, he pushes her against the door, collapsing the full weight of him against her, holding her there. He lowers himself so that he is planting a series of gentle kisses across the neckline of her dress, allowing his tongue to trace a line across the very top of her curves. And she knows she is going to let him do whatever he wants, there is no going back now. His breath is panting out of him as she starts to loosen his belt, they're not even going to make it into the room. Betsy closes her eyes and widens her legs so that she can pull him in between them. As he grabs both her hands in his with an intensity that makes her want to drop to her knees, she can feel her engagement ring dig into the soft flesh of his palm, sensing his grip recoil slightly as it does.

'Stop, Betsy, no. We can't.' The words might be escaping him but Dylan is making no attempt to halt his hands. They are around the back of her now, tugging at her knickers, teasing them even lower.

'I want to. I want *you*, Dylan.' There is no way she can stop this now.

Then he pulls back from her, a look of total anguish replacing the look of pure lust that was driving him a moment ago.

'Christ, Bee, you're getting married. I can't do this to you. I don't want to be *that* man. Shit. I'm sorry, this is entirely my fault. You're better than this.' He attempts to walk away but can't force his feet to do what his mind is obviously telling them to.

Betsy wriggles her dress back down, suddenly feeling incredibly sober and exposed in the corridor. Dylan is holding his face in both hands, trying to get his breath back, telling her over and over that he's sorry but he can't do it.

She finds the key, lets herself in and slams the door loudly behind. She can hear him still out on the landing, pleading with her to please not be angry with him. As she collapses on the bed, shaken by what just nearly happened, she knows it's going to. Not tonight, but soon. There's no way either of them will be able to stop it. As the glint from her engagement ring catches her eye, it's not Jacob she's thinking about now. It's her dad and what he'd think of her. The shame is enough to bring tears to her eyes – but not enough to persuade her that whatever started tonight should stop.

Chapter Twelve

Helen

It's a week after Helen called Nick and now the two of them are sitting at a table in the Coburg Bar at The Connaught hotel, allowing their hands to drop and find each other between the two wingback chairs they are nestled in. The room is dimly lit and alive with the soft murmur of all the discreet conversations going on around them. Shards of colourful light are being cast across the space from behind the rows of unfamiliar spirits lining the illuminated bar. They're both sipping a martini and letting the scent of fresh Amalfi lemons evoke all the romance of the Italian coast. Everything is perfect.

Betsy is early. She arrived unexpectedly with her boss Dylan and after some brief introductions, those two are perched at the bar to discuss some 'pressing work issues', which apparently just can't wait. No one, it seems, has registered that Jacob is nowhere to be seen. Helen's pleased, though – it gives her the just-the-two-of-them time she promised Nick he could have if he joined them for dinner tonight. He's being the perfect gentleman, not pressuring her or even mentioning their last lunch together, just allowing the evening to take them wherever it will. It's unrushed and indulgent and just wonderful.

Every time his fingers instinctively find hers and she feels his hold on her tighten slightly, there is a rush of something inside Helen that's thrilling and nerve-racking and everything in between.

'Can I see you this weekend, Helen? Are you free, or will you be working?' Nick is wearing a sharply tailored navy suit and a baby-blue shirt that makes his eyes sparkle in the candlelight dancing between them. 'Let's go and see a show? Or how about a long walk, just the two of us, through Hyde Park, then lunch overlooking the Serpentine?' He's so alive with ideas, Helen can't help but laugh and plot along with him.

'Sounds wonderful. It will have to be Sunday though because I'm working at the London shop on Saturday, it's so busy.'

'You need some help, Helen. You can't keep flitting between the two, surely? London one minute, Gloucestershire the next. I know you have someone who helps with the Cotswold shop, but still, it's too much for one person to oversee, isn't it? And you must be missing out on potential appointments, you can't be in two places at once.'

Maybe he has an ulterior motive and just wants a larger slice of her time, but he is right, thinks Helen, it's not sustainable. Although she has some solid staff now to help in the Cotswolds, bookings noticeably drop off when brides realise they won't be seeing her. 'It's true, I can't keep up with this level of juggling, it is a little exhausting but to get back to Little Bloombury, I need someone brilliant in London and, well, who? I've spent years building relationships with my clients, Nick, that's why they come. I'd have to be really sure someone else could do it properly. I knew finding that person was the one part of the new business plan I could never rush.'

'Let me help. I can put some feelers out, speak to some people who work in the retail business and put some suggestions in front of you…'

Helen should be jumping at this offer, but instead she's distracted by what's going on at the bar. Betsy and Dylan have turned to face each other. Their laptops haven't been opened, but they have managed to drain two glasses of champagne and order two more. Helen can see that her daughter's heels are resting on the foot bar of Dylan's stool and his legs are open so that hers are positioned snugly between them. She can also see she won't get a chance to raise the subject of Nat before Jacob arrives. She had hoped to mildly quiz Betsy on the subject, gauge her initial response to hearing Nat's name, but no, not now, not tonight. There is an intensity to whatever they are discussing that does not suggest work, not to Helen anyway. And now Nick is noticing it too.

'How is she?' Nick nods in Betsy's direction, doing exactly what Helen is, registering the intimacy between the two of them while desperately trying not to get caught staring.

'Enjoying his company, I would say, wouldn't you?' Helen looks at Nick's face, keen to see his response, hoping that Betsy knows what she's doing and that she isn't going to upset Jacob when he walks in.

'I wouldn't jump to any rash conclusions, Helen. Yes, they look close but remember, she brought him here tonight. She knows Jacob is on his way, doesn't she? I'd say it's probably a good thing she gets on so well with her boss. I hated most of mine before I had the guts to set up on my own.' Nick dismisses her worries with a shake of his head and another sip of his martini, then helps himself to one of the giant green olives from the pewter dish between them.

Still, they both watch as Dylan raises a hand and gently tucks a loose piece of hair back behind Betsy's ear. He does it slowly and deliberately and as he starts to pull his hand away again, Helen sees Betsy fleetingly close her eyes and turn her head towards it so that his fingers move gently across her face and down to her lips.

Nick and Helen lock eyes, neither saying a word, as a waiter approaches them.

'Mr Delaney, your table is ready. Would you like to follow me through?'

'We're waiting for one more guest actually, would you mind if we give him another five minutes, please?'

Jacob is now twenty-five minutes late.

Helen stands and approaches her daughter at the bar, mildly annoyed now that Betsy seems to be doing nothing to find out what's happened to Jacob. She is so engrossed in Dylan's company, Betsy doesn't see Helen until she is standing right next to them with Nick at her shoulder.

'Is Jacob on his way, Betsy? Our table is ready.'

Her irritated tone makes Dylan pull back from Betsy and sit up straighter. Betsy stays exactly where she is, slightly draped over the bar with her legs crossed now, one leaning against the inside of one of Dylan's.

'I've no idea.'

Helen can see the champagne has given her an air of nonchalance about the whole thing. 'Well, have you checked your phone – has he sent a text? Is he stuck in traffic, or train delays?' Why hasn't Betsy bothered to find out? She knows how important tonight is for Helen.

'Why don't I leave you guys to it? I'm sure you've got plenty to catch up on.' Dylan signals for the bill to pay for their drinks, then pulls his stool back to untangle himself from Betsy's legs.

Betsy reluctantly pulls her mobile from her bag and casts a quick glance at the screen. 'There's nothing from him.' She clearly doesn't want to initiate contact herself.

This is awkward, thinks Helen. *Do they wait for him and try to push the time of their reservation back, or do they move to the table now?* Betsy only seems concerned with the fact that Dylan is trying to excuse himself. Of course it's up to Nick to step in.

'Well, it looks like we're going to be a man down, so why don't you join us, Dylan? I can't be expected to entertain these two all on my own, surely!' He's joking, of course, but Helen looks disappointed. It's so important to her that Nick meets both Betsy and Jacob tonight; she's only made the suggestion because she's warming to the idea of Nick being part of their little family. Maybe what she really wants is his view on how Betsy and Jacob seem together. Does she really have reason to worry? With no emotional connection, Nick will be able to give her a rational response to all the questions troubling her. But only if Jacob bothers to turn up and he can see what they're like together for himself.

'Do you really think Jacob's not coming, Betsy?' Helen's having a hard job believing he could be that rude, or even just so late, despite his behaviour the last time they saw each other.

'I don't know, but I'm starving. Shall we just go through?' Betsy is off her chair now and gathering her things together.

There is a moment of hesitation from Dylan – this was clearly not part of his plan for tonight – but too late, the waiter takes his cue, and they're off, across the bustling lobby and into a smart wood-panelled dining room with heavily draped tables. It's definitely a special occasion sort of place, thinks Helen, trying not to let her disappointment at Jacob's no-show ruin the evening Nick has planned so well for them.

Within minutes Dylan is seeking Nick's advice on some renovations he needs to expand the London office space, and the two men are exchanging business cards. Then the subject of New York comes up.

'Yes, we're hoping to make a trip out there soon. I'm opening a New York office.'

'We?' Helen can see the delight on Betsy's face, but Dylan surely can't mean her?

'Betsy and I, yes. I couldn't do it without her. You have an incredibly talented daughter, Helen, but I'm sure you already know that.'

Perhaps any other time Helen would swell with pride to hear someone talk about Betsy this way but something about the look on her daughter's face, how she is hanging off Dylan's every word, is stealing all the pleasure from her.

'Well, please do me a huge favour, Dylan, and get her to use the long flight time to tick off some wedding planning because there is a lot still to do.' It comes out a little more clipped than Helen intends, but the point has been made.

Helen watches Dylan's face closely. How will he react to that? Does he even know Betsy is getting married in less than two months from now? And then she sees it. The very faintest falter in that perfect smile of his. A slight dip of the head – to hide his disappointment, perhaps. Then, the biggest giveaway, he changes the subject entirely.

'You must have been to New York, Nick? Anywhere you would recommend we stay? Ideally, somewhere downtown since I think the new office space will be in the financial district.'

'The newer Four Seasons is incredible, fabulous cocktail bar. Or there's the W, of course, if you want something a bit cooler.'

As Dylan is plugging this information into his phone, it's Helen who sees him first. She's on the window side of their table, with an uninterrupted view back across the entire restaurant. Jacob's suddenly standing in the entrance to the dining room, looking uncomfortably out of place and woefully underdressed. He has turned up to one of Mayfair's finest Michelin-starred restaurants wearing a pair of faded jeans and some battered old sneakers. The maître d' is having a word, furnishing him with details of the dress code, Helen can only presume. She's not even sure they're going to let him in. People are starting to stare and before she can adjust her face to look less alarmed, Betsy notices and spins her head around to see what has caught her mum's attention.

'*Bloody hell*, Jacob!' The words seethe out of her.

Helen doesn't miss the subtle sag of her daughter's shoulders and the slow, disappointed blink of realisation that, for her, the dynamic of the evening is about to change considerably. Before anyone can say another thing, Nick is up from his seat and joining Jacob, speaking quickly and quietly to the host, then slipping his own jacket off and over Jacob's T-shirted shoulders. Helen sees her daughter's cheeks flush slightly at that and she feels the embarrassment on his behalf too. Why didn't he look the place up, like anyone would?

As Jacob and Nick approach the table, it's obvious there is nowhere for their latecomer to sit. The restaurant is full, with no chance of simply squeezing another chair in – it's just not that sort of place. As Nick sits down, Jacob stands for a moment, looking like he has his father's ill-fitting jacket on. Betsy simply stares at him, a look of mild disgust lodged in her brow, before she remembers her manners and introduces Jacob to Dylan, who is clearly doing a much better job of pretending this is all perfectly normal behaviour.

'Sorry, no one told me it was this posh.' Jacob sounds like a petulant teenager, annoyed that he's had to put the iPad down and come out for dinner.

'Here, have my seat, Jacob. We haven't ordered yet, so no harm done.' Dylan takes control and vacates his seat, seeing that Jacob would stand there all night if no one solved the problem for him. 'Helen, it was charming to meet you.' He plants a kiss either side of her face.

'And Nick, please do drop me a line. I'd love you to come and take a look at the office, see what we can do to increase the space a little.'

'Absolutely, expect an email from me by Monday morning.'

'Betsy, I'll see you next week. Have a lovely weekend, everyone.' As Dylan turns to walk away from the table, Betsy goes to stand up but he cuts her off, placing a firm hand on both of her shoulders to keep her seated.

'No, no, you don't need to walk me out. Enjoy dinner with your family.' Then he's gone, back across the restaurant and out into the night. Helen feels a hint of disappointment that their charming dinner guest – well, compared to useless Jacob anyway – has had to depart. Perhaps in a different life Dylan would be exactly the kind of man she'd like to see sat around her own dining table for Sunday lunch, hearing how his and Betsy's week had been.

Betsy leans in closer to Jacob. She waits until Helen and Nick are ordering, then says spitefully, 'Don't you look attractive,' earning herself a hateful glare in return. It's barely audible but Helen just catches it.

They don't say another word to each other for the rest of the evening. And any attempt by Nick to ask about wedding plans is met with stilted silence and Jacob awkwardly shuffling in his seat. Betsy, notices Helen, doesn't look in the slightest bit awkward, too distracted by a flurry of incoming text messages, until the waiter reminds her the restaurant is a mobile-free zone.

When the two of them make their excuses at 9.30 p.m. to catch the late train back to Birmingham, Helen feels thoroughly let down. Not only that, she's embarrassed that her family has put on such a poor display in front of Nick. After some lukewarm goodbyes, everyone more than aware the evening hasn't been the jolly get-together that was planned, Helen watches Betsy stride out of the restaurant, three paces ahead of Jacob. The second the two of them disappear through the thick velvet drapes and out into the lobby, she apologises to Nick for them both.

'Think nothing of it, Helen. It's family.' He shrugs. 'Anyway, if you want me to be really honest, I'm happy to have you to myself again.' And he leans in to kiss her, letting his lips linger softly on hers, his hand cradling the back of her neck, so he can hold her in the kiss a little longer.

'I can't believe I left seeing you this long. I've missed you.' All Helen wants is to be kissed again by this man. Maybe it's the surroundings, the spoiling effect of plate after plate of beautifully presented food, the intoxicating headiness of the expensive bottle of Chablis they've shared, or every little attention he has paid her tonight, but everything about Nick is addictive.

'Come home with me.'

He says it so easily, so confidently. But the words make Helen's lungs fill with air that she suddenly can't release. She opens her mouth to respond but nothing comes, as the sensible part of her brain does battle with what her heart is telling her to do.

'Don't overthink it, Helen. Just do what you feel is right. I want to spend the *whole* evening with you. To fall asleep with you in my arms. I want you to be the first thing I see tomorrow morning.'

'So do I.' The words whisper out of her, but Helen means every one of them.

As the two of them curl up in each other's arms in the back of Nick's waiting Mercedes, Helen is alive with nerves, but she can't help herself.

'I have a problem, don't I? With Betsy?'

'Yes, *we* do. But I'm sorry, Helen, all I care about tonight is you. We can tackle that one in the morning.'

And she's happy with that. Nick is going to help and that's all she needs to hear for now. The evening has reached its perfect conclusion.

Chapter Thirteen

Jenny

It's a hard thing to get your head around – being motherless. All these years on, I'm still trying. She's gone. Forever. It's so final and immoveable and it doesn't matter how clever I might be, how determined or resourceful I try to be, this is one problem I'll never fix. She's never coming back. She exists now only in the pixelating memories my brain chooses to recall; the fading snapshots that turn up in an old shoe box, tucked into the jacket of a favourite book or at the back of an old photo frame. If I'm lucky, sometimes she briefly reappears in the smell of the first day of spring or the sound of the ice-cream van, or Lulu's sweet, unknowing face.

What do I miss? The list is endless, it swims away from me every time I think about her, swirling me around in a great tangle of sadness and regret. I'm sad about all the things I'll never hear from her again: *of course you can do it, let me sing to you, how's my beautiful girl?* I'm regretful of everything I never got a chance to say or to share with her, and angry she was denied all those moments she would have been so bloody brilliant at. What can I possibly compare her loss to, in a way someone unfamiliar with death will understand?

Is it like someone closing the book, snatching it from you before you can truly understand how brilliant that character is, leaving you empty and unfulfilled? A missed opportunity for greatness that you stuffed up because you overslept that morning and the sliding doors effect saw to it that you failed? That putrid, pit-of-the-stomach ache when you know you've done the wrong thing, hurt someone's feelings, lied your way out of something that will surely now come back to haunt you?

Yes and no. Yes, because all of these things hurt. No, because they are all so fleeting. They go away, but losing Mum is never-ending for me. A memory of her, lodged deep inside me, resurfaces from time to time, often when I'm not even thinking about her. I was eight and counting down the days to my first big school disco. Golden-haired Tony Hall was going to be there, I had nothing to wear, and I'd thrown a strop about it. Mum took me out and bought me a whole new outfit, not because she bowed to my tantrum, but because she could see how much it meant to me. The blue velvet dungarees that fastened at each shoulder with a shiny silver heart were so much more than an outfit. They were my passport into Tony's world, those pedal pushers, at least I had built them up to be.

Then I overheard the argument Mum and Dad had because we couldn't afford what she'd spent on me. *A nonsense waste of money*, he called it. I stood behind my bedroom door and listened to them going at each other; he was worried about the family finances, she was determined her daughter was going to walk into that disco feeling confident that I might just be in the game of winning Tony's heart. And then she said, 'I'll take my bike back.' She'd been saving for it for months. It was cherry red with a wicker basket at the front that she used to collect wildflowers in, the only possession I ever remember her caring about. She'd go out on it some afternoons, filling the basket with ham sandwiches and lemonade, to *clear my head*, she said, returning hours later, face all rosy and in one of those buoyant moods that usually meant we got whatever we wanted for tea.

And she was willing to give it up for me. I cried behind the door that day because even at eight, I felt so guilty that I was depriving my mum of something she loved. And that's it. If it has to boil down to one simple thing, the thing that she gave me that I miss so much now, it was her protection. From my dad's anger that day. From the school bullies, another. And against the whole world: every time she held my hand to cross a road, every time she made sure my scarf was tucked into my jacket to keep the wind out, every time she gave up an evening to help me with my homework, she was protecting me from harm and judgement.

Sitting on the sofa, now, with a stinking cold and half-listening to Marianne moan about the *pathetic* state of her sex life, it's Mum I need. Because who's going to protect me now? Marianne will shout me twenty quid if I'm running short one week. Lulu will make sure I've got someone to eat Christmas lunch with. Jean will defend me to management if I make a bad call on the maternity ward. But who will only ever see the good in me? Who will be my safety net, giving me the confidence to try new things, taking the risks because if all else fails, I've still got Mum? Her limitless love would always be there, that's what the naive me always thought.

'Is that rude fucker ever going to call me?' Marianne is shaking her mobile phone, as if a screw must have come loose inside and is stopping a string of juicy texts from reaching her. 'I'm not being funny, but I didn't schlep all the way to Manchester and perform what was undoubtedly the blow job of his life, only to be ignored by him now.

Do you know what he asked me to do, Jenny? Just after he ruined my new peep-hole bra? No? Well, I'm going to tell you. He…'

As Marianne takes the conversation to depths I thought impossible even for her, I write a letter to my mum, charting all the things I should have done – and plenty I shouldn't.

I'm sorry I never stuck at anything. Brownies, vegetables, the tough conversations.

I'm sorry all I ever seemed to ask you for was a lift somewhere.

I'm sorry for all the times I never asked about you.

I'm sorry my heart isn't as full of love as yours was.

I'm sorry I'm so disappointing, only half a daughter.

I'm sorry I don't always dream about you.

I'm sorry for all the times I wished it was someone else's mum who left in the ambulance that day and never came back.

I'm sorry for ever thinking you were embarrassing and for never bothering to hide it.

I'm sorry for all the lies I've told and the hundreds more I know I'll tell.

I'm sorry I only ever wrote you one letter from my French Exchange trip.

I'm sorry I don't love cycling.

I'm sorry I'll never place a gurgling grandchild in your arms.

I'm sorry I didn't believe you would ever get better.

I'm sorry I love you more than I love Dad.

I'm sorry I'll never get to say 'I'm her daughter' ever again.

I'm sorry the last thing I whispered in your ear was, 'can I stay up late?' when it should have been 'I love you'.

I'm sorry I opened your letters too soon.

I'm sorry I couldn't stop Dad marrying Sylvie.

I'm sorry you'll never read this.

I'm sorry, but I think I need a new mum.

Marianne hasn't noticed the tears that are silently dropping off my chin and onto the lined paper on my lap. The biro is starting to pool into an inky mess as some of the letters swim into each other, in danger of coming right off the page and onto the cushion.

I think about Helen, about her warmth, and wonder whether she has a daughter. Something makes me feel she must. She seemed so calm and patient, soft and forgiving, born for motherhood, to shape a small girl into a confident, inspiring young woman. I wonder, probably very irrationally, if she could love someone like me. But her phone call and Lulu's response to it has surely blown my cover. Maybe I should just call, see what sort of reaction I get?

'What's the most disgusting thing you've ever done to a bloke, Jenny? Come on, something really depraved that you've never told anyone before.' Sick of listening to the sound of her own voice, Marianne has suddenly remembered I'm in the room. She's cross-legged on the sofa opposite me, wearing a pair of gold hot pants that have more arse escaping than contained in them. She has seen fit to team this with a cropped top that has the words '*It's Not Going To Suck Itself*' spelt out in diamanté crystals across her tits. Then there are the purple leg-warmers, at least that's what I think they are, unless she has fashioned them out of an old pair of tights, I can't work it out. They finish mid-thigh, making her look like something out of one of those cheesy American cheerleader dramas.

'Marianne, there is more to life than shagging, you know.' I sound like her mum, I know I do, but seriously, does she *ever* think about anything else?

'Is there? Like what?' She looks genuinely confused.

'A career, friends… er… the arts!' That last bit makes her howl like a drunk.

'You are hysterical! Now, what was it? I'm not going to shut up until you tell me.'

I know why she's asking me this. Aside from taking her mind off the 'piece of dick' that's so far failed to text her, it's so she can look colossally disappointed with whatever I say. Like it's entry-level stuff, probably what she was up to on the other side of the school playing field at the age of twelve. Then she'll deliver another one of her dispatches from the frontline of depravity to show me how it should be done. Only last week she amused herself for a good half an hour telling me, in her own delightful way, that if I don't use it more often it's going to close over. Well, just for once, I'm not going to give her the satisfaction. Sometimes it pays to listen when the filth-ometer goes up in the staffroom.

'OK, since you ask, remember the two guys who came to replace the dishwasher last week? You know, that white thing in the kitchen that miraculously seems to eat all the dishes after a meal and then spits them out again, sparkling clean?'

'Hilarious. Yeah?' She's intrigued now. She's even put her phone down, one of the highest compliments she could bestow on another human being.

'Well, why d'you think it took them so long to do such a simple job? And didn't you noticed how flushed I was when they eventually left?'

'Are you serious? You shagged the pair of them? In our kitchen?' I can't tell yet if she's proud or affronted that it wasn't her getting it front and back by a couple of hairy workmen.

'Yep, and I didn't even spray the work surface with Dettol afterwards. And I can tell you, that fat one was particularly messy. Makes me heave a little just thinking about it, to be honest.' How I'm keeping a straight face, I don't know, but she laps it up.

'Well, bugger me. And I've been telling everyone you're a big lesbian!'

All I can hear is Marianne shrieking her lungs out as I close my bedroom door behind me. *When did I become such an excellent bull-shitter?*

I sit on the bed, a rather sad single one with six-year-old bedding from some closing-down sale, and swipe through my recent call list until I find the number I recognise as Helen's. I really hope she understands. Perhaps if I just explain what actually happened: she assumed I was a bride-to-be and then I felt too embarrassed to say otherwise in front of the customers with her that day. Then, well, it just gathered momentum… Urgh! *Just bloody do it, Jenny!* Then maybe I can drop by, take her some flowers. Perhaps we might even become friends?

As soon as I hear her kind voice, I'm reassured she's going to be nothing but lovely to me.

'Hi Helen, it's Jenny Archer. You called and spoke to my sister, Lulu, about my next appointment?' I can hear the nervousness in my voice and wonder if Helen can too.

'Jenny. Yes! My goodness, I have been meaning to call back. What a terrible mix-up.' She actually sounds more mortified than I do.

'I know and I'm sorry, if I can just explain, Helen. I never meant to cause any trouble.'

'Oh, it's me who should be apologising, Jenny. What a terrible mistake for me to make and honestly, I'm surprised at myself.'

'Sorry?'

'Making assumptions like that. I have to remind myself that not every bride lets her entire family in on her plans, or even that they've got engaged. It really was the most terrible error on my part. I should have just asked for you to call me back and not gone into any of the details. I hope I haven't messed things up for you, spoilt a big surprise or forced you to tell your sister when you didn't intend to yet?'

It takes me a moment to think this through. She's actually apologising to me, isn't she? She thinks she's in the wrong. She's giving me the out. I no longer need to confess, despite the fact I know I should. I'm trying to will myself to do it anyway but the imperative has gone. God, I am so weak. My determination to come clean evaporates quicker than one of Marianne's faked orgasms.

'Think nothing of it! Honestly, it's no problem.'

'Well, I have been thinking about it a lot, actually, and by way of apology, I'd love to offer you a discount on the beautiful Hayley Paige dress you chose. Would that go some way to making it up to you?'

Poor Helen, she has obviously been agonising about this. 'You are too kind.' And I am too much. Seriously, I am. I know I've only made things worse for myself now, but – *how tragic am I?* – it feels like the only way to be sure of seeing her again.

'Well, let's get you back in, try the dress on again and we can chat through any alterations that might be needed. Your last appointment finished in such a hurry. I'd love to hear more about the day you're planning, the man you're marrying, so I can do everything in my power to pull all the styling together beautifully for you.'

Oh shit! That's wiped the smile off my face. 'Perfect. I'll email you some dates and we can get it sorted.'

As I hang up, I know I'm now looking at another night in front of Pinterest, stealing all the best bits from other women's weddings, ready to pass them off as my own. I suppose it won't hurt to get ahead with this. Jean, Lucy and everyone at work will need to see progress on the wedding front too.

A couple of hours later, when my eyes have had enough screen time and are starting to blur all the bouquets into one over-the-top mess, I emerge from the bedroom to find Marianne looking extremely pleased with herself.

'Fucking brace yourself, Jenny, because you're not going to believe what I've done while you've been hiding in there!' She looks like she's about to explode with the sense of victory, her eyes are popping out of her head and her lips are pulled back over her gums like some sort of manic horse.

Whatever it is, it's not going to be good. There is smugness and mischief pouring out of her. *Please let it just not involve me.*

'Go on.' *I really don't want her to go on.*

'I called the company that fitted the new dishwasher, said we weren't at all happy with the way it's running and that they need to send the same two guys back ASAP to take a look. They're only bloody coming tomorrow night! But this time, I will be here, my friend. You don't get to have all the fun on your own. Didn't your mother teach you to share?'

I slump off back to my room and fire off an email to Helen. Does she by any chance have an appointment tomorrow, early evening? Otherwise, I'm going to be sat in Pizza Express around the corner from the flat, hugging a cappuccino for hours until Marianne has satisfied herself and it's safe to go home.

Chapter Fourteen

Nat

It's the wedding Nat has been looking forward to most this year: Heidi and Alex, a couple who met on day one of university and have been inseparable ever since. Helping Heidi finalise all the details for their party in the Kent countryside has been nothing short of magical. No dramas, no egos, no arguments over budgets, just one big happy family coming together to make it everything it should be. And as much as she's enjoyed it, it has made her heart ache a little more for Betsy, who is becoming more distant by the day.

And why did Heidi hire Nat? For the best possible reason. Because she wants her real friends to be stress-free with no obligations beyond attending the wedding and having the time of their lives. Heidi has been a dream to deal with, she and Nat often spending way longer than they needed to on the phone, chewing over all the details, genuinely sharing each other's excitement for the day that is now so nearly here. She'd love to be more like that with Betsy too.

The attention to detail has been impressive. This wedding is being held on a flower farm, where everything will happen outside, around giant fire pits – a nod to the couple's love of the great outdoors. The bride's father has been growing herbs all summer for them to display in vintage tins on the tables and there will be dahlias, peonies, roses and ripe pears hanging everywhere. All the invitations were painstakingly handmade by Heidi, featuring a watercolour map of the wedding site with a cute key denoting where to camp, dance and party under the stars. A log cabin will be filled with beautifully upholstered furniture, fur shrugs and a bar where guests can help themselves to hot toddies. Then, as a wonderful surprise for the couple and a thank you for all their hard work, Nat has co-ordinated the guests to bake homemade cakes and treats for an indulgent dessert table that will be covered with lamingtons, fruit scones, lemon curd tarts, fondant fancies, and a ginger cake smothered in butter frosting. Her mouth is watering at the thought of it all.

All Nat has to do now is finalise her dress. This should be straightforward enough, except it means an appointment with Helen – and Helen wants to talk about Betsy.

On the journey across London, through a congested and rain-soaked Wimbledon town centre and onto the eastbound District line, Nat is thinking about nothing other than how she is going to handle this. She needs to tread carefully. Helen may know a lot less than Nat fears she does. She may simply have worked out that Nat and Betsy know each other somehow so all Nat needs is a solid enough cover story to flick her straight off the scent. But what? The truth is, unlike many of the other brides-to-be Nat works with, she has struggled to get close to Betsy. Not because she doesn't want to, she can feel there's something between them that could be much more than one great night out together, but there is a reluctance on Betsy's part to let Nat in. What's she hiding? She didn't even want to choose Nat's bridesmaid dress. *Whatever you think is best*, Betsy said. Maybe Nat can get that done today, if Helen isn't too inquisitive. But she needs to protect Betsy too: it's not her job to fill Helen in on any of this.

By the time she's ringing the doorbell to The White Gallery, Nat is feeling jumpy and unsure of her facts and how this is all going to play out. She decides to focus on what she's really here for, to finalise the dress for Heidi and Alex's wedding in a few weekends' time. Everything else will just be question-dodging and hoping she hasn't woefully underestimated Helen's investigative skills.

Helen does at least seem very pleased to see her. 'Come in, my darling. This weather is appalling.' She scoops Nat in under the shop's smart striped awning and into the warmth, where she stands dripping all over the polished parquet floor, which already makes her feel like she's done the wrong thing.

'Don't worry about that, it will dry,' chirps Helen. 'Let's get you out of those wet clothes.' Helen is wriggling her free of her sopping wet mac and the useless bent-out-of-shape umbrella. 'I'll pop everything out the back. Why don't you take your jeans off too and slip on a robe? Then everything will be dry by the time you leave.'

What Nat wouldn't give to have someone like Helen around permanently – she's practical, organised and full of good ideas. Good mum material. But now that she's near naked under the robe, she feels even less confident about this meeting. The exposure somehow places her on the back foot and more at the mercy of Helen's questions.

'OK, so the wedding is soon now. I noted before you loved a few different looks, so let's narrow it down, shall we? I've put two in the changing room if you want to go through and get into the first one?'

'Good plan.' Nat disappears into the fitting room, hopeful that Helen may have entirely forgotten the reason she asked her to come today. She lifts the first dress from its hanger and starts to remove the robe. It's a long-sleeved navy jersey dress that's sashed at the waist and perfect for a winter wedding.

Helen steps into the fitting room and starts to help Nat belt it tight around herself. Nat's trying to pretend she's admiring herself in the mirror, but whenever she thinks she can risk it, she's flicking a glance at Helen, trying to read deeper into her mood, and ignore the slightly charged atmosphere she can feel building between them today – the sort of feeling you get when you know that once the pleasantries are done, there will be a more difficult conversation.

'What d'you think?' Helen stands back a little to get a better look. She's smiling. 'We'll need to pull it in across the chest a bit to stop the gaping, but otherwise, it's not a bad fit, I'd say. It looks great on you, Nat.'

'Yes! I like it. But let's try the Ghost one too, because that deep plum colour is gorgeous for this time of year.' *Has she forgotten?* wonders Nat. She seems so focused on the dresses, there is a possibility she has.

'Let me help you.' There is not one trace of annoyance or agitation on Helen's face. She is, as always, dressed beautifully, this time in a pale lilac shift dress that opens wide at the neck to reveal a delicate gold chain with a cluster of initials dangling from it. *Probably a love token from her husband and children*, thinks Nat. There is a stiff, double bow at her waist in the same thick satin fabric and her nails are polish-free, but buffed so well they catch the light from the crystal chandelier dangling above them.

The next dress has a thin halter-neck strap that sits on Nat's collarbone and a giant ruffle that fans out across her chest, before dropping super-low at the back.

'It's stunning on you, Nat! I love it, but you're going to freeze to death. There are plenty of cover-ups I can suggest, but the back is so low. Now I see it on you, I'm just not sure it works for this time of year. What d'you think?'

Nat can always rely on Helen to be entirely honest with her. Even when there's an opportunity to add more to the bill, Helen won't do it if she doesn't think the look is perfect.

'You're right, you're always right. Let's stick with the navy.' It's smiles all round, as this goes down as one of the quickest appointments Nat has ever had with Helen. And why would she ever go anywhere else? Helen's expertise is near-legendary on the wedding circuit and even if she may have privately questioned the frequency of Nat's appointments, she has never put her on the spot about it, never grilled her for answers she might not want to give. *Although,* Nat wonders, *is that about to change?*

As Nat is rushing out of the dress, keen to make her getaway, Helen disappears to retrieve her clothes. When she returns, her face has altered; she looks suddenly more solemn and Nat knows full well what's coming.

'Am I also right that you know Betsy?' She stands in front of Nat with her clothes draped across her arms, as if to say, *answer my questions, or you're not getting these back.*

'Betsy?' Nat's stalling for time, trying frantically to think of a response that will shut this down, refusing to make eye contact with Helen while she fumbles around with the dress.

Helen bides her time until Nat is down to just her undies and now has no choice but to face her.

'Yes, Betsy.' Helen says the words painfully slowly, like she has all the time in the world to hear the explanation that she assumes is coming. 'It's just, you never said that you knew her when her name came up in conversation the last time you were here. But then I found this at her house and, correct me if I'm wrong, but it's your business card, isn't it? And that's your mobile number? It's taken me a while to work it out, but there can't be many that end in triple five.' Helen holds up the card. *Her* business card. Nat immediately recognises the font and the discreet tiered wedding cake logo in the bottom right-hand corner.

'Nope, that's not me.' This is bare-faced lying. And it's not going to work, she knows it's not, and the rising panic she's feeling, intensified by the high-pitched scream of a police siren as it passes the boutique, is hampering all logical thought. Helen is like a gun dog on the scent.

'Really? This isn't your mobile number?' There's no anger in Helen's voice, just the weariness of someone who is being lied to and knows it. This conversation is about to reach its horrible, inevitable conclusion.

'No, doesn't look like it.' It's a real shame this conversation is having to happen with Nat wearing just her bra and knickers, her near-nakedness sapping her of the mental strength to cope with it. But she can't blab. Firstly, because she has a contract with Betsy that promises discretion but also because she knows that even if she confesses to merely a working relationship with Betsy, Helen's questions will not end there. It will be impossible to silence her once Nat has removed some of the doubt.

Helen places the bundle of clothes gently down on the fitting-room chaise longue and lifts the handset from the wall just above it. *Oh shit!* As she starts to punch the numbers from the card into the phone, Nat hangs her head. The only sound then is that of Nat's mobile phone, buried in her stiff radiator-dried jeans and trilling loudly between them. Despite the early confidence in her conviction, Nat can see the way Helen's face crumples at the sound, as her theory is proven to be right. Now she knows for sure there is some connection between Nat and Betsy. Nat just can't be the one to fill in all the missing blanks.

'Why does Betsy have your card? Why did you deny knowing her and can you *please* shed some light on why my wonderful daughter seems to be not the slightest bit excited about her own wedding day?'

'No, I can't. I have to go, Helen. Sorry.' Nat says the words far too abruptly, sounding mean and heartless, but none of this is her story to tell. She can't rat on Betsy, no matter how much pained concern is swamping Helen's face.

'Please, Nat.' Helen takes one small step towards her, then stops, perhaps not wanting to appear confrontational, then continues her plea. 'I'm her mother and something is obviously not right. I can't help her if I don't know what's wrong.'

'I think you should speak to Betsy.' She looks away from Helen, whose eyes are starting to fill with tears, and it's agonising. Nat knows she could quash some of her anguish in a few short sentences, but not without dropping Betsy right in it and she's not going to do that to someone she's hoping she might become friends with.

'I've tried speaking to her but as you'll know, if you know Betsy at all, she can be incredibly stubborn when she wants to be.'

Helen is standing between Nat and her exit out of here. She's dressed now and could run. She's seriously considering it. But then she'll never be able to return. And God, look at Helen's face, filled with all the concern of a mum who is in the dark and feels her daughter is slipping away from her.

'Call her, Helen.' Nat's trying her best to sound sympathetic and reasonable, like one quick chat is all that's needed to sort this out, while continuing to edge slowly and deliberately towards the door.

'She won't answer my calls!' There is the faintest hint of hysteria powering Helen's words now, a trait Nat has never seen in her before.

'Go and see her then.' Nat is trying a firmer tone. Helen needs to know she's not going to cave.

'She won't be honest with me! If she wanted to do that, I'm guessing you wouldn't be here on her behalf.' It's the first time Nat has ever heard Helen raise her voice. '*Please*, Nat, what is so bad that you can't tell me? Is she in some sort of terrible trouble? She hasn't lost her job, has she? Oh God, is it Jacob, has he done something awful to her?' Helen's head is in her hands now and she's stopped trying to keep a lid on her anxiety or a stop on her tears.

Nat lets the sound of another siren reach its peak volume outside the boutique, watching through the giant glass windows as cars swerve in sharply to let the police car past and listening as its urgent warning sound fades into the distance of the surrounding streets. She sucks in a huge, body-expanding breath, then turns back to face a teary Helen. This is one of those times, Nat concludes, when the adult conversation is going to have to happen. She's going to have to place Helen's feelings above her own need for discretion and risk whatever might come her way from Betsy later.

'OK, Helen, I'm going to tell you what I know, which isn't that much, actually. But I need your total assurance that it will go no further. And especially not to Betsy. I'd rather she didn't hate me and I have a reputation to protect in all of this, it's my livelihood.'

'Your livelihood? What on earth do you mean? What exactly has Betsy asked you to do?' It's the first time Helen's questioned whether any fault may lie with Betsy herself, not those around her.

Nat can see from the wideness of her eyes and the way Helen is barely breathing that her mind is going to a much darker place than it needs to, and so while it might be unforgiveable – and certainly unprofessional – Nat begins to tell her everything. 'Come on, take a seat.' The two of them sit stiffly next to each other on the chaise longue. 'I'm a professional bridesmaid.'

'A what?'

'Basically, it means women hire me to pretend to be their bridesmaid.'

'I know what it means, but why would any woman do that? I don't understand. I mean, I've read about this in the American magazines, but I didn't think it actually existed – not here, at least.' Nat can see Helen is still trying to work out how this can possibly be relevant to her and Betsy.

'I know it sounds odd but believe me, there are many reasons…'

'But Betsy's not lonely, she has plenty of friends. And she has me. We've always been so close. Why won't she talk to me, what have I done to push her away like this?' Helen turns to Nat, searching her face now for some indication as to how there could be so much distance between her and her daughter.

'I think Betsy's reasons for hiring me are quite different, Helen. You say she's not excited about the wedding and that's really been obvious to me, too. She's handed most of the arrangements to me so far. I designed the invites…'

'She told me she did!' The impact of the deceit on Helen's face is painful to watch, a horrible contorted mix of sadness and incredulity.

'I'm afraid not. I was supposed to be choosing my bridesmaid dress while I was here with you today. She just told me to choose whatever I wanted, no steer on colour or style or anything. She's asked me to think about cakes and flowers too.' Nat stops because she can see the tears are starting to flood Helen's eyes.

'She told me her bridesmaid was a friend from work.' The words are sobbing out of her now.

'Oh God, I'm so sorry, Helen. Maybe it would be kinder if I just shut up and you chat this all through with Betsy. I really don't want to lie to you, but I have loyalties to Betsy too. I've already said far too much.'

'Is she paying you to do all of this?' Now that they've started, and exactly as Nat predicted, Helen seems determined to extract as much information from her as possible.

'She is, yes.' Urgh! With every word she utters, Nat feels her betrayal of Betsy more and more strongly.

'And why do you think she's doing that? Why doesn't she want to plan this wedding with me?' Helen is trying to wipe the mascara clear from under her eyes but is just smearing it further down her face. 'Have you spoken to her much about it? Maybe it's all my fault, there's a man I've been getting close to. Maybe she feels neglected. I've paid too much attention to him and not to her, haven't I? Is that it?'

'She hasn't confided in me much. In fact, I'd go as far as to say, she's probably the most evasive bride-to-be I've ever *tried* to work with. If it makes you feel any better, Helen, I wouldn't say she's gained any pleasure from any of this.' Despite the disgust at her own treachery, at least the nerves are starting to dissipate from the pit of Nat's stomach, now that the beans have been well and truly spilled.

'So, she hasn't mentioned Nick?'

'Not at all. I don't think this is about you or anything you may have done. I think it's about her.'

'What about her? Has she given you any clue about what else might be going on in her private life?'

'Not exactly, no.'

'But there's something? Are you keeping something from me?'

Just then a young woman tries to enter the locked door of The White Gallery, forcing Helen to break away from their chat to speak to her. She's dressed impeccably in a smart black-and-white checked coat that flatteringly hugs her curves, black cigarette pants and soft grey suede ankle boots. She looks like she's just taking ten minutes out from her successful job in one of the neighbouring fashion boutiques to seek the benefit of Helen's limitless wisdom.

'I'm so sorry, I'm just with a client. Can I take a number and I will happily call you back later?'

Nat can see the smile is there on Helen's face, perhaps not quite as broad as usual, but she's determined not to let this future bride down with any hint of her own trauma. The girl hands over a business card, double-checks on a number of designers she's hoping Helen stocks and then she's on her way. It's so sad, thinks Nat, that a woman as lovely as Helen is having to grill her, a relative stranger, for answers about her own daughter. She deserves better than this.

'Please, Nat, go on.' She returns, this time sitting a few inches closer to Nat on the chaise longue.

'It's probably nothing, just a small thing really, it just struck me as quite odd at the time.'

'What did?' Helen edges even further forward so that their knees are just touching.

'She called one night, it was late and I think it had finally dawned on her that I needed some urgent answers on a few things.'

'Yes…'

'She was in a bar, I think, because I could barely hear a thing she was saying so we switched to texting each other.'

'Go on.'

'Well, maybe she'd had a few or something but all the way through the chat she kept referring to her partner by a different name. I know she's marrying Jacob, but that's not the name she used.'

'Can you remember what name she did use?'

'No, but I can probably check back through my texts if you think it's important?' Nat picks her phone up and starts to enter the security code that will allow her to access her messages. Helen's hand touches hers and she is shaking her head from side to side, telling Nat not to bother.

'I don't think you need to. I'm pretty sure the name you'll find will be Dylan.'

Nat pauses for a moment, wanting to be completely sure of her facts, and then, 'Yes, you're right, that was definitely it.'

*

Nat sits entirely still, registers the sad sag of Helen's shoulders and doesn't say a single word as Helen unleashes everything: about the surprise visit she paid to Betsy's house when she knew she wouldn't be there; about the expensive lingerie receipts, the new clothes, the luxury make-up habit her daughter has acquired. She doesn't hold back on anything – Jacob's appearance, the state of their home, the excruciating dinner with Nick and how relieved she was when the two of them finally left the table and Betsy presumably decided to mistakenly text Nat about Dylan – until the two women are both slumped, side by side, the story finally finished. Helen has kicked off her shoes and got through half of the box of tissues.

Nat can't help but think about the women those tissues are really intended for. As she glances around the boutique, her emotions steadied by the effect of all that calming white, she thinks about the happy mothers-of-the-bride, crying tears of pride and joy at seeing their angelic five-year-old blossom into a beautiful woman right there in the fitting room. Helen's sorrow seems so out of place in the shrine to future happiness that is The White Gallery, with all its sparkle and decadence and blemish-free perfection.

Nat wraps an arm around Helen and allows Helen's head to drop onto her shoulder. 'I've worked with so many different women, Helen, all with different reasons for hiring me. All with a different vision of how their married life will be, the kind of wife they'll make, the sort of husband they want him to be. The one difference with Betsy is that I don't think she wants to get married. Perhaps what you have to figure out now is why.'

Before Helen has a chance to respond, they are interrupted by the sound of the front door opening and closing – Helen must have forgotten to lock it again after their earlier visitor – and quick footsteps moving closer towards them across the wooden flooring. Who could be that familiar with the place? And then the call '*Mum!*' fills the air between them. There is no time to react, nowhere for the two women to go that won't immediately place them in Betsy's path. So they sit, for what seems like forever but is a matter of mere seconds, until Betsy's face appears around the corner of the fitting-room drapes.

One look at her mother's tear-stained cheeks, her companion and the pile of used tissues around her, and Nat watches the smile on Betsy's face switch to a look of utter betrayal. An angry, short sigh escapes her before she turns and makes straight back for the door. But not before Helen briefly halts her with a powerful reminder of who is in the wrong here.

'If you're feeling hurt right now, Betsy, I would ask you to take a moment to consider what the past hour has been like for me, your mother. Hearing everything that I have and feeling for the first time in my life that I barely know my own daughter.'

Shame is painting itself all over Betsy's face before she is off again.

It's Nat who moves next, jumping to her feet and jamming them quickly back into her Converse while Helen sits motionless.

'Aren't you coming?' Nat is grabbing her bag, determined to catch up with Betsy.

'No, I need time to think about everything you've said. She's angry. No good will come of anything we say to each other right now.'

Betsy is nearly all the way down the end of Connaught Street by the time Nat gets level with her.

'Betsy, please, *stop*.' The words are breathlessly panting out of Nat.

'What the hell d'you think you're doing? You've totally blown it for me, haven't you? I'm guessing by the look on Mum's face that she knows everything about the arrangement we have. So much for a discreet service!' Betsy looks so angry that a woman walking her dog past them deviates into an exaggerated semi-circle, creating some distance, sensing perhaps that slaps might be thrown.

'Whatever you're doing, Betsy, whatever is going on, it's unravelling. She's been to your house, she's spoken to Jacob, and I'm pretty sure she thinks there's something going on between you and some bloke called Dylan.' Nat is calm. She has no desire to fight with Betsy, just to help her feel that she can share everything with her mother, that Helen is waiting for her to do exactly that.

But the mere mention of Dylan's name makes Betsy's cheeks flare red.

'You just need to talk to her because she can't understand how she's failed you and why you could possibly want a stranger to arrange your wedding when she loves you as much as she does.'

'Like you actually give a shit! This is all just bad for business for you, isn't it?' Wow, it obviously hasn't occurred to her that the very last thing Nat is obliged to do with her time is stand in the middle of the street and fight someone else's battles.

'Listen, my relationship with your mum goes way back to long before you decided to call me. No one's taking sides here, I'm just trying to help.' Nat raises an arm to Betsy's shoulder, trying to smother some of the anger, then feels the shock as Betsy's own arm flies through the air, batting it painfully away.

Before Nat has a chance to do anything other than wince, Betsy explodes into tears and runs off at a speed Nat knows she'll never match.

Chapter Fifteen

Betsy

For the first time in as long as she can remember, Betsy wakes to find Jacob is not lying, open-mouthed and spread-eagled, in the bed next to her – that way exhausted people sleep when they've lost all control over their own bodies. It's early and still dark outside. She has to get to the London office today so it's nothing short of extraordinary if he's beaten her out of bed. Maybe he never actually made it there in the first place and he's still attached to the laptop in the spare bedroom. He'll be grumpy as hell if he is. She'll need to slip out undetected.

As she rises, head sore and heart heavy from the deep-down guilt she's been carrying with her since the showdown with Mum and Nat, Betsy knows she can't go on like this. In the past two weeks, she's dialled her mum's number, disconnected it and dialled it again countless times without ever letting the ringtone kick in. By now, the idea of making that phone call is so much worse than the reality of what they might have to say to each other.

Betsy is distracted by the chemical – or is it citrusy? – smell, carrying up to the bedroom; it's novel enough to send her sniffing the air out on the landing and down the stairs. As she nears the bottom, she can see through into their old-fashioned pine kitchen. Jacob is there, showered, dressed and with a tea towel flung over his left shoulder while he puts the last of all the freshly cleaned crockery back into the correct cupboards. There is a tray laid out with a pot of tea, two matching mugs, some pastries he must have gone out to buy from the twenty-four-hour garage this morning and a single iris in one of the glass bud vases she'd forgotten she owns. Betsy can tell from the few puddles yet to dry that he has mopped the lino floor too and for the first time in weeks, the Venetian blinds have been yanked up and the window thrown open, breathing new life into their stale surroundings – and into him, apparently.

She barely knows what to say and stands there, slack-jawed, until he spots her.

'I was just about to bring you breakfast in bed!'

'Really? It's not my birthday, you know that, right?'

'Does it have to be? I'm sorry you think that.' His eyes move to the tray and Betsy immediately feels bad for being anything other than enormously grateful for the loving gesture. 'We're celebrating!'

Oh God, what has she forgotten? The anniversary of when they first met? No, that's an easy one, Christmas Eve. It's not his birthday. So, what?

'When I got up this morning, there was an email in my inbox from my agent. Another publisher has read the first third of the book. They love it, Betsy, and they're going to make an offer!' He doesn't even wait for a response before lifting her off her feet and spinning her around the kitchen as if she weighs nothing at all. For one brief moment, she is thrown back to their first Christmas Eve and her wild predictions of all the fun they might have together. When he places her back down, both their eyes are welling with tears of happiness, relief and, in Betsy's case, a little more guilt – for silently concluding weeks ago this moment was never going to happen.

'Oh my God! This is the most amazing news. Congratulations, darling! How shall we celebrate?' This is exactly what they need, what their relationship needs.

'Well, let's wait until it's all signed on the dotted line but I thought I might take myself off somewhere for a little R&R – I could do with a change of scenery.' It's months since she's heard him sound so decisive. And OK, it might only be a few days away together he's suggesting, but this constitutes forward planning, something that has been entirely absent from him.

'Great! Where do you fancy? Shall we stay in the UK or somewhere short haul in Europe?' Betsy is freeing herself from his arms and glancing around the kitchen for her phone, she's going to start Googling options right away. This is the perfect opportunity to switch it up a bit. Break her out of the routine and get her away from all the questions, deception and guilty thoughts that have been stuck to her like a second skin for weeks.

'Actually, I think it's probably better if I go alone, Betsy.' He's going at the work surface with a J-cloth now, determined to finish what he's started. 'I've still got fifty thousand words to refine and you'll just be bored. But it does mean you can crack on with all the wedding planning, now we know the money is coming. I know you'll *love* that.' The slight lilt in his voice makes her question if he's being sarcastic… and why are his eyes scanning hers so carefully? To check her reaction? Or is she just paranoid? Either way, it's not a suggestion, he's not even asking how she feels about coming, or not, he's made up his mind. This is going to be his trip and there's no room for her on it.

'Right.' Perhaps she should just be grateful he's referencing the wedding at all.

'And they're already talking about a book tour so I could be away a lot in the new year. And I'll need to get the synopsis for book two sorted.' He really has got it all worked out, and Betsy is not part of his grand plan.

'Anyway, I'm going to get back to the laptop, so enjoy breakfast.' And with that he strides past her, swiping his own mug of tea and pastry from the tray, out of the kitchen and back to his makeshift office.

The croissant sticks in the back of Betsy's throat a bit after that. Is this how it's supposed to work? She gets to put up with the strops, the constant need for ego stroking, hours spent reading words that make no sense to her – bore her, even – just so when it all finally becomes worthwhile, she can sit and watch from the sidelines like his loser girlfriend?

She glances up at the kitchen clock. Great, she's going to miss the 7.54 a.m. to London now and look like the last slacker to arrive at work while everyone else is hard at it.

*

Avoiding your boss is harder work than Betsy ever imagined. Their early-morning chats have dried up; she's timing her arrival with the rest of the team so there is no chance of any awkward stepping around each other. When you've had your boss's hands up your dress and come dangerously close to having a lot more of him up there too, you think the whole world can tell, just from one quick glance at you both. It feels like Anton has crawled inside her mind and can read what now feels like an embarrassingly juvenile script, one where she actually imagined a man like Dylan would risk public and professional ridicule to be with a woman like her, a woman who gets engaged, then tries – and fails – to take her boss to bed. It's one thing to have been rejected by Dylan, quite another to have the entire team know about it.

As she slumps down into her seat this morning, willing herself not to look up at his office, where she knows he'll already be, Betsy thinks about how much she's changed since she took this job, and about how she's started treating work like the place to play out her sexual fantasies – even if they were only ever in her head. It all seems so mortifying now. Those red shoes! When she changed into them that night, it must have seemed all so horribly obvious to Dylan. Then she remembers the excruciating performance she put on in front of Nick and her mum. Everyone at the table that night must have thought nothing of Jacob's lateness compared to her open contempt for him, the man who's supposed to be her soulmate for life.

Meetings with Dylan have become perfunctory, professional and devoid of gags. It's ages since she's caught him looking at her absent-mindedly from his office, like he'd forgotten she could see in just as easily as he could stare out. She's way behind with her workload too, thanks to hours and hours wasted plotting mini-encounters with Dylan that would see them brush up against each other in the tiny work kitchen, or orchestrating a ride in the lift with only him, fantasising about how he might hit the stop button and… it's like she's regressed to a giddy seventeen-year-old girl who's never been shagged.

Well, today is the day she is going to put it all right. With enough effort, she might convince herself there are some tentative signs at home that things *could* improve, even if Jacob is now morphing from truculent teenager into selfish bastard. Plus, she has a super-keen team at work, who have been coming at her with great ideas for weeks. This is it. A new beginning.

Betsy kicks the day off with individual back-to-back meetings with her team. She restates their objectives through to the end of November, checks they are all on course to hit their targets, deals with a couple of inevitable foul-ups on Anton's part and agrees to pick up the slack on one of Kirsty's accounts so she can skip off early to watch her three-year-old take the lead role in her first nursery performance. With the team fully recharged and raring to go, she tackles her own workload, checking in with Mark and Jonathan. The contracts are signed, a hefty retainer has been agreed and she sends a series of diary invites for their monthly catch-ups. Then she's writing job ads, trawling her database of candidates and shortlisting a selection of the ten best to interview over the phone this afternoon. This account needs to get off to a flying start. After so much initial legwork, there's no way she's going to see it falter now.

At four o'clock, Betsy looks up from her keyboard, realising she hasn't had lunch, and concludes it's too late to bother. But she has successfully avoided all contact with Dylan so far today and just as she's thinking she'll keep it that way until home time, his name pops up in her inbox:

Subject: we need to talk about New York.

Acutely aware that Dylan is still her boss and that if he asks for a meeting, she's hardly in a position to say no, she pings one back.

Of course, just shout when you're ready.

His response lands almost instantaneously.

Pop in now.

She knows this is going to be painful because he asks her to close the door. He might think he's being discreet but now every pair of eyes in the place is trained on that glass cube, watching and straining their ears, making amateur attempts to lip-read. Is she being told off? Is one of *them* about to be told off? What is it that warrants the closed-door intimacy? She knows they'll all be sending each other speculative emails. It's exactly what she'd be doing if she was the one still at her desk.

'The itinerary is all planned. The flights are booked and two days' worth of meetings are scheduled. I just need to check that you are still happy to go, Betsy?'

Someone took their efficiency pill this morning. She'd thought an impenetrably cold businesslike approach to each other would be for the best, but now she's on the receiving end of it from Dylan it's hurtful. How can he stand there, firing worky things at her and not be thinking about where his hands have been and how his hot breath on her neck made her melt into him outside the hotel room that night?

'I am, yes. But only if I go alone.' Well, two can most definitely play it cool. But as Betsy's saying the words, she can feel the imprint of his strong hands on her thighs and she hopes to God her face isn't giving away the surge of longing she's feeling to have them right back there.

'Oh. OK. Why is that?' He's standing now, facing her full-on, giving every indication that he wants to get to the bottom of this.

But does he really need to ask? 'I think it's probably for the best, don't you?' The stronger the physical pull towards Dylan, the colder Betsy's responses are becoming and she can see he's startled by this. He looks frustrated, slightly angry with her even, maybe with himself for messing up his chance with her. His arms briefly move towards her, like he just wants to grab hold of her, but then he thinks better of it, perhaps remembering that this conversation is actually happening in front of an audience.

There is a fleeting moment when she could say sod it, and make the move herself, but Betsy lets it pass. Surely there has to be a limit to how much messing about any one person can take and Betsy is pushed right up against hers. It's hard to be this blunt with him, it really is. Especially when he's now sitting on the edge of his desk, his hands either side of him, making his arm muscles tense under his shirt, leaving himself completely open for her approach. But he blew her out, left her standing there in the corridor with that beautiful new dress hitched up over her hips. He made her feel stupid. Does he really think they can just pretend it never happened? She can't.

'Is that really what you would prefer?' His question feels loaded, like what he's really asking is, *do you want me or not*?

And of course she does. But what does he expect her to say? Yeah, let's go to New York together and you can humiliate me all over again there. And while we're at it, let's not forget who started this whole thing with all the whispering in her ear that night.

She can see she's wounded him. He looks like he has so much more to say but she's yet to take a seat herself and is now edging backwards towards the door, not brave enough to risk any more rejections and fire up the office rumour mill to critical levels.

'If you could just send me the schedule and hotel details and I'll take it from there.'

'OK. Would you prefer it if I—'

Betsy is already on her way out the door and heading back to her desk, feeling like she's wrongly drawn a line under the one thing she might actually really want, trying hard not to think about how it won't be the two of them boarding the plane together now for a few days of who knows what.

She's got to refocus on her workload, no choice really. There's plenty to do and she's going to put in a late one tonight, clear everything, so that next week she can hit the ground running and enjoy that immense sense of satisfaction that comes from being on top of it all.

It's gratifying to notice that Dylan achieves very little with the rest of his afternoon. Pretending to be looking at the clock on the wall above his office, she watches him pacing back and forth, picking up a newspaper and putting it back again unread, fidgeting in his chair, then spending ages gazing off into the distance while she deflects nosy enquiries from the team about what's wrong with him.

By six o'clock everyone's legged it, except the two of them. Dylan is on the phone in his office, has been for about an hour, and Betsy is finally getting to the bottom of a very long To-do list. Maybe another hour and she'll be done.

Dylan hangs up and sticks his head out of the office.

'I'm ordering a pizza. D'you fancy some?' He looks nervous, like he's not sure what sort of reaction he might get from a simple offer of food.

She's starving and could murder a slice or two. 'I'm fine, thanks.' Such a pointless snub, but still.

By the time it arrives, forty minutes later, the smell wafting tantalisingly across the room to her, she's ravenous and starts to pack up her things. Maybe she'll pick up something nice for her and Jacob on the way home.

'I got you a pepperoni and olive.' Dylan is standing in the doorway to his office, holding the square cardboard box aloft, looking like he might not be able to cope with any more rebuttals today.

She just wants to go home but is it churlish to say no and leave? Will it just create more awkwardness between them if she does? Probably. She can't avoid him forever, she has to be able to get on with her boss or she'll be adding job hunting to the list of things to stress about. At least there are no prying eyes at this time – and her belly is screaming for food.

'OK, thank you.'

Dylan disappears to grab the last remaining beer from the office supply and splits the contents of the bottle between two plastic cups, handing her one.

She's spread the pizzas out on the small meeting table in his office and grabbed some paper napkins from her desk. She starts to dig in, as he takes a seat opposite her, determined she won't be the first to diffuse the air floating sourly around them. She gets most of the way through one whole slice, wishing she could dynamite herself out of there, before finally he speaks.

'Did you ever ask yourself why I invited myself along to your family drinks that night?'

OK, here we go. 'Not really. I just assumed there was some air to clear. Or you wanted to flatter yourself, by watching me make a fool of myself again.' Her tone is so much more poisonous than she intends, all the weeks of embarrassment pouring out in one accusing sentence.

'Wrong. I wanted to meet him.'

'Nick?'

'Jacob.'

'You wanted to meet Jacob? Why?'

'I wanted to see if he was worth it, Betsy. To see if he deserved the absolute home run he didn't even know he'd scored. If the answer was yes, that would have been fine, I might have been able to step away.' Dylan isn't touching his pizza, too focused on her, his eyes never leaving her face.

'And what did you conclude?' No! This was supposed to be a quick bite to eat, humour him, then home, why is she letting herself get drawn in again?

'Christ, you were there! Your mum's boyfriend had to lend him his jacket. And I noticed the way you looked at him. It wasn't love I saw in your eyes that night.'

What he's saying is flattering and she knows he intends it to be, but in putting Jacob down like this, Dylan's also saying what lousy judgement she has. And who the hell is he to decide that?

'Why don't *you* have a girlfriend?' *Let's turn that judgement on him for a second.*

He chuckles slightly at her directness and pushes the pizza box away from him, knowing he has to comply with an answer, having delivered his critique.

'I never wanted one. Until now. I was always too busy setting up the business. It consumed me for years and I didn't want a love affair diverting me away from that.' He slows his speech now, choosing his words very carefully. 'Maybe it just took the right person to come along. Someone who would make me want to meet her mother, to be liked by all her friends, to put someone else first. But…'

'But what?' Betsy stiffens in her seat and he senses it, reaching a hand out across the table to her.

'But in a colossal bit of mismanagement, I seem to have chosen someone who's engaged to someone else.' Betsy can't help it, she lets her fingers find his, while acknowledging to herself how pathetic her resolve is.

Something her mum said to her years ago is forcing itself back into Betsy's head. Infidelity is the only commandment that is mentioned twice in the Bible: once for doing it and once for thinking about it. In which case she's certainly at least halfway to being a double sinner. And how did she get to this place? The girl who worked hard, was honest and decent and knew where the line was drawn, and never, until now, stepped over it. If Dylan could so easily see her disgust at Jacob that night at the family dinner, then couldn't everyone else, Jacob included? If their relationship has soured so much, why hasn't she had the guts to just call it off? She knows why. She's a good girl, she doesn't do this sort of thing. It's wrong. She doesn't run around hotels in the middle of the night, letting a man who isn't her fiancé see, touch and taste parts of her that should be for Jacob alone. But if someone else instigated it, made all the play, forced the difficult conversations on her, then that would be different, wouldn't it? She could become that woman then, couldn't she? One who allowed her life to be filled with passion and didn't settle for the empty husk of a relationship that was once good but is now bland and unfulfilling – right at the point when it should be making her heart soar. Dylan's directness is giving her all the confidence she now needs.

'She might be engaged, but she's not married yet, is she?' She doesn't hide from the words, she looks him straight in the eye as she says them, owning them completely.

'Do you know what you're saying, Betsy?' Dylan's up, on his feet and pacing back towards his desk before spinning back around to hear her response.

'I'm saying I don't want to go into a marriage thinking I can consider it successful if we just don't get divorced. I want to be *seen* again.' She hopes that last bit doesn't sound too needy, but it's true and she doesn't want to hold it back from him.

'I see you. I *love* seeing you, I always have. Surely you know that? Didn't you ever think it was odd, that day you announced your engagement in the office and I bollocked you for going on and on about it with the team?' A thin smile has returned to his beautiful face at the memory of that day.

'No, I thought it was probably fair enough, when we should all have been working.'

'It was because I was jealous, more jealous than I've ever been about anything. But I backed off because I assumed he must be incredible, this man who had won you over. Then when I met him, it made no sense to me at all.'

Having this conversation with nothing more than a couple of mouthfuls of beer to bolster her courage is so liberating. There's no pretence between them tonight and no chance of either of them misconstruing anything. Dylan walks slowly back to the table, this time taking the seat right next to her. He takes hold of both of her hands, pulling her onto his lap, and she doesn't even care that there is tomato sauce smothering her lips and probably a clump of basil stuck between her teeth.

What happens between them tonight, on the floor of his office with the sound of the cleaner hoovering next door, is so tender and slow and so much more honest than how it might have been a few weeks ago. There's nothing to prove. Betsy always knew this was going to happen, probably from the very first moment she laid eyes on him. And while she should be full of regret, she's not. Not yet. She needed to try Dylan on. To completely lose herself in him.

Now she'll have to tell Jacob. Perhaps if there had been no Dylan, she might have muddled through. But not any more. Dylan or no Dylan in her long-term future, there's no way she can marry Jacob.

Chapter Sixteen

Helen

As the end of November draws near, Helen has so much to think about. Betsy, of course, is top of her list. The two have exchanged a few brief texts after she stormed out of the boutique that day, but this is the longest Helen has ever gone without speaking to her beloved daughter. She misses her so much – their chats, the feel of Betsy's soft hair in her hand, her smile – although it feels like much longer since she's enjoyed seeing that. And her company. Just having her potter around the shop between clients, admiring some of the new pieces Helen's brought in.

Months ago, Betsy had arrived one lunchtime, unannounced, to persuade Helen out for a break. While she finished up with her bride, she watched her daughter pick up a new Swarovski crystal and mother-of-pearl crown and place it delicately on her head, its intricately arranged jewels catching every shard of light shining through the perfectly clean glass windows. She saw the smile break across Betsy's face and the faraway look in her eye. Betsy was standing just a few feet away, but Helen could see she was gone, off to another time and place where she was happy – and that crown was central to everything. Helen had assumed she was daydreaming about her wedding day, thinking about her first step down the aisle, her vows, that first self-conscious kiss in front of all their guests confirming her new status as Jacob's wife, and then celebrating long into the night. Now she's not so sure. Something, or someone, was making her smile, but was it Jacob? It all seems so unlikely now. Helen and Nick both saw that same blissful look creep across Betsy's face that night at the bar with Dylan – when she should have been more concerned with what had happened to Jacob. As Helen pictures them, their legs entwined under the bar stools, she can feel the corners of her mouth dip. She's not ready to consider what any of this might mean for Betsy.

As Helen circles the boutique, making sure everything is as it should be ahead of her final appointment of the day, she is also thinking about Nat – and how she has somehow replaced Helen as Betsy's confidante. At least she had before Helen blew Nat's cover. She's thinking about the job Nat does, how sad it is that there's even a need for it, then chastising herself for being so old-fashioned in her thinking. She knows there is a need, she's read about it several times; she just never really believed it before. Maybe Nat's providing a vital service? Maybe there are plenty of women who need her? Judging by the number of visits she's paid to Helen this year, the number of dress orders rushed through for her, that must be true. She just never imagined her Betsy would be one of them. Or that Nat is the sort of woman to provide that service. It's probably a stop gap, thinks Helen, and Nat's working her way towards something more, dare she say, credible. Helen has failed her daughter. It's the only reason she can think of why Betsy would choose Nat over her own loving mother's advice and guidance.

The thought depresses her as she straightens a run of Vera Wang gowns, ensuring none of the delicate glass beadwork is catching a neighbouring dress. And can Helen really say she is blameless in all of this? Has her daughter's life been quietly unravelling behind the scenes, while she was... doing what? Going out to lunch with Nick and losing hours to her own private daydreams? Indulging herself with thoughts of sharing a life with him. Reliving that wonderful night at Nick's apartment, everything he so gently said and did to her, and the way she felt more alive and wanted in those hours than she has in the past five years. How a completely new Helen is emerging, a woman no longer satisfied with just making it through the day, dodging intrusive memories of Phillip. One who wants to be held and loved and desired, and who doesn't want to feel bad about it. Goodness, how many hours has she lost rereading Nick's exquisite love notes, thoughtful handwritten ones that arrive unexpectedly to completely throw her off-focus for the rest of the day? Just as the thought of them is now.

Helen pauses near a display of pretty rose gold necklaces and starts to untangle them. But her fingers hesitate as she thinks about the last note that arrived a few days ago, simply saying, *There is no room in my head for anyone but you, Nx.* It arrived with a promised bundle of CVs for prospective managers for the London boutique that must have taken him days to source and edit. But Helen knows before she even looks at them that none of them will be right. It was lovely of Nick to offer to find them, and she didn't want to seem ungrateful, so she let him. But this is her business. Only someone Helen finds herself is going to be good enough, although she needs to be quick – the journeys back and forth between London and Gloucestershire, juggling capable but imperfect staff in the Cotswolds can't go on for much longer. It's just all this trouble with Betsy is eating into her thinking time, making it impossible to formulate a proper plan.

Poor Helen's heart should be so full of happiness, but her head is swamped with guilt. Coming at her thick and fast in the dead of the night, it's sometimes so strong it actually yanks her free from sleep. Has she taken her eye off the ball at the precise moment Betsy needs her the most? Perhaps this is the price Helen has to pay for all the joy being a mum has brought her over the years. Maybe it's selfish to expect to experience those intense highs without the all-consuming lows. Maybe she just needs to accept that her daughter must always come first, even now, all these years on.

The guilt is making her stomach turn and without further hesitation, Helen makes a grab for the boutique phone. She so badly wanted Betsy to be the one to call her. For Betsy to *want* to call her. But she fears that moment is never coming, and she doesn't want the gulf between them to stretch any wider.

But she's too late. The doorbell is ringing, and her next bride-to-be is here. Helen needs to refocus, and quickly. She can call Betsy later.

'Jenny! Come on in. I'm so glad I could fit you in today. You sounded like you badly wanted this appointment.' She allows herself a small smile as she recalls the slightly panicked email Jenny sent, begging Helen to fit her in tonight. The truth is, there was no free slot, she should be closing now, but something in the tone of Jenny's words made her decide to see her.

'Hi Helen. I did, yes.' Jenny's panting hard, as though she ran all the way here and is just about ready to cough up an internal organ. 'As well as wanting to… get myself back… into that incredible dress…' She's struggling to make it through the sentence, her lungs grabbing for air. 'I'm also avoiding my lunatic flatmate. But trust me, Helen… that's one story you don't want to hear.'

Jenny looks so harassed, thinks Helen, as she moves towards the back of the boutique to the small kitchen where she'll make them both a cuppa, giving Jenny a vital few minutes to catch her breath.

'Well, I'm very happy to help. How d'you take your tea?' she calls over her shoulder.

'Milk, no sugar, please… and some water would be great. Thank you.'

When Helen returns with two beautiful vintage floral teacups and saucers, two sugar cubes balanced on the edge of hers, the two women settle down on a blush velvet chair each, surrounded by everything a woman could need to create the outfit of a lifetime.

'OK, let's have a look at your paperwork. We never really got much chance to chat last time, did we?' Helen is wading through her trusty concertina file, trying to locate Jenny's brief notes.

'I know, I'm sorry, I think I just got a bit emotional.'

Jenny is not looking entirely comfortable now, thinks Helen, as she watches her fiddling with her phone and shifting nervously in her seat. 'Everyone does. At some point, it happens. It can be on the first appointment, or the very last, but I promise you, Jenny, every bride before you has wept on me and you're not the first to run out on me either, I'm afraid. I am entirely used to it – I shed a few tears myself sometimes.' There is something different about this girl, thinks Helen, that doesn't seem quite right. She can hear the cup and saucer rattling as Jenny lifts them, her hand shaking. Helen needs to unpick her a little and see if she can help at all.

'So, you said your wedding date was…' Helen's fingers can't locate the relevant piece of paper quickly enough to accurately finish her own sentence and she looks to Jenny to fill in the blank.

'Um… it's, oh, what did I say, er, July the 20th. Yes, that's it. July 20th.'

'Great. Plenty of time for you to choose pretty much anything you like. Oh, hang on…' Helen raises Jenny's form aloft. 'I've got June 20th here. Sorry, let me correct that. I must have jotted it down wrong. Definitely *July 20th*?' She wouldn't be the first stressed bride-to-be to give Helen the wrong wedding date. Others have even managed to get their own venue details completely wrong, until Helen double-checked them.

'OK, perfect. I know you loved the Hayley Paige embroidered ballgown but is there anything else you would like to try on? If that's the sort of silhouette you like, then I would also suggest you look at some of the gowns here by Rosa Clará, Suzanne Neville, perhaps Naomi Neoh and Alice Temperley?'

'Let's do it, yes, please! But, er, I don't need to pay anything today, do I?'

'Not until you decide on the dress, then I just need a small deposit. A few hundred pounds usually.' She can see Jenny's eyes widen, but like most brides, it's the most expensive dress she'll ever buy, so the fear normally comes from knowing it needs to be just right. 'And my offer of a discount still stands.'

The first dress Helen helps Jenny into is one of the very prettiest in the new Rosa Clará collection. A lace bodice with long tattoo lace sleeves, it dips low at the neckline with beautiful scalloped edging before a skirt that billows out into layer upon layer of the lightest tulle. It's one of those shapes that seems to look beautiful on most women and Helen is right, it looks so elegant on Jenny, too. As Helen is straightening the neckline, ensuring the waistband sits just where it should, she uses the time to fill in a few more details and gain a clearer picture of the kind of day Jenny is planning.

'Are you having a church wedding? The sleeves on this gown might feel very appropriate if you are.'

'Um… yes, it is. Most people do, don't they?'

'No, actually. I'd say most of the women I see are going for something different now. There is so much choice – and I think the idea of a formal walk to the altar puts a lot of them off a religious ceremony.'

Helen is on her hands and knees now, fluffing the skirt from below, so that all the layers sit neatly on top of each other. 'Will it be your father walking you down the aisle?'

Helen has to stand and ask the question again after getting no response from Jenny, who's absorbed by her reflection in the fitting-room mirror.

'He is, yes.'

She doesn't elaborate any further and Helen fears she may be treading on difficult ground here. 'I don't want to make you talk about anything you'd rather not, Jenny, so please don't feel you have to answer any of my questions. It just helps me build a picture of your day, that's all.' Helen moves round to the front of her so Jenny can see from her face she's sincere.

'Actually, I was just thinking how much Mum would have loved this dress.'

Helen can see she's trying to be brave, but Jenny's face is giving her away. The smile doesn't last quite long enough before she swallows hard, trying to force the emotion back down inside her.

'I'm sorry, it must be tough, planning your wedding without her.' Helen can't help but make the mental comparison; this poor girl being forced to plan alone, when Betsy is choosing it that way.

'Everything is hard without her.'

Helen watches as one single tear teeters on the very edge of Jenny's left eye, balancing there sadly. She makes no attempt to wipe it away. Does she cry so often, she doesn't even realise she's doing it? 'Here.' Helen hands her a tissue from the pretty white porcelain box she always keeps to hand.

'Thank you.' Jenny relaxes, like there is little point trying to remain composed any more. 'I was only sixteen when I lost her. A long time ago, but it doesn't get any easier. I think about her every day. Her voice is there, inside my head, wherever I go, whatever I'm doing. It's hard to separate it from my own some days. I feel like she could be with us right now.'

'I don't doubt for one second that she is. A mother's love is so strong, I don't think even death could dilute it. She would want to be here and so I bet she is.' Helen is squeezing Jenny's hand now, letting her know that she is happy to talk about this, that they can forget the dresses and just get to know each other, if that's what Jenny would prefer. 'What's her name?'

'Angela. She wrote me letters.' Jenny has moved towards the chaise longue and is perched there now, looking hopeful that Helen will join her.

'Really?' Helen understands the invitation immediately and takes a seat beside her.

'Yes, lots of them, before she died, so I could open them at important times in my life. But I haven't stuck to the rules, Helen, I've opened some of them earlier than I should have. Does that make me an awful person? Would she be disappointed in me?'

The need for reassurance is etched all over Jenny's face, in the downcast sadness of her big blue eyes and the defeated dip at the corners of her mouth. 'My goodness, no! I'd say it makes you human. I expect it was simply not in your mother's make-up to be disappointed with you. How could she be? Look at you. You're a beautiful young woman, you have a job, a man who wants to marry you, you're succeeding. She did a wonderful job in the time she had with you.' Helen means the words to be comforting but they are having precisely the opposite effect and now the tears are pouring out of Jenny, like she saved them all up for this appointment today. Helen gathers her up in her arms and just holds her there for a few minutes, not saying a word, but feeling the sharp sobs shake out of her. She's wondering how this girl made it all the way through the day. All the people she must have encountered, all the missed or ignored opportunities to help her. Then feeling the swell of pride that she can gladly offer Jenny that kindness.

Helen notices, but doesn't mind at all, that some of the tears have dropped onto the dress, dotting the skirt with tiny wet patches. She can get it dry-cleaned.

'It's just a thought, but is there something of your mother's we could work into the dress, Jenny? A piece of fabric from a treasured item of her clothing, her own wedding dress even, or a special piece of jewellery? We could use some of the stones or look at ways to actually attach it?'

The mention of her mother's jewellery sends Jenny's right hand shooting towards her engagement finger, where, Helen can see, there is no ring today. She couldn't help but notice the emerald-cut aquamarine last time Jenny was in, but now it's absent. She surely couldn't have lost it? No, she would be on her feet and heading for the door by now if that was the case.

'OK, don't panic. Did you take it off this morning when you were washing? Or at work?' She must have hit the nail on the head because she feels Jenny's body give way and relax back into her arms.

'Is it harder for you at Christmas time?' ventures Helen. 'That's when I used to really struggle, after losing my husband. It feels like a selfish thing to say now but when everyone else was moaning on about the shopping they still had to do or the number of people they had to feed, all I could think was how I would have traded places with them in an instant to have Phillip's shopping list back in my purse. You know, one year, after he was gone, I bought all his presents as normal. Wrapped the lot of them and put them under the tree. I even bought his favourite cream sherry. It made me feel better, like he was watching me, and I needed to show him he hadn't been forgotten. Then I had to unwrap them all again and take them to the charity shop, months later.' She can smile a little now, knowing she is a long way from those dark days.

'I keep seeing things in shop windows that I think she'll like, then remembering I can't buy them. Or I'll hear her favourite Christmas song and see her dancing around the kitchen – *like you know Jon Hamm's watching*, she used to say – glass of advocaat in hand, while the house filled with the smell of cloves, citrus, onions and eventually – because she never got the timing right – roast turkey.'

Helen's pleased to see Jenny's smiling a little now, that for a moment the lovely memory of her mum is stronger than the pain of losing her. She can also feel every word of this pricking at her own memories, the ones she has time-locked away and visits only very occasionally now.

'I was crying over the dates in M&S the other day because she only ever ate them at Christmas time. The day after, it was an old kids' film that happened to be on, because I remember the day we curled up on the sofa together and watched it, working our way through a mountain of salted popcorn. I ate so much, it made my lips go numb. The way she planted a kiss on my cheek or hand every ten minutes without even realising she was doing it.' Helen could kiss Jenny right now, and actually considers it for a moment, but gives her the space to keep talking, knowing how good it is for her to do just that.

'It never felt much like Christmas after we lost her. Dad never made an effort with the decorations – I understand why – and the day was always tinged with a sadness no one could shift or ignore. In the end we just started treating it like a normal day. Dad would spend it catching up on a bit of DIY and my sister and I would try to land an invite to a friend's house.' Helen can see how tightly clasped Jenny's hands are in her lap, perhaps a distraction to prevent the tears from welling up again.

'And what about now that you're older, how is it now?'

'I'm on my own this year, so it will be harder.' Helen can hear the tremble in her voice. 'Dad and Sylvie, his new wife, are going skiing and it's my sister's turn to spend it with her husband Will's family, so that just leaves me.'

'But what about your fiancé? Won't you be spending it with him?' Helen is confused, surely he won't leave her on her own?

She watches Jenny jolt like she's just remembered something important, then hang her head, saying nothing, before finally adding, 'He's busy.'

'You couldn't join him and be together, even if it's a work thing, just for some of the day?' There must be some way for this poor girl not to be left alone at Christmas time? It's a reminder that Helen's own Christmas is shaping up to be a little fraught if Betsy and Jacob don't sort themselves out. And where might Nick fit into all of this? She's yet to work that out.

'I'm afraid not.' Jenny quietly shakes her head.

There is a pause while Helen seriously weighs up the appropriateness of inviting a near-total stranger to spend it with her. She knows she can't, not when she's spent less than two hours in her company. She decides to try and lighten the mood a little.

'And that must get pretty confusing, mustn't it?'

'What's that?' Jenny lifts her head to look at Helen, whose eyes are back scanning her paperwork.

'You and your sister, both with partners called Will? I mean, what are the chances of that?' Helen watches Jenny search for and fail to find an answer. She can also see her cheeks flush and a startled look return to her eyes – the one she recognises from all the times she caught a teenage Betsy attempting to fib her way out of trouble.

There's definitely more to Jenny, Helen knows that for sure now, and wonders if a little more time in her company might help her understand this girl better.

'What are you doing tomorrow, Jenny? Fancy some help with a little wedding planning?' She's made the offer before she's even really had time to consider how above and beyond the call of duty it is. But then, Helen could do with some fun too. It will be good for both of them, if Jenny doesn't think it too weird a suggestion.

'Really? I would absolutely love that!' She looks like she can't believe her luck.

'OK, perfect. I know just where I'll take you.'

Chapter Seventeen

Jenny

It's Marianne's backside I see first, as I'm trying to slip back into the flat, unnoticed. I make it inside, close the front door painfully slowly on the icy November evening, not making a single sound. Then I tiptoe down the hallway, stepping over what looks like a pair of her hold ups and an up-ended empty wine bottle. Edging closer to the safety of my room, and glancing briefly in through her open bedroom door, there it is – thrust skywards, wobbling away, free from any underwear. She is bending right over, completely naked from the waist down, and I panic, thinking she can't have finished with the workmen yet. I stumble backwards slightly, very nearly revealing my presence. Bugger it! After The White Gallery, I killed as much time as I could on the way home, walking at a snail's pace to the tube, then pottering around M&S, examining things I had no intention of buying, but, argh, maybe it wasn't long enough?

I watch, horrified, as she moves about her room, pulling various items of clothing off the bedroom floor, sniffing and discarding them, until she finds something she deems clean enough – that is, something that doesn't smell repulsive. It's a pair of my fake leather Zara leggings that have been missing for months. Of course it is. She pulls them straight on, without bothering with knickers. She can keep them, I'll buy another pair. I can't risk a sixty-degree wash not killing whatever might be making its home in the crotch fibres.

Much as I want to, now is not the time to make a scene – and she won't care if I do, anyway. She still hasn't spotted me and by the sounds of it, the blokes have gone. Oh, thank you, God! I'm past her opened bedroom door, easing my weight across the floorboards, avoiding the ones I know always creak, down the hallway, until my hand is extending out towards my own bedroom door handle. If I can just make it into my room, then I'll slip into bed, turn off the light and avoid hearing all the gory details, at least until tomorrow morning when I might have the stomach for it.

But no.

'Ahhh, there you are!' Marianne appears in her bedroom doorway, glaring at me. She's pulled on a black string vest, not mine, both of her nipples poking aggressively through the holes. I'm tempted to ask what exactly is the point of wearing it, but, ugh, whatever! She looks a mess, more so than usual. Her lipstick is feathering out way beyond the natural line of her lips and she looks dirty, like she needs an hour-long soak in the bath. Maybe it's just because I know what she's been doing. What she thought I'd be joining her for.

'Oh, hi, Marianne, sorry I'm so late. Killer of a shift. I did mean to call, but it was just so busy.' I drop my bag, and, a little over-dramatically, the few groceries I've picked up on the way home, to the floor, as if to demonstrate my exhaustion. Maybe she'll take pity on me. I'm really not in the mood for a confrontation tonight. I'm also struggling to find somewhere for my eyes to fall that isn't her nipples being strangled by the cheap thread of the vest.

'Well, that was *a lot* for me to deal with on my own. I gave it my best shot, obviously, but God!' She looks genuinely clapped-out and I have to stop myself imagining what sordid acts might have gone on in the hours before I sneaked in.

'Sorry. Listen, I've got a banging headache and it's been one hell of a day so I'm going to turn in, if you don't mind. Let's chat tomorrow, yeah?' I muster a half-hearted smile that isn't returned.

'Sure. But, Jenny?' She steps closer to me, into the hall now.

'Yep.' I'm gathering my things up, ready to close the bedroom door on her, which is the only way she'll understand that this conversation is over.

'Why did you lie? Nothing happened between you and those guys, did it? They didn't have a clue what I was talking about when I mentioned what you said – you know, the threesome. You made me look like a right nutter.' Her hands move to her hips and I can see from her rarely serious face that she is annoyed.

I should have known she'd work it out – it wasn't going to take a genius, was it? There's no point in trying to talk my way around this one.

'I don't know, Marianne. Why does anyone lie? Because it's easier? Because just for once I wanted to exceed expectations? I didn't realise you were going to call them, did I?' I'm trying to muster the sort of expression that looks apologetic but also tells her to leave it alone. The way my voice is wavering must warn her not to dig any further because she backs off.

'Are you OK? You know, there's plenty of wine in the fridge, if you fancy a chat?' She looks sheepish, which is rare, not her usual arrogant self at all. And she's bought wine, instead of just helping herself to mine. Progress. 'Wouldn't mind one myself, actually… after that.'

It's the first sign of vulnerability I think I've ever seen her show. She's placed a needy hand on my shoulder and is doing that thing where people make their mouth form a smile, but everything else about their face begs, *look after me, please*. I should be doing the decent thing and responding. After all, I caused whatever she has had to deal with alone tonight. But I can't, my head is full of too much else. Her timing is off.

'Not tonight, Marianne. I just need to crash out. Sorry.' And I close the bedroom door on her.

*

There is a letter of Mum's that I've wanted to open for a long time, but the six words scrawled on the front of the envelope always told me not to rush this one. I'm guessing from the handwriting that it was penned in her final days. Just looking at the way the letters dip downwards across the paper, jagged and uneven, make me think there was pain involved in writing them – physical *and* emotional perhaps?

'*When you're old enough to understand.*'

Helen gave me such a lovely flash of motherly love today, but now I need more. I want to read this letter and feel grown-up and capable. Like I can handle whatever's in there. I need to feel like Mum could have told me herself and I would have understood – just like I understood and shared Helen's pain today. I decide I can't face this one without the aid of something full-bodied, red and at least fourteen per cent alcohol, so I duck quietly into the kitchen and pour myself an obscenely large glass of Shiraz, ignoring the pair of men's boxer shorts that I can see languishing on the floor under our tiny dining table. How long will it be before I crack and have to drop them in the bin with a pair of kitchen tongs? I return to my room, pull on my warm fleecy pyjamas and yank the duvet up under my chin. Then I force my thumb in under the envelope that has remained sealed for all those years.

This is a difficult one to write, Jenny, and I question, now, whether I should be writing it at all. But if I was alive, being a real mum to you, I think we would have had this conversation. So, I am committing it to paper in the hope that it will help you, give you a more rounded view of the world. More than anything, I hope it won't make you think any less of me.

Before I got ill and was confined to this bed for days on end, I decided I was going to leave your father. I know this will come as a big shock to you but let me explain. It took me a long time to get there but I know it was the right decision. I felt like I was dying in our marriage and I should have done something about it before that became horribly, prosaically true. He was such a kind man, the kindest of them all, and I think he guessed how I was feeling because he tried so hard to please me, every day. I never stopped loving him for that.

But I had lost sight of myself. All those years in the chorus line, the supporting act, knowing how he would end his sentences before he did, the routine, the perfectly repetitive pattern of our lives, all that sameness. It comforted me once, I actually longed for it before I had it. Then I let it swamp me and eventually I started to crave the spotlight again. Something, anything, to surprise me. Does this make me sound selfish? I hope not. I just couldn't be truly happy being someone else's person the whole time. It starts small, Jenny. I instinctively always took the passenger seat. I stopped asking questions. I deferred. Then I woke up one day and wondered where I went. I can't honestly name one thing in my life that is just for me.

It's not his fault, please don't ever think that. It was my mistake. And it was such an easy one to make, creeping up on me over the years before the error was so big, stretched right across the page of our daily lives, there was no way of rubbing it out.

Fly in your own sky, that's what I always used to say to you, do you remember? Well, I didn't, but you must, Jenny. Live your life like you are ten times yourself. I wish I had before it was too damn late to do a thing about it. This might be the most selfish letter I've ever written to anyone and I'm sad it had to be to you. It makes me feel better to commit it to paper, but I know it might make you feel worse. It's important, though, and you need to know.

Put yourself first, just sometimes. Even when everyone else needs you more. You deserve it, my beautiful, beautiful girl.

Love Mum x

It's the hardest of her letters I've had to read. I can't bear to think of her being so unhappy for all that time. And I'm shocked, deeply shocked, that in my childish naivety I looked at them both every day and didn't see what was really there, plastered all over her face, in every stifled sigh, in every avoided touch. But I'm angry too. What a thing to dump on me, when I can do nothing about it. I can't ask her a single question that might help me understand how the vision of my perfect family life just got rewritten in the time it took to read that letter.

When I wake the next morning, still clutching the letter to my chest, my cheeks are wet. Was I crying in my sleep? Part of me wishes I'd never read it. All that sad resignation is going to weigh me down for weeks, I know it. The other part of me feels so sorry for Dad. To be married to someone that long, knowing they weren't really in it with you, not any more. How could he cope? Maybe it's what made moving on to Sylvie so much easier than any of us could understand at the time. His marriage was over, long before Mum died – and he knew it, not that it stopped him caring for her, right until the end. What a love-filled man he is, when all I have done is despise him for transferring all that love to Sylvie so quickly.

I pull my phone off the bedside table and text a quick message to him.

Dad, I'd love to come and visit and see the new place, if that's OK with you and Sylvie? Love Jen x

His response pings straight back:

Fantastic, we would love to see you, just name the date. And have you ever been skiing, Jen? I could do with some tips! Love Dad x

Then I have no choice but to haul myself out of bed. It's ten o'clock and I'm meeting Helen at a café on Park Lane in two hours.

Elan Café is so pretty, it's hard to believe its purpose is merely serving coffee and cake. Helen has already grabbed us the perfect spot and as I step through the front door, passing under the branches of a silk blossom tree that is stretching its petal-heavy arms above the tables, she waves fondly at me.

'Oh my goodness, Helen, this place!' I find myself kissing her on both cheeks, which should maybe feel weird, given how long we've known each other, but doesn't at all.

'I knew you would love it – a client told me about it a while ago and I've been dying to come. I'm so glad you could join me.' She looks just as excited as I feel, and I notice she has made the effort to dress up in a pretty caramel-coloured cashmere cardigan with a mix of different vintage floral buttons dotted down the front. She's the vision of a soft, warm, gentle mum and I momentarily force the memory of last night's letter out of my head. Then I'm envying the wardrobe of a woman who is so much older than me.

'Thank you for inviting me!' My eyes are everywhere. There is a pale blue bike, the sort a beautiful French mademoiselle might cycle through ripe summer vineyards, positioned near the door, its wicker basket filled with pretty soft pink and white blooms. The chairs have expensive-looking gold frames and are upholstered in nearly-nude fabric and there are light grey mini Christmas trees dotted around, with fairy lights in them gently twinkling away. Behind our table is an entire wall of silk flowers in various shades of pink, blush and rose, and more flowers suspended from the ceiling.

'I could get married right here,' I tell Helen, actually believing for a second that could be a possibility, overlooking that as well as having no mum, I am also without the crucial fiancé.

'Just wait until you see the cakes. Go on, go and have a look.' Helen's nodding in the direction of the window, where they are all displayed in neat rows or on individual marble cake stands.

It's so funny the effect this place is having on Helen too, she's clapping her hands together like someone just told her she's won the EuroMillions. I take off my duffle coat and hang it over the back of the chair, aware that it is totally ruining the indulgent aesthetic we're all enjoying, and step towards the cake display. Everything is dusted with the finest shower of icing sugar. There are perfectly formed mousse domes and fruit piled so high on top of tarts that they look like they could topple over at any moment.

We order and when the food arrives, I'm glad to see Helen has not held back but has gone for a layered chocolate cake that I seriously doubt she is capable of finishing, and a ruby latte that's an intense deep crimson colour. My red velvet cake comes covered in pretty pansies that, apparently, I can also eat, and a rich creamy coffee blended with sweetened condensed cream. Can you *even* imagine!

'Have you seen the sign?' Helen tilts her head backwards.

'*Adventure awaits, but first coffee*,' I read aloud.

'That is our mission today, Jenny. After this, I'm taking you to Selfridges to look at Phillippa Craddock's flowers, and then we'll hop in a cab to Islington, for a final treat.'

'Wow, thank you so much! I know you must be so busy.'

'I was always planning to come here with Betsy, that's my daughter, she's engaged too, but…' She doesn't finish her sentence and I wonder if it's OK to ask why.

'Is she not around much?' I venture.

'Well, it's not so much that, she's just showing a little less enthusiasm for wedding planning than you are – I'm supposed to be walking her down the aisle on Christmas Eve, but I'm seriously starting to wonder if it will happen.'

Poor Helen, she looks a bit crushed by that thought. I'm not sure if the disappointment comes more from the possible lack of a wedding or the feeling of disloyalty that she's been so mildly critical of her own daughter.

'Is that what you were planning? Wow, how wonderful!' I pause for a minute then ask her, 'Have you ever thought of re-marrying?' She's so easy to talk to, like I don't need to pretend with her at all – which is a bit of shame, all things considered.

'Not yet.' She smiles a little as she says that and tucks her expertly styled hair self-consciously behind her left ear, which I take as an indication that there must be someone special on the horizon at least.

'But… you could?' I glance down at my plate, realising I've polished off nearly all the cake, just a glorious big dollop of butter frosting to go.

'Well, let's just say it's an option but I'm really not sure it's the right thing to do. Betsy needs me at the moment and I should be there for her.'

She seems pretty definite about that and it makes me sad to think that she's sacrificing another chance to snatch some happiness. 'What's his name?' I think my nosiness is being fuelled by the sugar rush.

'Nick. He's wonderful. Cut from a very different cloth to my first husband, but kind, *so* kind, and far more patient than I probably have a right to expect.'

Helen is so precise in the way she's eating her cake. I somehow managed to spread mine across the entire plate, but she is using her little fork to carve hers up, only ever raising to her lips what she can delicately eat in one small mouthful.

'I think you're completely deserving of him, Helen.'

She smirks like she thinks I'm just paying her a hollow compliment, which I'm not.

'I mean it. You're kind too, you sound well-matched to me.' I wish I could appoint myself Helen's borrowed daughter and share happy times like this with her every week. Maybe make her my new mum. Do we both need each other a little? Is she feeling that too? I know she couldn't replace my mum, I'm not *completely* mad, but I so badly want to have moments like this in my life. Feeling so comfortable in another woman's company – with none of the competitiveness and comparison that seems to fizz between women my own age.

'Enough about me. Come on, tell me about Will. Better yet, show me a picture, you must have plenty on your phone.' She motions towards my iPhone on the table between us and which I now instinctively make a grab for.

I feel my jaw tighten and I sit back in my chair, forcing a less intimate space between us. I don't mean to, it's just instinctive. I see Helen's head twitch slightly and her eyebrows shift a fraction as I do, the smallest registering of her surprise at my reaction, I fear.

'Er, let me see if I can find one.' It's painful, I actually sit there flicking through my images, knowing damn well I'm not going to find one. She wants to see the two of us together, doesn't she? Arm in arm on a weekend away, curled up in bed with the Sunday papers or clinking glasses on a night out. I'd show her one of Sam and me, but I deleted them all one night after he dumped me and Facebook surprised me with one of its unwelcome picture memories. I can't deliver the goods and I start to panic. Think, *think*.

'Oh bugger, my battery is really low! I better save it, Helen, or I won't have enough to snap everything later.' I feel awful lying to her. I wonder if she can tell. What might she say if I just confess all, right here and now? I'm tempted, but it sounds like she's had enough disappointment with her own daughter. I don't want to add to her problems, I'm already too fond of her.

'OK, let's get cracking then. Lots to see!' She insists on paying and we jump straight in a cab to Selfridges, me feeling every bit the bride-to-be about to choose her wedding bouquet. God, wouldn't it be handy if we could bump into someone from work while I'm at it?

*

Selfridges is rammed, full of tourists meandering around too slowly for the aggressive London pace and stressed workers on their lunch break, impeded by people like us with no stopwatch on them today. It's years since I've been in here, despite working so close to it, and the sheer size of the place is intimidating. Helen is in her element though, she knows exactly where she's going and takes us straight to the flowers.

It feels entirely inadequate to refer to what we're looking at as *a bouquet.* There are literally dozens of stems, all expertly twisted and bound together, held in place with a heavy ribbon, the colour of which perfectly matches the sage green leaves within it. And the smell! I lower my head to it and it's like I've face-planted into a bowl of sherbert. It's so sweet and fills me with happy memories of after-school hours with Mum in the garden.

Helen introduces me to Philippa – impressive – and we get an impromptu lesson in seasonality and perfume combining. The three of us are going on a glorious journey together through our scent memories – mine all outdoorsy and earthy, Helen's more refined and complex. It's fascinating and before we know it, two hours have slipped by and we're back out on Oxford Street and into another black cab.

'Cross Street in Islington, please.' Helen is on top of our itinerary and it's just so wonderful to sit back and let someone else look after things. I'm not having to think about anything, she has it all under control. Proper mum behaviour.

'Where are we going?'

Helen still hasn't mentioned the specifics of our final destination.

'Oh, just you wait and see!' is all I can get out of her.

*

The façade of Tallulah's is a bright, shocking purple. There's going to be no slipping in here unnoticed, that's for sure. But, oh my, once we are inside, it's like stepping into the dressing-up box I've always dreamed of. The tiny boutique is filled with the sort of lingerie that just doesn't exist in my practical knicker drawer. There is not an inch of wall space or a cabinet, table or rail that isn't covered or draped with something so exquisite it could transform even the most prudish amongst us into a leg-spreading goddess. I can't help but think of Marianne as my gaze falls on a leopard print basque – exactly the sort of thing she'd wear to watch TV on a Tuesday night.

'Isn't this place just *everything*?' sighs Helen. 'I stock a few of their pieces in The White Gallery, but I'd have it all if I had the space for it.' She is greeted by a tall elfin brunette wearing pale blue ripped jeans and a pink wrap top that gives us a hint of the something special she has on underneath. She pulls out a few new items for us to see and then leaves us to it. I take a moment to really absorb it all.

Hangers are covered in Japanese silks and there are frilly knickers framed and mounted on the walls. Every surface is covered in something I want to touch and take home with me. Not sure why exactly, there's no one there to appreciate it, but still. Marabou feathers seem to waft out from everywhere, there are masks begging to be taken to a masquerade ball, multi-coloured tassels in all the colours of India and a cream leather vanity case, lined in deep rose-coloured silk with internal elasticated pouches that have all sorts of treasures tucked into them. I walk around the room, careful not to let my handbag knock anything over, especially the vintage jugs filled with fresh gypsophila. I bend to take a closer look in an antique glass-fronted cabinet, wondering about the kind of home it might once have lived in and what sort of woman may have stored her precious possessions inside it. It's in such perfect condition, the key still balancing in the lock.

I'm absolutely determined not to let the thought of my own baggy pants and bras that lost their wires years ago destroy this experience. And I can see Helen is loving it just as much. She is burying herself in a rail of long negligees and kimonos – maybe something Nick might be on the receiving end of sometime soon? I lift a pair of cream lace knickers off a small glass table for a closer look and, oh, there's a single row of pearls instead of a – I hate to use the word – gusset. Oh to live the sort of life where I might prance about my fabulous interior-designed home in just these all day, while some equally naked man tries – and fails – to keep his hands off me! The girls from work would have a field day in here, I must tell them about it.

'I hope this is giving you a little food for thought.' Helen smiles at me from the till, where the assistant is wrapping up a couple of pieces for her. 'For the wedding night and the honeymoon, perhaps? Aren't you going to buy a little something?'

'No, not this time.' What would be the point? I know Marianne will only swipe it as soon as she can. But then I change my mind. 'Actually, you know what, Helen? Yes, I love this!' I'm holding up a pale blue camisole that is edged with a deep band of the softest cream-coloured lace. It's ninety-five pounds, but I'm having it. I'll take it in to work next week and show it off. The first piece for my honeymoon wardrobe!

As we step back outside, and Helen insists on putting me in a cab and paying for it, I give her the tightest hug I can. I don't want to let go of her.

'Thank you so much for today, I can't even begin to tell you how much I've enjoyed it. And your company. Can I see you again?' I realise how creepy this sounds and start laughing at myself.

'I was hoping you'd say that. Yes, please. It's been wonderful for me too.'

Then she's off, and, to be perfectly honest, I am missing her already.

Chapter Eighteen

Nat

The wedding is off.

These are not the words Nat usually likes to wake to, but that's all Betsy's text says. She saw it the second she stirred this morning. It must have been sent through the long, drawn-out frustration of a sleepless night, or an early-hours confession – screaming match, maybe – with Jacob.

As Nat is trying to work out whether to call Betsy straight away, another text pings through, reassuring her that she will be paid for everything she has done so far. Relief is definitely Nat's first reaction, but she's deflated too. She had hoped they might be nudging towards friendship, but Betsy has just planted them firmly in business-only territory. Then Betsy is asking if she can come and see her today. If they were keeping it strictly business, this would definitely not be part of the contractual requirements. On the other hand, it's the perfect opportunity for Nat to redeem herself and convince Betsy she had absolutely no alternative but to speak to Helen about what's been going on. Maybe she can persuade her to talk to Helen too, then everyone will be happy. Something in the conciliatory way Betsy has phrased the second text, *I know I don't deserve it*, has her tapping back, *ok, fine*, before Nat can decide against it. Betsy is adamant she will come to her, *the least I can do*, so she has two hours to get dressed and ready for whatever further revelations are coming her way.

Nat pads through to the kitchen, up-ends nearly a quarter of a box of chocolate-coated cereal into a giant breakfast bowl and then heads to the sofa, deciding to ease herself slowly into the weekend. That is until she hears her neighbours kick off their usual Saturday morning sex routine. Every weekend, without fail, it starts up at 10 a.m. sharp. She turned the TV down and listened the first time she heard them, laughing to herself, wondering who she should call and put on loud speaker to howl along with her. But over the weeks and months, it's become as mundane as the radiators starting up in the morning; the same rhythm, duration and grunting thumping through the walls, always sticking to their preferred repertoire as they hammer away at each other. Round one will be over in about the same time it takes to lightly brown and butter two slices of toast. Whatever they're doing, thinks Nat, as she's splashing semi-skimmed milk all down her striped jim-jams, it sounds horribly forced, like someone laughing too hard at a joke. The sort of exaggerated noise you make when a firework goes up, or someone puts a big slice of cake in front of you.

If that's what married sex sounds like, then no thanks. There's no denying Nat's on a bit of a downer at the moment. Last weekend's wedding – the beautiful love-filled homemade one that had easily topped her list of favourites this year – had an unexpected sting in the tail. Heidi and Alex had one of those weddings where no one seemed to care about formality, all their interest focused instead on celebrating this one crazy cool couple. The day drifted easily along through cider brandy and rhubarb cocktails, wooden boards laden with Welsh rarebit and wild mushroom brioches and into the chill of the evening, before the fairy lights started to twinkle in the branches above them all and everyone was drawn to the warm, smokey glow of the fire pit. One of the groom's best friends appeared with a guitar and started strumming out the crowd's requests as the volume rose and every last inhibition drifted upwards with the fire embers.

Heidi looked heavenly in a Claire Pettibone dress with beaded silk flowers blooming across the bodice and down both sheer sleeves, finishing at a waistband of pearls and delicate crystal stones. The skirt was a blush silk that draped across the floor as she walked, blending in perfectly with the deep coloured backdrop of the flower farm – purple and red violas, primroses and ivy berries. She looked like she had stepped straight off the pages of one of those flower fairy books from Nat's childhood, as if she wouldn't be going home this evening but would curl up later under some dew-covered petals or a toadstool.

Just so romantic, remembers Nat, as her neighbours are reaching their predictable, underwhelming crescendo. *Uh. Uh. Uh. Done*. She pictures them, sitting up in bed, discussing who's going to collect the dry cleaning and remind the milkman they're away next week.

Only one girl hadn't been smiling last weekend, and it took Nat all day to work out why. She tried to chat to her a couple of times, but after getting sharp one-word answers, she gave up. Then, as the temperature dropped, and guests started to make their way into the cosy log cabin the couple had built especially, she saw it happen. Alex hung back, so it was just him and the girl in the pale mint silk dress left by the fire – and Nat, watching from a safe distance. He tried to whisper something in her ear and, as he did so, he let his hand slide over the smoothness of the silk, pausing at the sexy curve of her hip, like he might have done a million times before. It was so deliberate and brazen, it took Nat's breath away for a second. She spun around quickly to see if anyone else was witnessing what she was – no, thank goodness – then the two of them pulled apart, Alex heading for the cabin, the girl stomping off in the direction of the parked cars.

It completely killed the evening for Nat. Knocked the wind right out of her, like the night all those years ago when she opened her eyes too soon and saw her mum stuffing presents into the stocking at the end of her bed. She'd never said anything then, finding it too sad to put it into words, and the feeling was the same this time. Now, soggy cereal finished, she's flicking back through her phone at pictures of Heidi and Alex; him all duplicitous smiles, her totally lost in the happy abandon of it all. It's making Nat wonder how many other weddings she's helped orchestrate this year that were somehow less than they should have been. Although she doesn't have time for it, she grabs her laptop from the bookshelf and starts to look back through some of her recent client records.

There's Miranda, who approached her wedding like she was brokering a business deal; Grace and all her insecure trust issues and ludicrous red wine throwing antics; Susie, the influencer, who saw her big day as just another pay day; Betsy, who doesn't want to marry at all. Nat lets her fingers tap forward to the weddings booked in for next year. Can she see any signs of positivity there? No. One bride-to-be who is hiding the fact that she will never get pregnant from her fiancé, through fear it will halt their wedding plans; a gay couple who are devoted to each other, but have had endless rejections from suppliers who don't recognise real committed love when they see it, and a woman so uncomfortable with her own company that she is now planning her fourth wedding. None of it makes sense – and yet Nat is so central to making it all happen. Whether she's simply pulling on a bridesmaid dress or being asked to orchestrate the whole thing, why does something that was once so fun, now feel so meaningless and wrong? Why doesn't she feel proud of what she does any more?

Another text from Betsy confirms she's already in Wimbledon. Nat needs to get a move on, she'll be here in less than half an hour. While the hot shower is pricking her skin, she thinks seriously about the value of what she does all day, every day, how she chooses to pay the bills. Unlike Helen, who is so honest with her judgement, where does Nat's moral compass point? Straight to her bank balance, apparently. Susie was the first client whose offer of work she ever turned down. Why has she agreed to help marry so many couples who were clearly not meant to be together? More than anything she just wants the next wedding she attends to be authentic, honest and maybe, just for once, not wrapped up in a novel's worth of deceit.

⁂

Twenty minutes later, as Nat is pulling on a pair of boyfriend jeans and a white t-shirt, the intercom pings, telling her Betsy is here. She buzzes her in, and having decided her entire career is founded on something paper-thin, she's not in the mood for trouble. More than anything she just wants the tables to turn, for Betsy to cheer her up. Now the two of them are ripping up the business contract, can't someone else come up with all the ideas for once, tell Nat how to make her life more fulfilling?

'Hi. Oh, you'd better come on in.' The bags lodged under Betsy's eyes immediately tell Nat this is going to be no jolly visit.

'Hi, Nat. I'm sorry to just land on you like this. Thank you for seeing me, especially after… last time.'

Betsy looks awful, like she hasn't slept properly for a week. Her hair is matted and her face completely make-up free. She's nervous too, her eyes are darting around the room, settling on Nat's laptop, then shifting off through to the bedroom, like she expects someone else to appear. Nat stands there for a second, registering how pitiful she is, then gets hold of her. It's a proper bone-crunching squeeze, one that's long overdue, and she can feel Betsy drop her bag to the floor so she can fully reciprocate.

'Don't say a thing, just park it on the sofa and I'll make a cuppa. How d'you have it?' The one benefit of doing what Nat does for a living is that she is great in a crisis.

'Thank you. Milk, no sugar,' Betsy is using the heel of each hand to smudge away her tears, creasing the skin around her eyes, instantly ageing herself.

She stays in the lounge for the four minutes it takes Nat to make their drinks, not saying a word, but Nat can hear the quiet sobs she's trying to stifle.

Nat hands her a mug of piping hot tea, knowing full well that she'll now be writing off the morning. Whatever's going on here, it's not going to be resolved quickly.

'I'm sorry, Nat. I behaved so badly the last time we saw each other, and you didn't deserve to be on the receiving end of all that. I just saw you and Mum together and, well, I didn't exactly handle it very well.' Betsy looks nothing like the ranting mess that screamed Nat down in the street that day. She looks broken, like every drop of energy has been hoovered out of her. Helen would be distraught if she could see her.

'She's really worried about you, you know.' Nat takes a seat on the sofa, sinking deep into its cream linen cushions.

'Mum? I know, we've spoken. I called her. I can't say it was the easiest chat we've ever had, but we cleared the air a little. I promised to sort myself out. But what she doesn't know is that the wedding is off. I just can't bring myself to take the wind out of her sails just yet. And… Jacob doesn't know yet either.'

'Betsy, I hope you're not here because you're expecting me to deliver the killer blows? That's really not what I do.' As much as she wants to help, Nat is going to have to draw the line at being the one to officially confirm all of Helen's worst fears about her daughter.

'Oh God, no! That's not what I meant at all. I just need to be able to tell *someone*. I can't speak to my friends, because so many of them are Jacob's friends too, and I obviously can't tell anyone at work because…' She trails off like she's just realised she really can't finish that sentence, and slumps down lower on the sofa.

'Has this got anything to do with Dylan, by any chance? Do you work with him? We may as well cut to the chase. Nothing ever got solved from dancing around it for twenty minutes.'

'He's my boss.' Betsy keeps her eyes glued to the mug of tea she's holding in her lap, too embarrassed, apparently, to make eye contact with Nat now.

'Right. And what? You fancy him? He fancies you? I know that would be majorly inconvenient timing right now, but it doesn't make you enemy number one. There are worse things you could be telling me.'

'It's more than that.'

Betsy clearly isn't going to elaborate and it's going to be up to Nat to tease this confession out of her. 'You wouldn't be the first or last woman on earth to snog the boss, Betsy. I'm not sure it's worth getting too bent out of shape about – certainly not worth calling a wedding off for – unless…' She can see the tears are starting to make their way down Betsy's cheeks again. '… unless there's more to it than that?' She moves to sit alongside Betsy, curling a leg up under herself so she can turn to face her directly.

'We slept together the other night in the office and I haven't been able to stop thinking about him since.' Betsy glances up through her fringe, perhaps waiting to see if the judgement she might reasonably expect is there on Nat's face: it's not.

'I think you need to be really careful, Betsy. How many years have you been with Jacob?'

'Too many.'

'Well, are you going to throw all that away for an office affair that might fizzle out before Christmas – or become so awkward, you end up having to leave?' Nat's seen enough brides-to-be wobble in the run-up to their weddings, then regret it later, a classic symptom of her *slide, not decide* generation who can have another date lined up on social media the same afternoon they call the wedding off.

'I think it might be more than that.'

'But you're not sure?' Nat's trying to channel a bit of Helen's calm inquisition.

'Well…'

'Has he had affairs with women in the office before? What d'you know about his previous love life?'

'Not a lot, really.'

'Who started it all? Did he make all the play?' She can see Betsy hasn't asked herself any of this stuff, too distracted probably by the *should she, shouldn't she?* lusty thrill of it all. Nat watches as Betsy's cheeks flush a deep rose and she sucks in a huge lungful of breath.

'I did. I feel like I made all this happen. I wanted it, I dreamt about it. It's consumed me for months. I want *him*, so badly. Everything else in my life – Mum, work, Jacob and this wedding – has just faded into the background. And I've had to tell so many lies to cover my tracks.

I can't keep up with it all. I know I'm going to break people's hearts but how can I avoid that?'

'You can't, and you won't. Do you think Jacob is onto you? Because your mum certainly is.'

'In a way I wish he was, but there's no chance. He's too wrapped up in his own world to even notice me half the time. He's shown about as much interest in this wedding as I have, and I couldn't tell you the last time he tried to touch me, get close to me. And thank God, because I know it sounds so awful, but the thought of it now makes my skin crawl.'

'Maybe you need some time away, Betsy. Out of the office. No Dylan, no Jacob, just a few fun days to clear your head and work out how you're going to handle all of this.'

Nat watches as Betsy's mind ticks over, piecing something together, trying to work out if something might be possible, then a small smile starts to ease across her lips.

'What are you doing next Wednesday?' Betsy looks at Nat, full of hope, like her answer to this question might just solve everything.

'Nothing, actually. I was just checking through my bookings and now that you've cancelled me, the diary is looking quiet until the end of the year.' Oh God, maybe she should have heard what's coming before she answered that so conclusively.

'Great. How d'you fancy coming to New York with me? No hotel costs. I'll cover all our expenses, even your flight.'

Nat's mouth starts to move to politely decline, but then she stops. Hasn't she got a bit of thinking to do herself? A few things to work out about her own future and where it's going? This could be a very useful trip. And, despite all the drama that seems to surround her, she likes Betsy. She could make it her mission to ensure she has some fun, gives up all the angst for a few days. Sounds pretty appealing, actually.

'Why are you going?' Nat drills down on the details.

'It's work, but I'll have plenty of spare time for sightseeing and no plans for any of the evenings.'

'How long are you going for?' Because once Nat and her plastic hit Greenwich Village it's going to be carnage.

'Three nights. And all moping will be banned. I really don't fancy going alone.' She needs saving, Nat can see that. She also knows she has the skills to make this happen for Betsy. The two of them could rampage all over Manhattan without a care in the world. She can also see the wide-eyed expectation in Betsy's face, how if Nat just says the word, it's going to make everything better.

'You could ask your mum, you know?' Helen would love the chance for a bit of mother-daughter bonding.

'I think we both know that's not the sort of trip I need this to be.' Yep, she's got a point. Helen will be all about Vera Wang and Kleinfeld's, while Betsy will want cocktails and bottomless brunch. God, that does sound tempting. It's a free trip to New York. When the hell is anyone going to throw that at her again?

'You know what, Betsy, that sounds like just what I need too. Sod it, I'm in!'

The two of them sit there, smiling deeply at each other, like they've just hatched the plan of the century, knowing big things could happen on this trip. Then they collapse into hysterics as Nat's neighbours start round two of what she imagines they might call 'rumpus-pumpus'.

Chapter Nineteen

Betsy

There is something so immediately thrilling about landing in New York, thinks Betsy, knowing that once she's through the airport's sliding doors and out into the dense, gasoline-enriched air, there is a sprawling, hectic, famous city waiting to be explored. New cocktails to down, spontaneous encounters to have, living the life of someone else for a precious few days. That's what she's hoping for, anyway.

But the queue at customs is ludicrously long, snaking all the way across the arrivals hall and back up the ramp. There are hundreds of bleary-eyed, slightly crumpled people just staring off into the distance, too tired to talk, waiting for the progress of the person in front of them to dictate their own slow passage forwards – towards passport control, where the gateway to Manhattan's unlimited fun will be thrown open. Betsy and Nat's flight left London at 5 p.m., it's now 1 a.m. according to their body clocks, but 8 p.m. local time. Why didn't she nap on the plane when she had the chance, thinks Betsy, before she was penned into this hot, harshly illuminated vacuum of body odour, bad manners and fraying tempers. Just as she's reminding herself it could be worse, there could be a toddler or two brutalising a worn-out parent, one unleashes hell, a few metres back from them in the queue. The wail for *my bed* is shattering the numbness she's feeling at least, but it's like an alarm clock that won't turn off, one that only gets louder the longer it's ignored. The verbal assault continues for the forty-five minutes it takes them both to reach the front of the queue, as their emotions swing between empathy and incredulity at the kid's stamina to downright hatred for someone for spawning a creature so vile.

Never has Betsy been so pleased to hand her passport over the counter. Never has she been so brusquely dismissed as she was by the large male official whose face didn't alter expression throughout their entire four-minute exchange. All thoughts and perks of their business class flight are fast fading. An unexpected extravagance on Dylan's part, the tickets were obviously booked when he believed it would be him sitting next to Betsy, enjoying the menu, with proper cutlery and endless top-ups of fizz that they never needed to ask for. The treat was not wasted on the pair of them, though. Nat spent nearly the entire flight eating, Betsy noticed, working her way through every conceivable snack they could put in front of her before, after the fourth mini box of chocolate truffles, finally declaring she felt sick. Then she cocooned herself in two cashmere blankets, spread out a selection of glossy mags on her table and asked one of the cabin crew if there was any chance of a head and shoulder massage. Only in first class, apparently. *Next time*, the flight attendant mouthed, not a hair out of place in her tight bun, not the slightest smudge to her bright red lipstick. She looked just as perfect as she wiggled her way up and down the plane's aisle to hand them a complimentary bag rammed full of beauty products as she had at the beginning of the flight.

Now, as she's waiting for Nat to make it through customs behind her, Betsy thinks for a moment how grateful she is for this uncomplicated few days away with a new friend. How energising it is to be around someone with no sense of your history, as you edit yourself to appear your most appealing, show them only the bits you want to. And there will be none of the trauma of wondering what might happen next with Dylan, having to remind herself to stay professional, the constant second-guessing about how he might feel after *that* night in his office. She's thinking about the text he dangerously, stupidly, sent to her mobile later the same evening, saying, *please can I do that to you again soon?* She also knows that the force of what she feels for Dylan is going to dictate the conversation she has to have with Jacob when she gets home. The wedding can't happen, she knows that. But is there any sort of future for them? It's making her dread the return flight before they've even had a chance to buy their first street hotdog, sit in their first diner, order their first *cwoffee*.

After grabbing their luggage – first on the carousel, thanks to the speedy business class priority – Betsy and Nat step out into the loud madness of their first New York evening, fellow tourists clattering cluelessly around them, and straight into the path of all the unlicenced cab drivers touting for business. It's Nat who takes control, diverting them left and to the official yellow cab rank. Betsy is starting to lose the power of logical thought and collapses in the back seat, fighting the urge to let her head drift backwards as they pull away. She's only vaguely aware of Nat directing the driver to The Mark hotel on the Upper East Side as they slide into the speeding traffic heading for Manhattan and all the promise it holds for the next two days.

As the buildings start to climb up around them, Nat is running through a checklist of everywhere she wants to go, everything she wants to do in the short time they'll be here.

'I know you're working, Betsy, but we must find time to see the Christmas windows at Saks Fifth Avenue and go ice skating in Central Park. I'd love to walk the High Line one afternoon, then there's shopping at Barneys. We've got to have lunch at Balthazar, cocktails at The Blond and brunch at Jack's Wife Freda. A bride flew me out here in June to help plan her wedding and she took me to loads of cool places. Are you getting all this?'

Betsy has entered that twilight place that exists on the very edge of sleep. She's catching about every third word coming out of Nat's mouth, wondering where the hell all her energy is coming from. Then she remembers the seven thousand calories Nat scoffed on the way out here.

'Yeah, yeah.' Betsy's eyelids are refusing to stay up and so she musters all the energy she has left to extend an arm and press the small black button on the passenger door that lowers the window and lets a blast of cold air hit her face.

'I want to walk down Fifth Avenue like money is no object. We need to hang out in the West Village, then get our nails done at Tenoverten.'

Nat's got a proper case of verbal diarrhoea but then again it will be handy to have her own personal tour guide and nothing to think about herself. And, gloriously, someone to look after her. Despite how little they know about each other, Betsy gets that sense. Nat's strong, she won't put up with any nonsense. The sort of girl who no doubt has spent her entire life putting mates before meat. She could probably learn a lot from her. Betsy has missed that so much. Having someone in her life who made their own life revolve around hers. She needs someone to think about her for once – someone who isn't family and therefore biologically obliged to play that role – and maybe for the next two days, that's Nat.

Betsy's legs are jammed right up against the back of the driver's seat, forcing her to sit sideways, her view of the road completely obscured by the back of his head and the partition separating them both. Her seat is so low, the ads on the inbuilt TV in front of her blaring so loudly and he is driving *so* fast, weaving in and out of vehicles, regardless of their size, without bothering to indicate, that she is starting to feel violently sick, and just a little bit in fear of her life. The thought of hurling all over the cracked leather seats is at least keeping her awake. And she slightly hates herself for it, but in this moment of need, her thoughts turn to Jacob and the first and only time they came to New York together, all those years ago when romantic foreign city breaks were everything. Before Jacob thought writing novels was everything.

She's thinking about the tiny, overpriced hotel they stayed in, just off Times Square, the eternal lightbulb of the city. How they threw open the door to their hotel room with great expectation, then struggled to manoeuvre themselves around the bed to unpack, such was the total lack of space. How they opened the minibar and baulked at the price of even a Diet Coke, then set about grabbing as much food as they could from the breakfast buffet each morning, wrapping a secret stash into a paper napkin each, and making it count as lunch.

Why is she getting so wistful about all this? Why is she wishing suddenly it was Jacob in the back of the cab with her, stroking her hair and telling her to breathe deeply, they'll be at the hotel soon. But the fact is, Jacob didn't give a toss that she was coming on this trip, he just saw it as an opportunity to get the word count up, without having to feel bad about neglecting her again. Nothing new there.

As Manhattan starts to appear ahead of them like some giant pop-up book, the instantly recognisable movie set slowly unfurling in front of her eyes, Betsy makes herself a promise. She's going to enjoy this trip, it's going to be for her. Yes, she'll tick off everything on Dylan's itinerary, the meetings, the site visits he wants, but beyond that she wants some uncomplicated fun. And Nat is the wing woman she needs on this mission.

*

Betsy didn't have time before they left London to Google the hotel Dylan had booked. But now she and Nat are here, she's breathless at the choice he's made. As their cab pulls up outside, on a beautiful tree-lined street that leads directly to Central Park, Betsy gets her first glimpse of the Art Deco entrance to The Mark. It's like the Manhattan townhouse of every girl's dreams. There are help-yourself liveried bicycles with monogrammed bells, black helmets and matching baskets ready for them to use or pedicabs if they want someone to do the cycling for them. How very bloody New York!

Their bags magically disappear ahead of them as they step onto the shiny black and white striped marble lobby floor dotted with vibrant pops of amber-hued furniture. She can see immediately the sort of break Dylan had in mind for them both. Glamorous. Discreet. Luxurious.

There are all sorts of arty objects suspended from ceilings, protruding from walls or balancing on expensive-looking furniture that Betsy makes a mental note not to touch while she's here. None of it makes much sense to either of them, but it sets the tone immediately and they exchange a supercharged grin. Are they really about to hang out here together for two days? Betsy glances through to the softly lit, mirrored bar full of beautiful people – she's guessing film execs, supermodels, Russian oligarchs, power players from the art world, owners of fashion houses – the sort of people who have the confidence to spend three thousand dollars on an outfit and then finish it off with a pair of white sneakers. They're perched on low-slung ponyskin sofas, or mocha-coloured leather bar stools, sipping a rainbow of cocktails and lapping up each other's company. There's a bar-to-ceiling spirits cabinet glittering like a collection of vintage jewels and everything is bathed in a soft pink glow.

As they're checking in, a tight-faced woman glides past them, the flattering lighting making her cosmetic surgery look just a little less severe. She's all diamonds and perfect black tailoring, forcing Betsy into a quick mental assessment of what she's packed. Nothing nearly swanky enough, it seems.

'I'm so pleased I threw in some of my old bridesmaid dresses,' chirps Nat. 'I was determined to wear them again and this is my chance! Do you mind doing the honours here, Betsy?' She's nodding towards the reception desk. 'I'm busting!' Then she's gone, off over the shiny floor, skidding a little on the way.

'Welcome to The Mark, Miss Whittaker. I'm Ethan and I'll help you with anything you need during your stay with us.' The elegantly suited man addressing Betsy from behind the black lacquered desk has surely just stepped straight off a catwalk somewhere. There is not one blemish on his chiselled face, his teeth are blinding, his hair styled just enough not to look vain. And as he leans forward with some paperwork for her to sign, Betsy is engulfed in a cloud of fresh floral scent, too feminine for most men but strangely enticing on this one. It's 10 p.m. now (3 a.m. London time) and much as Betsy wants to respond to his lightly flirtatious grin, she's struggling to remember the basic details required for the registration form in front of her.

He disappears from view for a few minutes just as Nat reappears, tears streaming down each cheek.

'Oh my God, what's happened?' Betsy is suddenly, brutally, awake again.

'I can't breathe. Just give me a minute.' She's actually sobbing.

'You're scaring me, Nat. What is it?' *Please God, let her not have knocked over anything expensive.* Dylan's generosity will only stretch so far and Betsy's not sure even he will cover the cost of a broken artwork or two.

'I just saw Oprah in the ladies'!' Nat holds a calming hand to her chest.

Betsy raises a disbelieving eyebrow and looks to Ethan for confirmation.

'She has been known to have that effect on people,' he whispers, nodding discreetly at them both before busying himself with another guest, subtly drawing their conversation to a close.

Then Betsy notices a shift in Nat's expression. Her hand drops, along with her mouth and she's unable to stop herself staring at… what? Ethan, with their room cards? With Betsy he was all professional slickness, and she watches now to see how he will respond to Nat, who is doing nothing to contain her obvious delight at seeing him. He falters slightly, just for a second, but not before Betsy sees a flash of something cross his crystal blue eyes. Lust? Maybe it's the way the waistband of Nat's joggers has slipped downwards slightly to reveal a strip of flesh or the vulnerability in the tears she is wiping onto the sleeve of her sweatshirt. Whatever it is, Ethan clearly likes what he sees.

It's up to Betsy to shatter the moment, grabbing Nat and directing her towards the lifts.

'Can't we have just *one* cocktail before bed?' Nat pleads, pointlessly, with Betsy, who has already decided to unpack in the morning, too whacked to think about anything other than bed now. 'OK,' accepts Nat. 'But first thing tomorrow, I'm into their hair salon. I can't risk Oprah, or Ethan, seeing me in this state again! Sleep well, Betsy.'

*

Betsy lies on her super-king bed for the next two hours, her mind on spin cycle through her turbulent love life. Maybe it's the effect of being so far away from home, in a city where anything is supposed to be possible, but her own movie is playing out in full colour well into the early hours of the morning. Despite everything that has happened, who is it she really wants to see play the leading man for her? Who would she like to open the door to tomorrow – a surprise visitor standing there, barely visible for the giant bouquet he'd be holding, asking to be chosen? Her old Jacob? Or her new Dylan?

Chapter Twenty

Helen

Hyde Park in December is just magical. Helen has always loved it; the clean, earthy smell in the air, the sense of space and escape just moments from the frenzied pulse of Knightsbridge and its relentless stream of tourists flowing in and out of Harrods, proudly swinging their iconic green carrier bags.

Despite the chill, Helen takes a seat on the terrace at the café that overlooks the Serpentine lake. It's the first Sunday in December, ten o'clock, and already the park is full of activity. Joggers with thighs reddened by the cold are belting around the running paths, their frozen breath trailing behind them, bodies steaming like racehorses. The boating lake is already teeming with young families, driven out of bed early, now rugged up in scarves and bobble hats and trying to master the bright yellow pedalos. Their laughter is drifting across the water to Helen as she turns up the collar of her cream wool peacoat and warms her fingers around the cappuccino she's ordered.

Nick isn't due to meet her for another half an hour, but she's arrived early for a bit of calm thinking time. She's looking forward to seeing him, taking a romantic walk along one of the footpaths that will pass

Diana's memorial fountain and all the way through to Kensington Gardens and the Palace. They'll look like any other couple, thinks Helen, as she wipes the frothy milk from her top lip. No one will guess at the scramble of emotions she's feeling as he leads her by the hand past the rollerbladers and power-walkers.

As the minutes tick by towards Nick's arrival, Helen is thinking again about his proposal and what it means. She's a woman who's wanted. Loved. Desired. And that feels so good, but does accepting Nick mean she will have to close the door finally and permanently on her old life? Will it still be OK to think about Phillip, talk about him as affectionately as she knows she'll always want to? And what might be the alternative if she declines Nick's offer? Will he want to move on, to find another more committed relationship? And if he does, where will that leave her? Trying to maintain her dignity while battling her way through the undignified midlife dating scene? Constantly on the receiving end of pitiful remarks like, 'It will happen when you least expect it'?

Her mind flicks back to the passionate night they shared together at his Mayfair apartment a few weeks ago – and how everything seemed to flow so naturally between them. But can she really hope it will stay that way if her answer is yes? Is she ready for the level of self-consciousness a new relationship will bring? Nick seeing her knickers drying on the washing line? The day-to-day mundanity that was such a comforting framework when she had a young family to scramble through life – will that become a source of dullness to them both after this first flush of excitement? Will she ever again feel the deep peace that comes from being so happily married?

She's distracted for a moment by a young couple at the next table, their limbs casually wrapped up in each other, faces so close they are almost touching. Despite everything there is to love about him, is Helen capable of building that level of unguarded intimacy with Nick?

She can see a line of near-naked swimmers across the lake, about to make their heart-stopping leap into the water, cheered on by a bigger crowd of sensible spectators. Their bodies are pale, rounded and real. Some of the men have boobs bigger than the women. Some of the women have strong, muscular thighs bigger than the men's. They're lined up, about twenty of them, apparently not giving a hoot who sees them and what judgement they might make.

It reminds Helen of her own soft, imperfect body, her wrinkles, curves, physical flaws, and how Phillip was not just accepting of them but loved them, loved every single inch of her. How it took a lifetime to build the bond between them, how entirely comfortable she grew to be with his eyes on every part of her, never seeing anything other than love and admiration in his face. She knows how lucky she is to have shared her life with a man who every day showed her so much kindness. How, more than anything else in this world, she wanted to grow old with the man she met when she was young. How now it can never be the same; there are other people for her to consider. Will Nick be capable of loving her children as dearly as she herself does?

She can see Nick approaching from the far side of the Serpentine. She's watching him, knowing he will never be that man. They simply don't have time to acquire all that shared history. He hasn't spotted her yet and she enjoys being able to secretly study him for a few minutes. He looks happy, wrapped in a long fawn wool coat, a checked scarf swinging from his neck as he strides along. She can feel the nervous wave of tension build in her, knowing that in a couple of minutes he'll be by her side and she wants to be good company for him. She watches as he pauses, just a few metres off from the café now. He runs both hands down the front of his coat as if to straighten out any creases, then he ruffles his hair free, takes a huge intake of breath and sets off again, eyes scanning the front of the café for her. He's nervous too.

Helen shoots an arm into the air, keen not to get caught unhelpfully staring at him, and then he's there beside her, pulling her in close to him and burying his face in the warmth of her neck. She feels his lips part slightly on her skin as he plants a series of little kisses there, his body pressed tightly up against hers, warming Helen's cheeks into an anxious blush. Both his hands are up into the back of her hair and he's enjoying holding her for a few blissful seconds.

'You're beautiful.'

It's a pretty special hello and for a moment Helen wonders if the walk they've arranged is going to happen at all, or whether he's going to suggest they jump straight into a taxi back to his place. Her cheeks flush a little deeper. Is that what she's hoping for?

'It's so good to see you.' She laces her hands in his and they stand smiling at each other until she giggles at the silliness of it all and they take a seat.

'What a glorious day to be spending with you! What would you like to do? Walk through the park, or we could see what's on at the Serpentine Gallery. Maybe lunch at Corrigan's?' Nick is full of ideas, clearly revelling in having Helen's undivided attention for the whole day.

'Let's just walk for now, shall we? The park is so pretty at this time of year.'

As Nick's waving for the bill, Helen's eyes move skywards, blinking into the hazy sunshine through clouds that look heavy with snow. She imagines getting snowed in with Nick, forced to dive into one of the cosy log cabins dotted along the main park road at this time of year, selling Christmas treats and hot mulled wine.

'Come on, then!' Nick pulls her out of her seat and they're off.

They start to make their way along the path back towards Hyde Park Corner, following the noise of the Winter Wonderland fair that appears here every Christmas, its colourful Ferris wheel dominating the skyline. Everywhere around them people are eating pretzels big enough for two, or foot-long hotdogs made from no one's quite sure what, and excitedly pushing sticks of marshmallows into an erupting chocolate fountain. There are stalls selling over-priced tree decorations and sweets in every colour. Nick guides Helen through the labyrinth of walkways until they reach the main fairground, where children are already hurtling down the helter skelter and adults are being spun, flown or dropped from a great height.

Before Helen can voice her lack of desire to go on any of the rides, Nick pulls her up the steps to the carousel and helps her on top of one of the horses, sliding in behind her. When the ride starts to move, she lets out a squeal of delight and he wraps his arms around her even tighter. As they gather speed, swaying up and down, she can hear him laughing behind her and waving at some of the children who have gathered to watch them. She can't remember the last time she was on one of these things, but it must have been decades ago with her own small children. She closes her eyes, feeling the cold air sting her ears, and Nick's hands moving around her waist, her whole body alive to every movement he's making: his thighs gripping hers, their knees bumping together and his breath on the back of her neck.

As the horses gather pace, she's starting to feel a little giddy and isn't sure if it's the effect Nick's having on her, or because she's trying to focus on the happy faces of the children as they flash by. Then she's aware of a man, noticeably on his own, towering over the children, not smiling like they are but looking at Helen and Nick just as intently – and with no apparent reason to be there. The speed of the ride isn't giving Helen long enough to get a proper look at his face but the shape of him is definitely familiar. It's the stoop of his shoulders and the way he's pulled his flat cap down over his ears that she knows she has seen before. But if he was a friend he'd be waving, calling out her name, wouldn't he? As the ride starts to slow, she readies herself to take a longer look at his face, but as they pull around again, he's gone, leaving Helen feeling uneasy about his identity.

Nick's head drops over her shoulder and he kisses her on the cheek. 'I love you, Helen.' He whispers the words into her left ear, letting his lips linger there, where she can feel all the passion behind them. It makes her think about how different this is to her first date with Phillip – because there wasn't one. They went from being neighbours to classmates to boyfriend and girlfriend and a married couple without ever planning it or seeing it coming, yet knowing it would. The closest they got to a date was sitting together on her parents' uncomfortable leather sofa, having their every move watched, not even daring to hold hands. Later, when they were older, they retreated to the darkness of the cinema in the days when there were double seats in the back rows and where Phillip could finally steal all the kisses he'd been waiting for. Helen doesn't know how to date, she's never done it. She doesn't understand the rules that will be all the more familiar to Nick.

They walk some more then, leaving the buzz of the fair behind. They make their way up towards Speakers' Corner, falling into the sort of easy conversation she'd hoped they would.

'Did you get a chance to look through the CVs I sent you? There were some good ones in there, I thought.'

'Yes, thank you. But they're not right. I know what I'm looking for, Nick, and it wasn't in any of those CVs, I'm afraid. I've got someone in mind. I just need to sound her out, see if it appeals to her.'

A comfortable silence falls between them as Nick's arm moves up around Helen's shoulder. She can sense the subject he's dying to raise but is far too gentlemanly to do so. She decides to put him out of his misery.

'I have been thinking a lot about what you asked me, Nick. I hope you know that, it isn't something I've just moved on from.' She glances sideways at him, keen to gauge his reaction, and watches his nervous smile and the way his eyes dip to the floor, as if expecting the worst. 'Please don't tell me you're about to shatter my hopes, Helen, not yet. Not before I've even had a fighting chance to win you over today.' He's forced her to stop walking and turns her around to face him.

'I just don't want to keep you dangling like this, it seems so unfair, but I have so many unanswered questions filling my head and I just don't know…' Maybe it would be kinder just to say no. Maybe they can still see each other, continue to get close.

'Just don't say no. Please.' Nick's hand is on her face now, his fingers smoothing her cheek, his thumb across her lips trying to stop the rejection that might be forming there.

'I barely know you, you barely know me.' She hates to sound like the sensible one in all of this, but there's so much she doesn't know about him.

'That's not true, I know more than you think—'

'Nick—' She tries to cut him off so she can say what she needs to, explain her reticence at such a lovely offer, but he's marching her towards a bench, sitting her down and taking both of her hands.

'I've had months of getting to know you, when you didn't even realise I was doing it. You were never just another client, Helen, I wanted you from the very first moment I saw you. As I walked across the hotel lobby that day, there you were. I haven't stopped thinking about you since. I've never felt this way about another woman in my life. There has never been anyone else. I'm not some habitual proposer that just never got a yes. It's you, and only you.'

She can see the irritation in his face now, at himself, not her, worried he's failing to make his point well enough. She attempts to reassure him that he is, but as she opens her mouth to respond, there he is: the man in the flat cap, standing directly in front of them, staring down at them. Still not smiling. Helen instinctively tightens her grip on Nick's hand and, registering her nervousness, he goes to stand.

'No need to get up, mate.' The man raises a hand to halt Nick. 'I don't want to cause any trouble. You don't recognise me, do you?' His eyes are back on Helen now, who is completely at a loss to place him.

'I'm sorry, um, I do, yes, I saw you over by the carousel. But I'm sorry, I just can't recall your name or how I know you.' The fact that he hasn't offered an immediate introduction is making her very nervous.

'It's William. Bill… Bill Edwards.'

Still, Helen is blank.

'It's OK, no reason why that name should mean anything to you, love. We only met a couple of times. But I looked at your picture every day on Phillip's locker door. We worked together for nearly twenty years and I don't think there was one shift when he didn't talk about you, the soppy bugger!' Bill's gaze has fallen to Nick and Helen's hands, registering the intimacy between them. Helen pulls hers sharply away.

'One of the nicest blokes you could ever hope to meet, he was.' Bill's focus is back on Nick. 'Really one of a kind. It killed us all the day he got sick.' He lets the words hang in the air, no one, even Nick, quite sure how to respond to them. 'Anyway, I hope he'd be pleased that you've moved on, Helen. He must have known any other man would be honoured to have you.' And with that, he drops his gaze to the floor and silently walks away, leaving Helen flustered and flapping around in her bag to find a tissue.

Nick doesn't speak for a few minutes, but looks considerably more defeated than before their interruption. 'I'm sorry that had to happen.'

Helen just shakes her head, like she is in the wrong and there is nothing anyone can do about it.

'Helen, just let me love you. That's all I ask. I know you can feel what we have between us too. What do you need to know?' He's determined to pick up where they left off. 'That I never go to bed before midnight? I have a relationship with the novels of P.G. Wodehouse that borders on the obsessional? I rarely eat breakfast and can't get out of bed until I've read *The Telegraph* every morning. Ravello is my favourite place to holiday. I never drink on Sundays. I can't live without Tignanello. I hate everything about Jeremy Clarkson and the last film I cried at was Al Pacino in *Scent of a Woman*. Everything else, you can discover for yourself. Isn't that supposed to be the fun bit?' He wipes her tears away with his fingers, pushing her hair gently back off her face and then dotting her forehead with the softest of kisses.

She can't help but smile at him and it dilutes the tension a little.

'What would make this – *us* – work for you? It could be a long engagement if you wanted it to be, we don't have to rush that. We could move in together and then you can decide. Whatever makes you feel comfortable, I will do it. But if you're going to reject me, do it for the right reasons and not just because you're scared. There will always be a Bill who wants to remind you of the past.'

'And what if my answer is no? Could we still see each other? Have lunch and do fun things together at the weekend? Would you be happy to take it that slow?' Helen's face is full of hope. Maybe this is the answer: forget the proposal for now and just concentrate on building their relationship.

Nick turns away from Helen, lets his body fall back onto the bench, runs both hands through his hair and expels an exasperated breath, like everything he just said hasn't been heard at all.

'I need you to know that I'm not trying to replace anyone that's gone before me. I'm not trying to be a father to anyone who doesn't want me to be. On those things, I will be whatever you want me to be. I will play it however you want me to. But I can't sit in a restaurant with you, Helen, casually eating lunch and pretending I don't want to have you, in every way possible. I can't just dilute my feelings for you. It would be torture, frankly.' His face is full of sadness. His eyes make one final plea to Helen to think about what she might be about to throw away.

'I understand.' Helen composes herself and takes Nick's hand back in hers, sliding closer to him again on the bench. His arm is around her and she lowers her head to his shoulder, where they sit for several minutes, neither saying anything, but Helen's mind is busy plotting.

'What are you doing for Christmas?' she eventually asks.

'Sorry?'

'Do you have any plans?' Of everything she could be asking him, this is probably the last thing he is expecting.

'Some friends have invited me to their place in the country, but I haven't committed to anything yet.'

'Do you think you could keep it that way. Just for a while?'

'If you're saying there's a chance I might get to spend it with you, Helen, then yes, of course I will.'

Helen buries her face a little deeper in the comforting softness of his coat, smiling privately to herself. As the first translucent snowflakes start to flutter down around them, she wonders if this Christmas might just be one of her happiest yet.

Chapter Twenty-One

Jenny

'Whatever you thought you were doing tonight, cancel it!' Lucy is holding court again in the staffroom, bellowing the words at me, ensuring everyone else can hear too. 'Christ knows how Jean managed it, but she's reworked everyone's rotas so that we can all take you out for a belated celebratory drink, Jenny. Call it the pre-hen do, if you like.'

Fantastic! A proper night out. There's going to be gossip and whispered confessions and boy talk and shared intimacies and proper female bonding. Perhaps I can show them all I'm good fun, they'll see qualities in me beyond being a reliable co-worker.

'Thanks, everyone. Thank you, Jean. I'm really touched, I had no idea you were planning anything.' Bugger, I wish I'd worn something a little smarter today than a cotton jumpsuit! It's at least a year old, colour faded and really not something I want everyone's camera phones snapping later. If I get a chance, I'll pop out at lunchtime and grab something else on Oxford Street.

'No need to thank me, lovely.' Jean is doing the same as the rest of us: talking through quick open mouthfuls of cereal bars and scorching coffee in the ten minutes before the day shift starts. 'I'm just looking forward to a few drinks and catching up on how all your planning is going.'

She's going to be so impressed when I tell her about the lovely Phillippa Craddock flowers and the trip to Tallulah's lingerie boutique. I bet none of them has heard of it. Well, they'll want to go when I describe that pearly thong! But I haven't updated the Pinterest boards they set up for me. I really need to find some time today to get on with that. Just ten minutes should do it, if I get a break. I don't want them to be disappointed or feel let down by my lack of effort.

I'm transferred to the postnatal ward and it's manic. I have three bays of beds assigned to me, four women and four babies in each bay. That's twenty-four people in my care. Sometimes I find it hard to believe I am given that responsibility. Me? Trusted to make sure every one of these people will leave the hospital safe, feeling ready, supported and with as much advice and guidance as I have time to give them.

As I'm speed reading through the handover notes for each woman, I'm trying to remember the names of all the flowers Phillippa recommended for my summer wedding, in case someone asks. There were garden roses and foxgloves, but she mentioned others that she said would retain their scent all day in my bouquet. Why didn't I write them all down? I'll have to Google them later.

In many ways the postnatal ward is my very favourite place to be. After all, it's where the babies and new families are – the very thing that all our hard work is designed to produce. Some days, I will sit in one of the bedside armchairs, allowing a new mother to sleep for half an hour while I cradle her newborn. Even now, it still shocks me how small they are, swamped in the crook of my arm, their soft heads barely the size of my fist. I'll listen as they gurgle, burp and wriggle their way through their first few hours of life… Stocks! That was the fragrant flower. I pull out the little jotter pad I keep in the front pocket of my tabard and scribble it down before I forget again.

Sometimes I'll look at their tiny wrinkled faces and try to predict what will become of them. Am I holding a future scientist? How many babies will this baby have? Will they lead a happy life or a troubled one? Will their parents love them in the way they deserve to be loved? Will they be clever, creative, a big thinker or a quiet genius? Perhaps it's best that I am left to imagine their futures. The truth isn't always as palatable, is it? I try not to think about my mum when I'm at work, but I can't help it today. Maybe because I'm tired and lacking the mental strength to force my emotions back down to that place deep within me, where they simmer gently. I'm wondering how she must have felt on her first day being my mum, when she held me in her arms and looked down at my plump face. I know I was loved, but did she ever have a moment of self-doubt? Just one fleeting thought about whether I was actually a good idea after all? I like to think not. I can feel my eyes starting to water at how the hands on the clock were spinning far too fast from our very first day together – and how she might have done things differently, had there been any way of knowing that.

As I'm finishing the notes and preparing to make my first round of visits to the bays, I'm reminded of how lucky I was to have her – if only for those sixteen years. I helped deliver a baby last week to a woman who screamed at me to 'get this little bastard out of me' at the top of her voice. She was so sadly detached when he eventually appeared, fourteen hours later. She never cuddled him, leaving that to me. I try not to judge, but as I watched her walk through the double doors of the maternity unit the following day, the baby being carried by her own mother, I could see from the nervous look on that grandmother's face how frightened she was for the future too. I wanted to run after that mum and remind her how bloody lucky she is.

I can see today is going to be one of those days when I have no time to do anything well. My first visit is to Mrs Ferguson, who had a traumatically long birth overnight that ended with a full blood transfusion this morning after her placenta refused to follow the baby and she haemorrhaged. As the tiles on the floor of the labour room flashed from white to shocking red in the time it took me to hit the emergency button, I could feel my head swim with the rising panic. As I glanced down, I could see my scrubs had turned a deeper shade of purple and my skin beneath them was wet with her blood. Seconds later, Jean was there, dismissing the sobbing father. The trauma team followed, crashing around the room, making no allowances for anyone who got in the way, their total priority getting this mum to theatre. I watched over the baby then until dad was composed enough to return, his eyes swollen and his whole body shaking from the adrenaline surge, immune to the intense heat in this place.

Now the baby boy is sleeping soundly in the clear Perspex cot next to her, but I can see that Mrs Ferguson is not in a good way; she is shattered, emotionally and physically. I struggle to sit her upright in bed and give her as much time as I can. She needs to talk about it, to try to make sense of what happened to her – how someone who was prepared and well-researched ended up so far from her idea of a beautiful birthing experience. She's teary and defeated, with dead eyes that have no enthusiasm for what lies ahead in the coming weeks, the last remains of numbing morphine probably still floating through her bloodstream. I spend eight minutes with her – barely enough time to do all my vital checks, nowhere near enough time to convince her that today is just one day, and how she feels now will be quickly forgotten once she gets her baby boy home.

Then I have to move on, checking another baby isn't jaundiced, helping another emotional mum who's frustrated at her failure to breastfeed to hand express her milk, showing a dad how to change a nappy. I sign for an antibody injection for one of my mums, Mrs Marks, as it arrives from the lab. Her blood group has tested as incompatible with her baby and the jab will protect against the possibility of future miscarriage. Glancing around the room, I can see every midwife here is flat out – checking blood pressures, taking temperatures, examining for signs of DVT, asking if mum's milk has come in yet, has the baby pooed, are mum's stitches healing properly? There is so much to remember. Wait, what did I say my wedding date was? And did I tell the work girls it will be in Wiltshire, or was that just Helen? I need one of the other midwives to double-check the injection before I can administer it to Mrs Marks and there's no chance now, so I pop it in the fridge for later. There are buzzers to answer, paperwork to process, doctors to liaise with, and calls coming in from the labour ward: they need the beds. I have to keep these women moving through the system and discharged otherwise everything will back up and we'll have women in labour in the antenatal department, terrifying the living daylights out of the mums-to-be there.

By the time I have seen everyone at least once it's nearly midday and I have to make a choice: it's either a new outfit for tonight or some rushed wedding updates. I opt for the latter, knowing it's going to be the subject of a lot of questions later on. I duck into the staff loo, breathing deeply from the stress of it all, noticing to my shame that my armpits are starting to pong a bit already. Have I got time to Google the top ten most popular honeymoon destinations – I know they'll ask where we're going – and who does the best gift list? I lock the door behind me and call up the Pinterest board on my phone. I'm frantically dragging images of Philippa's flowers onto my *dream wedding* board and – very cleverly, I think – a shot of her and me together that I got Helen to take last weekend. All too soon I am right down a black hole that leads to hand-painted, watercoloured stationery, place settings decorated with a rainbow of individual rose heads, and mini maids with fresh flowers trailing from their hair down the back of white silk dresses tied with bows. Then it's macaroon towers, sunset coloured cocktails, and open-sided marquees, with proper crystal chandeliers suspended from their ceilings and mismatched glass vases filled with all-white countryside blooms running along their lace-covered tables. I'm copying and pasting as much as I can as fast as I can, watching the battery life on my phone diminish, trying not to think about what Jean will say if she catches me with my phone on the ward.

Then bloody Lucy is hammering on the door.

'We need to free up some beds out here, Jenny. Labour ward is really struggling down there! Any of your ladies free to go now?'

There is literally nowhere around here for any peace. I glance down at my watch and realise I have been in here for twenty-five minutes. Shit!

'Yes, just give me one second. Mrs Marks is next, I think.'

You can always tell the determined mums: they're the ones who don't usually wait to be asked to shower or get dressed, they just force themselves up and out of bed – sometimes when they really shouldn't. They want to get out of here and home to clean sheets and tea on demand, and who can blame them? As I tear back into the ward, Mrs Marks is stood by the side of her bed, overnight bag packed, and at her feet, baby in clean clothes and securely locked into the car seat, husband impatiently jangling the car keys and smiling hopefully my way. I have to laugh a little – it's like my opinion on whether she should go home or not is irrelevant.

'Looks like you're all set!' If only every woman's experience of childbirth was this positive. Mrs Marks has been admitted, given birth, established a strong feeding pattern and is about to be gone again in less than twenty-four hours. And she's smiling. Then I see why as she pulls an enormous gift bag out from behind her back.

'For you… For all your help. James picked it up for you this morning.' She nods towards her husband, who raises his eyebrows as if to say, *this surely now confirms we can get out of this hell hole.*

'That is very kind of you. And quite an upgrade from the usual supermarket chocolates – not that I'm complaining!' I can feel my cheeks starting to warm, and I wish I was better at these moments of gratitude.

'We figured after a day here, you might like to go home, run a bath and wallow in something expensive! You deserve it.' And with that, James places an arm around his wife's shoulders and starts directing her towards the exit.

I shout *goodbye and good luck* to the backs of their heads.

*

Our table at the wine bar around the corner from Queen Mary's is covered with a round of luminous cocktails when we arrive. This lot mean business and have clearly planned ahead to get me sloshed tonight – thank God there's no repeat early shift for me in the morning. Jean, who has busted out some sequins for the occasion, and Lucy, still wearing the sunglasses atop her head, are quick to grab the seats either side of me and then there is minor scrabble amongst everyone else to get as close as possible. Get me! Everyone is here, from our two student midwives, Annie and Samantha, to everyone from my usual shift pattern and even some of the temporary casual covers. I'm veering between the enormous sense of excitement that popular people must feel all the time – all these people are here just for me – and a raw, shake-inducing fear that I'm about to be exposed as the biggest bullshitter of all time. All I can think about is what the hell I would say if Marianne happened to walk in here now, or my sister Lulu. I know they won't, but the thought that they *could* is doing terrible, acid-producing things to my insides.

It's also driving that first cocktail down my throat at some speed. I don't know what's in it, but I can feel the alcohol lighting the skin at the back of my throat and its vapours tingling at the insides of my nostrils every time I raise the martini glass to my lips. I've eaten next to nothing all day beyond a handful of Hobnobs and some Pringles and so the mood-lifting effect is almost immediate. I notice we're already attracting the attention of a table of suited men, who are all trying to talk over each other about the kind of crap no one is ever really interested in. For a fleeting moment, I wish Marianne was here to witness it. I can feel my head already start to lighten as loud, excited chatter is breaking out around me. Then Jean gathers everyone's attention by tapping her glass with a knife.

'Quiet please, everyone! Pipe down for a moment! Can we all raise our glasses to our lovely Jenny, who has kept so quiet about her engagement, perhaps hoping that none of us would make a fuss. But we were never going to have that, were we?' A big chorus of *no* goes up. 'Huge congratulations, Jenny. You deserve every happiness and we can't wait to help with all the planning!'

'To Jenny!'

Even the blokes are raising their wine glasses. This is just incredible. I'm on to my second drink when Lucy starts to quiz me on what I'd like for the real hen do.

'Any ideas? Something in London, or further afield? Or would you prefer two? One overseas and then one local, like lots of women do today?' She's asking me all this in between huge slurps of her cocktail, then signalling to the barman to refill the jugs on the table with more of the potent concoction. I don't think anyone knows what they're drinking, or cares.

It occurs to me that Lucy might be offering to organise the hen do for me and I need to dispel that idea before she starts taking deposits off people, booking flights and making hotel reservations.

'My flatmate, Marianne, is taking care of it all, I think. But since you ask, what would I like?' I drain my glass and think about all the fun things that are lacking in my life. All the sort of stuff that girls do after work together, that couples plan for carefree weekends away, that a woman like me, nudging thirty, really should have ticked off by now.

'I want to do all those pointless things, Lucy. Spend forty minutes badly icing a cupcake. Learn how to arrange some flowers properly, or how to make perfect pasta and then never make it again. I want to fly up the Thames on a speedboat, play dodgeball, whatever that is, and learn how to put eyeliner on without looking like I've just been thumped. I want to learn how to tell the difference between a good and a crap bottle of wine, how to look sexy when I dance and then I want to spend the afternoon pretending to be arty while staring at the usually concealed body parts of an extremely fit bloke and call it art… I could go on.'

'I might be able to help you with that one, luv!' One of the suits from the neighbouring table has got brave enough to come over and chat, egged on by his equally lecherous mates.

'Oh, bugger off, Mark!' Annie, our student midwife, seems to know this cretin and despite being exceptionally shy at work, has no qualms about telling him to do one. 'I mean it, Mark, sod off!'

Everyone else is starting to howl as he's forced to retreat to his sidekicks. I'm the only one not laughing. The lovely couldn't-care-less escapism created by the cocktail has been replaced with a deep sense of worry. Something's wrong. What is it? I just can't remember, but I know it's going to hit me any second now. Everything was fine until Annie started having a go at Mark.

Then I can picture it, clear as if it were on the table in front of me. The syringe, loaded with Mrs Marks' vital antibody injection, one that has to be given within seventy-two hours of birth to be effective. It's still in the fridge at work while she is probably tucked up in bed, listening to the soft, muffled snores of her baby boy, believing all is well with the world. I stop drinking. Jean is going to hit the roof when she hears this, I might be sacked. Certainly bollocked. I need to do something. But what? I can't think of anything effective through the fug of all that alcohol.

It's a thought that will keep me awake long into the night, rigid with worry but incapable of doing a single thing about it.

Chapter Twenty-Two

Nat

It's three o'clock in the morning, the hotel room is in total darkness and there's a jet-lagged, panic-filled moment when Nat can't quite remember where she is. But even at this time and eleven floors up, the aggressive blast of yellow cab horns below confirms her location. The sink-into bed is huge and so comfortable, it's pulling her back into sleep, before her brain is forcing her out of it again, over and over, until by 6 a.m., she has no choice but to wrestle back the heavy duvet and get up.

This morning Betsy has some meetings downtown with a couple of real estate executives and so they've arranged to meet for an early dinner at an old school Italian place. Until then? Nat has the whole day to explore. And she's going to start it with a stroll through Central Park. She showers, throws on some jeans, a soft baby pink roll-neck and a pair of Converse and hoovers up some of New York's finest room service. A mountain of avocado on toast, two perfectly poached eggs and a coffee so strong she can feel it start to shake her awake as it travels through her.

She needs a map and heads to reception where, oh yes, the beautiful Ethan greets her with that smile dancing naughtily across his lips. It travels all the way up to his eyes – eyes that are trained on Nat, and only Nat, as she exits the lift and makes her way towards him. She's suddenly nervous and surprised that this man is having such an effect on her.

'Morning, Miss Baker. I hope you slept well. What can I help you with this morning?' The formality is weirdly erotic and she can feel her cheeks warm as she tries and fails to stop the image of a naked Ethan from filling her head.

'I'm going to do a bit of exploring. Do you have a map I can take, please?' She can think of plenty of things she'd like him to help her with, but for now she's keeping the chat purely practical.

'Sure. Where did you have in mind? Do you need some suggestions?'

'I was going to start in the park, then I'm not sure. I thought I'd tick off a few of the tourist things, you know?'

'OK, so turn right out of the hotel and you'll enter the park near the boathouse. Then pick your way south, maybe, towards the zoo and the skating rink?'

They're both leaning over the reception desk, heads and hands almost touching as he points to her location on the fold-out map with fingers that look freshly manicured. When she thinks she can get away with it, Nat lets her gaze travel upwards from the map to Ethan's face, untouched, as hers is, by the ravages of tiredness. Despite the number of men she encounters through work, she doesn't always find it that easy to connect with them. Men at weddings are usually either drunk or overexcited, misbehaving and showing off, offering a far less appealing version of themselves. Lovely, uncomplicated, easy encounters are pretty rare these days.

'OK, sounds good, then I'll come out on…?'

'If you keep going all the way to Central Park South then you'll be close to some really cool stuff – The Museum of Modern Art, Radio

City Music Hall, Grand Central Terminal. Then a little farther on you've got the Chrysler Building and the Empire State. Are you up for plenty of walking? The best way to see New York, I always think.'

'Definitely! OK, wish me luck.' Nat swipes the map from the desk and heads out of the hotel into the morning hustle before she can do something as embarrassing as ask Ethan to join her. It's still early and the streets are full of locals doing the power-walk to work, full of intent, everyone with somewhere to be. *The stride of pride*, Betsy called it.

The walk to the park entrance is a short one, with too many people on not enough pavement, all chasing the infrequent free cabs. As she hits Fifth Avenue, the road is lined with smart office-bound New Yorkers, their right arms all thrust skywards in the hope of claiming one of those taxis. Giant black SUVs with no place in the city speed past, the rush of air forcing her backwards a little. She glances left and right, seeing how the expanse of perfectly straight road goes on forever, then looks up – something no one ever seems to do in this city – getting an immediate sense of her tininess in it. All that sunshine, bouncing off all that concrete and glass. She's keen to get into the park and out of the madness, but even there she's far from alone.

There are runners *everywhere*; old ones, fast ones, painfully slow ones that have no business calling themselves runners, some not wearing nearly enough clothes, one running in his jeans. Some are pushing triple buggies full of babies. Another is shouting motivational advice at himself as he sprints towards the central reservoir. Most are doing something as well as running – boxing, bellowing into a mobile phone, skipping, singing along through headphones. Nat passes a small patch of grass littered with dogs of every possible breed and size: doggy training. She notices the man hosting the session is wearing a faded sweatshirt that says 'Say no to drugs and yes to pugs' across the front in loud orange type. For a city with so little spare space, why do so many people have dogs? Nat wonders what they do all day in their tiny high-rise apartments while their owners are at work.

By 10 a.m. she's made it down to the ice rink, where she pauses to watch the first early-morning skaters gliding around its glossy surface, framed by a backdrop of the city skyline. It's mostly couples, holding hands and laughing as they skid from one side to another, some gripping the edge, desperate not to fall and get soaked in the first ten minutes. It's a magical sight, but Nat can feel her smile fading. She wants to get on and have a go, but no one is skating alone. Everyone on the ice has someone to hold onto and she doesn't. She suddenly feels really disappointed that she's going to miss this because she has no one to share it with.

'Aren't you going on?' She recognises the perky American enthusiasm immediately and spins around to see Ethan standing there beaming, while her face is a less attractive mix of confusion and shock. She feels her heart rate immediately pick up and the momentary awkwardness that comes from suddenly being confronted by someone and having nothing clever or funny to say. *Why is it so hard to channel detached coolness in front of him?*

'Oh, er, aren't you supposed to be at work?' She's obviously ecstatic he's not.

'Nope, I've been on all night. This is my usual route home. I love walking through the park and, well, I knew you'd be in here today. So, are you considering it?' He's close to her now, resting both arms on the barrier around the rink, but grinning sideways at her. He looks even more beautiful beyond the dimly lit coolness of the hotel and out in the mid-morning sun.

'Er… I'm thinking about it. I mean, I'd like to, but I've never done it before and everyone's in couples. I'm not sure it will be much fun on my own.' She nods towards the romantic scene on the ice behind her.

'Well, how are we going to solve that for you?' He edges even more closely towards her, hands now thrust deep in the pockets of a black wool coat with the collar turned up, framing his face perfectly.

'Maybe I'll just watch for a while, build up to it? You never know, someone might take pity on me and offer to hold my hand.' What the hell, she may as well throw the hint out there. He's here now, seems a shame to waste him.

'Come on! I can't let you miss out on one of the great New York traditions, can I? What sort of man would that make me?' His confidence is completely intoxicating, like he truly believes the two of them are about to step onto that ice and have the most romantic dance of all time, even if he might not yet have guessed at her level of captivation. *Where do people learn how to be this self-assured*, Nat's wondering, as Ethan's hand is on hers and he's pulling her towards the kiosk, where everyone is swapping their warm winter shoes for uncomfortable skates.

Ethan steps onto the ice first, then spins effortlessly back towards Nat, holding two hands out towards her. He has clearly done this before. The second the tip of her first blade touches the ice, Nat can feel her whole body thrown off balance and Ethan slides forwards to steady her. He takes her left hand in his, holds it tight across her body, then slides his right arm around her waist, holding her close to him. They're off, him far faster than she's comfortable with, her doing that awful skate-walk thing that people do when they don't trust themselves to stay upright.

After a couple of circuits, she's getting the hang of it and Ethan loosens his grip so the two of them are skating wide apart now, just holding hands. He doesn't take his eyes off her all the way around the rink as Nat whoops and screeches every time another skater gets within a metre of them. Then, with no warning, he takes her into the centre circle where some giant show-off is pirouetting, pulls firmly on her arm so she spins into his chest and then kisses her full on the lips while the two of them continue to slowly turn together. She can feel how soft his lips are, how fresh his breath is, and how much he wants this kiss. She's returning it, allowing every bit of tension in her body to melt into him, holding him tight with both arms around his waist, while his hands are cradling her face. Her eyes are closed, forcing her to focus hard on every sensation she's feeling. Then their tongues are gently exploring each other, and she can actually feel herself go weak in his arms. It's the stuff of pure fantasy and even as the kiss is lingering, she knows it will never happen to her again. Not like this. Not in this lifetime. She is kissing a total stranger, on the ice rink, in the middle of Central Park, and it feels incomparable to anything else.

Finally, Ethan pulls his lips away from her and whispers in Nat's ear, 'I just knew that was going to be good. Can I do it again?' And he does, without waiting for her answer. By the time they are making their way back to the side of the rink, Nat's not sure she can handle much more of this.

'Fancy some company today? I don't want to let you go just yet.'

Is he actually kidding? Nat can think of no better plan than to hang out with this beautiful creature all day, allowing him to kiss her whenever the urge strikes. No British man has ever made her feel so desirable so quickly and it's a feeling she wants to wallow in for as long as she can hold onto Ethan today. They exit the park and continue to walk in the direction of downtown, holding hands like they've been dating for months.

'So, is there anyone special at home, Miss Baker?'

'I think you can probably call me Nat now, don't you? And no, there hasn't been for a long time. I've been too wrapped up in work for the past few years to really focus on starting a relationship.'

'And what's work? What do you do, Nat?'

'Um…' She really doesn't want to tell Ethan the truth. He might not understand, think it's a bit weird or that she hasn't got a proper job, and she cares about his opinion.

'I'm sort of a wedding planner, kind of.' Hopefully, that will satisfy him.

'Great! You'll be brilliant at planning our wedding then.' He doesn't laugh at all as he says it, just continues to direct her through the crowds that are building now they're back on Fifth Avenue and approaching the New York Public Library. 'Shall we grab a coffee?'

He buys them two flat whites from a nearby coffee cart and they take a seat on the huge stone staircase leading up to the library entrance, surrounded by school groups and tourists taking a pit stop.

'How about your love life?' Nat asks, as they get settled next to each other.

'Nah! Despite all evidence to the contrary, it's actually quite hard to meet women in the hotel business. Well, I meet plenty of them, but not necessarily ones you want to take home to meet Mom, you know? I also travel a fair bit. I'm training, so I move across different countries, doing placements in different roles. I guess it would be hard to find a girlfriend who would be happy with that. Life gets a little lonely.'

It's incredible, thinks Nat, she has known this guy for barely a few hours and he's being more honest and open with her than men she's dated for months back home. Why? Because he knows she'll soon be gone so what does it matter? Maybe. But who cares? For now, he's hers and she's going to enjoy every moment with him.

'I get it. Isn't it when you're surrounded by the most people that you often feel the most alone?' She allows her head to drop onto his shoulder and feels him do the same, resting his head on hers, then tilting his face to plant a few soft kisses across her forehead. Two kindred spirits that fate has thrown together for a fleeting moment in a foreign city. Nat takes as long as she can to drain her coffee cup.

'Well, I'd better get home for a shower and freshen up.' Ethan sits upright. 'I'm in again tomorrow, so maybe I'll see you then?' He looks hopeful, but Nat is suddenly struggling to remain composed. She wants to shout *NO!* at him. *Stay with me – forever if you like.*

'If you keep heading south from here you'll hit Madison Square Park and the Flatiron Building. Then, if you've had enough walking, hop in a cab to Greenwich Village, Soho and Little Italy. There are some great restaurants there too. Do you have plans to meet your friend later for dinner?'

'Yes! Join us! We're going to a little Italian place on Cornelia Street. The reservation's for eight o'clock.' Oh God, she sounds desperate. Would it be too rude to text Betsy and tell her she'll have to make do with room service on her own tonight because Nat's got a date?

'Not Palma?'

'Yes, d'you know it?'

'It's my favourite restaurant in the whole of New York City. They have the most amazing courtyard that's always full of flowers, whatever the season. I'd love to go with you, Nat, but I don't want to crash your evening. Won't your friend be annoyed?'

'God, no! She'd love to see you, I'm sure.' Nat doesn't know this at all, but if she doesn't see Ethan tonight, she might not see him ever again and she wouldn't mind a few more of those kisses before then.

'OK, here's my number.' He hands her his business card. 'If it's any problem at all, just call or text. I won't be offended. Otherwise, I'll see you there.'

'It won't be, I promise. See you later.' This time it's Nat who kisses Ethan. She starts on his right cheek, but he isn't satisfied with that. He pulls her to her feet and kisses her on the lips. It's passionate but brief this time. 'I have to go,' he says, 'before I try to convince you to come home with me.' Then he's gone, before Nat even has chance to say she'd love to.

*

Palma is every bit as beautiful as Ethan suggested it would be; its pale terracotta walls bathe the whole restaurant in a romantic glow. The main restaurant, where they are seated, has about a dozen trattoria-style wooden tables and chairs and a bar that runs nearly the entire length of the room. There are tea lights flickering all along the bar and an oversized urn stuffed with branches of flowering pink camellias, while each table has its own little earthenware pot of white gardenias. It's so pretty. Perfect, in fact.

Nat texted Betsy to let her know Ethan would be joining them and while she sounded all breezy with her *no probs, I'll change the booking* response, it's not until she sees the two of them together that Nat really relaxes. Ethan's chatting Betsy through the menu, asking about her day and offering all the advice he can on real estate opportunities in the city. All the staff seem to know him and make a point of coming over to shake his hand and let him know what's good to order today.

They're two bottles of Chianti and three plates of meatballs, risotto and pappardelle in, when Ethan excuses himself and moves to the bar briefly to chat to what Nat assumes must be the owner.

'Nat, he adores you!' Betsy looks every bit as excited as Nat feels. Or maybe that's just the effect of the bottle of wine she's polished off by herself.

'Really? D'you think? Oh my God, I love him! I can't even try to be cool about it!'

'I can see that. You've got to invite him to London, I bet he'd come.' Betsy is slurring her words and it's only now Nat is registering that she's not really eaten much, preferring the wine instead.

'I'm so sorry, Betsy, I haven't even asked about your day. Was it OK? Did you get everything done?' Nat spoons the last of the buffalo ricotta cheesecake into her mouth, full already, but unable to resist its rich, creamy gooiness.

'Yeah, all fine.' But Betsy doesn't look particularly fine. She's got the fuzzy glaze of someone who needs to stop drinking, all her focus gone now that Ethan has taken his inquisitive charm to the bar. 'Well, I'm not really fine. Work stuff's all good, but I've been fending off irritated texts from Mum all day. She's really running out of patience with me. Jacob's busy booking a week away without me and Dylan has broken his promise to leave me alone this week, so I can get my head around everything.' Betsy pours more Chianti down her throat and Nat can see they're going to need to call time on this evening soon.

'I know it might look impossible now, Betsy, but you'll sort it all out. Just try to enjoy your last day tomorrow and then tackle it all when you get back – one thing at a time.' Nat's talking to Betsy, but her eyes are wandering across the room to Ethan. He's leaning over the bar, enjoying a joke with the guys behind it, but every few seconds he glances over his shoulder and smiles at her. How bad would it be to stick Betsy in a cab and go home with him tonight? She can't remember the last time she felt so instantly, insanely, attracted to someone. It's painful. Urgh! But she knows she can't abandon Betsy, it wouldn't be fair.

Her phone pings and against her better judgement she decides to read the email that lands. It's from a bride-to-be, keen to get an initial meeting in with her. The wedding is next spring and she wants to hire Nat because both sides of the wedding party are already at each other's throats and she needs a neutral referee to navigate them through the planning and up the aisle. It's another job Nat won't be accepting. She needs to make some changes in her life, she knows that. But what? If she's not going to be a pro bridesmaid anymore, what is she going to do? Preferably something that will allow her to make more time for her totally neglected love life.

'Let me just say goodbye to Ethan and we'll get going, shall we?' Betsy is really starting to fade, the jet-lag and emotions of the day all catching up with her, as she's distracted by more messages on her phone.

Nat moves to the bar, where Ethan's hands are immediately on her. 'I don't want to go home without you,' he whispers in her ear. 'Let's stay up all night together.' But one look at Betsy slumped over the table tells him it's not going to happen. She's beyond just being plonked in a cab so the two of them can spend long, lusty hours devouring each other.

'Let me at least see you tomorrow then. Please?' Then he's kissing her again, not caring for one second that everyone behind the bar is openly staring at the two of them and shooting each other surprised grins.

'Of course, yep, let's do that.' Nat turns to gather up Betsy and sees that tears have started to roll down her face.

'Leave the bill to me, you need to get going,' offers Ethan. 'Go on, get her back to the hotel and I'll sort this out. Unless you want my help?'

'I'll be fine, thanks. But tomorrow's on me, OK?' More kisses, then they have to part.

As soon as Nat and Betsy step out into the bracing night air, Betsy loses what little composure she has left and is crying all over Nat as they both bundle into a cab.

'I've just sent the most stupid text message to Mum,' she sobs.

'It can't be that bad. Come on, you're just tired, you need a good night's sleep.'

'Trust me, it is. I'm screwed. She's never going to forgive me.' Betsy has her head in her hands now, totally inconsolable.

It's a bad end to a wonderful day. Nat knows she should ask what the hell was in that text, but her head is too full of Ethan and Betsy's sobs are fading quicker than the passing headlights.

Chapter Twenty-Three

Betsy

The last thing Betsy needs with a headache this thunderous is a perky, optimistic American, especially one who is on full audition mode and doesn't seem to know the meaning of the word *modesty*.

She's interviewing potential managers for the New York office all morning. Well, pretending to. What she's actually doing is thinking about Dylan, Jacob and the crass text she sent to her mum last night, knowing how disappointed she'll be to read it. Words that were bashed out when the Chianti convinced her she didn't care.

I can't do it. I don't want to marry him, Mum. I can't face it. I'm sorry.

When she woke this morning, it was a full hour before she remembered. She got up, thrust some painkillers down, saw off a litre of ice-cold water from the minibar, scrubbed away the stench of last night's booze in the shower and confirmed her plans for the day with Nat. Then, as she was about to order room service, it hit her. The memory came firing out of nowhere. *The totally unretractable text.* All those weeks of pretending to her mum that everything was fine and when she is finally ready to admit it isn't, she chose the most cowardly way possible to tell her. Causing her mum any sadness, when she's had more than her fair share in life, is what's really making Betsy feel so lousy. The reply was immediate and ambiguous, at least Betsy's paranoia tells her it is.

Oh Betsy, come home, darling.

'You'll see from my résumé, I am more than qualified to run this business for you. I have the experience, the motivation, the perfect personality and all the contacts you need to headhunt the best people. I will be looking for a package that reflects that and…'

Oh, please do sod off, Ashley! Betsy badly wants to say it, but lets her disinterested face do the talking instead – not that it's making this interviewee break stride. While Ashley takes her through the salary, perks and incentive scheme she will demand to come on board, Betsy's wondering what her mum is thinking. Is she feeling horribly let down? Disappointed? Is she feeling nothing but great sympathy for Betsy right now? Is there going to be a serious dressing-down when she gets back, for wasting everyone's time and money? It's just impossible to tell from those five words.

She casts a look at her phone messages. Worryingly, there's nothing more from Mum, but there is one from Dylan that makes a flare of excitement sweep up through her entire body.

I miss you. There are things I need to say. Things I need to do. x

Ashley may as well not be in the room for all the attention Betsy is paying her now. Mercifully, she's the last candidate she's seeing today. And she has precisely no chance of landing this job anyway. Far too much ego, too little humility; too many forced good manners, not enough natural sincerity. Then again, who is Betsy to be so judgemental?

And why hasn't Jacob made contact? She's heard nothing from him since she left London and it hurts, actually. Long gone are the days when, if work or their social lives forced them apart, they would send constant text updates on their whereabouts. There was a time when she would have told him she was about to take off, that she'd just landed, was in the cab, arriving at the hotel. Not any more. And neither does he. As Betsy is having her fingers near-crushed by Ashley's handshake as she's finally leaving, she's trying to work out if there was ever an obvious downhill turning point in their relationship, or has it been a steady slow decline into not caring? Maybe that's what happens to all once-happy couples. First, they stop sitting at their respective desks each day daydreaming about each other. Then, before they know it, they're only making themselves a cup of tea, forgetting birthdays, and she's not bothering to put make-up on at the weekends. Next thing you know, he's on Rightmove and they're arguing over custody of the bird table. And all because one morning they just stopped kissing each other goodbye before work.

Thank God Betsy is off to meet Nat at Saks department store, ticking off one of those great Christmas-in-New-York moments. She needs to get off this downer and hang out with someone who will take her mind off the misery she's wallowing in. As she's being thrown all over the back of the yellow cab, she's wondering whether Jacob is even still hers to lose. Maybe not. And how does that feel? The sweet memory of how it used to be with him seems too diluted now compared to the fix she's craving from Dylan. But what if in two weeks that fizzles to nothing and there's no Jacob to fall back on? Can she face the thought of being alone? No. Does she want to accept that she and Jacob are a failure together, to give up on them completely? No.

Another text from Dylan.

I was going to pretend I had a work question. But I don't. I just can't stop thinking about you. All of you. x

There is a large part of Betsy that wants to drive straight to the airport, fly home immediately to Dylan and reacquaint herself with the floor of his office. But then, she is supposed to be using this trip for some undistracted thinking time. And how can she do that with texts like this getting her all revved up? So much for him leaving her alone. The fact that Jacob is managing to do so is only making Betsy think about him more. She's going to be home in less than twenty-four hours and she is still so torn, so far from making any sort of concrete decision.

'Betsy!'

As her cab is pulling up, Nat is already waving at her from the pavement. 'Over here!' She is wedged between a swarm of jostling tourists, made wider by their huge padded winter coats. They're all waving camera phones above their heads, desperately trying to capture a shot of whatever Christmas explosion is going off in Saks' windows.

'Hey, have you had a good day, Nat?' Betsy is pleased to see she's come alone. She's not sure she can handle the embarrassment of seeing Ethan after her drunken display last night. Or the two of them flirting when she herself has no one to snuggle up to on this cold night away from home.

'Yeah, it was *amazing*!' Nat looks sensationally pleased with herself.

'*How* amazing?' Betsy's guessing Nat didn't just wander the mid-town streets, shopping for bargains like she'd planned to.

'Ethan delivered breakfast to my room this morning, then got someone to cover his shift. I've only just got back out of bed!'

'Bloody hell! You only met each other yesterday!'

Betsy and Nat link arms, laughing aloud, as they inch their way towards the front of the crowd.

'When you know, you know! Honestly, I've never felt this way about a guy before. I can't stop thinking about him, Betsy. And we're going home so soon.'

'Yeah, I know.' Much as she doesn't want to be a total Debbie Downer, it's hard to share Nat's wild enthusiasm for the opposite sex right now.

'Oh, God, sorry! That was totally insensitive of me.' Nat pulls Betsy into a tight hug.

'No, don't worry. I got myself into this mess. I just wish to God I hadn't sent that text to Mum last night, telling her I can't marry Jacob.' In that moment, it's just all too much for Betsy. The happy families and couples crowding her, all celebrating the last few weeks before Christmas. The cheery Disney music filtering out of Saks. The completely over-the-top fairy-tale sets she can see in each of the store's windows – every one displaying a cheerful version of life that is so far from her reality. As they nudge closer to the glass, she can see Snow White in the window. The kiss scene: her animatronic prince is actually bending over her, planting one tender kiss on her lips before he rises again. It's being repeated over and over to appreciative coos from the crowd. Betsy can't take her eyes off it. It's so creepy and yet so lovely. All couples go through bad patches, right? Why should she and Jacob be any different? She's looking at the faces of the strangers around her, all so absorbed by it, as if collectively thinking, yes, this is what life is all about. Finding your someone special. This is what we all want, deep down, whether we know it or not.

The throng behind them is impatient for their moment with Snow White so Betsy and Nat move along, making their way along the full length of Saks' windows. Every one of them is paying homage to the Disney princess – that's fourteen windows looking out onto Fifth Avenue that are crammed with lavish scenes that must have taken all year to create. Dwarves are astride baby deer, woodland creatures are singing to and dancing with Snow White, the Wicked Queen even gets a look in. Then, when they turn the corner onto 49th Street, the windows have been filled with different designer interpretations of what Snow White might wear today. One is a beautiful white dress by Marchesa, a label Betsy recognises from her mum's boutique. And just look at it! It's the most beautiful dress she has ever seen: a silk-tulle ballgown with embroidered silver stars falling down the skirt and flutter sleeves that billow out romantically from the mannequin. It's exactly the sort of dress she might have been wearing in a few weeks from now if… if everything had been so different. If she hadn't caved into the first real challenge her relationship had ever been thrown.

Betsy can feel her cheeks get colder and realises it's because tears are starting to run down them.

'Come on, let's get back to the hotel, get packed and get to the airport for a glass of something expensive before we get on board.' Nat doesn't need to say anything more. She can probably tell none of Betsy's problems are going to get resolved until she is back in England and facing them. Perhaps with the immoveable deadline of the seven-hour flight home, Betsy will finally be forced to decide how this story is going to end.

*

She wasn't expecting to sleep on the way home and she doesn't. But by the time the wheels touch down at Heathrow at 11 a.m., Betsy has a plan. She is getting off this flight, into a black cab and going straight to the office. Nat looks as fresh as a daisy, having snored pretty loudly most of the way home, and as they say their goodbyes, Betsy fights back more tears. How she wishes she was Nat, going home for a hot shower and a day on the sofa, sending harmless flirty texts back and forth across the Atlantic to Ethan.

'Listen, it's all going to be fine.' Nat squeezes her hand as they make their way through to baggage reclaim. 'It always is, in the end. No one has died, you just need to have the difficult conversations and move on. Just imagine how much better you're going to feel when this is all over.'

Betsy wishes she shared Nat's confidence. She's right about one thing, though: the next conversation is going to be very difficult.

*

She's willing the black cab to go slowly, but for once, they are round the airport one-way system and onto the M4 in no time at all. All too soon the cab is climbing over the Earls Court flyover and past the Natural History Museum – not even a building this beautiful can lift her spirits today. By the time she is passing Buckingham Palace Betsy feels like she's drunk six double-shot coffees. She can feel her heartbeat fluttering, all that nervous energy at the thought of seeing Dylan, and then telling him she has to make a go of it with Jacob. She's going to have the conversation as quickly as possible, make her excuses, then get home and start repairing all the damage she's caused. Jacob will probably be writing so she'll make him cups of tea and tidy the house.

Damn it! Dylan's at lunch. Of *course* he is. He's texted to say he'll be back as soon as he can – hopefully, by 4 p.m. Bang goes her surprise afternoon with Jacob, but it does at least give Betsy a chance to reconnect with her team – and to have a much-needed shower.

Kirsty is working from home today because her daughter is sick, and Lauren is out at meetings, so that just leaves her and Anton on their bank of desks. Not ideal. But remarkably, he has landed a new piece of business while Betsy was away and is overflowing with even more than his usual dose of self-importance.

'I just knew they'd go for it. I worked bloody hard on that proposal, it was too good to turn down and they would have been idiots to have walked away.'

The half-hearted smile Betsy's managing is only making Anton work harder to impress her.

'They did say, actually, Betsy, that it was by far the most professional and competitive approach they've had. D'you think I should get a meeting in with Dylan when he's back and tell him all about it?'

'No!' She shrieks the word a lot louder than she intended but there's only one person getting into Dylan's office this afternoon and it's not this wannabe.

'Oh… OK.'

Betsy can see from the incredulous look on Anton's face and the sarcastic arch of his eyebrows exactly what's going through his mind. Something unfavourable about irrational, emotional female bosses. He's probably thinking he knows more than her, now that he's claimed one solitary deal in the six months he's been working here. He's disappointed he's not getting the verbal back-slap he feels he deserves. And it's mean of Betsy not to give it. She knows it too, but she's too distracted practising the little speech she's going to give Dylan in a few hours from now.

By 5 p.m. and still no sign of Dylan, people are starting to drift off home, which is a good thing. This chat is going to be awkward enough and the less people in the office to potentially see any of it, the better.

His last text at 4.45 p.m. said he was on his way so she has no choice but to wait it out.

Finally, nearly an hour later, he walks in, eyes looking directly over at Betsy's desk. Then he scans the room quickly, sees that she is alone, drops his bag and walks straight over to her. He must clock the pained look on her face because halfway across the room he slows and his smile fades slightly.

'Are you OK?' He's at her desk now and goes to embrace her but changes his mind at the last second. He can surely tell from the way she doesn't rise from her chair but lowers her gaze to her keyboard that she's not OK.

'The trip was good.' She nods gently. 'I saw everyone that you wanted me to and all the interviews went—'

'That's not what I mean, you know it isn't.' He doesn't sound angry or worried but there is the slightest nervous edge to his voice like he knows something is wrong, but isn't quite sure of the scale of it yet. He sits on the desk, right next to her, and uses his right foot to move her chair so that she is directly facing him.

'Shall we go into your office? It's more private.' Betsy's still not smiling. It's clear she's not suggesting the privacy for what Dylan might have had in mind. She's timid now, doubting how on earth she is going to get the words out.

'No! What's wrong? Tell me, Betsy. I've been desperate to see you all day and now you're acting like I've done something wrong.'

'Well, we both have, haven't we? I've been doing some thinking while I've been away and I've got to try and give things a go. With Jacob, I mean.'

'Jesus!' The word roars out of him and while Betsy tries to gather herself, he explodes. 'Do you have any idea what this is doing to me?'

He's on his feet now, pacing around her desk, hands pulling at his hair. 'I can't concentrate on anything else but you. I've been trying so hard not to love you from the very beginning. And when I finally have hope that you might just give me a chance, you tell me this?' Then he's gone, back into his office, where he slumps into his chair.

Betsy sits for a moment, pondering her next move. Should she be gutless, take the easy option and slip out of the office to give him chance to calm down? Perhaps call him later? But she'll have to pass his door to make it to the lift and she's guessing he won't let that happen. She takes a moment, gets her breath back, then slowly approaches his office. He's reclining in the seat now, watching her.

'I'm so, so sorry, Dylan. I'm just trying to do the right thing. I never meant to hurt you – or anyone.'

'So, you're going to marry someone who is not worthy of you at all just to avoid hurting him. I love you, Betsy, doesn't that count for something too?'

Hearing him say those words sends such a heave of emotion up through her that she can't control the tears and they start to slowly seep out of her. He sees it and is out of his chair and across the room to her in seconds.

'Don't bloody do it! I love you, I want to be with you. We can make this work, I know we can.' He wraps his arms around her and buries his face in her neck, letting his lips travel along her skin to her shoulder, pushing the strap of her bra down as he goes.

She doesn't have the will or the desire to stop him and as their lips meet, she starts to unbutton his shirt. Betsy closes her eyes and hears herself saying his name over and over again as their clothes are dropping to the floor, and his hands are exploring every nearly naked inch of her. Then, just as everything is feeling so right, and Dylan's started to tease her knickers down over her hip bones, she can feel him tense and pull back from her. There's a clattering sound from outside on the main office floor, as if someone is trying to make an exit at great speed before they are seen. But Dylan *has* seen them, through the giant glass wall of his office.

'Oh my God, who is it?' Betsy is mortified, trying to gather her things from the floor with one hand and shield herself with the other. Laura, she could handle, but not Anton, or any other of the people that share this office.

'Christ! What day is it?' Dylan is clearly panicking too.

'Wednesday, why? Who was that, Dylan? *Tell me*!'

He's at his desk now, bashing away at his keyboard while trying to get his shirt back on, then he glances down at his watch before collapsing back in his chair, defeated.

'Argh, what an idiot! How could I forget? I was so distracted by the fact you were coming back today, Betsy, it completely slipped my mind. I'm so sorry.' He's actually blushing, she's never seen him look embarrassed before.

'I arranged for him to come and look at the office space. You know, when I had drinks with you all at The Connaught.'

'Who? What do you mean?' She's getting cross now, unable to follow what little information Dylan's giving her.

'Nick.' Dylan's head is in his hands, knowing there is no way to make this better.

'Not Mum's Nick? No! It can't be.'

'Yes. He saw everything, Betsy.'

Chapter Twenty-Four

Helen

Is there any better feeling than being brilliantly in demand? Today, Helen's got a full schedule of appointments in the Cotswold boutique – six brides who all need her at the top of her game – and she can't wait to get cracking. Plus, Nick has already called this morning to say he's driving over to see her with something to talk about that can't wait, which she hopes will be as exciting as it sounds. Then a text from Betsy, saying she has taken the day off work – unheard of – and is also on her way. Helen's not sure who will arrive first, but she's rather hoping it will be Nick. She could do with chatting through the Betsy situation with him before her daughter gets here.

She cried when she received Betsy's text last week, brutally confirming her worst fears that the wedding is off. It was all she could think about that day; her poor Betsy was way beyond reach of the cuddle Helen knew she'd need. There was a fleeting moment when she actually considered getting on a plane to New York herself but then she was reminded how Betsy hasn't wanted her advice and support for a long time. Would she want it now, when they feel further apart than ever?

She can't even bring herself to look at the Bruce Oldfield dress that's hung, protected by its thick, clear plastic bag, in her bedroom upstairs. The gentle ping of her mobile woke her at seven o'clock that morning and she felt nauseous as the words started to slowly make sense. First, because a quick calculation confirmed that it was very early hours in New York and Betsy was still awake, no doubt agonising over the whole thing. Secondly, because her words sounded so dramatic. Helen can tell the message was written through tears. But thirdly, and most significantly, she cried because of what that text says about her relationship with her daughter. Have they really grown so far apart that Betsy felt she could break that news in the most casual way possible? Did she even care as she was sending it that it would crush Helen for so many different reasons? That its arrival in her inbox is confirmation that she's failed her daughter; the joyous family occasion they all need is cancelled, a painful reminder there is no Phillip to help talk Betsy through all this? The best of dads, as well as husbands, he would have known exactly what to say. Is her daughter really that cowardly? And now that she's on her way, is Helen going to share all these feelings with her?

Helen is preparing for her first appointment today – a young girl called Tabitha whose emailed brief was typed in multi-coloured letters, littered with unicorn emojis, and simply saying, *make me shine like a diamond*. But now she can feel the heaviness start to weigh in her chest. Being a good mum is the one thing she's always felt no one can take away from her. She might be useless at confrontation, defenceless in the face of a sad story and often shy when it comes to making new friends, but being a good mum? It's her calling. At least she always thought it was.

There's a tightness in her jaw as she wonders what happened to the sweet, sweet girl Betsy used to be. The one who saved her pocket money to buy a cheap potted pansy at the garden centre for Helen's birthday every year. Who charged out of school each day like the starting pistol had just been fired, her face beaming at the first sight of Helen at the school gates, never once late. And the one who told Helen she needed her to hold her hand on her wedding day, to walk her down the aisle when it really should have been Phillip's honour. Helen had planned how she was going to plant the softest kiss on her daughter's cheek, give her fingers a reassuring squeeze, tell her how much she loves her one more time before she stepped aside and surrendered the keys to Betsy's heart to Jacob. Now, none of it will come to be. And Helen wants to know why. She *needs* to understand how the version of Betsy she holds so dearly in her heart bears so little resemblance to the indifference she has shown.

She's trying her hardest not to obsess about all of this when a text lands from Nick: he's fifteen minutes away. Then she's welcoming a visibly overexcited Tabitha – quite the vision in pink over-the-knee socks and a sequinned batwing top – who is bouncing from one foot to the other.

As soon as Helen opens the door to Tabitha and her equally ebullient mother, they both rampage through the boutique, grabbing at everything that sparkles, pulling fine pearl decorated accessories off Helen's perfectly straight silk hangers, forcing their feet into crystal-embellished sandals and loading their heads up with Swarovski-dotted veils and crown-like tiaras. Helen takes a deep, calming breath. They are, at least, a welcome distraction.

'OMG, this is TDF!' Tabitha shouts at the top of her tiny lungs as she forces her fist into a sheer sequinned glove.

'Is that a good thing?' Helen's not sure she has the energy to work this out.

'To. Die. For. I love everything in here. Get me into that fitting room. NOW!'

Helen dutifully does as she is told. She can feel her phone vibrate in the pocket of her plaid wool trousers and sneaks a quick glance: Betsy will be half an hour. Great. She excuses herself for a moment and sends a quick message back.

Lovely, Nick on his way too. We can all catch up.

Helen has a break of an hour after this appointment so perhaps the three of them can grab a coffee together. Then she flicks her phone to silent, knowing these two are going to demand her full attention, just as Tabitha bellows from behind the curtain, 'So, if I do a load of tweets about my dress, will you give me some money off, then?'

It's not the first time she's been asked this question, far from it, but it always astounds Helen that anyone has the gall to do it. Would she go into a restaurant and haggle over the price of a main course, or try to pay less than the cashier requested for her weekly supermarket shop?

'I'm afraid not. There just isn't a large enough margin in the cost of these gowns to allow me to do that. Sorry. But I do have some very competitive payment terms if you'd like me to talk you through them?' Helen says the words very clearly, and definitively, killing any suggestion that this might be up for debate, but still with her usual gentle, professional tone. She's not in the mood for anything even approaching an argument.

Tabitha and her mother are looking at Helen like she's insane, their lips curled back over their excessively white front teeth, heavily painted brows forming a quizzical arch before Tabitha audibly snorts and returns to burying herself in the rail of dresses.

'The Bridal Closet said they would.' The mum, dressed all in black, has turned to face Helen, arms folded tightly across her chest. She lets the words hang unpleasantly in the air while she fixes her gaze on Helen, her daughter seemingly unaware of the standoff that is developing around her. When Helen refuses to be drawn on the subject, she adds, 'I thought you might at least match their offer of thirty per cent off.'

'It's not something I do. I never have, I do make that quite clear on the website.' Still Helen remains friendly, busying her hands and deflecting her gaze to a row of beaded sashes that line one wall of the fitting room.

'Why on earth would we shop here then?' The mum raises her voice and Helen can tell she is going to have to react. Calmly. The flush in the mum's cheeks is telling her there is a level of anger under all that foundation that she is not keen to see unleashed.

'Well, of course you don't have to. If you feel there is a better offer waiting for you somewhere else, then I understand that.'

'Get your clothes back on, Tabitha! We're going!' The words growl out of her, making Helen stumble backwards slightly into a glass-topped side table. A vase of blowsy pink carnations rocks back and forth and she has to steady them quickly.

'I want to try on the Hayley Paige!'

She's brave, thinks Helen, taking on the might of her mother.

'You can, but we'll do it at a proper bridal boutique. One that actually appreciates its customers.' The woman throws the filthiest look at Helen, it's pure venom.

And just as Helen opens her mouth to protest she can hear Nick's reassuring loud voice out in the main shop: 'Can I borrow you please, Helen?'

She needs no further excuse and leaves the two women raging at each other.

Seeing Nick's concern-filled face – he's obviously overheard the entire thing – makes her long for a big protective hug. She can feel her heartbeat jackhammering inside her and the energy drain from her legs. Nick directs her into a chair as the two women stomp back through the boutique, slamming the door so loudly that one of Helen's beautiful framed photographs topples over. He immediately moves to straighten it as Helen watches closely. She knows which one it is, the image that Nick is holding in both hands now, studying. It's herself and Phillip on their wedding day, laughing as if they had not one care in the world – they didn't. She can see a small smile force itself across his lips as he replaces it; he knows she's watching him. 'Wow, you look so happy! Beautiful, too.'

He's so kind and measured, thinks Helen, paying her a compliment even though she can tell from his slight stiffness that he's not entirely happy to see the picture there.

'Look, I hate to bang on about it, but have you decided about getting some help with the boutique yet?' Nick takes a seat beside her, obviously keen to move the conversation on. 'I don't want to push you on this, but equally, I don't like to think of you here alone, dealing with women like that.' He nods towards the door, thankfully still secure in its frame.

'Yes! I'm going to make someone an offer. I just need to pin her down, see if she's interested.'

'Perfect! Who is she?' He looks genuinely thrilled at this news.

'Well, let's see if she's interested first, shall we? Then I'll tell you all about her.' Helen isn't ready to let him in on her plan just yet; the big reveal will have to wait. 'Now, what did you want to talk to me about that's so pressing, you had to drive straight here?' Helen is all smiles, thinking Nick is probably about to suggest something romantic, spontaneous. A mini-break to a European capital city, perhaps?

'Betsy.' His face is so serious, no flirtatious little smirks now, and when he takes both of Helen's hands in his, she knows she isn't going to like what's coming.

'What about her?' Helen's mind is whirring on ahead, trying to work out what Nick could possibly know that she doesn't. 'Have you heard from her? Seen her?'

'Yes, I have seen her.' He struggles to hold eye contact with Helen, taking his time, looking like he's trying to work out if he can say what he intended to.

'You need to talk to her, Helen. And soon.'

'Well, that's not a problem, she's due here any minute.' The words have barely left her lips when the door to the boutique bursts open and Betsy comes hurtling through, flushed, panting and in the sort of rage that Helen has never seen before.

'Shut up! Just shut up!' She screams the words at them through angry tears, obviously not caring for a second that there could be customers in the shop, and sending Nick immediately, defensively, to his feet.

'Betsy! What on earth is wrong?' Helen stands up too, her palms raised, protectively open, trying to physically take the sting out of her daughter's anger. She's assuming that anger is being directed at her until she sees the accusing look Betsy is shooting at Nick.

'Calm down, Betsy. There is absolutely no need to get upset about this.' Nick is clearly trying to remain composed, but Helen can tell from the startled way his eyes are pinned wide open that he is not used to being spoken to like this.

'What gives *you* the right to interfere in my life?' Betsy throws her bag at the floor and focuses every ounce of her fury at him.

Helen starts to sob, at a total loss to understand how the two people she cares most about can be so violently opposed to each other. What on earth has happened?

'You couldn't wait to get over here, could you? Score yourself some brownie points by telling her everything! It's not going to make her love you, you know! What did you think, she would thank you for telling her what a slut her daughter is?'

'That's enough!' It's Helen's turn to shout now. 'Get out, Betsy!'

That silences her. Betsy's frozen for a moment, eyes flicking between her mum and Nick, stunned by the realisation that her mother is siding with him over her own daughter. She doesn't move.

'I mean it, I've had enough of you. The way you treat me. Your lack of respect. Everything. Until you can treat people with the kindness they deserve, you are not welcome here. And for your information, I do already love him!'

Nick's arm is suddenly around Helen's shoulders as she buries her face in a fistful of tissues.

'No.' He says it quietly. '*I'm* the one who needs to leave, you both need to talk. Stay, Betsy. Sit down. *Talk* to each other.' He plants the briefest kiss on Helen's cheek and is gone, without looking back.

*

Helen has no choice but to cancel her next bride, something she has only ever done once before. She tells Betsy to go upstairs to her flat above the boutique, makes the call, then follows her daughter, full of trepidation.

Betsy is sat with her legs curled up under herself on the sofa. Her face is a puffy, tear-stained mess. But for once, it isn't working with

Helen. She's not about to cave in and say everything will be OK. Not this time, not after the show Betsy just put on in front of Nick.

'Just start from the beginning, will you. Tell me everything. What was all that about?'

'Nick saw me and Dylan together. My boss. You met him at dinner.' The sting has left her. No one, not even a fully petulant Betsy, can stay *that* angry for long.

'Yes, I know who he is. But saw you where?'

'In his office.'

'Right. And…?'

'It's not where we were that's important, Mum, it's what we were doing.' Betsy says the words quietly, perhaps guessing Helen is seconds away from fully understanding what she is guilty of.

Helen doesn't say a thing. She sits down next to Betsy on the sofa, turns to face her and simply lets her eyes quietly fill with tears, knowing what her daughter is about to confess.

'We've been having an affair. Not for long, but long enough for me to know I can't marry Jacob and…' She's sobbing hard now, her voice travelling up an octave or two. 'And I'm so sorry I'm such a terrible daughter. And you're ashamed of me. And that you deserve so much better than the way I treat you.' Betsy's smearing tears and mascara across her face with the back of her hand.

'I've tried to stop it. I came back from New York determined it would end, but when I got back to the office and saw Dylan, that all changed. Then Nick arrived. I'm so sorry I've let you down, Mum. What must Dad think of me?'

It's the first time Helen has ever heard Betsy reference Phillip in this way since his death. They've reminisced about him endlessly, revisiting their favourite memories of the world's best father and husband – Helen often sharing stories from Betsy's babyhood that she couldn't possibly remember. But Betsy's never spoken about him as if he was watching over her still, forming an opinion, making judgements. It's so sad, and it's opening Helen's heart up all over again.

'He loved every part of you, Betsy. And he would *still* love you, if he were here now. Try as hard as you like but there will never be anything you can do or say to change that. He idolised you, would forgive you anything. And I'll never stop loving you, Betsy. You are part of me, my most treasured part. I hope you know that.' Helen uses her fingers to gently sweep Betsy's tears away, then guides her daughter's head onto her shoulder, and tries to hug all the misery out of her.

'People have affairs and their relationships survive. Have you thought about that? About what you are giving up?' Helen's saying it because she feels she must. But she's seen Betsy and Jacob together. And Betsy and Dylan. It's a futile question, one she already knows the answer to. Helen, of all people, understands the pull Betsy is feeling, the thrill of being desired and adored.

'I don't want to marry Jacob. Ever.'

'That's very final.'

'Not as final as getting married. Surely, it's OK to be thirty-four and not married?'

Helen gently nods her head. Her daughter is finally talking to her and she doesn't want to interrupt her.

'I think we've been on our way to being over for a very long time, Mum. I've just been making excuses and hoping we'd turn a corner.'

Helen isn't going to argue. She remembers all too well the surprise visit she paid to Jacob that morning and his total disinterest in her, Betsy and the wedding.

'I want what you and Dad had, what you and Nick might have one day. Someone who is going to put me first. Someone I'll want to put first too.' She pauses, clearly imagining the worst, then confirming it. 'Everyone's going to hate me, aren't they?'

'What you're doing is very brave. It would be easier to plough on, wouldn't it? But yes, everyone will have an opinion on it – from the guy who serves you your morning coffee to every colleague and Jacob's family. You'll have to be ready for that. Looking at this positively, at least the invites never went out.'

Betsy sits up to face her mum again. 'How did you know that?'

'It doesn't matter, it's a long story. But would you still feel this way if nothing comes of you and Dylan?'

Betsy pauses, for a lot longer than Helen feels comfortable with, and she can see the sigh rise and fall in her daughter's chest.

'I think so, Mum. More than anything, I'm just sick of pretending.'

'Nick didn't tell me, you know? I don't think he ever intended to. He came here today to try and spell out how much we needed to talk. I think you owe him an apology, when you're ready to face it.'

'I know. But how can I make it up to *you*, Mum?' Betsy is talking to her mum's soft, perfumed chest, hiding her face again.

'That's easy. I want you to spend Christmas Eve with Nick and me. We're having drinks for close family and friends, I want you there.' Helen is smiling down at the top of her daughter's head, running her hand lovingly over her hair. 'I think, as a family, we are due a special get-together.'

'Well, it's not like I have any plans that day now, is it?' Betsy's sarcasm is misplaced but Helen knows it's just her way of trying to lighten the mood, to let her mum know she's going to be OK.

'You do now.' It's the first proper smile Helen has felt like sharing all day but it's fleeting. 'Betsy, does Jacob know any of this yet?' Helen fears that a man so self-absorbed and apathetic as Jacob won't have considered for a moment what is coming his way.

'No.'

'Then that's your next job. Whatever you think of him now, you have shared some beautiful times together and he deserves your honesty. Do it soon. As soon as you can.'

'I'll do it tonight. The second I get back.'

Chapter Twenty-Five

Jenny

'I really can't see what you're so worried about. It sounds like a load of nonsense to me.'

I don't know how many times I've suggested to Marianne that she might want to put on more than her mesh bra and knickers before she joins me for breakfast in the morning. I'm starting to wonder if she's doing it just to wind me up. It's working. There is zero chance of enjoying my soggy cornflakes when, out of the corner of my eye, I can see all sorts escaping down her thigh.

I also don't know why I bother to share my problems with her. She has absolutely no idea of the gravity of what I've done. And even if she did, she still wouldn't give a toss. In her world I'd be slapping on some lipstick, tossing my head in the air and finding someone else to blame. Well, it's not going to be that easy. I need to confess all about Mrs Marks' injection to Jean the second I get to work this morning, and maybe even go to her home to administer it, if Jean will let me. Then take the roasting that is presumably coming my way.

'If you ask me, maybe you should invest a bit more time planning where your next shag is coming from, Jen. Because, I'm not being funny, but you haven't had it for, what? Six months?'

She clocks my hard swallow and the way I immediately try to busy myself sweeping crumbs off the tablecloth and into my palm.

'Shit! It's even longer than that, isn't it? How are you getting through the day? And who the hell is Will?'

I see then that she's got something in her hand. A heavy white envelope with *Jenny & Will* in black swirly calligraphy across the front. 'This came in the post this morning. I made a point of opening the door to him, just to see how he would react to my new undies. And I'm pleased to say he flushed even redder than usual.' I have no idea why Marianne does this to our elderly postman every morning, but the poor bugger must dread coming here.

Mmm, a congratulations card from someone at work, maybe? Christ, I can't open it in front of Marianne – that will take *way* too much explaining.

'Oh. How weird. Maybe it's for Lulu and Will and they just got us confused?' I'm casually reaching for it across the table but not quickly enough.

'Only one way to find out!'

Before I can say another word, Marianne tears the envelope open and is reading aloud the gold-embossed card that's inside:

Nick & Helen
Would love you to join them for
Christmas Eve drinks & canapés
The Hamilton Penthouse
Corinthia Hotel
6.30 p.m.
RSVP: Helen@TheWhiteGallery.co.uk

'Do you know a Nick and Helen? You've never mentioned them before?' Marianne has put down her toast and is eyeing me. She knows something's not quite right but I'm not about to give her any more opportunity to dig.

'Nope.' I snatch the invitation from her. 'I'll ask Lulu if it means anything to her.' I can see from the sideways stare she's giving me that my flatmate doesn't believe a word. To be fair, I probably wouldn't either. But I've got more important things to worry about this morning, so I drain my coffee cup and head out to the tube station, filled with a sense of impending doom.

*

Midwives are amazing. That's what I'm thinking as I'm being physically body-bumped away from the last remaining seat on the eastbound District line by a man who is using his hard, rectangular briefcase as a battering ram. I feel it connect sharply with my hip bone and wince. I turn, expecting an apology, but he's already in the seat, flapping open his newspaper and pretending to be unaware of what he just did. He probably aims to sit in that same seat every morning and can't handle a day that begins any differently, throwing him off his naturally comforting course.

As exhausting as work can be, I do love it. In many ways it centres me, even in the most testing situation – and I never know when that might come. Today, I might assist in a water birth; position myself just back from the pool and watch as the woman surrenders her swollen body to the warm cocooning effect of the water. I'll barely be needed at all, until it's time to ease the baby gently up to the surface and into the arms of Mum. Or I might be running alongside the bed as a woman is wheeled into theatre for an emergency C-section. The last time this happened, the mum was stuck at four centimetres dilated and we needed to get the baby out. The problem was, by the time we got her to theatre and onto the operating table, she had rapidly progressed to being fully dilated: the baby was coming. I'll never forget that day. We got his head out but his shoulders were stuck, for eleven minutes – too long. We had to resuscitate him – sadly, not quickly enough to save his delicate brain from damage. I cried all the way home on the tube that night. Baby Archie stayed with us for four months until he was well enough to go home, and I loved getting to know him. He liked having his neck tickled. I was the first person he ever smiled at. I felt on top of the world that day, like there was nothing that could bring me down. How could it, when his mum was fighting so hard to keep her little family together?

This is all going to make my confession to Jean much harder. I don't want her to think I don't care, that I can't be trusted. I need her to know it was one stupid mistake that I will never make again. It's just getting the first words out that will be difficult.

*

Jean is waiting for me. I was *not* expecting that. I can tell from her face that she already knows. I won't get a chance to put this right myself now. She looks stern but also massively disappointed, like she knows she's got to unleash hell on me but really doesn't want to and now despises me even more for putting her in that position. I can also tell that other people know. I don't even make it as far as the staffroom. The second I lock eyes with our receptionist, I see how hers widen and flick straight to Jean – as if to say, *here we go.*

'Can you step into my office please, Jenny.'

A wave of pins and needles radiates up my back and everything physically sinks downwards inside me. Oh my God, I'm going to cry before I even get in there. If she sees how upset I am, might she go a little easier on me? But the sobering effect of the fear I'm feeling is cancelling out all my tears. What if I just say, *No, I can't come in. Sorry. I don't want to*. Is that an option? I seriously consider making a grab for the mobile in my pocket and pretending there's an urgent call I need to take. A big family problem that will mean I have to go home, *right now*.

Why am I behaving like a child?

I glance across the hallway to the staffroom and see several heads turn. They all know and have obviously been waiting for my arrival. Would it have killed someone to text me a warning?

'Have a seat.' Jean shifts a couple of box files off a chair so I can sit down and I hope for a fleeting moment that she's going to ask me about wedding cake trends. As it happens, I'm quite up on that. The flavours of the English countryside are super-popular right now – red apple, elderflower, peach, strawberry and anything rose-scented. *Oh God, focus Jenny!*

'You know why you're in here, don't you?' Jean sits down too, in the chair opposite me. Her office – actually more of a storeroom – is so small our knees are nearly touching, which is just making this even more awkward.

'I think so.' I'm holding out, allowing myself futile hope.

'She came back in. Very early this morning and in a total panic that something dreadful was going to happen.'

That confirms it. Why didn't I just say something there and then in the bar when it first occurred to me? Yes, it would have sucked the life out of the evening, but anything is better than this, than looking incompetent and uncaring. She would have seen for herself how mortified I was. But it all seems a bit hollow now, like I'm apologising purely because she's caught me out.

'I'm so sorry. It was so busy yesterday when she left. I was looking forward to the drinks and it just completely slipped my mind.'

'It's always busy, Jenny. That can't be an excuse for doing a less than vigilant job. *She* managed to remember. A brand-new mum, full of worry, on no sleep, and she still remembered. Which means there really is no excuse for you forgetting, I'm afraid.' She's looking over the top of her specs at me in proper headmistress mode.

'I know. I'm sorry. Should I call her?' I really don't want to do that. I don't want to hear anyone else be cross with me and I've got nothing satisfying to offer her by way of an explanation. After she gave me such a lovely gift, too.

'No, I've dealt with it. But I'm disappointed. It's a silly mistake to make and one you know could have had very serious consequences if it hadn't been picked up. The fact that it wasn't picked up by you only makes it worse.'

I can't even tell her I knew now, otherwise it poses the even more stupid question of why I still didn't say anything. I just thought I could get in here and put it right before this conversation had to happen.

'Whatever is going on in your private life, it can't detract from the very important job you do here. I thought you knew that.'

'Of course, yes.' If only she knew how much of my headspace this non-wedding is taking up – having to plan, or rather unplan; it is so exhausting.

'I am putting you in room six today with Mrs Marshall. Her waters broke twenty-four hours ago, no spontaneous labour. She's had the prostin gel and was moved to the delivery suite very early this morning. Lucy has just set up the Syntocinon drip and she's one centimetre dilated, only very mild contractions so far. Go and relieve Lucy, she needs to go home.'

To the untrained, this statement would mean nothing. But I know what Jean is saying: she is asking me to look after a woman who will, in all probability, take hours and hours to start labour fully. While her husband sits mute in the corner, eyes never looking up from his phone screen, my long, laborious job will be to watch the CTG that monitors baby's heartbeat. I'll take hourly blood pressure readings, and check the epidural level to make sure it is still strong enough. Then every fifteen minutes I'll record the foetal heart rate and any contractions she may be having. It will be long, slow and drawn-out. It's continuous and repetitive monitoring and I'll have to get someone to cover for me if I need so much as a wee – and knowing how busy we always are, how likely is *that* to happen?

Some days you'll hit it off with the woman and the two of you can have a lovely chat. This is when I feel really useful, dispensing endless advice on the best nappies, making the transition from breast to bottle, sleep routines. I feel needed and valued. Others, like today, I walk in the room and she's fast asleep and he can barely manage a grunt in my direction. I enter the room at 9.35 a.m. and by ten o'clock, I am climbing the walls with frustration. My mind flicks back to the invitation and how I am going to navigate my way around that one. I'd love to go to Helen's drinks. I've got nothing else to do on Christmas Eve with Dad, Lulu and Marianne all away. And it sounds so luxurious; all that five-star spoiling is something I'm never likely to be offered ever again. Couldn't Will just be busy? How believable is that?

I watch the hands on the clock on the wall slowly creep round as I sit in the opposite corner of the room from the dad. The darkness is making me sleepy and I can feel myself starting to drift mentally out of the room. Have I really been in here two hours? It feels like six. I start to worry I'm actually going to fall asleep and I have to set the alarm on my mobile to buzz every fifteen minutes. I honestly did mean to put my phone in my locker – the last thing I need is to give Jean a single other reason to be cross with me – but now I'm glad I have it.

I notice a new text from Helen.

Can you call me urgently please, Jenny. I must speak to you, Helen

No kiss. *She knows.* She knows I'm lying to her and have been for months. She's going to be furious. She's going to shout at me. Will she report me to work? Perhaps she'll think I'm so mental, my employer should know. I work in a hospital, I care for people. I can't be unhinged or irresponsible. Lives will be put at risk. Oh, shit! I'm going to have to call her. But how?

I try to bash out a quick covert response, desperately attempting to gauge any level of anger she might be feeling, but the text won't go. The signal is too weak in here and I know I'm not going to get a break for hours. I look at Mrs Marshall. She's relaxed, drifting in and out of sleep and comfortable, and her readings are all fine. I stick my head out into the corridor. Who is free to cover me for fifteen minutes? No one, obviously. I sit back down. I know I shouldn't leave her. It's wrong and Jean will hit the roof. And rightly so. But… perhaps if I tell the dad I'm popping to the loo, I can duck down the corridor, past the staffroom and out towards the far end of the department where we store the old equipment and no one ever ventures. I just get a terse 'yep' from him and then I pop my head back out into the corridor. One of the student midwives is passing and I know she's my only hope. I can't leave her in the room alone, but I can ask her to find someone to cover me quickly.

'Annie! Can you get someone to sit with Mrs Marshall, please? I'm busting and I've got to leave the room now, I can't wait.'

'Oh, um, right, yes. The only thing is, I've just been asked to—'

'Seriously, it has to be now, please. I won't be long. Just whizz back round to the staffroom and grab someone, will you please.'

I can't wait for a response. I'm off, as fast as I can, without drawing attention to myself, walk-running all the way there. All I need is five quick minutes.

As soon as I round the corner on to the back corridor, I slide my mobile discreetly out from the front pocket of my scrubs and pull up Helen's number. The second she answers, I make it clear I've got no time to chat.

'Helen, it's Jenny. I got your text. I'm at work so I've only got a couple of minutes…'

'Hello! OK, I've got someone with me too, so let me call you back ASAP. Two minutes OK, bye.'

The call disconnects and I'm pacing back and forth, shooting the occasional glance back round the corner to check no one else is heading this way. She didn't sound angry. Otherwise she would have just flown at me, right? But I need to be sure. Come on, Helen, *come on*. I lift the small silver fob watch on my scrubs and see I've already been gone eight minutes and it's another six before she calls me back.

'OK, so today is the deadline to pay the deposit for your dress. I had a feeling you'd forget. Am I right?'

Oh shit! I'm instantly regretting calling her. I could have dodged this. This conversation definitely could have waited and now I'm stuck on the call when I should be with Mrs Marshall. I don't even need a bloody dress – not that I can tell her that, obviously. I'll be straight off the Christmas drinks list.

'Let me see. It's the Hayley Paige embroidered ballgown… you decided against the extra crystal embellished belt… you need it for July 20th… and the alterations we decided on were largely to lift the hem, pull in the waist a fraction, and the shoulders needed slimming a little too. So, let me think, the total cost is going to be…'

I can hear Helen trying to tot up the figures, mental arithmetic clearly not her thing, and then she's talking me through calendar dates.

'So, if you're paying the deposit today and we confirm the order, that gives us one, two, three…'

She's counting out the weeks until my imaginary wedding and I can feel my breath start to shorten. 'And how much is the deposit, Helen?' I have to cut her off or I'll be here all day.

'It's fifty per cent of the total cost, so in your case, that will be about £2,300. Are you paying on credit or debit card? Oh gosh, someone's hammering on the door, Jenny, just give me a second.'

I hear her put the handset down. *Think, think, think.* As I'm considering just hanging up, she's back.

'OK, sorry about that. I do make it clear we're by appointment only, but you always get someone who tries to drop in on the hop. Now, where were we?'

'So, my dad was going to come in and pay the deposit. He's been saving up for a while and I think it's something he really wants to do. Is that OK?'

'Umm. I really should take the deposit today.' There's a painful pause that I make no attempt to fill. Helen is obviously working out how reliable my father might be. 'It's the 12th December today and my last open day before Christmas will be next Thursday, 20th. He'll need to call me ASAP. Actually, do you want to give me his number and I can liaise with him directly?'

'Oh, it's OK, I've given him yours.' I don't know where I think this is going or how it can possibly end well. He's obviously not going to call. Helen's going to chase me again. And then what? I can't worry about that now, I need to get back to Mrs Marshall. I glance at my watch: I've been gone twenty-four minutes. Far too long.

'OK then, that's agreed. I hope to see you and Will on Christmas Eve, Jenny? You did get the invitation?'

'Yes, of course! You will, you will! Er, although it may just be me. Let me get back to you. I must go! Thank you, Helen, bye.'

I stand there for a second, just taking a breath and composing myself, slightly terrified by the enormity of the lies I've just told, and hot, very hot, from the stress of it all. I can't think about it now. There must be a way to salvage all this without losing Helen's friendship but there's not enough space in my head to work it out. I'll sit down tonight and go through it all.

*

Was that someone shouting my name? I'm sure I heard it. Did I? I freeze until it comes again. It's Jean. Without another thought, I belt back around the corner, down the corridor, past the staffroom and towards room six. Annie is at reception, casually chatting to another one of the students, and when she sees me, her mouth drops open and she jerks to attention. Oh no! I can tell instantly from her reaction that she never found the cover for me.

As soon as I see the door propped open and hear the high-pitched CTG alarm going, it's obvious something is wrong. Jean comes out with a look of sharp focus that confirms there is definitely a problem – something she shouldn't be seeing before me. She looks straight at me and too late, I notice her gaze falls to my right hand. The one still clutching my mobile phone. I thrust it guiltily back in my pocket, but the damage is done. Her face contorts into a look that's part confusion, part rage.

'Call theatre now!' she shouts at me. 'Emergency C-section.'

As I enter the room and yank the phone from the wall I see Lucy is here too, firing details at another midwife, who is documenting everything on the patient notes. 'Foetal heart rate 165 bpm, mum's temperature 38.5.' At the same time, she's doing all the things I should be doing: turning off the Syntocinon drip and switching it for fluids to make sure Mrs Marshall is properly hydrated. 'Time is 12.16 p.m., last recorded observations were 11.40 a.m.' She looks accusingly at me when she says that. No one is saying it yet but we all know this is my fault.

Mum is surprisingly calm but her husband is glaring at me: he knows I should have been here. The sheepish look on my face and the quick efficiency of everyone else around me is giving the game away. The room is full of activity now. A doctor is getting mum to sign a consent form while Lucy is pulling on the knee-high white stockings she'll wear to theatre and giving her the antacid tablet she needs. Then the anaesthetist arrives to top up her epidural. In the fifteen minutes it takes for all this to happen, I am rooted to the spot, feeling incapable of making a positive difference to anything that's happening. My room has been taken over by people who would never leave Mrs Marshall alone.

'You're going to need to explain to me why you felt it was OK to abandon a labouring woman, who was on continuous monitoring, for what appears to be well over thirty minutes.' Jean is half-whispering the words in my ear, mindful, I'm sure, that it won't help the situation if the mum or her husband overhears us. 'I hope for your sake there are no further complications. And that the call you felt couldn't wait wasn't about something as trivial as wedding planning.'

'I didn't leave her alone! I promise I didn't. Well, I asked Annie to get cover and she clearly didn't because—'

Jean cuts me off. 'You're telling me you asked an unqualified student midwife to handle the situation?'

'No, no, that's not what I mean. I just asked her to find cover, not to look after Mrs Marshall.'

'I see no difference, I'm afraid, Jenny.'

'There is, there is! I never abandoned her, it's not my fault.' I'm trying so hard to keep the tears from falling. If mum or her husband see me crying now it will only inflame the situation, make me look even less professional.

'This…' Jean is struggling to control her anger now, 'is absolutely not the time to try to justify yourself. We will talk later.'

Something in me snaps then. Maybe it's the culmination of all those lies, pressing down on me, the lack of understanding about how much effort this has all taken. Or the delayed realisation that I have put a woman and her unborn baby at risk. How could I? This is not who I am. I step out of the room, closely followed by Jean, who can see I'm about to crack. I drop my face into my hands and say sorry over and over again. Not to Jean, though, to my mum. She would be so ashamed if she could see me now.

'Pardon? Stop mumbling and make yourself useful, Jenny. Get Mr Marshall into some scrubs. He'll want to go to theatre too. Lucy will take them down, I'm not at all sure you're up to the task.'

The fact I have nothing to say for myself only seems to irritate her further.

'There's more to life than three-tiered cakes and honeymoon shopping, you know.'

That's it. I've had enough.

'There is no bloody wedding! There never was!' That floors her. I spit the words straight at her and she shudders to a halt.

I'm rooted to the spot, waiting for a big reaction that doesn't come. She just stands there, shocked, silently shaking her head at me, telling me loud and clear what a pathetic joke I am.

Chapter Twenty-Six

Nat

Something will go wrong. It always does, thinks Nat, as her final wedding of the year gets underway. It's Lucy and Sam, two of those people with a string of bad choices behind them, resigned, almost, in their late-thirties, to never meeting The One. Then, bam! The sliding doors effect kicks in. She oversleeps one morning, he's taken the day off; two entirely inconsequential acts that place them both on a later train. Call it fate that they stepped into the same carriage and she dropped her book, so the two of them dipped for it and banged heads.

So, now it's only right, thinks Nat, that a meeting that started with them both guffawing together like idiots should end in a beautiful winter wedding day in the Surrey countryside.

That first chance encounter was just six months ago, and Nat loved Lucy from the moment she shared her story. There is something so uncomplicated and honest about it. Just as this is the only wedding of the year where the bride hasn't hidden the fact that Nat is a professional bridesmaid. Why would she? There are no lies to conceal and no awkward relationships for Nat to navigate everyone around, just a need to have someone take care of everything – and a great personal recommendation, which convinced Lucy that Nat was better than any wedding planner she might Google.

Isn't this how it's supposed to happen? wonders Nat, standing behind them, listening to them exchange their vows. Just a bit of unpredictable animal attraction when you least expect it? As Sam is calmly stroking Lucy's arm under her veil, Nat's thinking about Ethan. This romance-filled day inviting comparison with Nat's own chance meeting in New York. Except her story had a very different ending. Two hours on their last day together spent exploring each other's bodies, rolling around on her king-sized bed with not one inhibition between them, while elsewhere, Betsy mainlined coffee and planned her speech to Helen. Then followed a surprisingly fervent promise from Ethan that they *will* see each other again – that Nat quickly dismissed as flatteringly unachievable – followed by a stiff talking to herself for the entire flight home.

Everything about her brief relationship with Ethan is passionate, all-consuming, mind-bending. It's also over and she can't lose sight of that. She needs to concentrate on the ceremony she's supposed to be part of today, knowing the memory of him is going to make her body tighten and tense for months to come, taking her out of the room and back into bed with him whenever she allows herself to wander back there. But that's all it is: a memory.

Right now there's Lucy's lace-edged train to straighten and her bouquet of deep burgundy blooms to hold while all the pictures are being taken. And, after today, Nat has a website to close down and a future to plan. While Lucy and Sam are having all their couple shots taken on the frost-covered lawn at the back of the stately home in which they were married, Nat moves to the terrace and perches at the hot chocolate bar. *Such a lovely idea*, she thinks, as she's handed a warm mug. She helps herself to a handful of soft marshmallows and caramel sprinkles, then looks back down across the lawn to Lucy and Sam.

Now the scary official bit is out of the way, she can see the tension has lifted from their shoulders, and the relief is powering their wide smiles as they're jostled together in the swell of well-wishing guests. Nat scans the crowd. Lucy hasn't said a word about any potential troublemakers on the guest list, but Nat lets her expert eye travel over everyone, looking for any telltale signs. A lone guest hanging back, not wanting to be part of the celebrations. A face that's not lit from within. Someone who only has eyes for the bride or groom. Or a mother who looks furious that this went the distance. No, there is none of it here today. And there is still no sign of it as they are filing inside for dinner in the house's private library.

Polished wooden tables run the length of the room, each with its cream silk reading lamp left in place. There are loose floral arrangements dotted along each table, vases filled with emerald green wintry foliage and plum anemones with their deep chocolate-coloured centres; a scattering of cinnamon sticks, pine cones and cranberry branches alongside. There is a fireplace with a mantelpiece covered in sprawling eucalyptus, trailing vines, jewel-coloured dahlias and pomegranates, which perfectly match the colour of the velvet ribbon around Lucy's bouquet. The smell is heavenly. Everyone is happy, loudly toasting the couple with huge goblets of red wine and helping themselves to the feast displayed around the room – a lamb, steak and salmon carving station is positioned next to a raw bar serving oysters, prawns and ceviche.

But Nat isn't hungry and oddly, none of this is moving her today. She's stepping through her duties, like they are just that – things to tick off the To-do list until she can disappear upstairs to her room at the agreed 8 p.m. She's being professional, of course: helping Lucy with make-up touch-ups, chatting to all the family, instigating introductions, making sure the itinerary is running to schedule. But more than anything she wants to get away, out of what she hopes will be the last bridesmaid dress she'll ever wear, and start really thinking about her future.

While everyone is eating, she tells Lucy she has a quick call to make and steps into an adjoining drawing room: she wants to call Helen. She knows Betsy will have spoken to her by now, confirming the wedding is off, and Nat wants to check Helen's OK. She also needs to thank her for the beautiful card, inviting her to drinks on Christmas Eve. It is so lovely of Helen to include her and, hopes Nat, a sign that she is more than just a valued regular client.

'Helen, it's Nat. Are you OK to talk?' Nat settles into one of the deep, cosy couches, feeling the throbbing in her feet as she takes the weight off her heels.

'Yes! I've got a few minutes between clients. How's the wedding going? I assume you're at one?' She sounds cheerful enough.

'You guessed right. All good, surprisingly straightforward, in fact. I've spent most of the day trying to work out what the big "but" is that must be coming. I can't help myself, I feel like I've missed something and it can't be this easy. Anyway, I'm really just calling to see if you're OK? Have you managed to chat to Betsy yet?' There is a slight pause now and for a moment Nat fears she has overstepped the mark, calling Helen about a personal matter, not a professional one.

'I have, yes. I think everything's going to be fine but… I don't envy her that conversation with Jacob. It's going to be very difficult and to be honest, I'm struggling to concentrate on much until I hear from her about how it went.'

'Anything I can do to help?' Poor Helen. Nat knows she would have that conversation on Betsy's behalf in a second if it was the right thing to do. But not this time. This one is all Betsy's to squirm her way through.

'Just look out for her, will you, please? I know you two have grown close and she may prefer to come to you, rather than me.'

'Of course I will. I also wanted to thank you, Helen, for your lovely drinks invite. I'll definitely be there.'

'Ah, I'm so pleased to hear that! It's going to be very special. Actually, while I have you, Nat, there is something I need to ask you too.'

'Anything, fire away.'

'Well, do you think you might be able to pop into the boutique next week? Sorry, I know it's very close to Christmas, but this can't wait.'

'I can. But, Helen, you must know there is no way I'll be able to wait that long to find out what this is all about. Come on, whatever it is, you can blab! It's giving me a good excuse to duck out of the wedding duties for a bit longer anyway.'

'OK, fair enough.' The sound of Helen's soft laughter tells Nat this can only be a good thing.

'I have been thinking for some time about getting some help in the boutique. It's really becoming too much for me to handle on my own, between London and the Cotswolds. And, well, I've seen how brilliant you are with brides, how they warm to you and you've been to more weddings than any other person I know. So, I was really wondering if you might be interested in—'

'Yes! One hundred per cent yes, Helen. It would be an absolute dream to work for you! Oh my goodness, sorry, is that what you were going to ask me? How embarrassing! Maybe it wasn't?'

'It's exactly what I was going to ask you, don't worry! I need a manager to run the London store and I was very much hoping that someone would be you.'

Without realising it, Nat has risen from the sofa and is pacing around the drawing room, her heart pounding in her chest. 'I'm not a businesswoman like you, though, Helen. I've never worked in retail, I'm not sure I can do it.'

'You've been running what looks, to me, like a very successful business for years. You're discreet, professional and honest. That's what I need. Everything else, I can teach you. What d'you say? Can I tempt you in to talk hours, salary and all the other bits?'

'Yes, you can! I am so honoured. I've been thinking about making some changes for a while and this just feels like the perfect opportunity, thank you so much.'

'OK, great, let's chat next week. I'd better let you get back to the wedding. I'm so pleased, Nat. I can't wait to have you on board.'

*

That's it! For once, Nat is going to make it through an entire wedding day without any dramas, frayed emotions or infighting. She steps back into the library just as the speeches are drawing to a close and everyone starts to file back out onto the heated terrace. She has an hour to go until she will be off duty so she grabs her fur shrug and enters the throng of people, all now helping themselves to colourful cocktails and frosted glasses of ice-cold champagne.

My last wedding, Nat thinks. This is what today will be, the very last time she will pull on a bridesmaid dress and have to pretend to be someone she's not. Will she miss it? No. Not when it comes with the need for a four-page spreadsheet reminding her of the politics and deceit fuelling it all. As she ducks and squeezes her way through the throng to the edge of the terrace she perches on a stone wall and looks back to the house, lit up like a Christmas tree. She can see right through it now, through the crowds, into the grand hallway with its enormous glass chandeliers, twinkling into the night. Chicly dressed bodies are draped over sofas, propping up fireplaces and perched languidly on the edge of drink-covered tables. Huge hats have been discarded and abandoned on stone statues and potted trees, and as the music climbs louder, so the wedding party dances into its final throes.

Only one man stands out from the crowd. Nat can just see the outline of him, the casual silhouette as he enters from the gravel driveway into the main house, through the giant stone door frame. He's the only man not wearing a tux. His hair is dishevelled and there is a small suitcase at his side. He's either incredibly late to the party or… Or this is it. The thing Nat has been waiting for all day that is going to knock this perfectly planned party off its course. The thing that is going to stop her flying up the stairs in ten minutes to pull on an elasticated waist and start hoovering up the minibar treats.

She can feel the tension spread across her chest as she starts to make her way back up the stone staircase. Whatever it is, she'll be the one sorting it out. Every step she takes closer towards him is tightening her throat and forcing her to steady her breath. Nat pushes her way through the boisterous crowd, fending off questions about local taxis and lost handbags, and into the relative calm of the reception hall. She knows what she can see but her brain won't let her believe it. It *can't* be him. He's more than three thousand miles away, his shape somehow not fitting here in her world.

She stands right in front of him now and can see the nervous anticipation all over his face.

'Great dress,' is all he says, through a smile that suggests he wants to get it off her as quickly as possible.

'You've come a very long way to say that. FaceTime would have been considerably cheaper, you know.' Surely there must be another reason he's here? This is some monumental coincidence, something he just neglected to mention the last time they were naked together.

'I figured I would give us a chance.' Ethan steps forward and takes her hand. 'Just give it a shot, you know? And if it all comes to nothing, it doesn't matter.' He's waiting for a sign from Nat that he hasn't called this all wrong. That he's not going to have to pick up that suitcase and call the cab back, the quickest return journey to the airport of all time.

But all Nat can think is, *what a pain in the arse*. She was going to dine out on the memory of him forever, keep him perfectly preserved in her mind, where nothing could ruin him. Now there might have to be changes and openness and honesty and putting her heart out there to risk getting it crushed.

'But how did you…?'

'Betsy. I know I shouldn't, but I got her email from the hotel registration form and she told me you'd be here tonight.' Ethan's eyes are all over Nat, failing to notice the member of staff who is trying to take his case away. 'Did I get it wrong?'

'Nat! Nat?'

She drags her eyes away from him.

'You're needed on the dancefloor!' It's Lucy and she's made so few demands of Nat today, she can hardly decline the request now.

'OK, I'm right there!' she shouts over her shoulder, but she's smiling at him. 'I have to go. Here's my key. Room eight. I'll see you up there as soon as I can.'

Chapter Twenty-Seven

Betsy

How can she want something so much and yet feel so incapable of doing the one thing that will achieve it? That's what Betsy's agonising over as she slowly turns her key in the lock of their front door. Knowing that Jacob is the other side of it, she also knows there is no escaping this conversation now. It's happening. Tonight.

The house is a tip. As soon as she pushes the door open, she can feel it connect with something hard behind it, probably another mountain of research books delivered from Amazon. Jacob has a habit of letting them accumulate, climbing higher up the wall until he can ignore them no longer – or Betsy cracks and throws them in his office. She walks through the hallway towards the kitchen, thinking she will confront him right now, before there is time to dither, change her mind or just bottle it completely. But there's no sign of him, just a stack of washing-up that smells as though it's been there since this morning, a pile of untouched Sunday papers from last weekend and two carrier bags of groceries that have been bought but not put away.

He must be in his office. Betsy moves back into the hallway, pausing at the bottom of the stairs, straining to hear any noise that will indicate where he is and what he's doing. Nothing. She looks at her reflection in the mirror hanging on the wall there, just above the little shelf where they throw their keys and loose change. She's trying to see herself as Jacob will in a few minutes' time: not the woman she was, but the woman she has become, one capable of all those lies and of stamping all over the feelings of someone she once loved. Betsy doesn't like what's looking back at her: there is a hardness and determination in her eyes that doesn't suit her.

She carefully climbs the stairs, up to the landing, where finally she can make out the click, click, click of his keyboard through the spare bedroom door. The words are obviously pouring out of him today. There is no pause, and she stands for a minute, guessing how many pages he must be steaming through, wondering what has inspired such an unusual level of productivity. And knowing it won't be anything to do with her. Should she push the door open, storm in and shout the bad news at him? No. He'll be out soon.

Betsy decides to retreat into their bedroom and pack a few things quietly before the raised voices start. There's no way she'll be able to stay here tonight. Not once he realises what's been going on and that everything between them is over. Dylan said that she should go over to his place and spend the night once this is finished. He offered to park outside and wait for her to emerge, but she's decided against that, feeling it would add to the duplicitous and premeditated agony of it all.

She's trying to find the large carry-on case they normally ram under the bed but it's not there. Bloody hell! Where is it? She hasn't got long until he hears she's back and comes out. But after checking behind the wardrobe and in the cupboard under the stairs she gives up. She hastily places everything she thinks she might need for a few nights in a carrier bag and puts it down the side of the bathroom cabinet, where she knows he won't look. A few spare pairs of knickers, some work clothes, jewellery, make-up and a framed picture of her and Mum. It's not much, she thinks, considering she has no idea how long it will be before she can face coming back for more. Then she sits on the bed and tries very hard not to cry.

Is she going to regret this in the days to come? Is she doing something tonight that will alter the course of her life, taking it down a path full of regret and bitterness? What if she never marries now and Jacob was her one chance to get it right? She thinks about the invitation to her mum and Nick's drinks on Christmas Eve – what should have been her wedding day – knowing that she will have to go alone. Christ, Jacob doesn't even know it's being planned! Betsy hasn't been alone for so long. She hasn't been the single woman in the room, having to be extra-interesting to break into all those closed couple conversations, and competing to find her place in the natural rhythm of other people's familiar, established relationships. It's an uneasy thought.

She had so much love for Jacob once. It's impossible not to feel a little wistful about the times she'd dream about him all night and still it wouldn't be enough – she'd wake, longing to see him. She thinks about all those long, lazy days, walking, holding hands and not even registering where they were going; the way he used to sit and stare at her, listening to every word she said like it was the most insightful thing ever uttered; getting so close to her on the sofa that their bodies became a permanent tangle of limbs. Then, when they were serious enough to know there would be one, plotting their future. It was all so flattering. Neither of them knew *this* was how their story would end: spare knickers and half a tube of toothpaste stuffed into a plastic carrier bag, ready for a quick getaway. And would Betsy have bothered, back then, if she had known? Would she have taken a few happy years for one miserable one? Right now, knowing the conversation she's about to have, the answer would have to be no.

Betsy's given a lot of thought to what she's going to say. She's just not sure how to package it up so it sounds less brutal. She doesn't love him any more. That's the truth. Because you can't love someone who shows their keyboard more attention than you. But can she say it? Should she? Will it crush him, making it impossible for him to find someone else to have a better life with, or will he appreciate the can't-argue-with-that clarity?

How can she live with someone this long and not know the answer to these questions, how Jacob is likely to react?

She heads downstairs, opens the fridge and pours herself the dregs of a bottle of white wine that must have been uncorked more than two weeks ago. It tastes sour, vinegary. It should be going down the sink but instead it's coating her throat, detaching her ever so slightly from the nervous anticipation that's making her head start to hum.

She's not going to tell him about Dylan. Not unless she absolutely has to, but if he asks the direct question, Betsy knows there will be no point lying. He'll see it in her face and then detest her for not crediting him with the intelligence to work it out.

As this awful scenario is playing out in her mind, she can hear the office door open upstairs.

'Betsy? Is that you?' Jacob hollers down to her.

Her eyes close and she lets a slow, controlled breath escape her. There is an angry moment when she scolds herself for not taking the cowardly way out. She could have scrawled a note, an email even. It might have been gutless but at least it would have avoided standing in front of the man she said she would marry and admitting she's let another one touch every part of her. Her face will give away that she didn't just enjoy it, she craves it. And in a way she never did with Jacob.

'Oh, you've already started on the wine then?' Jacob steps into the kitchen, his eyes falling to the glass she's clutching hard enough to shatter.

'Yeah, busy day, needed it.' She can't look at him and distracts herself, fiddling in the cutlery drawer for nothing in particular.

'Right. I'll just grab a beer, then shall we have a chat about some... wedding stuff?'

Really? He wants to talk about this now? *What a colossal mess*, thinks Betsy as she's walking through to the lounge, wondering what sort of relationship carnage they'll both be fighting their way through, ten minutes from now. Can he really believe the wedding is still happening, when so little has been planned? When they've had so few conversations about it in recent weeks? Yes, they always agreed to keep it low-key but they haven't even decided on a menu, for Christ's sake! But then again, a venue has been booked, a not insignificant deposit has been paid. Who knows what conversations he's been having without her? Maybe he just never noticed the pile of now dust-covered invitations still stuffed under the sofa? Maybe in his neurotic pursuit of writing a bestseller, he hasn't noticed *anything* else going on around him. She takes an armchair so there is no chance of him sitting next to her. Then waits for eight painful minutes while he clatters around the kitchen looking, presumably, for the bottle opener she knows is in the sink. She just can't face going back in there to help him locate it.

When he eventually appears, he's carrying a beer and a new bottle of wine he's opened. He tops up her glass without asking if she wants another, then perches on the sofa opposite her. She watches him drain nearly his entire beer in one controlled go and is struck that these are the last few moments she can consider them a couple. When he finishes, he places the bottle very deliberately at his feet, takes a deep breath and looks directly at Betsy, clearly building up to something. He's right on the edge of the sofa, legs wide open, hands gripped together in front of him.

'This wedding's not happening, is it?' It's more of a statement than a question and catches her completely off guard.

'What d'you mean?'

'Come on, Betsy, it's time for a little honesty, don't you think?' There is no anger in Jacob's voice at all, but his irritated tone does suggest that now would not be a good time to play the innocent.

'You don't want to get married?' She's carefully trying to work out what he may or may not know, what it is that has sparked this confrontation.

'Oh no! You're not pinning this one on me, I'm afraid. You're the one who doesn't want to get married. At least have the decency to admit that.' He's smirking and it's totally unnerving. Betsy can't think of anything to say in response.

'Well?'

He's not going to let her off the hook. It's like he needs to hear her say it, confirming he hasn't been imagining whatever it is he thinks he knows. The sneering annoys Betsy, giving her the confidence to deliver the answer he's looking for.

'No, I don't.' The words sound so spiteful left hanging in the air between them. Betsy curls her legs up under herself in the chair, much like an animal might roll into a ball to protect itself.

'And why is that? And were you *ever* planning to tell me?' He's getting chippy now. Like he's realised all those wasted weeks of trying to work her out were exactly that – he should have just asked her directly.

'I don't know.' Pathetic. What's happened to the speech she's been planning all the way home?

'I think you do.'

She's never seen Jacob like this before. He's being unkind, and while she's hardly one to talk, it's so unlike him to make her squirm like this.

Silence.

'Let me help you. Could it be something to do with the security code that suddenly appeared on your phone? The increasing number of nights you've needed to stay overnight in London? Or how about the way you've completely reinvented yourself – right down to the ridiculous, expensive lingerie that definitely wasn't bought for my benefit. I mean, look at you, Betsy! You look nothing like the girl I proposed to.'

He lets his eyes travel over her for a moment, working their way down the dress that's tightly skimming every inch of her, making her suddenly very conscious of her lips she's painted a deep red.

'I wonder if any of this sheds any light on why you have shown zero interest in our wedding day. Could it be, perhaps, because you knew there would never be one? You hired a professional bridesmaid, whatever that is, then left her business cards lying around. Why? Because you couldn't even be bothered to choose your own wedding dress – and you couldn't care less whether I would find that out?'

'How d'you—'

'I'm not nearly as stupid as you think I am. You've obviously been busy thinking about other things – other *people* – but it's been glaringly obvious to the rest of us. Your own mother worked you out weeks ago. She came to see me, Betsy. Did you even know that? Stood in this very room, clearly believing it was all my fault that everything was going tits up.' He's almost hanging off the sofa now, his body thrust towards her.

Betsy's cheeks flare with embarrassment and she can see the flicker of enjoyment pass across Jacob's face as he registers it. She never imagined this was a conversation he would dominate. Just how much evidence has he been mounting? She's sitting here, feeling completely exposed, desperate to bolt for the door, but knowing these things have to be said. He's going to say them, whether she likes it or not.

'I'm sorry.' It's all that quivers out of her.

'Are you? Or just sorry you're not nearly as devious as you needed to be?' He hasn't taken his eyes off her once throughout this whole conversation, not given her a second to visually compose herself. She's wondering how long he might have been planning this little speech. Longer than her one journey home from work, that's for sure.

'I didn't think you cared. You've been so engrossed in the book and—'

That makes him angry. 'Don't try and lay this on me! I've been doing that for *us*! Hoping it would be the pay day we need, to make life a little easier. But I've seen the way your eyes glaze over every time I've tried to talk to you about it, how bored you look. I've had to practically beg you to read any of it.'

Funny, it never felt like he was doing any of this for them and it's a convenient argument to make now, when they both know it's over. But she can't deny she's hated having to give him feedback on something she honestly doesn't care about. Not recently, anyway. First, she resented the fact that the book took him away for days, sometimes weeks, into a self-indulgent obsession in the spare room. But more recently? She's been glad of it. Glad that his book deal has wedged them ever further apart and his deadlines have given her an excuse to disappear out of the house for the day.

'You never rated it, did you? Do you know how hard it's been seeing my own girlfriend have no confidence in what I'm doing? It's hardly inspiring! You never thought I'd get anywhere with it, did you?'

She really can't answer that one and lets her head sink towards her lap. Having all her failures as a human being laid bare like this is making Betsy's eyes fill with tears of shame. She can't think of a single thing to say to justify herself. Because however righteous she may have felt at the time, she just looks a coward now for never speaking up and saying what she really felt about Jacob, their life together and their joke of a wedding.

'What happens now?' She knows he'll have an answer. He can't have thought this far through everything and not known how they will resolve it all. She's totally on the back foot.

'I've cancelled everything that needs to be cancelled – which was depressingly little, actually. We're going to have a real battle on our hands to see any of the deposit back from the venue, but that's hardly surprising.'

'Oh, right.' She's not sure whether to feel grateful he's had the awkward conversations with suppliers or even more ridiculous that while she's been tiptoeing around him, he was ensuring this wedding was never going to happen.

'I did it weeks ago, Betsy.'

She's nearly at the bottom of her second glass of wine, knowing she'll finish the entire bottle tonight. 'How are we going to…?' Her eyes are moving around the room, trying to convey what her mouth doesn't seem capable of.

'How are we going to live together now? Is that what you're trying to ask?'

'Yes.'

'We're not. I've rented a small flat a few miles from here. It's in the opposite direction to the station so there is no chance we'll be bumping into each other.'

The tears are flowing down her face now, powered by humiliation more than anything.

'It's a bit late for all that, don't you think?'

The fact that Jacob is being so heartless about all of this, not giving her an inch, is making Betsy feel so sad. He obviously mentally checked out of their relationship some time ago. So did she, of course, but there is something mortifying in the realisation that he seems to care so little about the fact they're over. There is nothing sensitive about the way he's delivering his revelations tonight. She had at least spent some time wondering how she would break the news to him gently, with the least amount of damage to his feelings. He doesn't seem to care how much any of this is upsetting her.

'There's still a lot to sort out with the house and everything, so I suggest we communicate over email, since I won't be here. Might be less awkward.' He's on his feet now.

'You're going now? Tonight?' Betsy rises from the sofa too, almost feeling like she needs to stop him. Like there must be more to say and she wants to find a way to end it more pleasantly than this. She wants a hug or a good luck, or something that tells her there will be no hard feelings.

She's not going to get it.

She follows him out into the hallway and watches as he flies up the stairs in a hurry to grab his laptop and a couple of notebooks. Then he's back, standing next to her, and that's when she sees what was hiding behind the door, impeding her entrance earlier. The suitcase she was looking for. Already packed with all *his* belongings.

'Let's just try and keep this as civilised as we can, shall we? I'll be in touch.'

Then he's gone, out the door and out of her life. She's been dumped and the tears are choking out of her in a way that is totally unexpected.

They are officially over, but what's really shocking is how much better he's handled their demise than she has.

Betsy returns to the lounge, slumps down onto the sofa and instinctively makes a grab for her phone, wanting more than anything to speak to her mum. Then she sees a text from Dylan.

You on your way yet?

She won't be going to his place. That will mean reliving tonight's humiliating events and that's the last thing she can face right now.

Chapter Twenty-Eight

Helen

'I can't decide, Betsy. The rose red or the café au lait. What do you think?'

'Both are lovely, Mum, but what are you wearing? Do you want your nails to match with it, or contrast?'

Helen and Betsy are side by side in one of the manicure booths in Fenwick's department store. And Helen is suddenly incapable of making a single decision.

'Actually, that's a surprise. You'll see tomorrow, but I'm just not sure if it should be…'

'OK, it's just your nails, Mum. Stop fussing. No one will be looking at them, except you. I'll decide for you. Go for the café au lait, it's more classy.'

'Yes, you're right. That's best.' Helen nods towards the beauty therapist opposite them, who looks highly relieved to finally be able to proceed.

As she starts to shape and buff Helen's nails, two glasses of champagne appear in front of them and Helen leans sideways in to Betsy, smiling, feeling more content than she has in a very long time.

'Thank you for coming today. It means everything to me that you're here.' Helen's spirits are lifted skywards by the gentle tinkle of Christmas carols being piped through the beauty hall and the it's-nearly-Christmas fever that seems to be gripping everyone around them. There is tinsel draped across every shelf, gift boxes full of co-ordinating beauty products screaming to be bought, enormous green and red garlands suspended in loops above their heads and delicate glass baubles, in every colour, neatly placed on every spare inch of counter.

'You're so soft, Mum!'

'I know, but I mean it. You've had so much to deal with and I'm touched you found the time to come today. Have you spoken to Jacob since last week?' Helen's not entirely sure whether to take the conversation in this direction but it's the first time she's seen Betsy since she called the night Jacob left. Nearly an hour was lost on that phone call, as Helen struggled to understand a word Betsy was saying through uncontrolled sobs and wails of, *I've made such a fool of myself, Mum!*

'A few terse emails. Demands to get the house on the market as soon as Christmas is out of the way. Some dates and times when he's planning to come and collect his things and instructions for me not to be there when he does. He's obviously moved on, Mum. And, well, I can hardly blame him for that, can I?' Betsy's eyes don't leave her champagne flute while she's relaying all this to Helen, who can see the therapist is trying, and failing, not to listen.

'How do you feel about it all?' She needs to have this conversation with her daughter and if it has to be done in front of an audience, then so be it. She needs convincing that Betsy is going to be OK at the drinks reception tomorrow – Christmas Eve. That there won't be any further outbursts.

'A bit hollow, really. And embarrassed.' Betsy manages a vague smile through a sideways glance at her mum. 'You know, for thinking I was being so clever, for not crediting him with the intelligence to work any of it out and for stupidly believing I could fool anyone. When I look back over the past three months, it's like I'm seeing a different person. I went to such lengths to put myself in Dylan's path and out of Jacob's. I'll just never understand why Jacob didn't stop me. Why he didn't say something, challenge me, give me some awful ultimatum? Anything would have been better than letting me humiliate myself, day after day.'

'I'm guessing he didn't think he owed you that.' Betsy's her daughter and Helen loves her deeply, but she also wants to be honest with her. Betsy broke the trust she and Jacob had and therefore has no right now to moan about his lack of consideration. Helen drops her free left hand to Betsy's thigh and gives it a quick rub, just to let her know that despite what she's saying, she'll always be on Team Betsy.

'Thanks, Mum. I just hope one day I get a chance to properly apologise to him, when he stops hating me as much as he does right now.'

'That day will come, I'm sure it will.' It's so reassuring for Helen to see the old Betsy is returning; one who cares what people think of her and is determined to do the right thing, no matter how awkward it might be or how long it takes. 'For now, he has the book deal to think about, which will be a brilliant distraction, until someone else comes along, and she will.' Helen's also reassured to see that last comment raises no reaction from Betsy, not one flicker of regret or jealousy that another woman will inevitably end up sharing Jacob's life.

'And what about Dylan? How are things between you both?'

'I've barely seen him.' Betsy shakes her head and allows her shoulders to visibly drop a couple of inches. 'I know he's just trying to give me the time and space to deal with all the Jacob stuff, but I miss him so much. The two weeks before Christmas are always manic for him, he's trying to lock everything down before everyone disappears for the holidays. And I've been needed in the Birmingham office more.'

'Yes, of course.' Helen's not entirely sure she understands this. Wouldn't Dylan make time for Betsy, no matter what, given what she's going through? Betsy, perhaps sensing how inadequate her explanation sounds, continues.

'He was mortified about Nick walking in on us – we both were – and there is a part of me wondering if he just thinks the whole thing is better left. I also wonder if he's still stinging from the fact I had said I should make a go of it with Jacob. He doesn't know how that conversation really panned out and I'll have to be honest with him about it when we talk properly.'

'Maybe just give it time? It's a funny time of year, isn't it, Christmas? Everyone's emotions heighted, stress levels through the roof. Maybe just give him a bit of space, allow there to be some distance between you both, then tackle it in January with a clear head and fresh eyes, if you know what I mean?'

Helen can tell from the sad nod of Betsy's head that this is not what her daughter is hoping for. She wants a big, romantic gesture, Helen can see it in her eyes and the way this turn in the conversation is encouraging the champagne to disappear quicker. Betsy wants a sign that someone out there can't live without her; the Hollywood ending where Dylan swoops in, makes everything OK, confirming all the highs and lows of the past few months were worth it in the end. But is her daughter going to get it? Is she going to get a surprise gift on her doorstep Christmas morning, or an unexpected ring of the doorbell later on tonight – something that might confirm his adoration, despite everything?

'More than anything, I'm just relieved. Whatever happens now, at least I'm not living a lie – not doing a daily battle with the guilt of all that bullshit.'

Helen shoots her daughter a frown. 'Betsy!'

'Shit, sorry! Argh! Sorry again. You know what I mean.'

The therapist starts giggling. 'Oops, I'm sorry too! I have been trying not to listen but it's not easy when we're this close.' The three of them share a few laughs before the therapist adds, 'Actually, it's so lovely to see a mum and daughter get on so well. Usually they sit here and don't say a word to each other for forty-five minutes. One will be glued to her phone, the other all stroppy because she's feeling ignored. Top-up, ladies?' Then she excuses herself to fetch the bubbles and refresh her tools for Betsy's mani.

'So, Nick mentioned you two met for a coffee. To clear the air.' Helen can feel herself smile at the mere mention of his name.

'We did. He's so lovely, Mum. I really like him. After you gave me his number, I called and fluffed my way through some pathetic attempt at an apology. Then he suggested we grab a coffee. I think he knew that seeing each other was the only way to rub out all the awkwardness I caused. And he was right. I'm so sorry, Mum. I'm not sure I can ever say it enough to make you forget about that awful afternoon in the boutique.' She buries her head in her hands, reliving the aggressive confrontation with Nick all over again. 'Are you serious about him?'

'Very. I love him, Betsy, and that's not something I ever imagined I would be able to say about another man.' Helen is facing Betsy now, looking intently at her, studying her face for any sign that this wounds her daughter, feeling tense that despite her obvious approval of Nick, she might not be ready to fully accept him into their little family. 'Is that OK with you? It doesn't make you sad in any way that

I'm moving on with my life?' Helen looks at Betsy, like the answer to this question can't possibly be more important. 'Be honest, please.' She holds her breath.

'He's so good for you, Mum. Don't lose him, too.' Betsy chokes out the last few words and then, without warning, and as much as she's trying to keep them in, tears stream down her face.

'Oh darling, I'll never forget him, you know that, don't you? I'll never stop loving him. Half my heart will always belong to your dad.' Helen's eyes glass over, and she is close to weeping herself, knowing what a bittersweet moment this is for both of them. 'I still dream about him sometimes. And he's so vivid, so alive to me, I feel like I can almost touch him. But they're happy dreams now. I wake up smiling, not crying.' She pulls Betsy in to her, being the strong one. She's not going to cry today, not when she's on the verge of something so exciting with Nick. There is too much to be happy and grateful for.

Four more glasses of fizz and two perfect manicures later, Helen and Betsy stumble out into the crisp early afternoon sunshine and the swarm of last-minute demented Christmas shoppers. Helen waits until Betsy has started her walk up Bond Street towards Oxford Street and the tube, her heart aching slightly at the thought that her daughter will wake up on Christmas morning alone. Then she heads down Brook Street, past Claridge's, pausing only to collect a frothy all-white bouquet of garden roses from a tiny florist on Davies Street. She decides against taking a taxi and walks back through the brilliant December sunshine to the boutique, where she knows Nat will be waiting for her.

*

'The Bruce Oldfield dress you asked me to steam is all done and hanging in the fitting room. I found some time to buff the shoes you laid out next to it and— wow, what beautiful flowers! Can I pop them in some water for you?'

'Thank you, you're an angel.' Helen's already wondering how on earth she coped before Nat agreed to come on board.

Nat is every bit as efficient as Helen was hoping she'd be. She's not even officially beginning her new role managing the boutique until the new year but insisted she had a clear diary and should come in and start learning the ropes. It's the only reason Helen was able to spare the time to catch up with Betsy today – and she already loves Nat for that.

Once the flowers are in water in the kitchen at the back of the boutique, Nat fills Helen in on everything she's done today.

'Miss Jenkins collected her Freya Rose shoes and paid the balance. Then I updated all your diary appointments, copying them from the emails into the concertina file, just as you said you like it. The whole place has been hoovered and polished and I've added some new appointments to the diary for January. Seems a few people have already opened diamond rings this Christmas, because we've had quite a few calls. Will you let me do some fittings with you in the new year, Helen? I'm really keen to get cracking!'

Helen doesn't answer. Instead, she steps forward, wraps her arms around a clearly startled Nat and thanks her over and over again for *being the right-hand woman I know I need.*

'You really don't need to thank me. I think it's you who has saved *me*, actually. Although our orders of bridesmaids' dresses may plummet a little now. Anyway, if there's nothing else, I'd better get going.'

'Yes, of course, off you go.' Just as Helen is closing the door behind Nat, she spins back around and holds her hand out.

'I almost forgot to ask. Would it be OK if I bring a friend to the drinks tomorrow, Helen? Sorry, I hope you don't mind me asking. It's an American, an… er… a surprise visitor and, well, they don't know anyone else here.'

There's something in the way Nat coyly tucks her hair behind her left ear and tries and fails to stifle a giant smile that makes Helen smirk. 'I can't wait to meet him – I assume it is a him?'

'Yes. It's Ethan. Ethan Miller. He's staying with me for a while. I think you'll like him.'

'Great. Make sure you introduce me.' She watches Nat disappear up the road as the familiar figure of Nick is approaching the shop. Even from a distance she can see he's full of beans, his walk more of a bounce than a stride. He's perfectly groomed and wearing the sort of smile that makes Helen's heart swell with love and pride.

'What a lovely surprise!'

Nick steps into the boutique and plants a passionate kiss on Helen's lips before she's even had a chance to step back out of the doorway.

'Well, I have a Christmas present to deliver, don't I? I'm not going to have time to monopolise you tomorrow, so I thought I would hand deliver it this evening, along with this.' He pulls a bottle of pink champagne out from behind his back and Helen catches herself thinking once again, *is this really happening to me*?

'Oh no, in all the rush to get everything done, I haven't bought you anything! I feel terrible now.'

'Don't be ridiculous, Helen. I never expected anything and, actually, this gift is sort of for the two of us anyway. Go on, sit down, get opening and I'll pour the fizz.'

When he returns from the kitchen with two full glasses, Helen is already breaking through the thick metallic wrapping paper, being careful not to chip her freshly painted nails. She can feel it's a heavy silver photo frame, then sees it's inlaid with pretty mother-of-pearl detail – he's obviously chosen something that will work perfectly in the boutique. He's placed a picture inside for her, too. It's of the two of them together, taken in Hyde Park by a passer-by, that day on the bench, just as the first snow was starting to fall. Helen is smiling directly at the camera so hadn't appreciated at the time the way Nick is looking at her like nothing else in the world matters. They both look so happy.

'I love it.' Helen holds it between her fingers, feeling herself fill with emotion. She knows what Nick is hoping for and she's ready to do it. She turns to face him, placing her hand on his left cheek, then giving him the sweetest thank you kiss. Without saying another word, she places the photo on the central table, next to the others she's collected over the years. Then she lifts the one of her and Phillip on their wedding day and moves it close to the till, next to a roll of crisp white tissue paper that she uses to carefully wrap accessories before her brides take them home.

They enjoy the champagne together, running through last-minute canapé orders and timings for tomorrow.

'Are you ready, Helen?' Nick is so full of excitement it's sending a wonderful spike of nervous energy right up through her. She takes a deep breath.

'Yes, I think I am.' Helen moves closer to him, allowing her head to gently topple onto his shoulder. 'I love you.'

'Then I wonder if you would let me give you this, too?' Nick has pulled the red Cartier box from his pocket and opens it to reveal the pear-shaped diamond ring that he first offered her over lunch in Scott's that day. She smiles to herself now, remembering how she had bolted from the restaurant, regretting her actions almost the second she was outside.

'I wouldn't mind at all.' She sits up straight, not taking her eyes off Nick's face as she feels the coolness of the ring sliding onto her finger.

The perfect fit. When her gaze drops to her lap, it takes her breath away. It's the most exquisite piece of jewellery she will ever own. Then, without realising it, her hand moves up to her neck, her fingers reaching for the necklace she wears every day, feeling for the initials of her little family and the two rings from Phillip that sat for thirty-five years on the finger Nick is still holding.

'It's OK, Helen, I'd never ask you to take it off. I understand Phillip will always be part of your life. He helped shape the woman you are, the woman I love, and if he were here now, I'd thank him for that. I'm going to look after you, Helen, just as he would want me to.'

They sit then, wrapped in each other's arms, each of them occasionally throwing out reminders of things the other one said they'd organise for tomorrow.

'Cake napkins?'

'Don't worry, the hotel is providing them.'

'Did you confirm the cocktail choice?'

'Yes, all sorted.'

'And the numbers that are staying the night?'

'All taken care of.'

'We're ready then,' Nick says finally, draining the last mouthful of champagne from his glass.

'I'd say we are. Yes.'

They share one last conspiratorial smile.

'And I can't persuade you to come home with me tonight?' He raises an eyebrow, his face full of hope.

'No. Let's do this properly, shall we? I'll see you tomorrow, don't be late.'

*

After waving Nick off down Connaught Street, Helen closes the door and steps back inside the boutique. She circulates one last time, making sure everything is as it should be – she won't be back for nearly two weeks. She switches off all the lights and turns the sign on the door to 'closed'. In the near darkness she returns to the till, picks up the framed image of herself and Phillip and holds it close to her chest.

'Goodbye, Phillip,' she says aloud. 'Wish me luck for tomorrow, my darling.' Then she wraps the beautiful old frame in three layers of white tissue paper and places it in the drawer under the till, next to a selection of her favourite Estée Lauder fragrances and some loose pictures of her favourite brides.

She steps out into the twilight of London, on this most exciting of evenings, seeing the light bounce warmly off her engagement ring. It already feels completely at home on her hand.

Chapter Twenty-Nine

Jenny

Can this really be happening? Can I really be going to Helen and Nick's gorgeous Christmas drinks wearing something that belongs to Marianne? Sadly, yes, I can. It's only happening because she buggered off to Victoria train station this morning with every decent thing I own, rammed into three Sainsbury's carrier bags. When I yanked open my wardrobe doors this afternoon, ready to carefully select my outfit, it was almost bare. A few well-worn summer dresses – that haven't fitted me for at least three years – looking tragically rejected on their tangled wire coat hangers, plus a highly flammable nylon nurse's outfit I wore to the work's Christmas do last year. That's actually the one thing I thought she might have swiped, considering she's off for another one of her liaisons with heaven knows who. Because there's no pause for Marianne, no moment of reverence while we celebrate the Lord's birthday.

So, I have no choice but to plunder her own fashion cast-offs and the choices are terrifyingly limited. Once I discount anything dirty, see-through or just too complicated to work out how to put on, I'm left with two options: a purple velour jumpsuit that is extremely tight around the crotch and has a comedy thick band of silver sequins running down the outside of each leg, or to go shopping for something I can't afford. I opt for the jumpsuit but add some sensible black block heels and a smart boxy handbag I've had since early job interview days. It will have to do. I am just about getting away with it, I think.

Thank goodness for the distraction of these Christmas drinks. I am trying to put all thoughts of the shitstorm at work behind me. I'm not due back there until mid-January. After *the incident*, as it was referred to in the days that followed, Jean suggested it would be in the best interests of everyone if I took a bit of time off. It broke my heart to hear her say that. She added she would *square it away* with management and that it would give me some time to think about what I did and hopefully negate the need for an uncomfortable official inquiry. I think she also wants to see if Mr and Mrs Marshall make a formal complaint too. I'm a goner if they do and I've accepted that.

The good news is Baby Rudy is fine, and the family were discharged as normal, in plenty of time for Christmas together. But a week on, whenever I think about the moment I let every professional responsibility follow me out the door of the labour room, I can feel my heart banging so fast, like it's trying to overtake itself. I have to physically stop myself thinking about all the different possible endings to Mrs Marshall's story. Conclusions I could have created in one fleeting moment of stupidity. I still can't quite believe I did it. Maybe this was someone's way of saying enough's enough*? Step away from the buttercream towers now, please, Jenny. Close the Pinterest account. Stop making appointments at bridal boutiques, you mentalist!*

This is why I need a mum. Someone who would sit quietly and listen to all this madness, then cuddle me and love me just the same. All I've got is a pile of letters – well, one unread letter left, to be precise.

I open it today, even though the words on the front couldn't be further from my own feelings. *When you're feeling brave*, it says. Urgh! Hardly. Why didn't she ever write one called *When you've been a dick* or *When you've made a massive arse of yourself*? The handwriting is barely legible, shaky, maybe she had to write it over several days. And even now, twelve years on, I can see the page is watermarked with her tears. It's crumpled and creased. Did she screw it up? Write the whole thing through all that pain and then debate whether or not to keep it? I'm glad she did, even though I can feel the sorrow in every one of her words.

Sweet Jenny, I think this is the last letter I will ever write to you. I so wish I could take all the love I feel for you and find a way to let it flow from my pen straight to your heart, to keep you warm when I'm gone. I want you to feel it. To know how much I loved you, will always love you. I look at you sometimes and the easy, uncomplicated way you approach life and I wonder if you have any concept of how big my love is. Perhaps when you have your own children you will get some sense of how the worst thing about any of this is letting go of you. Nothing else matters to me. I feel so damn cheated, Jenny. Not for all the special moments I will miss, but for all the times you'll never be able to pick up the phone to me. Angry that it will be someone else's advice that you're forced to seek. Find a friend, Jenny. Someone older and wiser who will always have your best interests at heart. You are so easy to love, someone else will be honoured to do that. All of this will be easier for you when I'm gone. There will be less disappointment.

I wanted to pull you onto the bed with me today and whisper a thousand I love yous in your ear, but I just couldn't risk you sensing how very close the end might be. I wanted to give you just a few precious more minutes not worrying about me. I see the way the concern clouds your face every time you sit with me, not realising just how much comfort you bring. Just feeling the softness of your hand in mine has lifted me to a beautiful pain-free place. Thank you, Jenny. You've given me a memory full of wonderful pictures of you. Every time I close my eyes, there you are. I will never be lonely.

Keep an eye on Lulu for me, will you? She's clever and sensible but she's never been good with her own company – and she lacks your boundless capacity to love. Watch over her for me, please. Be the sister she needs. And always remember I would take all that life has thrown at me, a hundred times over, to have you as my daughter. You are the one thing I will never regret. Being your mummy is the greatest honour of my life. Now live your life, Jenny. Live it honestly and people will love you just as much as I do.

Your devoted mum x

I don't know exactly how long I sit on the edge of my bed, holding the letter, sobbing, but it's hours, and by the end of it I feel like I have nothing left to give. I just sit there picturing my sixteen-year-old self like it was yesterday. The pretty blue and white striped Breton dress I was wearing the day Mum finally let go and how I didn't brush my hair for three weeks afterwards because I just couldn't see the point of looking pretty. Why bother brushing my hair when everything else about me said *keep away*? Dad didn't even notice.

Then I start to think about some of the other women I know. Helen and her ungrateful daughter, Betsy. Lulu and the sacrifices she's made for her career. Lucy and the husband she only mildly tolerates. Jean and her childless home. Everyone is handling life without the need to try on big wedding dresses or buy honeymoon lingerie that will never be worn.

The thought of Jean reminds me that she knows there isn't going to be a wedding. What I don't know is whether she's told anyone else – although I screamed it so loudly at her at the time, I suspect everyone in the department knows it. Not one person texted or called afterwards. All those women who were happy to sit downing cocktails with me a few days before don't want to know me now, and it's making me think I can never go back. How can I face them all? I'll be a pariah. Maybe some of them, now that the circle of trust has been broken, will refuse to work with me.

It's 5.15 p.m. and I need to get going. The drinks start at 6.30 and I don't want to be late for Helen. I cast a quick eye over myself in the full-length mirror in the hallway and realise, too late, that there's a nasty brown stain on the jumpsuit around the left boob. I pause, debating whether to sniff it, knowing there is no other option to change into. Then I retreat to my room and grab a brooch I inexplicably bought years ago in a car boot sale for three quid and have never worn. A giant ladybird with shiny glass stones clustered in red and black, it covers the stain perfectly. I look ridiculous, but I'm off – looking a berk is the least of my worries right now.

I have no idea what I'm going to say to Helen about the lack of Will, my fiancé. The only sensible option is to come clean. It's what Mum would have wanted, but perhaps surprisingly, it's what I want too. I haven't got the energy to keep up with the story-telling anymore, I don't want to be that person. My only hope is that there will be some shred of understanding from Helen, that she'll hear me out and not just ask the hotel security to escort me to the door.

*

The Hamilton Penthouse looks like an extension of The White Gallery – like it was designed and decorated with Helen herself in mind.

Everything is white, or a shade of, and as I step onto the bright marble floor, I am hit by the sweet smell of an impressive floral display that sits on a high silver table in the entrance hall. About thirty crystal vases of all shapes and sizes are filled with the purest white flowers, broken only by an occasional branch or stem sprayed silver. It is all impossibly elegant, and I feel my hand move upwards and over the brooch. I was, at least, wise enough to ditch the duffle coat in the cloakroom off the lobby. Bloody hell! Just as I'm wondering how many drinks I'll need before I stop caring how weird I look, a waiter wearing white gloves places a perfectly chilled flute of champagne in my hand. I'm already thinking purple velour's not half as rank as it sounds.

So far, I don't recognise anyone, but I'm happy to wander. To my right is a small dining room with one central circular table, framed by heavy silk drapes and mirrored walls. It is covered in a crease-free white tablecloth that sweeps the floor and enough Christmas canapés to feed a hundred guests, despite there being less than thirty that I've seen so far. Tapered white candles flicker delicately in glass candelabras, sending the softest light bouncing around the room. Further into the penthouse, there is a larger drawing room dominated by a white Christmas tree. Its branches look heavy with snow and are filled with hundreds of tiny glass domes, strings of expensive-looking oversized pearls, life-like feathered doves and cascading silver stars. Across the room there is a log fire burning and it's here that Nick introduces himself to me.

'You must be Jenny?'

'Nick?'

He confirms it with a nod, then plants a kiss on both my cheeks.

Once again, I have to admire Helen's taste. Nick is super-handsome in a black tux with a small white rose attached to his left lapel. This is a major effort for Christmas Eve drinks and definitely beats the microwave meal and crap telly that was my planned evening.

'Helen will be over the moon that you made it. Did you come alone, no Will?'

Helen has obviously briefed him but I'm not ready to get into all that just yet. Perhaps after another glass or two of fizz.

'I'm afraid not, but thank you so much for having me. This place is incredible! Do you always do something so glamorous on Christmas Eve?' I'm glancing around, taking in how impeccably smart everyone looks. All the men, perhaps work associates and close friends of Nick's, are wearing lounge suits and are dotted around the room in clusters of three or four, easing into the party and excitedly chatting about their plans for tomorrow. The women must have looked this place up in advance because all of them are blending seamlessly with the muted décor, wearing a uniform of soft greys, caramels and rose golds. No one else is in purple velour. All the glittering Quality Street colours of Christmas have been left outside in the mad bustle around Trafalgar Square.

Nick chuckles. 'Not always, no, but this year feels extra special.' His smile is so warm, I can see how Helen would be completely seduced by it.

'I haven't seen Helen. Is she here yet?' I was relying on her to introduce me to a few people and I'm starting to feel a bit panicked at the prospect of Nick leaving me.

He nods skywards. 'She's upstairs in the bedroom, just putting the finishing touches to her outfit, I think. She won't be long. We're just waiting for a few stragglers, then I'll make a toast. Don't miss it! Ah, can I introduce you to Betsy, Helen's daughter?'

Betsy is suddenly beside us and not at all what I imagined. She lacks all the warmth of Helen and, to be honest, looks a bit bloody miserable, like she's only going to smile when she thinks she must.

'Hi, Betsy, Helen has told me so much about you. I'm Jenny, one of her, er, clients.' I hold my hand out and study her face for any sign that Helen may have discussed me with her, but she looks entirely disinterested. Her handshake is weak, and her eyes are away over my shoulder and back towards the door. I wonder who she might be missing. There are none of Helen's exquisite manners here.

'Nice to meet you…' She clearly fails to remember my name.

Nick excuses himself to chat to the one woman – other than me – who looks out of place here. She's in the corner near the Christmas tree and looks vaguely corporate in a black trouser suit. She's glancing at her watch and conferring with Nick on something, perhaps the timing of his toast.

As I'm starting to think I may have to stand here all night with Betsy – in silence – another woman bounds over to join us.

'Betsy! Get that down you.'

If I'm not mistaken, this ball of energy thrusting some fizz at Betsy appears to be wearing a bridesmaid's dress. It's lilac, full-length, and while it lacks the potency of the bright purple I'm wearing, it is at least different to all the other women. Thank goodness, a comrade – I hope.

'Nat, you came! Brilliant!' That seems to have snapped Betsy out of her melancholy at least. Then she turns to the man at Nat's left shoulder. 'And hi, Ethan. Don't worry, I don't plan to get nearly as smashed as the last time I saw you. You're safe.'

The three of them are busy embracing each other, forgetting I'm here too, and so it's left to Ethan to include me.

'I'm sorry. I'm American, so excuse the total lack of manners. Ethan. Fantastic to meet you…?'

'Jenny, hello.' He has hold of me by both shoulders and hugs me so tightly, he is in danger of impaling himself on the ladybird.

'Jenny. Where's the food? Have you sniffed it out yet? I'm starving!'

I direct Ethan back to the dining room and Betsy follows him, leaving Nat and me to chat.

'So, how do you know Helen? Or are you a friend of Nick's?' Nat is guzzling her own fizz so fast, splashes of it are spilling onto the bodice of her dress and fanning out, making it look much worse. She notices, but just raises her eyebrows like this is totally normal behaviour.

'I'm a client of Helen's. Well, I *was*.'

'Oh cool, when did you get married? And what did you wear?' Her interest in me is raised.

'I chose the Hayley Paige embroidered ballgown, but I'm not married. The, um, the wedding's off, actually.' *Surely she will move on and not question me any further on it?*

'Oh, right. What did you say your name was? Jenny?'

'Yes.'

'Jenny Archer?'

Where is this going? 'Yes. How did you—?'

'I'm Natalie Butler. Nat. I'm the new boutique manager at Helen's London White Gallery. I was looking at your order the other day and wondering what was happening there. I just haven't had a chance to talk to Helen about it.'

'Oh, right.' *What are the chances?* Of all the people to get chatting to tonight, it has to be Nat. I can't think of a single other thing to say so I just let my mouth dip and my eyes find the floor between us.

'Listen, don't worry about it. Whatever's wrong, I'm sure we can work it out.' Her hand lands on my shoulder and there is something in the confident, understanding way she looks at me that makes me feel like unloading everything to her.

'It's all a bit of a mess, really. I haven't exactly been that honest with a lot of people and, well, it's catching up with me. The last thing I want to do is upset Helen, I'm just not sure she'll understand when she finds out what's been going on with me. I was going to try to chat to her tonight.'

Her face opens up into the warmest smile that reminds me of Helen, far more so than Betsy does.

'Jenny, you don't know this about me yet, but I am somewhat of an expert when it comes to talking my way out of things. Trust me, whatever it is, we'll get you out of it. In fact, I'm having drinks at the boutique next week. It's a bit of a relaunch to mark me taking over. Why don't you pop along, and we can chat properly then, if you like?'

'Really?' Yes! *Maybe this is it? The moment I've been waiting for. I can come clean to Nat and come up with a plan to break all this to Helen in a way that won't make her think any less of me.*

'Of course!'

Before I have a chance to thank her we are rejoined by Betsy and Ethan and I notice the room has got a little more crowded while we've been chatting. Nick is still with the woman in the black suit and suddenly he's tapping the side of his glass with a knife. The room silences and no one looks quite sure why, until he says, 'Come and join me, Helen.'

In one fluid movement, we all turn back towards the hallway. Helen is standing there, holding a bunch of snow white roses, tied with a thick cream ribbon. Her hair is neatly tucked in under a beautiful ivory teardrop hat, with a delicate face veil that stops just short of her rose-coloured lips. She stands perfectly still for a moment, letting everyone in the room register the surprise. Then there is the most wonderful collective gasp as we all start to make eye contact, sure now of what we're seeing. The only movement Helen makes is to let her gaze travel across to Betsy. The two of them look at each other and I see a tear run down Betsy's face as she slowly nods her head, allowing herself the first genuine smile of the night. Only once Helen sees it does she start to walk towards Nick, as we all part, forming the natural aisle of which she is so deserving.

I can't help it, I start to cry. Nat does, too. And I can see Nick isn't far off either. We've all been completely duped. We all believed we were simply here to nibble a mince pie or two before it was time to race home for some last-minute present wrapping. As Helen reaches Nick, he places a tender kiss on her lips and holds her in his arms, making their audience wait while he enjoys the anticipation of what is about to happen. Then, in front of the twinkling Christmas tree and a room fizzing with emotion, they exchange their wedding vows: Nick promising to devote the rest of his life to protecting her heart and keeping her safe; Helen thanking him for filling her life with a joy she never thought possible. It is the most magical, meaningful thing I will ever witness.

Just as Nick is delivering his first married kiss, I see something change in Betsy's face as she does an audible intake of breath. It's loud enough to send even Nick and Helen's eyes back towards the entrance, where I can see another man has quietly joined our party. He's older than Betsy, greying slightly. My heart lurches a little at the thought that something might be about to upset this perfect evening, until I see Nick mouth the words 'I invited Dylan' to Helen and I relax again. I watch as Dylan picks his way through the crowd to Betsy, who looks like a different woman to the sullen one who greeted me earlier. There is a joy in her face now, like she just unwrapped the best Christmas present imaginable.

I spend the next forty minutes trying to get close enough to Helen to congratulate her, but I'm constantly beaten to it by other guests and all we've managed so far is a wave across the room. Then Nick announces there is one more surprise.

We all head up a wide marble staircase to a terrace on the top floor of the penthouse, where there are wrap-around views of the city skyline. It's surprisingly mild outside tonight and none of us needs the cosy cashmere wraps Helen and Nick have thoughtfully provided. More champagne is served and then, without warning, the sky explodes above us into a colourful firework display that has everyone squealing with delight. I'm still trying to locate Helen; the evening is drawing to its conclusion and I must speak to her before it's all over.

Then I feel an arm slide across my shoulders. Helen pulls me in to her and I allow the comforting familiarity of her powdery floral perfume to envelope me completely. I can see Nick is looking across the sea of heads for her and she nods at him, letting him know she's needed here with me for now.

'I'm so happy for you, Helen. You deserve all this, and it's wonderful being part of it with you.' I can hear the blurred edges of my words rolling into each other and feel my legs buckling slightly beneath me.

'I'm not sure it would have been the same without you, Jenny.' She plants the softest lingering kiss on my forehead and I feel nothing but total gratitude for this incredible woman.

'Even though there's no Will tonight?' I wasn't going to go there but more than anything, I want this evening to be genuine, for both of us.

Helen pauses. I sense her head shift so she's looking at me but I can't look back at her. Not yet.

'Even if there never was a Will.' She says it so softly, tightening her grip on me as she does so.

I swear, my heart stops beating while I wait for her to continue. She must feel how my body has stiffened under her hold because she starts to rub her hand up and down my arm, like she's trying to loosen me up.

'I think I've known for a while that your father was never coming to pay for the dress, Jenny. I was just hoping you would tell me yourself. I wanted to give you that chance.'

'And I blew it.'

'No, darling. You haven't blown anything. Perhaps it was just more obvious to me than you realised. No pics of Will on your phone, you stumbling over the wedding date, then the phone call that your sister answered. I thought I'd let the cat out of the bag but there was never any secret to reveal, was there?' She's manoeuvred herself in front of me now so there is no avoiding her gaze.

'No.' All around me people are cheering and whooping but the thought that Helen might be disappointed in me is stopping me sharing in the collective joy.

'Tonight is not the night for explanations.' She's holding my face in her hands now, smoothing my hair back behind my ears. 'But I want you to know you are not alone. I can see you need someone and I would love it if you would consider letting that be me? I am here for you, if you'd like me to be. I will love you like you are my own daughter, Jenny. Honestly, I think I already do. Everything else will follow, when it's ready. One day, some day, you will find true happiness, because you deserve it.'

And for the first time since I innocently pulled that Breton dress over my shoulders that awful morning, I think everything might just work out OK.

'One day, some day. Yes, you're right, Helen.'

We both gaze upwards, allowing our heads to move together. No more words are needed, on this, the night I discover the true meaning of love.

A Letter from Jade

I want to say a huge thank you for choosing to read *What I Didn't Say*. If you enjoyed it and want to keep up-to-date with my latest releases, just sign up at the following link. Your email address will never be shared with anyone else and you can unsubscribe at any time:

www.bookouture.com/jade-beer

If you've ever posted a picture on social media that makes your life look a little bit more together than it is, this book could be for you. If you've told the odd little white lie to gloss over something, make a niggling problem disappear or expedite your way out of trouble, this book could also be for you. If you're planning a wedding, are already married or have somehow found yourself in a bridal boutique, helping a friend into a wedding gown, and stood there questioning what it's all about, this is also a book for you. It's also a book for me, since I have done all of these things, some many times over.

The reaction to my debut novel, *The Almost Wife*, was so heart-soaringly positive, you all connected with the women in my story so well, how could I not bring a couple of them back for more? So, Helen and her daughter Betsy have returned in *What I Didn't Say*, but this time they're joined by a whole new cast of characters that I hope will make you laugh and cry just as hard. Their experiences are, in part at least, the culmination of seven years editing *Condé Nast Brides*, witnessing all the emotions that a woman goes through. Not just on her journey to the aisle but in her professional life, her private relationships and when it comes to working out what kind of woman she is, how much she likes that woman and the sacrifices she's prepared to make to get where she wants to be.

I hope you enjoy reading this story of love, passion and friendship as much as I loved writing it. And if you did, please get in touch, let me know what you think, write a review if you like. I would be thrilled to hear from you on **Instagram or Twitter or via my website**. Everyone knows someone who is planning a wedding and as well as being a bittersweet emotional read, this book is also chock-full of inspiration for the big day – so spread the word!

Thank you,
Jade Beer

@JadeBRIDES

@jadebeerbrides

www.jadebeer.com

Acknowledgements

To Anne Hamilton and Erin Kelly, for the thoughtful and ruthless copy editing. Your experience, humour and clever advice has made this story so much better than it was. To my Bookouture editor Kathryn Taussig, aka the bad language police, for climbing back inside the mind of my reader and knowing exactly what she will like. To my agent Alice Saunders for helping me birth this book at the same time as her own tiny human and never missing a beat. How do you stay so sane?

To Caroline Long, friend of old, mother and midwife extraordinaire. While I'm obsessing over model castings, shoot dates and whose dress to put on the next cover of *Brides*, you are pulling new babies into the world. You, and everyone in the maternity department at St Michael's Hospital in Bristol, were so generous with your time and knowledge. Never stop caring – I know you couldn't.

To women everywhere. Those who are throwing a crap sandwich into a kid's packed-lunch box at midnight or tapping away at the laptop into the early hours because when were there ever enough hours in the day? For all the missed deadlines, broken promises, late arrivals, early exits and inventive stretching of the truth that somehow keeps it all chugging forwards. For all the mums and daughters trying to understand each other, to love one another and value each other in the time you have left. To my own wonderful mum. How easy you are to love. I think about you every day, thankful that I got one of the very best.

To Laila and Clara, my school-age bosses. Thank you for reminding me every day what is important. Laila, our girls' nights in are the ones I look forward to most. Clara, our dawn tea-parties will still make me smile when I'm a little old lady. My time with you both is golden. When you are old enough to read this book, I hope you will spot the bits that you both inspired. You fill my life with love and I never want to let you go.

Manufactured by Amazon.ca
Bolton, ON

27756521R00192